Thomas Rain

The Life and Labours of John Wray, Pioneer Missionary in British Guiana

Compiled chiefly from his own mss. and diaries

Thomas Rain

The Life and Labours of John Wray, Pioneer Missionary in British Guiana
Compiled chiefly from his own mss. and diaries

ISBN/EAN: 9783337426644

Printed in Europe, USA, Canada, Australia, Japan

Cover: Foto ©Raphael Reischuk / pixelio.de

More available books at **www.hansebooks.com**

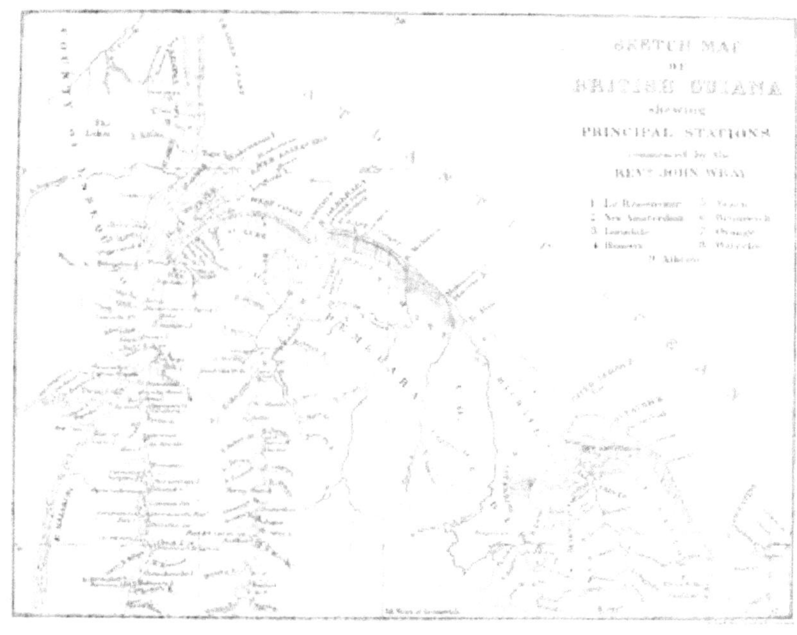

SKETCH MAP
OF
BRITISH GUIANA
shewing
PRINCIPAL STATIONS
commenced by the
REV. JOHN WRAY
1 La Resouvenir
2 New Amsterdam
3 Lonsdale
4 Bearers
5 Yassu
6 Plaisance
7 Orange
8 Waterloo
9 Athlone

THE LIFE AND LABOURS

OF

JOHN WRAY,

Pioneer Missionary in British Guiana.

COMPILED CHIEFLY FROM HIS OWN MSS. AND DIARIES,

BY

THOMAS RAIN.

WITH MAP AND PORTRAITS.

"Is not this the fast that I have chosen? to loose the bonds of wickedness, to undo the bands of the yoke, and to let the oppressed go free, and that ye break every yoke? Is it not to deal thy bread to the hungry, and that thou bring the poor that are cast out to thy house? when thou seest the naked, that thou cover him; and that thou hide not thyself from thine own flesh?"—ISAIAH lviii. 6, 7.

"And he said unto them, Go ye into all the world, and preach the gospel to the whole creation."—MARK xvi. 15.

(Profits from the Sale of this Work will be devoted to Missions in the Colony.)

London

JOHN SNOW & CO.,

2 IVY LANE, PATERNOSTER ROW, E.C.

1892.

PREFACE.

Some account of " John Wray, Pioneer Missionary," by the present writer, appeared in the *Evangelical Magazine* for 1887. Based upon an acquaintance, personal and otherwise, with the scene of his labours and with surviving converts, it was such a condensation of scattered printed matter as about twenty pages would allow. Yet, so far as the author is aware, the little attempt was the first of its kind; and certainly, so far as he was concerned, it seemed not unlikely to be the last. As of John Wray's own parentage and family, so of his widow and children after their return to England, the writer knew nothing. What inquiries he had made proved unavailing; and the brief history soon began to mingle with the stream of things behind, which are on the way to being forgotten.

A letter to hand, August, 1888, put a new aspect on matters. Written by a gentleman quite unknown to the recipient, but expressing, at his wife's request and in sympathy with her, thanks "for your kind remembrance of her father, John Wray," of which " remembrance " they had just been informed; it led both to a most interesting and valued correspondence, and to the loan, for a while, of such MSS. and Diaries as are herewith detailed.

The lady, Mrs. Tuckett, for the last forty years or so wife

of the Rev. E. H. Tuckett, retired Baptist minister of Exeter,* was previously wife and widow of the Rev. James Howe, of Berbice, fatally smitten in the same house and hour as her father. She is the second daughter of John Wray, and the elder of two surviving sisters, all that remain of his family.† Born in 1811, during the critical period in the history of the new Mission which determined her father's sudden return alone to England, and during the anxious time therefore of his absence; despite her many years and changeful experience; the perils, pains, and losses of earlier days, and the infirmities of later age; her intellect is clear, her memory good, her spirit truthful, and her hand steady enough for most legible penmanship, so that her long letter of reminiscences and the two shorter letters of reply to inquiries are as dependable as they are interesting.

John Wray's relation to the British Guiana Mission was such that the Directors of the London Missionary Society requested him to write its history. For this purpose they wished him to prolong his stay in England when (1831) he had returned in company with Mrs. Wray, seeking restoration to health and real rest. To their request he assented in part; he would undertake the authorship, but the pressing claims of his home and of the Mission led him not to delay his return to Berbice. The attempt was made, therefore, along with the care and burden of those claims resting upon him, claims increasing rather than diminishing with Negro Emancipation. Amid all he fell; his history, apparently in its first rough draft, not being more than one-fourth accomplished.

Papers and Diaries were then forwarded to the Missionary

---

* Removed since to Exmouth.

† Now sole survivor.

Society, the Directors placing them in the hands of their Foreign Secretary, the Rev. Wm. Ellis, whose prolonged illness, however, led ultimately to his resignation altogether of office. After a time their return was requested by Mrs. Wray, and with the family they have since remained.

So complete and expensive a work as would at that time have commanded a ready sale, is obviously now not to be thought of. Too late in the day for such a production, it is nevertheless believed that a record of the striking and peculiar incidents of such a course and of the chief features of such a character and conquest as John Wray's, can never be too late. Regretting, therefore, the non-appearance of the work in prospect fifty years ago for the service of the Church and of the world, the attempt is now made, *con amore*, to supply a record of this latter kind; and, omitting much that has since become well known, or that may be better gathered from more recent works of science, travel, or manufacture, to produce such a memoir as, notwithstanding its imperfections and shortcomings, shall at least constrain the feeling—*Better this than none, and " Better late than never."*

Cottingham, near Hull,
    January, 1892.

LIST OF MSS., &c.

I. History of the Mission, written in accordance with Resolution of Directors. About 200 out of more than 400 folio pages; the sheets in hand, barring loss of 8 or 10 intervening pages, reaching from 16th June, 1811, to 9th December, 1815.

II. Diary, January, 1824, to September, 1834; about 355 pp. Written in bound folio volume.

III. Diary, September to December, 1834; January, 1836, to April, 1837, in folio sheets; blank pages being left for 1835.

IV. Several Letters : John Wray to his children in England or elsewhere; to his friend and benefactor, John Thompson, Esq., Albion Street, Hull ; and of Rev. James Howe to his father-in-law.

V. Letter of Reminiscences by Mrs. Tuckett to Editor, 53 pp.; and two other Letters of reply to inquiries, 18 and 10 pp. respectively.

VI. Several subsidiary Documents, also Portraits and Engravings.

CONTENTS.

ILLUSTRATIONS.

LIFE OF JOHN WRAY.

INTRODUCTION.

Towering aloft in one of the most conspicuous and busy centres of Kingston-upon-Hull, surmounted by his figure at full length, and fronting toward the house in which he was born, the family home for many years,* stands the monument of William Wilberforce. A fine memorial of departed worth, enduring and striking, it forms as true and abiding a symbol of a noble career, far-reaching in aims and issues, as it is a handsome token of human esteem and love.

Naturally, with the intelligent and thoughtful beholder of such an object, associations, memories, ideas, crowd upon the mind; but, leaving all else, our present note is, and must be, only one of simple fact connected with the position, just remarked, of the crowning figure. Facing the merchant's mansion in the High Street, the gaze of the statue on its lofty pedestal is in an easterly direction, and thus is towards the neighbouring district of Holderness and towards that sea, a few miles away, beyond which lies Holland.

* "*July*, 1798.—It was a solemn and affecting scene to me, yesterday evening, to be in my mother's room; to see the bed where I was born, and where my father and mother died, and where she then lay in her coffin. I was alone, and I need not say to you, or seek to conceal from you, I put up my prayers that the scene might work its due effect."—*From letter to his wife:* "Life of Wm. Wilberforce," vol. ii. pp. 294-95.

Holderness and Holland must always, and generally have intimate and interesting relations with Hull; but two individuals, hailing respectively from these regions, as they together come into sympathetic connection with his work, so through peculiar circumstances must they, his nearer neighbour especially, have at times enlisted a deep interest in the heart and mind of its great and philanthropic citizen. These individuals were Hermanus Hilbertus Post, Esq., born at Utrecht in 1755, four years in advance of Wilberforce, and the Rev. John Wray, born at South Skirlaugh on the eve of 1780, the year in which Wilberforce himself came of age and entered Parliament.

But already, by the space of some six years, the Hollander, in 1780, had reached Demerara, shortly to become proprietor and planter of the estate Le Resouvenir; and in the long run, after years of effort in the direction, to be the introducer to the Colony, in 1808, of its first missionary. That missionary was John Wray, of Holderness, who thus entered upon his course, and, as events proved, became the pioneer of mission work, not only on Le Resouvenir and in Demerara, but also, and chiefly, in the neighbouring colony of Berbice.

Meanwhile, between 1780 and 1808, the anti-slavery agitation had commenced, progressed, and, in 1807, attained its first triumph—an Act of Parliament for abolishing the slave trade. Wilberforce, the first distinguished leader in that agitation, had been eight years in the House before he succeeded in laying his twelve propositions on the table with a view to abolition. This he did on the 12th of May, 1789 (a hundred years ago), at the close of a speech, one of his greatest (the only one that has the notes fully given in his published life),* which called forth the admiration of an assembly rich in famous orators. It was, however, but the beginning of a long, wearying, and bitter struggle. Though it dealt only with the trade—the carrying—*e.g.*, of slaves

* "Life, &c.," vol. ii. Appendix.

taken in Africa, to be sold in the West Indies—yet nineteen years, involving on occasions almost superhuman toil on the part of the philanthropic leaders, were needful to secure their object.

A still longer, and, if possible, more bitter and arduous conflict then gradually arose, concerning the regulation, and ultimately the entire abolition, of slavery in the British dominions. 1833 was reached before this became law, and only then at the cost, to the United Kingdom, of £20,000,000 sterling; when Wilberforce, too, had just breathed his last, having, about ten years before, resigned the chief leadership of the movement to younger and stronger hands, and, worn out with toil, retired altogether from Parliament.

Between the two great conflicts, or, more correctly perhaps, between the two divisions of the one great conflict, it was that the mission on Le Resouvenir was commenced, and John Wray went forth to undertake the work. In the details of his course there and elsewhere, occasions will be noted which bring him into intimate connection or personal intercourse with the now famous abolitionist. One occasion, in later years, may here be specially remarked, an occasion when the estate, the mission, the planter then long dead, the pioneer, as well as his successor there, would sadly fill the mind of Wilberforce. It has place among the closing days of the philanthropist's course as a senator, and the words he hoped to speak would be amongst the very last he uttered in the House.

Premising that the "Smith" referred to was John Smith, Wray's successor on Le Resouvenir, that John Wray, at work in Berbice and amid trouble there, was prevented only by the interference of its friendly Governor being found at the side of Smith when the latter became the victim of Demerara's crowning crime, we quote the last entry of Mr. Wilberforce's diary before confinement to his bed through illness:— "Poor Smith, the missionary, died in prison at Demerara. The day of reckoning will come!"

Again, premising that 1st June, 1824, was the day for a battle royal in the Commons' House over Smith's arrest, trial, and shameful sentence; and that "the first public business Wilberforce attempted after leaving his sick-room, was, '1st June, preparing for Smith the missionary's business,'" we again quote :—

"Was at the House the first time for eight weeks or more. Brougham made a capital speech, by Macintosh well termed impregnable. I doubt not he will be great in reply. Macintosh's own was most beautiful—his mind teemed with ideas."

" The decision was postponed till the 11th. In the interval he says " :—

"I very much wish, if my voice should be strong enough, to bear my testimony against the scandalous injustice exercised upon poor Smith. The case proved against him is greatly short of what I thought it might have been. I myself once saw a missionary's journal, and its contents would have been capable of being perverted into a much stronger charge of promoting discontent among the slaves. Had I happened, for instance, to correspond with Smith, that alone would have hanged him."*

His wish was gratified. On the 11th of June, 1824—

"Mr. Wilberforce rose amidst loud and long continued cheering, and, in a strain of impressive eloquence, vindicated the character of the missionary, and supported the motion."†

But it was *the last effort of his parliamentary life*. Yet never should this be recorded without the addition that the debate proved the beginning of a triumphant end; for, though the immediate decision was adverse, the speeches preceding it so rallied the scattered Abolitionists, and so enlightened and aroused the country, that freedom for the slave eventually prevailed.

To gain or to convey an adequate conception of the diffi-

* " Life, &c.," vol. v. pp. 221-23.
† " Martyr of Demerara," p. 168.

culties through which the friends of the negro, and of missions to the negro, had to make their way, seems at this day hardly possible. So many and great are changes for the better at home and abroad, so widely diffused are they, and, as to some, so long continued now, that another atmosphere is breathed, another code of language and of manners has gradually been adopted. Dividing the distance, however, and going backwards from more recent experiences, we may find some help in the attempt.

With, then, our improved methods of teaching, with elementary schools in reach of every home, and with easier access to schools or colleges of higher degree, already the state of instruction as it was less than a generation ago is a vanishing memory; so amid the abundance, and cheapness, and general prosperity following upon a Free Trade policy barely more than forty years old, few can vividly recall, much less impart to others, the sense of dearness, and famine, and fever, and squalor that was felt as, during the closing days of Corn Law monopoly, destitute Irish crowded in upon the destitute English of our great Lancashire cities. Yet men in 1860 and 1846 deemed themselves in advance, as indeed they were in advance, of the men of 1819. Were they not enjoying the benefits of a revised Penal Code, of a reformed Parliament, of a Catholic Emancipation Act, of the Abolition of Slavery, of Repeal of the Test and Corporation Acts, and of a Ten Hours' Bill?

The men of 1819, however, so unprivileged as they seem to have been, could lay claim to benefits enjoyed which were unknown to their fathers of 1789. The British slave trade had ceased to exist, nor could any slave ship be seen riding at anchor in our rivers, or docked at our ports for renewal or for being refurnished with its horrid gear; whilst every great modern Missionary and Bible and Tract Society had begun its career and got well on its course; as also had the great Educational Societies.

But the whole of this progress and all these privileges were unknown when Wilberforce, in 1789, rose in the Commons' House with his first measures favouring abolition. Says the Rev. Thomas Price in his " Memoir " :—

"Those who have witnessed the recent feelings of the nation on this subject, may imagine that but little moral courage was required for the adoption of the course which Mr. Wilberforce took. But the state of things was then totally different from what we have lately seen. The atrocities of the system were not known ; the moral sensibilities of the nation were blunted ; and a numerous, affluent, and unprincipled party was pledged to opposition. It was at this risk of party associations, and of personal friendships, that he determined on his course ; and the virulence with which he was assailed, and the foul aspersions which were cast upon his unspotted fame, bespoke the fear which his talents and virtues had excited. The nation, though but little informed and still less interested in this great question, was yet in advance of the House of Commons " (p. 25).

And again : —

"This motion being carried, was a signal to the West India planters, merchants, and others, to commence an unprincipled and furious opposition " (p. 26).

Once more :—

"Greater difficulties can scarcely be conceived than those with which the abolitionists had to contend. Their whole project was regarded as chimerical, and every means which wealth, power, and dishonesty could devise, was employed against them. The evil to be remedied was practised at the distance of some thousands of miles, and those who witnessed its enormities possessed, for the most part, a pecuniary interest in their continuance. It was well known that the highest personage in the state was opposed to their views, and that the revenues of the nation, and the prosperity of its commerce, were extensively regarded as threatened by them. Undeterred, however, by those circumstances, the friends of humanity determined on their course, and the rectitude of their object gave them success. Their labours constituted the seed from which an abundant harvest has been gathered in our day " (p. 44).

To all which, it may be added, a body more than usually frail, and health ever delicate, made the work of their chief none the lighter, or the conflict less easy to endure.

These are things as found in our own land, the land of which it had already been sung :—

> "Slaves cannot breathe in England ; if their lungs
> Receive our air, that moment they are free ;
> They touch our country, and their shackles fall."*

But what of the lands, our own distant possessions, in which slaves could and did breathe ; in which the creed was that it could never be otherwise ; and the destiny seemed in accord with the creed, as dark as it, and as determined for ages as human greed and arbitrary power could make it? Or out of such possessions, what, in particular, of those where "religion with its treasures untold," and "the sound of the church going bell," were widely and utterly unknown —possessions like Demerara, Essequibo, and Berbice, as they were both before and after they became, by conquest, our colonies? The differences there between the present and the past are of course more marked and striking, being differences between wider extremes. But all the more difficult, even on the spot, is it in the midst of one extreme to realise the other. How much more difficult then for those living at a distance !

The slaves, as a class, had not a single class as their friend ; all other classes were rather in league against them. If they fled, the scattered Indians of the interior were employed to track them, and if they rebelled, the troops of the mother country were summoned to crush them ; whilst by any person a reward could be obtained for the capture of a fugitive, or, if not taken alive, upon production—*e.g.*, of a right hand. Like their brethren in bondage in the West India Islands, they were Negro Africans or of African

* "Cowper's Task," Bk. 2.

descent; not natives, in the first instance, any more than were the few whites, their masters.

What is now known as British Guiana is a part of that larger Guiana which is bounded by the Atlantic on the one side, and by the huge rivers Orinoco and Amazon respectively on its two other sides—an extensive and wondrous land of multiplied rivers and streams, of countless forms of life, gorgeous beauty, and immeasurable fertility. Indians of various tribes possessed it, or rather roamed over it, when first discovered by Europeans; and, for a century after, expeditions—Spanish, Portuguese, French—went thither to seek El Dorado; the adventurers more frequently than otherwise perishing in the attempt. Our own Sir Walter Raleigh was about the last and most humane leader of any such-like enterprise.

Then came less dreamy and more matter-of-fact Dutchmen to seek gold by tilling the soil. They began about 270 years ago, in small companies, going some distance up the rivers to be out of the way of pirates or to lessen the risks of war; and importing negro slaves from Africa to be their labourers. Things made slow progress; the course was a very chequered one, and the work had its dangers neither surprising nor undeserved. A minister of religion might be found with each colony, but if so, he did nothing for the slaves. Heathens to begin with, some especially of more savage tribes and of greater strength, torn from their native shores and brought through the horrors of the middle passage, it is no wonder that, doubly degraded and with nothing to brighten their prospects or better their lot, despite the punishments inflicted or the cruelties threatened, they fled in numbers to the bush, and formed bands extremely dangerous to the community.

The Moravians in the early part of last century sent brethren up the Berbice river to instruct them; but all in authority opposed the devoted men, who, going further, laboured then, and not without success, among the Indians. Eventually, however, they suffered the loss of their station; and ultimately, through various causes, disappeared from the Colony. Rebellions took place, more or less easily suppressed; but an insurrection about 1760, was so general and successful as virtually, for some twelve months, to put the negroes in possession of Berbice. It was ended only by the arrival from Holland of a strong naval and military force, at a great cost to the Colony; its suppression being followed by shocking torturings of the chief insurgents.

Later on, despite the insect plagues, the pestilential miasm, and other dangers, the Dutch ventured more upon the alluvial soil lower down the rivers and on the ocean coast. Here was land that might well be the envy even of the fertile West Indies; and, accustomed to dig and dyke and dam in their own country, they ran their deep drains and formed their side-lines and their front and back embankments, so as to fringe the rivers and intermediate sea shores with a series of parallelograms, mostly two to four miles in depth, and from one-third to one mile in breadth. Here, if anywhere, El Dorado appeared. The crops, whether of coffee, cotton, or sugar, proved marvellously abundant and, for a time, were very remunerative.

But the slave was no sharer in this prosperity. With him, if anything, matters must have gone from bad to worse, the labour at the dams and trenches being very arduous and sickening. Their numbers were greatly added to, as also, in some measure, the number of whites and of free coloured people was increased. But nothing was done in the way of Christian worship and instruction. So late as 1796, there were only a small Lutheran Church in Berbice and a Dutch Reformed Church on Fort Island, Essequibo, a hundred miles distant from each other; and the services of the ministers were sacred to the use, not of the tens of thousands of slaves, but of the few whites, masters or merchants, who chose to attend. Somewhat later, a chaplain read the prayers of the Church of England in a small room of the Old Court-house, Georgetown, Demerara, which might have accommodated about thirty or forty persons; but if any black people ventured to look in upon the worshippers, sometimes not more than half-a-dozen, there assembled, they were driven from the door.* To teach a slave the art of reading, or to instruct him in the simplest religious truths, was reckoned a sin against the laws of the land. Thus, unless a master or manager of a somewhat better character did anything in his household, nothing was done ; and as communities do not stand still, society degenerated.

From the first, the whites generally had been immoral and sensual; with increase of riches and luxuries, they became increasingly so. Marriage according to law was more than unknown amongst the slaves, it was illegal; and among the free people it was almost unknown. The whip, a formidable one too, was the great motive to labour; how constantly, and excessively, and cruelly, and wantonly it was used, seems incredible. In a word, impiety and profanity, tyranny and brutality, the grossest immorality and licentiousness, drunkenness and duelling, superstition and murder, pervaded society. About 1792, there landed in Demerara one of the French nobility, a young Count, but a fugitive from the emissaries of the Revolution. This gentleman, Stephen Grellet by name, to be known in after years, and for more than half a century, both in Europe and America as an enlightened and devoted minister of the Society of Friends, was then not without some knowledge of God, and some uprightness both of thought and life, having been trained a Roman Catholic ; but the cruelties he witnessed so shocked him, and the impiety which abounded so hurtfully affected him, that he became for a while an atheist and a disciple of Voltaire.

* See "Martyr of Demerara," p. 14.

The fortunes of war at last put the Dutch colonies of Guiana into possession of Britain; and it was eventually settled that the French should have Cayenne, the Dutch, Surinam, and herself should retain Berbice, Demerara, and Essequibo. These, it may here be explained, are three important rivers, flowing in a northerly direction, and giving names, respectively, to three contiguous breadths of country —Demerara being the middle portion. They were governed, at the time of their capture and for many years afterwards, by two separate colonial governors and legislatures, Berbice having and keeping its own, and were designated, *British Guiana;* since 1831, however, under the same name, ruled as three counties, under one colonial governor and legislature.

With the advent of British power came, though very slowly and imperceptibly, the streaks which proved the dawn of better things. Not in the capital which now poured into the country, nor in the planters and officials of simply another nationality were they found; but, first of all, European women of some refinement and chastity appeared more frequently. Then Hermanus Hilbertus Post, Esq., had become a British subject; and when, years before, this gentleman quitted Holland, he did not leave, nor did he wish to leave, everything of the old country behind. Into the land of abounding darkness, impiety, and cruelty, he had taken with him habits of untiring industry, and feelings of humanity; germs of philanthropic enterprise, and influences of a Christian home, particularly of the prayers and efforts of a pious mother, and of his eldest sister, who had watched over him, and had sought to permeate heart and mind with the truth as it is in Jesus. To such truth, from early years, his mind had been tenderly sensitive; and such truth was to advance until he became a new man in Christ, and until all within became subject to its sway. In accord with which, therefore, and now under British rule, not unlikely it was that appeals for a minister of religion to go out and live on Le Resouvenir, made out of concern for his negroes, beforetime to other lands but in vain, came at last to be directed to England.*

Further, as British possessions, there was likewise the prospect of these colonies being included in whatever success might attend the efforts of Wilberforce and the Abolitionists to check the slave-trade, or to pass measures for improving the treatment and condition of those in bondage.

Yet, as has been said, the new influences operated and the brighter events came to pass but slowly. For years things seemed to be very much the same. A Wesleyan missionary from Dominica attempted to enter Demerara with a view to establish a mission. Mr. Wallbridge gives a short account of this matter, which cannot well be put in fewer words :—

"He arrived on the 30th September, 1805, and on the 2nd October he had an interview with the Governor (Beaujon), who, of course, questioned him as to what he was, and what was the object of his visit. Being informed that he ' was a missionary of the Methodist Connexion, and that his design was to instruct the negroes in the principles of Christianity,' he replied, ' If that be what you are come to do, you must go back. I cannot let you stay here, and therefore you had better return in the mail-boat.' Thinking that he would deliberate on the matter, the missionary said, ' May it please your Excellency, may I call on you another time ?' The reply was, ' No ; there will be no occasion, as you cannot stay. I suppose you will go back in the mail-boat ?' On the 8th October he accordingly sailed from Demerara ' in the mail-boat.' Such was the determined opposition to the instruction of ' the negroes in the principles of Christianity' in those days."†

Mr. Post's first letters to this country were lost, and so went unanswered ; but at last, when about to despair, one

* See Memoir of Mr. Post by Rev. J. Wray, *Evangelical Magazine*, 1811.

† " Martyr of Demerara," p. 16.

addressed to the London Missionary Society reached its destination, and was favourably acknowledged. Its offers were accepted, and it became settled that John Wray, then studying at Gosport, should be the individual to go forth, and, as Mr. Wallbridge expresses it, be "honoured to be the first Christian minister who ever opened his lips to show the way of salvation to the people then in slavery."

Under such circumstances, then, and into such a condition of men and things, long before William Ellis, or John Williams, or Robert Moffat, entered upon Mission labours, did John Wray enter upon his. All alone as regards fellow-missionaries, and one of the first of the Society's agents to proceed alone ; with two or three delicacies of digestion and disposition that might well have been pleaded in excuse ("from his delicate state of health when he left his native land, his friends hardly supposing he would reach the place of his destination") ;* but with qualities of soul and spirit that signified him as seemingly just the man for the work, he tried for twelve months, and was then joined by one well fitted and well worthy to be, as she proved to be, partner all along with him in life and toil. Their character and qualifications ; their trials and triumphs ; their adventures, sometimes so strange ; and how generally it fared with them, the following pages will in measure show, very largely, too, from his own words.

It seems a pity that friends and parties have not had the benefit of some such publication before now. But, as John Foster remarks to his friend Josiah Hill :—

"Have you wholly given up the project and task of making some use of the *diaries* of a pious man ? You may do so, and little more will be said. It is very curious to observe how the first eagerness for publishing something about a good man has quieted down after the project had been kept some time in abeyance. There is something melancholy in this, as showing how

* See Appendix A.

the warm memory of the good can decline by degrees to a comparative indifference, even when there is not a real change in the judgment of their worthiness. In a little while after our departure how very, very few will feel a painful sense of *wanting* us. It will be confined to some three or four (if not still fewer) who had a cordial, deep attachment to us, from relationship, or the most intimate kind of friendship." *

But John Wray, whilst a pious man, of a retiring nature too, was more than a pious man: he was a pioneer missionary and a public servant; an instrument also, in the order of Providence, for accomplishing and for helping others to accomplish in one of our richest possessions and one of our most important infant colonies, beneficial changes far beyond what he himself ever dreamt of, or thought of seeing. Consequently, in his case, there are reasons for a public record, or, if years delayed, for some like record, which do not exist in the case of an individual of private life, however worthy.

Little more than a bare enumeration of such reasons will close this Introduction.

(1.) Memoirs of Wilberforce, of H. H. Post, and of John Smith have been published; none as yet of John Wray. So, too, what Ellis, Williams, Moffat, missionaries of the same Society, were to their respective Mission spheres, that was Wray to his: their memorials have appeared; his is wanting.

(2.) The success of modern missionary enterprise has recently been markedly challenged. Verily, with little reason; but a hundred lands that men visit and deal with are now so Christianised, that it is forgotten how paganised they were found, and this not a century ago. British Guiana—*e.g.*, and the life of John Wray—will be one means of bringing to remembrance the fact, and of thus correcting the error.

* Foster's "Life and Correspondence," vol. ii. p. 275.

(3.) The history of the Christian Church in Guiana may yet be written. What he has read and heard leads the writer of this to think that, as to the British part of the country, it is not clearly remembered, or is sadly overlooked that John Wray first brought the Gospel to the negroes then in slavery. His published life will be a standing testimony—(a) to this; (b) a testimony also favourable to the efficiency of Christian Churches, though free from State connection or from State subsidies; (c) a like testimony to the fact that, be Independency or Congregationalism right or wrong, John Wray, himself an Independent, though a most catholic-minded man and ever ready to welcome and work with Christians of other ecclesiastical forms, proceeded on the Congregational plan in forming the churches with which he had to do.*

(4.) The abandonment of estates has been laid at the door of mission work and of slave emancipation. Readers of Wray's life will find mention of many estates abandoned long before a missionary crossed them or emancipation was purchased; and of others that afterwards came to be abandoned through the cruel greed of speculators.

(5.) Followers of Christ in the past are often judged as lacking in devotion to the interests of humanity. Wray's life will add to the evidence showing how wrong this judgment is; that, as there were missionaries to leper asylums

---

* These, it may be remarked, have stood firm, notwithstanding the presence of other Christian communities that depend more or less upon the Colony chest. They once led the way in education and in the efficiency of schools, and it is to be hoped they will be enabled in the midst of great rivalries and temptations still, as free Christian churches, so to maintain their position and usefulness that, following the example of several West India islands, the Colony may be led to see it right and best that all Christian communities should be maintained by the free-will offerings of their respective members. For a while, the Congregational Union of England and Wales is at equal charges with the London Missionary Society in rendering some help to their brethren in Guiana. (See Appendix B.)

long before a Father Damien saw the light, so there was a patient, persevering "Enthusiasm of Humanity" before "Ecce Homo" was written, and a young lady willing to enter a London hospital to qualify as nurse that she might go to help the neglected and teach the ignorant in a distant land before an ever-estimable Florence Nightingale appeared.

(6.) Present day readers of Guiana history and missions need the explanation of John Wray's position and procedure at the important crisis in both history and missions, of 1823, which the memoir affords.

(7.) It is right and dutiful, profitable and safe, for communities as well as individuals to consider their origin and history, as Israel was called to "remember all the way which the Lord thy God led thee, &c." (Deut. viii.); to confess, "A Syrian ready to perish was my father, &c." (Deut. xxvi.); to "look unto the rock *whence ye are hewn,* &c." (Isa. li.) In all which the Memoir will be a help to the churches and people of British Guiana, neither small nor uninteresting.

(8.) Slave trade and slavery are not yet ended. Oceans and continents have, thank God, within a few decades been swept clear of their curse and cruelty; but lands and seas remain in which they are still rife and ruinous; and the struggle for their extirpation still goes forward amid a thousand difficulties and discouragements. To weary toilers and in the use of lawful means, what cheer is to be drawn from memoirs such as those of men eminent in the warfare— William Wilberforce and Thomas Fowell Buxton! nor less, perhaps, from those of men of lower degree, or who were not so directly at work upon these great evils, such as John Wray!

CHAPTER I.

BIRTH TO DEPARTURE FROM ENGLAND.

DECEMBER, 1779—DECEMBER, 1807.

Birth and Family—Moral and Religious Condition of Holderness— Efforts of Hull Christians—Reaction between Foreign and Home Missions—Wray's Conversion and Church Relation—He Studies at Gosport—National Affairs—Efforts to Abolish Slave-Trade—Letter from Demerara—Hermanus Hilbertus Post, Esq.—Wray appointed Missionary—His Character and Anxieties—Rebecca Ashford—His Departure: Her Character and Enterprise.

VERY few are the particulars now known of the birth and earlier years of John Wray, even as reliable testimony to these particulars is but scanty and scattered.

That he was born at South Skirlaugh, near Hull, December, 1779, is the inscription on his tomb in lands far off; and that he was baptized at St. Augustine's, the parish church, we read, by the kind courtesy of the vicar, in its register, where the record simply is, "John, son of Robert Reay,* baptized 12th January, 1780." A brother was subsequently born and named Joseph, but as we find no second entry in the parish register, and as the Register of Missionaries of the London Missionary Society gives John as, "born in 1780, at Preston, Yorkshire" (slightly incorrect, it will be perceived, in two particulars), it seems likely

---

* A blunder of clerk or sexton, whose writing the entry seems to be. Reay, Rea, Ray, and Wreay, are all surnames; but Wray is very common in the Hull neighbourhood.

that the household had quitted Skirlaugh and settled at
Preston, about six miles south of their former home, and
somewhat nearer Hull.

But the gain of a brother proved the loss of a mother, she
dying at the time. "You inquire," writes Mrs. Tuckett,
"about my father's relatives. He had only one brother;
his mother died when this brother was born. His father
and brother both died before my sister and I came to
England to go to school. I know of no other relative."

As little do we know of John's training or of any intention with respect to future employment. An impression
that the family was not one of great means or of high social
position grows upon us as we read. Fond of nursery and
garden work, his native neighbourhood would certainly
furnish full opportunity of acquiring and cultivating the
taste. "My father was especially fond of his garden,"
writes the same daughter, "and often in the early morning
before the sun was hot, he was in his garden helping and
directing the gardener; he planted fruit trees of all kinds;
his garden was his only recreation."

More important, however, is the moral and religious
atmosphere by which he would be surrounded, and whatever
this was in the home, out of doors, if similar to much of
Holderness at that time, it would be noxious enough. A
few pages in our possession, headed "Brief Account of the
Religious and Moral State of Holderness," and printed about
1821, thus describes the condition of things as they were
less than twenty-five years previously :—

"Though this retired part of Yorkshire had once the happiness
to enjoy the faithful labours of some of those ministers who were
ejected by the Act of Uniformity, yet, since that period, it had
fallen into a notorious disregard of religious institutions. A
moral barbarism had overspread the whole region. The Sabbath
openly disregarded ; profane swearing ; intoxication ; ribaldry in
discourse ; scoffing at everything in the form of piety ; ignorance

of God, and entire destitution of the knowledge of Christ, were sufficient indications of the affecting state of the people.

"The sight of this moral waste, just bordering upon a place so highly favoured as Hull, excited the strongest feelings of concern in the minds of the followers of Christ in that town. The sense which they entertained of its deep destitution, when contrasted with Hull, may be best understood by a quaint but forcible expression uttered by a good man about thirty years ago. It was with feelings of hopeless lamentation that, on meeting a pious friend one day, he exclaimed, 'Satan still keeps guard upon the *North Bridge.*' Up to that bridge the Gospel had indeed shed its light ; beyond it, all was deep and frightful darkness, with scarcely a hope that it would be dispelled for ages. The first attempts of the Methodists were met by such determined opposition, that, courageous and persevering as they are, they were driven from the field."

Hull itself was indeed favoured with some truly devoted men and ministers both in the Establishment and out of it ; men not likely to rest content in presence of such a gloom on their borders and of such a sentry on their bridge ; or to cease attempts at passing or dislodging the one and dispersing the other. The influence of its eminent philanthropist too, himself indeed absent from his native town, but about to issue his long prayed-over and carefully prepared " Practical View of Christianity," would be all on their side ; and it seems that the forces of life and light in the town began, at that time, to carry the entire position of this region of darkness and death.

Among these, and apparently among the foremost, were the Rev. George Lambert, a man eminent in evangelic labours, and some members of the congregation to which he ministered in Fish Street Chapel ; and the " Brief Account " already quoted goes on to speak more particularly of the work undertaken by them in eighteen or twenty Holderness villages ; concluding its few but interesting details with the following, among other notes of progress :—

"Nothing can be more cheering than to contrast the present state of this extensive tract of country with that which it exhibited when the attempts above recited were first made. Its aspect is altogether changed. We behold churches collected and enjoying the administration of Divine ordinances ; Sunday schools in active operation ; several of those who owe their salvation to the instrumentality of these exertions employed in extending to others the benefit they have received ; opposition to the preaching of the Gospel now no more ; and a general impression, of a highly favourable kind, made upon the moral deportment of the people at large. The Methodists have now an active itinerary in the district, the Baptists have several congregations, and the light of evangelical truth beams from more than one pulpit in the Establishment."

We pause here to remark that the London Missionary Society, one of the earliest and most undenominational of modern Missionary Societies for conveying the Gospel to heathen lands, was formed in the year 1795 (prior to these successful attempts in Holderness), the Rev. George Lambert being among its founders and the preacher of its first anniversary sermon ; in all which he would have the sympathies of his congregation and of many of his Christian fellow-townsmen. A wave of unusual power and volume had thus rolled forwards in lands beyond—Was then, we may suggestively ask, this home-missionary attempt in Holderness its proportionately powerful backsweep? And when again came the onward roll, was John Wray borne along, not only as a convert to be left in membership at Fish Street, but himself to be carried forward to distant shores, a pioneer missionary to the heathen? For the spirit of prayerful and intelligent obedience to the Lord's commands—"Go ye into all the world and preach the Gospel to the whole creation ;" "Go ye therefore, and make disciples of all the nations,"—the true missionary spirit, like mercy as sung by our dramatic poet, "is twice blessed ; it blesseth him (the Church, the land) that gives and him that takes."

However, whether or not John Wray was himself among the "several who, owing their salvation to the instrumentality of these exertions, were employed in extending to others the benefit they have received," it would be natural and a thing of no rare occurrence that, influenced by the preaching and teaching at some Home Mission station, he should himself begin to take part in the work, and thus to acquire and to manifest the patience and faith, the graces and gifts, which marked him as fitted for the peculiar sphere he was afterwards so successfully to occupy.

As a certainty we know that the young man was brought to a saving knowledge of the truth about the year 1800, and that it was through the instrumentality of John Thompson, Esq., who lived in Albion Street, Hull, and was of the Messrs. Thomas & John Thompson, then well-known bankers in the town. To this gentleman and to his great kindness, as well as to his like-minded brother, there are several references in the journal; one or two remaining letters also are addressed to him.

An informing entry, taken from the diary of 1830, runs thus :—

"*Lord's Day, 24th January.*—Last evening I heard of the death of my long attached friend, Mr. Thompson. He died on 23rd November. He was nearly eighty years old, and has spent a long life in the service of the Redeemer. He has been useful to the souls and bodies of hundreds. Several through his instrumentality have become faithful and useful ministers of the Gospel, and a great number members of Christian societies. It is now almost thirty years since I had the happiness to become acquainted with him, and by the blessing of God on his exertions I was, I trust, brought to embrace the Gospel in sincerity and truth. I thank God for sparing him so long. He has ever been the sincere friend of my children."

Of little consequence does it seem to be told what local church-name such a Christian bore, or under what form of

visible church-government he was found; but Mr. John
Thompson was a Wesleyan Methodist, whilst John Wray
himself entered into fellowship with the Congregational or
Independent Church, meeting in Fish Street Chapel. With
regard to this latter fact, indeed, our measure of certainty
has to depend upon other documents than church records,
for the volume of these, belonging to the period, has
unfortunately, within the last few years, gone on its travels
and become lost to view. But the Register of Missionaries
gives him as in membership at Fish Street, and an extract
from the Rev. G. Lambert's private diary, we shall presently
see, supports the statement.

About the beginning of 1805 Wray went to Gosport,
where an establishment for students from the South of
England preparing for the ministry had been opened in
1789, under the superintendence of the Rev. David (afterwards Dr.) Bogue, and where

"the Missionary Society in 1800, having resolved to prepare
their missionaries for their future labours by a course of instruction, placed them under Mr. Bogue, who now gives to one class
lectures suited to form them for foreign missions, and to another,
education for the ministry at home. The latter class, according
to the wish of the original founder of the seminary, attend
principally to theology. Of the three years to which the course
of instruction is limited, the two first are occupied with lectures
on the principles of Christianity, and the last with lectures on
the sacred books. During the whole time, Latin, Greek, and
Hebrew are studied, and instructions are given in geography and
astronomy, in language and composition, in Jewish antiquities,
ecclesiastical history, and the pastoral office." *

Leaving him there in retirement for a season, we find an
opportunity for a needful glance at the world around, and
particularly at national affairs.

* "History of Dissenters," by Drs. Bogue and Bennett, vol. iv. pp.
281-82.

The preceding fifteen years had been filled pretty much with the French Revolution, the rise of Napoleon Buonaparte, and his threatened invasion of England ; as succeeding years were filled with him and his wars. But amid these, and all such excitements as culminated in a victory like that of the Nile or of Trafalgar, the efforts, already specified, of Wilberforce and of his friends to abolish the slave trade occasionally claimed attention, and sometimes came prominently into view. After the first great attempt of May, 1789, and after like attempts in the year 1791-92, when, though supported by the eloquence of Mr. Fox and Mr. Pitt, he was still defeated ; Mr. Wilberforce, in each of the five following years, " renewed his efforts, but without success."

"The House" (our quotations here and in some following sentences are from Dr. Price's Memoir), "the House appeared to grow weary of the discussion, and the country at large to have lost somewhat of its former zeal and vigour. The indefatigable Clarkson began to sink under the exertions involved. Considerations were not wanting to induce an abandonment of the cause." " Everything depended, at this crisis, on the decision of Mr. Wilberforce, and he was faithful to the occasion ;" but "every expedient having been devised, every form which the measure could assume having been put before the House and been rejected, he and his friends did not deem it advisable to bring the subject again into Parliament till some new circumstances should favour its introduction." Accordingly, "from 1799 to the year 1804, he contented himself with moving for certain papers, and with assuring the House that he had not grown cool in the cause."
" In the latter year the abolition committee determined on renewed exertions, having increased their number by electing James Stephens, Zachary Macaulay, Henry Brougham, Robert Grant, William Allen, and others, members of its body ;" men whose "subsequent history, so distinguished, has fully justified the committee in their election."
" The entrance of the Irish members into the British Parliament, which occurred in 1804, revived the hopes of the abolitionists. Most of them were known to be friendly to the cause."

"Mr. Wilberforce, accordingly, on the 30th of May, moved that the house resolve itself into committee, and he prefaced his motion by one of the most impassioned speeches ever made within its walls. We have generally understood it was his noblest effort."

The measure passed the Commons, but was postponed by the Lords to the following session :—

"Again introduced in 1805 by Mr. Wilberforce, with every prospect of success, it was unhappily lost in the Commons, through the excessive confidence of its friends," a loss which, "being quite unexpected, was a matter of severe disappointment."

"But the period at length arrived when this great question was to be decided. 'What moral principle failed to achieve, ministerial changes accomplished.' The death of Mr. Pitt (personally a supporter of abolition), in January, 1806, made way for the Fox and Grenville administration, and the question was immediately ushered into Parliament under their ministerial auspices."

The course for the next few months was one of triumph, and though not without threatening events, was finally crowned with most welcome and complete success. The death of Mr. Fox, in October, awakened some apprehensions, but

"the confidence of the abolitionists was restored by Lord Grenville introducing, on the 2nd of January, 1807, a bill for the abolition of the slave-trade into the House of Lords, which was immediately carried through both Houses, though against much opposition. 'Pressed forward with the utmost possible expedition, the friends of humanity and religion were far from being without anxiety. Even after it had passed both Houses, its fate was regarded as uncertain ; for the king, being displeased with his ministers, had determined on their dismission. But the force of public opinion prevailed, and the royal assent was given by commission to the bill.'"

"'This took place,' says Mr. Clarkson, 'the next day, Wednesday, 25th January, at half-past eleven in the morning, for His Majesty's message was delivered to the different members of administration that they were then to wait upon him, to deliver up the seals of their offices. It then appeared that a commission for the royal assent to this bill, among others, had been obtained. This was instantly opened by the Lord Chancellor (Erskine), who was accompanied by the Lords Holland and Auckland, and as the clock struck twelve—it was completed. The ceremony being over, the seals of the respective offices were delivered up : so that the execution of the commission was the last act of the administration of Lord Grenville."

"Thus ended one of the most glorious contests, after a continuance for twenty years, of any ever carried on in any age or country."

The few foregoing details show clearly that not all the excitement of the European war in which this country was then engaged, could keep the question of Abolition from coming more or less to the front. It occupied the thoughts of Mr. Fox even amid the struggles and pains of his final sickness. "Two things," said he, on his death-bed, "I wish earnestly to see accomplished—peace with Europe, and the abolition of the slave-trade ; but, of the two, I wish the latter."

That the question would be frequently uppermost in the mind of many a more private well-wisher of his species, we can easily conceive ; as we can conceive the subject to have been one of frequent converse, reading, and thought among the students at Gosport, during some of their few spare hours ; and that not the least interested of their number would be he who hailed from the same neighbourhood as the distinguished leader in the cause ; though yet little thinking what personal intercourse he would come to have with that leader, or what part he himself would be called to take on behalf of the enslaved and heathen African.

Amid all, however, and above all, a hand Divine was coming into view, beckoning the directors of the London Missionary Society in a new direction. During the twelve years of the Society's existence, it had sent forth missionaries in large companies to the South Seas, and in smaller detachments to the Cape of Good Hope, India, and one or two other regions. But it had done nothing yet in the direction of the West Indies or for the negroes in bondage, when a letter was received revealing the "man of Macedonia," in a new form, "standing and praying, Come over into Demerara and help us." He had long been standing and beseeching others in other countries, but in vain ; and he was now almost in despair. His signature was—Hermanus Hilbertus Post, of Le Resouvenir.

Into all the particulars of this gentleman's career since landing in Demerara we cannot enter ; but may here say that, after a brief experience of overseership, Mr. Post became possessor of virgin soil. Working alongside a few slaves he formed the estate Le Resouvenir, and made it one of the best and most neatly laid-out properties in the colony. He cared for his slaves and forwarded help to the old home ; constantly befriended widow and orphan, and sought to benefit neighbouring planters and their negroes ; at one period of long-continued drought, by his plans and exertions saving hundreds of men and cattle from perishing. At length, for health's sake, he visited the United States, and continued there some eight years ; travelling part of the time, and, during the remainder, following the plough on a farm which he had purchased · A non-resident proprietor so far as Demerara was concerned, he returned thither to find, like so many other non-resident proprietors, things in very bad order, and that a little longer delay would entirely have ruined him. He intended to remain only to put Le Resouvenir in order, or to dispose of it and return to Holland for the rest of his days. Happily, this was over-ruled. At last, one rainy season, through exposure and toil while assisting a neighbouring planter to repair a yielding back-dam, and thus to save his neighbour's estate from inundation and ruin, he brought on the disease which, in course of time, terminated his earthly life.

Mr. Post had long been concerned for the spiritual welfare of those under his care, and this had led him not only to personal efforts at instructing them, but to the employment of a catechist, then to inquiries after some minister who should live and labour on the estate; ultimately to the application just mentioned.

"Assuredly gathering that the Lord had called them for to preach the Gospel" in Demerara, the Directors of the Missionary Society responded favourably to Mr. Post's letter, accepting his offers of introduction, protection, and personal aid. But this involved the question, "Whom shall we send, and who will go for us?" and whether the Directors first approached John Wray, or John Wray first approached the Directors, is of little moment compared with the fact, that ready and willing he stood, saying, "Here am I, send me," and that their rejoinder was, "Go."

Now about twenty-seven years of age, perhaps of no very extensive educational attainments or striking literary gifts, he was a man of true Christian spirit and principle; prepared to be, as he had good need to be, "Wise as serpents, and harmless as doves;" a man of devotion to his work, and of quiet, steady perseverance therein.

Through a somewhat unexpected opening, we have a glimpse of the pioneer, during probably his last vacation, and possibly his last visit to Hull, before departure. It is furnished by the private diary of the Rev. G. Lambert, and is in accord with the statement of John Wray's fellowship at Fish Street. Not intended perhaps for more than a few eyes to see, it is quoted by the Rev. G. T. Coster in his "Pastors and People" (a centenary memorial of Fish Street Congregational Church), as illustrative of Mr. Lambert's thoughts on "Pulpit tone."

We must premise that the pastor was by this time an old and experienced minister, only eight years short of "finishing his course with joy." The preacher was speaking, not only in presence of pastor and people, from among whom he had gone to Gosport, but in view of shortly leaving all and of going far away to work and to experiences quite new, and such as promised trials to flesh and blood, neither few nor small.

"*Lord's Day, 30th August,* 1807.—Mr. John Wray, who is going abroad as a missionary, preached in the afternoon from Matt. viii. 2 ; but it was delivered in such a lullaby tone—the language so poetical, and the plan so diffuse—that I was not comfortable under the sermon. He is a good young man, aims at doing good, and I hope will be successful ; but I wish more care had been taken by his tutor to the forming him for a preacher."

Had that tutor been permitted a sight of the last remark when written, he would perhaps have gently reminded the venerable auditor, that Mr. John Wray had been in the class at Gosport, which had "lectures suited to form them for foreign missions," and little, we think, did either aged pastor or young preacher conceive the amount of "pegging away" with Dr. Watt's First Catechism, &c., &c., that awaited the pioneer.

One weight, in particular, on the mind of the missionary elect, would perhaps be as yet unknown to any beyond the parties immediately concerned. Rebecca, and such a Rebecca, proved willing, and even " willing to go with this man ;" but paterfamilias would not give consent. Nor, as to such and so beloved a daughter, and with the world and our colonies in such a condition as they then were, can we be surprised. With more excuse than had the Rev. Sydney Smith and the *Edinburgh Review* of those days, visions of cannibal feasts would recur to the paternal mind. John Wray's attempt in Demerara, too, was at first but tentative ; there was some prospect that he might not be able to continue, or, if spared, that he might not be allowed to stay.

The burden was not to be removed, the cloud lifted, or the way opened, until, like Israel in old time, moving onward, he was about to cross the sea, and had well nigh his foot in the waters. His ordination service at Gosport proved the occasion, not only of his own separation to the work unto which he had been called, but of his securing the companion and helpmeet he desired. We must, however, let Mrs. Tuckett tell all this and a few other family matters in her own free and affectionate way.

" My mother, Mrs. Wray, was born at Gosport. I have often heard her speak of Dr. Bogue as her dear friend and pastor, and that as an infant he baptized her ; also of the solemn time (before father left England), when in his study he talked and prayed with them both, commending them and the work in which they were to be engaged to the God and Father of our Lord Jesus Christ.

" Mother was the last child of a large family, and the darling of her father. He was much opposed to her going to Demerara, where, he said, she would be eaten up by cannibals, &c., &c., but as she was not to go immediately, the matter was left, and in God's goodness, when father was ordained, he was induced to go to the service, and there his heart was touched by what he heard, and before father left England he freely gave her to him.

" The Society promised to send her out in a year, if he found he could live there, for the Colonies had a dreadful name ; to go there was thought to be going to certain death, but it was war time, and she had to wait for a convoy, and thus she was a much longer time detained than was expected."

And so without Rebecca Ashford, but not without a mind considerably relieved as to their future, nor without the deep interest and hearty good will of many a friend of Christ and well-wisher of the enslaved negro, nor probably without the knowledge of Wilberforce, then in the joy of his first great success as to the slave-trade, whose acquaintance and friendly interest and help the pioneer, in after years, is found possessing, John Wray departed—" Single," as the

Missionary Register puts it in brief expression, "Sailed, 18th December, 1807."

Better here perhaps than elsewhere, may our last extract from Mrs. Tuckett be continued ; referring, as it does, to the preparation for future usefulness attempted by Miss Rebecca Ashford during her detention in England, revealing too, somewhat of her noble character, and also the many domestic claims amid which co-operation in missionary duties with her future husband had to be carried on ; or calls for neighbourly help and sympathy in the frequent sicknesses of an unhealthy region, amid the heat of a tropical clime, its insect pests, and the sufferings of a slave population, were ever willingly complied with.

"In the meantime, letters received from my father told her of the great mortality there was among the new born infants and often of the mothers, arising from the ignorance of the negro women who attended them. She at once made up her mind to acquire the art of midwifery ; she went to London, entered Brownlow Street Hospital, studied it and obtained her Diploma or certificate.*　This knowledge proved of great importance, not only to the poor negroes, but to many of the white ladies in cases of extreme danger ; when she would watch whole nights by the bedside, and by timely imparting nourishment, &c., saved many lives. She was a born doctor.

"Also after we removed to Berbice and went to live at Sandvoort (I believe Orange Chapel was afterwards built there or

---

* To her own great surprise, as she was not conscious of having seen it before, this certificate turned up a few months ago when Mrs. Tuckett was looking over some other papers. In the upper part is a view of the British Lying-in-Hospital, Brownlow Street, Long Acre ; and a symbolical representation of Providence, Britannia, Piety, and Plenty. It gives Rebecca Ashford as resident at the town of Southampton, and is unqualified as to her conduct, work, and capabilities. It is dated the 10th day of February, 1809 ; and is signed by :—

<table>
<tr><td>N. COMBE, M.D.,
ROBT. BATTY, M.D.,
RICD. SIMMON,</td><td>} Medical Officers of the Institution.</td></tr>
</table>

very near it ; there her first-born son, John Thompson Wray, was buried beneath a large mango tree), to the missionaries' wives she was a mother, always with them in their hour of trial. They always came to our house on their arrival, and it was her delight to encourage them, and explain things to them ; she, in fact, was a mother in Israel. What she was to my father, tongue cannot tell ; and to her children. She was of a very cheerful disposition, and Father thought her price above rubies ; she was all in all to him in the desolate, unfriendly land that he loved and lived for.

" I do not recollect anything of the removal to Sandvoort, but I have heard Father say that the roads were almost impassable at times ; yet she rode into town with him most mornings to teach as many children as they could gather together, free coloured children who were growing up in total ignorance. Father was then connected with the Crown estates ; mother's labours among the poor mothers and infants were acknowledged in high quarters in England, and she was asked to name anything as an acknowledgment for her services. She asked the freedom of six young girls (coloured), the daughters of white men, left in slavery, and it was granted.

"She had a large family herself; twins twice. My brother Robert, who died in Demerara at the age of twenty from a sunstroke, was a twin ; his brother William died at the age of four or five.

" Mother's maiden name was Rebecca Ashford. I do not know the year that she was born in, but have often heard her say that she spent her twenty-fourth birthday on board the vessel on her voyage to Demerara. Father used to tell us to read the 31st of Proverbs often, for there we would find a description of our mother ; to me particularly, when about to become a missionary's wife, he held her up as a bright example."

CHAPTER II.

LANDING IN DEMERARA, TO FIRST RETURN TO ENGLAND.

FEBRUARY 1808—JUNE 1811.

Voyage and Arrival—Encouraging Incidents—Mr. Post's Hospitality and Co-operation—His Erection of Bethel Chapel and Manse: Missionary spirit : School in Town : Views of Providence—Success of the Work —Opposition—Mr. Post's Letters—Mr. Wray's Report.

"ARRIVED in Demerara, *6th February*, 1808," is the record in Register, brief as that of departure. The two contain about all we know of the voyage—it was seven weeks long. Four weeks would then be accounted a fair passage as to time, for it must be remembered that steamships, telegraphs, and railways of the present day, were things unimagined. The season was winter ; not unlikely, therefore, squalls and gales in more northerly seas, would delay the vessel's progress until, the trade winds reached, all would be steady sailing to the Guiana coast. But at best we cannot think otherwise of the voyage than as of one trying to Mr. Wray, with whom, on account of his propensity to sickness, sea-travelling was no favourite. We fear that many wearisome days and nights were appointed him, a deep draught of others in store on future voyages, and a vivid type of the fever-sickness, physic-sickness, heart-sickness (if never home-sickness), personal and domestic ; amid which, to say nothing of

> " The sigh
> With that more fearful war within,
> When passion's storms are loud and high,"

his work had so often to be carried on, and his journeys pursued, when his utterly wearied frame was not actually compelled to rest, and his chafed yet patient soul compelled to wait.

But there would come healthier and brighter times, earnest of many such, that would cheer him on his way. The night scene of ocean phosphorescence and of the starry heavens in tropical latitudes would have charms for him; nor less so the new world of rich vegetation and animal life that would rise to view as he approached West Indian or South American shores.

And so with the darker world of sin and ignorance, of tyranny and woe, into conflict with which he was about to enter. Each turn of toil or pain seems marked with something of cheer or of relief, some quiet token at times of victory achieved, or of way being made.

As the ship bearing our missionary entered harbour, the last ship to import new slaves from Africa was leaving it. The horrid traffic, so far as the British colonies and British protection were concerned, was gone. John Wray observed the circumstance, and was often heard by his children to remark that "as he sailed into Demerara, the last slave-ship sailed out."

What kind of reception was afforded him by the Governor seems not to be reported. Perhaps silence signifies "nothing remarkable." The Governors just then were frequently changed, three appointments being made in fourteen months. The second of the three, Lieutenant-Colonel Nicholson, was actually in office, but as this was only *pro. tem.*, and as Wray entered under the wing of Mr. Post, though in after days the pioneer as well as his follower, John Smith, had to encounter the frowns and opposition of Governors, possibly now there was no difficulty.

An entire stranger, he landed not without a friend and a home prepared to receive him; nor without a few ready to sympathize with him in his plans and purposes. On 6th February he was at once made a guest at Mr. Post's own house on Le Resouvenir, some eight miles from town, and one mile from the shore of the Atlantic ; about as healthy a position as there was in that unhealthy region. "The missionary was received at his house," writes Mr. Wray, "with the greatest cordiality ; to whom, till the day of his death, he manifested the most sincere friendship and paternal affection." In fact more favourable circumstances for the pioneer's becoming acclimatized and making acquaintance with the plagues and pleasantnesses of Guiana soil and life, or for his entering upon such a life as he had gone to attempt, it would not be easy to conceive. With an host as active and willing as himself, much more experienced too and, in many things, abler, there was no delay. The newly-arrived guest would soon be fully occupied in the variety of employment which fell to his lot, as it does to the lot specially of a first missionary; and host and guest, planter and missionary, worked side by side in perfect harmony.

Sad must have been the labour when, within two or three years, that variety came to include the preparation of a memoir of this colonial benefactor. A printed copy of such lies before us, having annotations in pen and ink by one confessedly of somewhat different religious sentiments, but which more than confirm all Mr. Wray has said in favour of his generous entertainer's moral and religious character. Leaving, therefore, details of the missionary's own way and manner of dealing with the natives and with others until we can illustrate from his own journal, we will here draw largely from this brief memorial of his departed friend and founder of the mission.

The missionary's first efforts, of course, were with such of the household and with such of the slaves from that and neighbouring estates as were willing and were permitted to come and worship or receive Christian instruction. His mission was primarily and chiefly to the negro population. But, from the beginning, white or coloured persons from places near came also to worship. These grew more numerous, travelling up to Le Resouvenir even from town; and in a few weeks, Mr. Post, to accommodate them, had one of his estate buildings turned into a meeting-room, and "prepared seats for them according to their station in life." Two services were held on the Sabbath, Mr. Wray conducting worship and preaching; whilst teaching, catechizing the negroes old and young, or visiting the sick, went on as opportunity offered or other claims allowed.

The numbers of Sunday comers did not cease to multiply, and it soon became evident that the place of meeting would shortly be found too strait for the growing congregation. In the course of a correspondence kept up with the Directors of the Missionary Society, Mr. Post, therefore, arranged to erect a suitable building of a size to accommodate 600 persons, they contributing £100, and he the main cost. Named " Bethel Chapel," and opened on the 11th September, 1808, only a day or two more than eight months after the missionary's arrival—at the first service, builder and preacher had the joy of seeing it " crowded with people of various colours."

" Bethel Chapel," Le Resouvenir! how little did generous planter or missionary pioneer, or any of the varied throng that then crowded within its walls, dream of the foul injustice and monstrous cruelty associated with which, in a while and for years to come, its name would ring throughout and beyond the empire !

The erection of a minister's house on the estate and close to the chapel, followed immediately, and was completed in 1809; Mr. Post " expending more than £1000 on these objects, and about £200 being subscribed by other respectable inhabitants of the Colony." *

* Evangelical Magazine, 1835, p. 211.

"He soon discovered a missionary spirit, becoming very anxious to have the Gospel preached in other parts of the Colony and in the neighbouring Colony of Berbice ; but his bad state of health hindered him from being so active as he wished. It was his desire and intention to have travelled with me in different parts of the Colony, but sickness always prevented."

Preparations, however, were made for beginning work in town. Here, Mr. Post "freely offered ground to build a chapel upon, if permission could have been obtained ; but an express prohibition was sent from men in power." A school under his direction as acting trustee and " which had been kept in one of his buildings in town by a person who failed," was more fortunate. "Mr. Post hired teachers to carry it on, and when some of the children were taken away lest he should teach them *his* religion, it cost him for a considerable time £16 per month more than the income." Here again the Missionary Society was enlisted as co-adjutor, and by the end of the year another agent was far on his way, passage and other expenses liberally paid by the generous trustee.

This is certainly no light list of gift and work for the commencing year, pursued too, as we shall see, amid great and growing opposition and obloquy.

"But Mr. Post persevered undaunted, following his Master through evil and through good report." " He entertained exalted views of Divine providence. If his undertakings prospered, he ascribed all to the blessing of God upon them, rather than to his own creature wisdom or strength. If he met with crosses or losses in the world, he looked through second causes to the great Disposer of all events. At that season of the year when he built the chapel, he had a much better crop of cotton in one field that any of his neighbours, in consequence of a different method he had pursued with his trees. At another time he was greatly distressed for want of money, and knew not what course to take ; when, very opportunely, a gentleman came and lent him £4000. These and many events of a like nature, he looked upon as directions of Providence, but did not like to speak of them to the people of the world, lest they should think it enthusiasm."

However, "on Lord's Day, 23rd October, 1808," Mr. Wray says :—

" A few weeks after the opening of Bethel Chapel, I preached, at the request of Mr. Post, respecting the judgments of God that pass through the Colony; my sermon being from Hosea iv. 1-4, and chiefly taken up with some reflections of Mr. Post's on the awful state of the Colony in 1803, and the providence of God since that period towards the inhabitants. His mind is greatly affected because so many of his fellow-colonists oppose the instruction of the negroes in the principles of Christianity. This led him to reflect on the ways of God towards the Colony for four or five years back. He considers the preaching of the Gospel as the last trial God is about to make to bring the people to repentance."

All notwithstanding,—

" the fruits of Mr. Wray's labours began more than ever to awaken the attention of those who were interested in the continuance of slavery. The *Royal Gazette* (Demerara) of that period gave publicity to the following sentiments :—' It is dangerous to make slaves Christians, without giving them their liberty. He that chooses to make slaves Christians, let him give them their liberty. What will be the consequence when to that class of men is given the title of *beloved brethren*, as is actually done ? Will not the negro conceive that by baptism, being made a Christian, he is as credible as his *Christian white brethren ?*'"

For the preceding extract we are indebted to the Rev. E. A. Wallbridge, who goes on pertinently to remark :—

" Slavery thrives only in the dreary regions of moral darkness, where the light of truth must not enter. It loves to dwell in a land of spiritual death, amidst whips and chains and stocks, with all the odious instruments of punishment deemed necessary to compel incessant and unrequited toil. Disguise it as you may, slavery is still a system which 'loves darkness rather than light.'"*

* "Martyr of Demerara," p. 17.

Accordingly, Mr. Post

"was looked upon by many as a fool or a madman, and became the subject of their laughter. He was charged with introducing anarchy, disorder, and discontent among the enslaved negroes ; and was forbidden, by authority, ' to hold any riotous meeting of slaves on his estate.' Many said he was going to make Demerara a second St. Domingo ; indeed, numbers dated the ruin of the Colony from the day that the missionary arrived. But ' none of these things moved him.' He was determined to persevere in the path of duty, and leave the event with God." Yet " he studied, night and day, what method was best to be taken, and did all in his power to remove the prejudices of the people. He wrote letters to some, conversed with others, and endeavoured to receive all the information he could concerning the success of the Gospel among the negroes of Surinam, whence came the most pleasing intelligence concerning the preaching of the Moravians, and where, as well as in several of the West India Islands, from which also he sought and received reports, the missionaries appeared to receive every encouragement from the most respectable inhabitants. It appeared to be his continual study, and the chief business of his life, to promote the glory of God and the salvation of the negroes."

A few extracts from his letters of that time will show his anxiety in this respect. Writing, February 1808, he says :—

"My health and strength have failed me much for several months, and disabled me, in many instances, from being as useful as I could wish ; but I know that our Lord has no need of me. I am not worthy to serve His cause. Join with us in earnest prayer that the work here, as well as in other places, may continue and prosper to the salvation of many of every colour. God in His mercy has prepared a way for His minister, and will, I trust, continue to bless his labours with His Almighty power, and open the understandings of the people to whom the sound of every scriptural or spiritual expression is new. May his health be preserved, and the obstacles against future undertakings be removed."

When writing for a person for the School, he says :—

" My constitution is such that it does not promise me many more healthy days. The gout seems to continue my constant companion ; but I trust I shall, before my departure, see that long-desired work accomplished, of instructing the youth of all classes in the ways of true wisdom."

When 1808 had passed, and with it the first eleven months of the missionary's presence and work, dating 12th January, 1809, Mr. Post writes :—

" It would be ingratitude to our God and Saviour not to praise His name for what He has done. He has built His temple in this wilderness, and, I trust, has given us reason to call it *Bethel*, because many of the ignorant negroes have experienced the presence of the Lord. It is not possible that such a change could otherwise have been effected in their conduct, both on mine and other estates, but especially on the estate next to mine (Success). They were formerly a nuisance to the neighbourhood, on account of their drumming, dancing, &c., two or three nights in the week, and were looked on with a jealous eye on account of their dangerous communications ; but they are now become the most zealous attenders on public worship, catechizing, and private instruction. No drums are heard in this neighbourhood, except where the owners have prohibited the attendance of their slaves. Drunkards and fighters are changed into sober and peaceable people, and endeavour to please those who are set over them."

Mr. Wray, of course, amid all other duties, had his own correspondence with the Society, and with friends at home to maintain. Reporting to the former, about the middle of the year, he writes as one feeling that his coming to Demerara had been a right step, and as one growingly confident that he should be able, as certainly he was willing, to continue—re-assuring news to all parties, not least so to her who was expecting to follow. Very encouraging also would be the further intelligence that, after the opening of the chapel, the pioneer was preaching to a congregation of between 400

and 500 black and free coloured people, exclusive of
Europeans, and otherwise imparting religious instruction to
them; or, again, the Report at the end of 1808, that—

"A church had been formed consisting of twenty-four members;
150 persons appeared to be sincerely seeking salvation; 200
of the negroes had learned passages of Scripture, the Assembly's
Catechism, and hymns; and that the improvement affected
among the people generally, who received this Christian instruction, was such as to draw forth the approbation of the managers."*

1809.

*Arrival of Rev. John Davies—Continued Prosperity—Founder's Fatal
Illness—Arrival of Miss Ashford and others—Founder's Decease—
Funeral Solemnities—His Attainments, Character, and Generosity.*

In the first month of 1809 appeared the Rev. John Davies,
to undertake the school in town. He landed on the 22nd,
was cordially received by Mr. Post, and soon began his work;
residing, and preaching also, as occasion might allow, on the
site where Providence new chapel, house, and school now
stand. The new arrival so laboured and prospered, that
before long he had upwards of forty children daily under
instruction in useful knowledge and Christian truth, and
preached three times a week in the schoolroom to upwards
of 300 people.† Some of the latter came from distant parts
of the country on the Lord's Day to hear the words of
eternal truth; and many are the interesting accounts given,
long years after, by persons who used to attend his instructions; how they suffered the loss of sleep, and performed
long journeys to Georgetown; how they meekly endured
increased labour, and fearlessly risked being seized by the
constables as runaway negroes, if they might only hear their
beloved minister.‡

---

* Brief account, *Evangelical Magazine* 1835, p. 211.
† *Evangelical Magazine*, 1811, p. 7.
‡ "Martyr of Demerara," p. 18.

At Le Resouvenir the work of the Lord continued to prosper, though here, as perhaps everywhere, not all that were nearest at hand, or had the easiest access, or the greatest encouragements, were readiest to become partakers. Mr. Post rejoiced in God when good was done there among his own negroes or others; but he was at times cast down when, with all *his* great encouragement, only few of his own put in an appearance to learn the catechism or to hear the Word. He gave them Saturday to go to market that they might have the Sabbath to themselves; and garments, when lack of these was pleaded as an excuse for staying away. He would converse with them in the most affectionate manner, explain the Bible and pictorial illustrations of the Scriptures to his own people or to any who would come, sometimes spending a great part of the Sabbath in this work, and so do all in his power to bring sinners to Christ. Thus we find him writing in another letter:—

"I have not the pleasure to find that my own negroes attend so well as those on other estates, but I thank God that many of them do, and are very zealous indeed, and much concerned to have an interest in that Jesus who came to die for sinners. I asked one of my carpenters if his knowledge was much improved, to which he replied, 'Very much,' and said that he was convinced of sin. I asked him if he were to fall in a river and a plank were thrown to him what would he do, to which he answered, 'I would take hold of it very strong; so I do Jesus.' He and several more assure me that their only hope is on what Jesus has done for them, and that they pray daily for wisdom and the Spirit of God. Many express themselves with great thankfulness that they have an opportunity to hear the Gospel, when, surely, I point them to the First Cause, who showed His love to them in directing me and the hearts of the good people in Europe to do it. It is affecting to see so many black faces in the meeting, who formerly were not much distinguished from the brute creation, all directed toward the minister, especially when the subject is very serious; and in prayer, to see many kneeling, others standing, repeating with a sigh the word *Amen*, and to hear from their lips the words plainly expressed both in prayer and singing hymns. These are pleasing facts. I recommend us all to the prayers of the Christian people in England. We think it our duty to pray for the coming of the kingdom of Jesus over all the world."

Accounts continuing favourable, Miss Rebecca Ashford, according to arrangement and so soon as a convoy could be obtained, quitted home and England to join Mr. Wray, and for a first absence which proved to be of twenty-two years' duration. There sailed on the same day, 5th March, 1809, and for the same destination, Miss Sandars, to become Mrs. Davies ; the Rev. Isaac Purkis, going to Tobago ; and the Rev. Thomas Adam, who eventually went on to Trinidad. All landed safely in Demerara, 15th April, just in time to take off the edge from a great loss which the mission was about to sustain.

For already, four days before their departure from England, Mr. Post had been taken with a fatal seizure. His two or three last years had been years more or less of suffering from gout and asthma, with occasional attacks of great danger and severity. One such attack he had experienced just before Mr. Wray's arrival, and another shortly after it. Again, in the early days of January, 1809, he had a similar seizure, but was restored, being able after a short time to attend to business, when he was much employed about the school and the building of the minister's house. On 28th February he went to the back of the estate with Mrs. Post, a whole distance of several miles, and the next morning he was confined to his room, never to leave it again.

"On 8th April," again to quote at length the Memoir, "he endured very severe pain, both night and day, which sometimes rendered him impatient and fretful. About a month before his death he sent for his head carpenter, and with the greatest composure gave him orders to make his coffin. He gave also particular directions concerning his funeral. Twice or thrice he sent for the children brought up in his house, for his manager, and for some of his domestics, and took his leave of them in a very affectionate manner. At those times he was generally composed, and enjoyed comfortable prospects of eternity. At one of these seasons he recommended the children very affectionately to me, and requested that I would catechize them and attend to their spiritual welfare. To one of his oldest negroes, a driver of the name of Mars, who came to see him, he said, 'Mars, how are you ?' The old man, thinking that he asked what the people had been doing, said, 'Picking cotton, massa.' Mr. Post replied, 'I do not ask you what you have been doing. Picking cotton is nothing to me now ! I have done with it.' He then called the old negro to his bed-side, took hold of his hand, and bid him farewell, exhorting him to attend the preaching, to come to Jesus, to pray to Him, and charged him to meet him at the right hand of God, telling him he must shortly die, and that though he had been his master, and had sometimes been angry with him, there would soon be no difference between them. They both wept abundantly. This was a very affecting scene."

In a similarly kind manner did this dying Christian planter "frequently speak to the negroes who came to see him, exhorting them to seek Christ with their whole hearts." Himself experiencing varied feelings, " sensible that he was a sinner—a great sinner—and that he had nothing to plead but the sufferings and death of Christ," he derived comfort chiefly from those passages of Scripture "which give encouragement to the chief of sinners. These were greatly blessed to him." "Though often perplexed with doubts and fears he was, at other times, strong in faith, giving glory to God."

"One day he sent for me (Mr. Wray) from the dinner-table, and said, 'I have sent for you to tell you that I shall just enter in through Christ;' and at another time he said, 'Yea, though I walk through the valley of the shadow of death, God will be with me.' He frequently repeated the name of Jesus in a very affecting way, and would often say, 'Come and receive me to Thyself !' Once he told me he was very comfortable, and requested me to pray especially for the spread of the Gospel, and said, 'All will be well.' At another time he said, with great earnestness, 'Tell the people at my funeral that I am a sinner, but have obtained mercy through Jesus Christ.' Once, when I was speaking to him, he looked steadfastly at me, and said, in a very affecting manner, 'You have come so far to teach me how to die. I know you love me, and I will love you in Heaven.' When his spirits were good, and he was tolerably free from pain, he would converse cheerfully about preaching, religion, and what he had passed through in life. He would frequently request me to read to him, and when I asked him what he wished to have read, he would say, 'Something suitable. Some of the sayings of Jesus or Paul.' On the two or three last days of his life I had not an opportunity to converse much with him, for he was extremely weak ; but he was enabled to build on the rock Christ Jesus. The day before his death, I had some conversation with him on temporal subjects, especially about the chapel."

But Miss Ashford with her companions had now been landed some fourteen days, and much about marriage, missions, and missionaries, about this mission to Demerara in particular, must have demanded and divided Mr. Wray's attention ; so mingled, not seldom, is the cup of life ; as the bell of morn becomes the curfew, a wedding and passing bell, too, ringing merrily and mournfully, all in a day.

For at last, on 29th April, a great loss befell all except him, the Christian planter, who,—

"about half-past eight o'clock in the evening, fell asleep in Jesus. Loud were the lamentations of the poor negroes, who spent most of the night weeping for him. It was a very affecting scene. I suppose there were more than 500 negroes of his own and from other estates lamenting their loss. Mr. Purkis and the manager went among the houses to request them to be still ; but in vain. They continued to weep aloud, exclaiming, 'My massa, my massa !' I was much affected with the language of one poor woman who said she had been twenty years on the estate—not able to do any work ; but her massa had given her everything to make her comfortable."

Growth and decay are so rapid in that country as not to allow of burial being deferred beyond the day after death.

At five in the afternoon of Lord's Day, 30th April, therefore, Mr. Post was interred. His grave was on his own estate, in his own burial-ground, under a large mango tree; he having strictly charged, in response to a wish expressed to the contrary, that it should not be within the precincts of the chapel. The day proved very wet, thus preventing the attendance of many people of colour. Nevertheless a great number of such came to the funeral, besides a multitude of negroes in their deep sorrow. Eight of the latter, who were his own, whom he had selected for the purpose, some of whom he had enjoyed the happiness of seeing baptized and walking in the fear of the Lord, carried his remains to the grave.

At the door of his house the 63rd Hymn of Dr. Watts' second book, beginning—

> " Hark ! from the tombs a doleful sound,
> My ear, attend the cry,"

was sung; and at the grave, the 88th of the first book—

> " Life is the time to serve the Lord,
> The time to insure the great reward ; "

and the 107th of the second book—

> " That awful day will surely come,
> The appointed hour makes haste."

An exhortation also was given from Amos iv. 12, " Prepare to meet thy God, O Israel." On several succeeding days the estate appeared as though it were in mourning for its late owner; and on Lord's Day, May 14th, a funeral sermon was preached from Rev. xiv. 13, " And I heard a voice from heaven saying unto me, Write, Blessed are the dead which die in the Lord, &c."

A few more details of the character and attainments of this excellent man and founder of the Mission, before we finally cease mention of him, will not be out of place.

Master of the Dutch, French, and English languages, Mr

Post had not read many books on any subject, secular or sacred, with which he was familiar, but was well acquainted with what he had perused, and by travelling and other means had obtained a considerable degree of general knowledge.

He was an able and a practical agriculturist, and undoubtedly one of the most laborious planters in the Colony; himself, specially in times of emergency, working alongside while directing his slaves.

"He did not punish but when absolutely necessary, and a very respectable planter, who knew him many years, affirms that he never knew him inflict severe punishment, and that he never had any runaway negroes, except two or three, who were notoriously bad." "Nothing would cause him sooner to dismiss a white servant than undue severity with the negroes. Kind to them at all times, he was especially so when they were sick; sending them wine or soup or whatever else his house or table could afford, and paying them his own personal visits; Mrs. Post also giving the greatest attention to them, whether by night or day."

"His conversation was always edifying, his two favourite topics being Religion and Astronomy. He would have sat up half the night, in a gallery behind his house, to view and converse about the heavenly bodies; and when speaking of religion, he was never weary. He would often lament much that he found people in Holland and North America so little inclined to speak on religious subjects."

"In his dealings with others he was honest, upright, and faithful to all his engagements. His word was as good as his bond. None disputed that what Mr. Post promised he would fulfil if in his power; and he was careful not to promise more. Easily imposed on by others, in two or three instances he suffered greatly on account of this. Indeed, the trials and temptations altogether which he endured were very great and of a peculiar nature, and would have sunk many a stout heart to the grave."

"Taught to read the Bible at home, he brought it with him to Demerara, and read it every day, not merely as the effect of custom, but that he might derive benefit from it. Soon after his arrival, the gentleman with whom he then lived used to laugh at him, and say, 'Mr. Post, you read your Bible to atone for your sins;' to which he would reply, 'No, sir, I do not; but I read it to keep me from sin.' After he had a house of his own he read it every morning to his family before they rose from the breakfast table; nor did company or occasional visitors hinder this practice. I have heard a gentleman say, 'I used to call upon Mr. Post when I went to town, but I left it off, because he always detained me by reading the Bible. Not that I have anything to say against reading it, God forbid! but I wanted to be in town about my business.' In private, Mr. Post diligently studied the Bible, meditating upon it, and thus becoming well acquainted with its sacred contents."

His doctrinal sentiments were formed from the Bible rather than from any human author. As after he was made acquainted with the Assembly's Catechism he greatly approved of it, these sentiments may, in brief, be described as coincident therewith.

"His mind had formerly been much perplexed about the inspiration of the Holy Scriptures; and the more he read on the subject in human authors, the more he was confused. The reading of the Word alone confirmed his mind in this glorious truth. Especially did the sayings of Christ, the Epistles of Paul, and the fulfilment of the prophecies; also the majestic language of the Scriptures and the holy precepts they contain; the effects which the Gospel produces and its progress through the world by the mildest means, in the midst of the greatest opposition; finally establish him in their truth."

Gradually, however, it was that he was cleared of the meshes of serious error and consequent sin, which he not only had forsaken but bitterly lamented, long before his death.

"He professed an uncommon esteem for the more public ordinances of religion," and thought those persons blessed indeed who dwell where these are observed.

"Such opportunities he could not enjoy for more than twenty years, but to supply the deficiency, he or one of his friends used to read a sermon every Lord's Day. His strongest objection to Demerara was his not having an opportunity to hear the Gospel and to converse on spiritual things. The last three or four years before the Gospel was preached on his estate, he used to retire, as soon as breakfast was over, to a small house which he built at the seaside, to read and pray; that he might be free from visitors who came to his house, and worship his God in spirit and truth.

" After my arrival he diligently attended preaching twice every Lord's Day, and also in the week days when business did not prevent him. He was always extremely attentive during public worship, and frequently shed tears. Singing was a part of the service in which he took peculiar delight. He was strongly attached to Dr. Watts' Psalms and Hymns. At the administration of baptism he was also much affected, especially when he stood up to present his little Creole slaves ; and engaged to bring them up in the fear of the Lord. He considered this undertaking of the greatest importance, and his indispensable duty. On the 26th December, 1808, when thirteen men and seven women were baptized, he shed tears of joy during the whole service. He was also very anxious that the Lord's Supper should be dispensed among the pious negroes, and to sit down with them at the table of the Lord ; but used to say he thought it would be too much for him. This, however, was not accomplished during his life ; but he requested on his death-bed it might be as soon as possible."

" Undoubtedly he had his imperfections, which he daily lamented ; but if we consider him in every point of view, and make proper allowances for the country, &c., in which he lived, he appears to have been a truly excellent man, and almost a miracle of grace."

" In his death the negroes lost one of the kindest masters ; his bereaved widow, a most affectionate husband ; her child, one of the best of parents ; the fatherless and the widow, a kind protector ; the Colony of Demerara, a respectable, useful, and benevolent inhabitant ; and the writer of this Memoir (Mr. Wray), one of the most sincere friends—a friend who will ever be remembered by him with the warmest gratitude. Above all, the Church of Christ has lost one of its most useful members—one whose life appeared almost absolutely essential to the promotion of the Gospel in this country ; but God sometimes removes such useful persons, to convince us that He can do without them, and sometimes lest we should put them in His place."

With consistent thoughtfulness, Mr. Post "generously secured to the London Missionary Society, so long as it should continue to provide a missionary preaching the doctrines of the Reformed Church, the chapel on Le Resouvenir, together with a dwelling-house for the minister, a garden, and the sum of £100 annually towards the minister's support;" but should the condition cease to be fulfilled, the property was then to be transferred to a Scotch society.*

The Missionary Society, on its part, records its loss in the same 16th Annual Report as that "of one of their warmest and most useful friends," declaring it "impossible to express the obligations under which the cause of religion in the Colony was laid by his influence, contributions, and exertions;" and that "the Society will long cherish the memory of their generous benefactor," and hope likewise that it may prove a stimulus to "others at home and abroad, to emulate so worthy an example."

1809–1811.

General Character of Mr. and Mrs. Wray's Work—Prosperity of the Mission—Their First-born—Appearance of Indians—Serious Ill Health of Mr. Wray—Governor's Troublesome Proclamation—Wray's Appeal and consequent Departure for England.

A FEW weeks, and things that were to continue had settled again to their usual course on Le Resouvenir. But not all these exactly as before. One difference was in the friend at John Wray's side. The first and former had gone, the second, and more intimate and future, had taken that place in which she long proved a help-meet indeed, and was highly favoured in some respects. For, if he had the somewhat unusual experience in Guiana missions, of being spared thirty years to found station after station, Mrs. Wray had

* Report of the Missionary Society, 1810.

E

the almost unique experience among missionaries' wives
there, of sharing, as a wife, so long a period of life, and toil,
and peril ; yet withal of surviving her husband, and, as a
widow, returning with her family to England.

Much of their work, it may here be said, was of the
simplest, but none the less laborious character. The slaves
that came for instruction had to be taught as the veriest
children, and without the advantage of teaching them to
read. They might of themselves, in process of time, pick up
the art, as some of them did ; else, teaching was very much
by means of repetition—hymns, passages of Scripture,
Watts' Catechisms and the Assembly's First, being thus
committed to memory. It was literally "precept upon
precept, precept upon precept; line upon line, line upon
line ; here a little, there a little ;" until the learners could
for themselves say verse or answer, and in turn convey like
instruction to others. This, with singing, quite as much as
preaching (which itself had to be of the simplest character),
was their occupation—work pursued by Mr. and Mrs. Wray
whenever and wherever there was an opportunity, and from
the first not without good results. These grew, as we shall
see, year by year, multiplying fast in later years ; some of
which results were to be witnessed in the sterling stamp of
men and Christians taught by them, and to be found here
and there in the churches long after their instructors had
been laid in the dust. It was, indeed, the thin edge of the
wedge ; a long thin edge, too ; but none other was possible ;
a wedge however, which, when the long end had securely
entered, was to be driven home to its fullest extent much
sooner, and with effects upon the social state of Guiana much
greater, than what even John Wray or many a one else then
thought.

At the close of 1809, Mr. Wray was able to write of the
cause of Christ as continuing to prosper, and of many
persons old and young as being anxious to hear the Word of

Life. There had been many pleasing instances of the power of Divine grace on the hearts of negroes, the alteration produced in their moral conduct being such as to recommend the Gospel of Christ. Referring to the Christmas holidays, he says :—

"What a great and glorious change has taken place among them since the last year ! Instead of following their vain amusements, numbers have turned to the Lord, sing His praises, and glorify His name. They now hate the things which they once loved, and delight in the things of Jesus of which many of them never heard till lately." *

From sixteen to twenty children attended almost every day to learn to read ; and, generally in the evening, a great many women. On the Lord's Day there was a school often of fifty children ; also more of the owners of estates seemed disposed to promote the instruction of their slaves, having observed the good effect produced on those already taught.

In the course of 1810 this improvement continued, and encouragements were multiplied. Though a few who appeared to set out well became lukewarm and indifferent, the congregation progressively increased to between 500 and 600 persons. About 200 attended public worship regularly, and of these many were inquiring the way of salvation. At the close of the year Mr. Wray was pastor of a church numbering thirty-seven communicants, and, 12th December, 1810, writes :—

"It gives me pleasure that some of the negroes are able to conduct the singing without the assistance of any white person ; a few have been able to read sufficiently well as to make use of their hymn-books. A man named Romeo, about fifty years of age, is able to read fairly well in the New Testament ; and one much older, though he cannot read, can pray with great fluency and propriety. It is astonishing to hear what use he makes of Scripture in his prayers. His name is Jason : he comes from a great distance ; and bad weather never stops him.

* Society's 16th Annual Report.

"At —— I frequently preach on the Lord's Day in the afternoon ; but find it too much to ride ten miles in the hot sun and preach thrice ; yet I do not like to neglect a field of labour when it is open. About 400 frequently attend, of whom perhaps 100 sometimes attend at Le Resouvenir and elsewhere."

Several events of this year must have special if only brief mention.

On 18th May came their first-born, a little daughter whom her parents named Elizabeth, and who, spared through many perils, grew up to be their life-long companion and to survive them many years, remaining unmarried. After a useful and well-spent life, she fell asleep in Jesus at Exeter, so recently as August, 1885.

A much different appearance was that of a chief and other principal men from one of the far inland tribes of Indians, who, after a journey of six weeks, arrived in town and, during their stay, attended Divine worship, behaving with great reverence. Through an interpreter conversation was held with them. After being informed as to what had been said at the service, an earnest desire for a teacher to be sent into their country was expressed by the chief, a lord of eight other tribes besides his own. On the other hand, a young man of education and piety, by repute well qualified for the undertaking, was already known to Mr. Wray, and when, willing to go, he applied to the Missionary Society for the requisite assistance, had the pioneer's recommendation.

During the year, Mr. Wray compiled the brief memoir of his friend Mr. Post, from which we have so largely quoted; with conscientious care submitting it to the widow and to two most intimate and long-attached friends of the deceased, Messrs. Van Couten and Sample, who approved and accredited it as correct ; he then forwarded it in time for publication in the January number of the *Evangelical Magazine* for 1811.

But already indications were not wanting that the

pioneer was being overtasked, and the opening months of 1811 saw him a comparatively helpless invalid; having narrowly escaped the loss of an eye through inflammation, being threatened with serious disorder of the liver, and under doctor's orders to cease a-while so much speaking or reading. In this dilemma, Mrs. Wray read a chapter or sermon to the negroes when her husband was unable to say more than a few words; she still continuing her school, her women's prayer-meetings, and frequently catechizing both children and adults.

In addition to these effects of toil and climate upon Mr. Wray, came increasing anxieties on other accounts. For if the goodwill of some as they witnessed the beneficial results of his labours was being gained, opposition to mission-work and hindrances in the country generally were also growing. These at length culminated in a proclamation by the Governor which led to a corresponding movement on the part of John Wray, seemingly quite in harmony with his character. He could endure much, not, however, to be needlessly shorn of his work. Any who thought so patient and harmless a man would sit down and submit to anything when a legitimate way was open for redress, must soon have been led to a different opinion.

Three changes of Governors had taken place since his arrival in the Colony, the last of these being when H. W. Bentinck, Esq., who had held office, May 1806 to May 1807, and retiring, had returned to England on account of ill-health, resuming the reins in May, 1809. Two years afterwards, on the 25th of May, 1811, he issued a proclamation prohibiting the negroes assembling before sunrise and after sunset, be the object of such gathering what it might. As of course they had to work during daylight, this greatly interfered with the religious instruction of the people, and though designed as a measure of civil precaution, there are more than appearances that it was meant also to interfere with their attendance at places of public worship. It followed on the lines of such proceedings as had been adopted in Jamaica, where a "disposition had been repeatedly manifested by the island Government to suppress the preaching of the Gospel." Though checked by the interference of the British Government,

"the rulers again had had recourse to regulations plainly intended to prevent, if possible, the instruction of the negroes by those who alone would take the pains to bestow it ;"*

and, 14th November, 1810, had passed an Act for licensing preachers, places of worship, and forbidding assemblies of the negroes except in the daytime, with long terms of notice to elapse before application, and exorbitant fees, all to be enforced by penalties fearfully heavy, and, in the case of slaves, by punishments terribly severe. Thus a preacher was liable to a fine of £50, and each hearer to one of £10, if found together for worship before sunrise or after sunset. Again, if the house or preacher was not licensed, the preacher was to forfeit £50, or be imprisoned three months in the common jail ; each person attending the meeting, if not a slave, to forfeit for the first offence £5, and for every subsequent offence £10 ; if a slave, he or she was to receive a public flogging. And that these enactments were not to remain a dead letter is manifest, for it is recorded that :—

"On 30th May, 1811, Mr. J. Wiggins and Mr. J. Toland, two preachers of the Methodist Connexion, were convicted at Kingston for preaching without a license and after sunset ; they were fined £50 each."†

Details in Demerara might be different, but the interference with missionary work was much the same ; an interference, too, which continued to spread—Trinidad being next reported as following suite. ‡

---

* *Evangelical Magazine*, 1811, p. 395.
  †   "   "   "   439.
  ‡   "   "   "   436.

To meet the emergency, Mr. Wray took his own course, or rather we should say, and may be sure, the course which, as in the sight of God, approved itself to his conscience, painful in many ways though it might be. He appealed to the Governor, and having failed in his appeal, leaving wife and child at Le Resouvenir, getting Mr. Davies to preach there at times, he came straight away home to His Majesty's Ministers for redress. The particulars were often narrated in after days within hearing of his children, and Mrs. Tuckett has not forgotten them. She writes :—

"In 1811, before I was born, he came to England to appeal to His Majesty's Ministers for the removal of certain hindrances thrown in his way, &c., as you know. I have often heard him speak of his interview with Governor Bentinck (I think it was Governor Bentinck—he was a thorn in my father's side in after years in Berbice). 'Your Excellency,' my father said, 'I have come to speak to you about this proclamation which prohibits the negroes from assembling before sunrise and after sunset.' His Excellency cut him short :—'If I catch you breaking the law, I will banish you from the Colony.' My father told him he had no intention of breaking the law, but as with such a law he could do nothing in the way of teaching the slaves, he should at once go to England and appeal to His Majesty's Ministers.

"My father left his Excellency, and at once proceeded to the waterside to look for a ship about to sail for England. There was but one, taking in cotton, and it would sail in a few days. 'Captain,' he said, 'I want to go to England.' 'Oh,' said the captain, 'I can't possibly take you ; every berth is filled with cotton bales.' 'But,' said my father, 'I will do without a berth ; I will sleep on the cotton bales—only let me come on board, and I will put up with any inconvenience.' The captain yielded ; my father rode back to Le Resouvenir, told mother of his interview with the Governor, and that he had taken his passage in a ship which would sail in a few days ; and so, mother has often said, the promise she made before God in her own heart when she accepted my father, that she would never in any way hinder him in what he thought it his duty to do, flashed on her mind, and she always kept this promise as sacred."

The first item, which has survived, of Mr. Wray's MSS. containing a rough draft of his history of the mission, is dated 16th June, 1811 :—

"Having been at Mr. Davies's two or three days, annoyed by the mosquitoes so much that we (himself and Mrs. W.) could get no rest, I went on board the ship *Demerara* very early this morning, accompanied by Mr. Davies.　My dear wife was much affected.　In the afternoon, about four o'clock, we weighed anchor."

CHAPTER III.

FIRST RETURN TO ENGLAND, TO SETTLEMENT IN BERBICE.

JUNE 1811—JUNE 1813.

Landing in Liverpool—Intercourse with Spencer—Death of Spencer—Reception in London—Success of Appeal and of other Work—Return—Slave Ship—Arrival and various Receptions—"Cushoo," and Consequences.

"A PLEASANT passage," writes Mr. Wray, and "I landed near Liverpool, in a boat that came alongside, 31st July."

Liverpool, of course, was not the great city it is to-day; but man is the same, and any who have sympathetically followed our missionary so far, will not be unprepared to read further:—"When I set my foot on my native land I was deeply affected. My feelings I cannot describe."

The then town, and much besides, was about to be plunged into mourning: very modestly does the newly-arrived one record his intercourse with him, the loss of whom was the occasion of such sorrow :—

"I remained a few days in Liverpool, and was kindly entertained by Mr. and Mrs. Hurry. I preached three times on the Sabbath (4th August), and supped in company with the lamented Spencer,* the night before he was drowned. In the evening of that day, the first Monday of August, we were to have united in prayer to God, at the missionary prayer meeting, but his soul had taken its flight, to unite with happy spirits above."

* For some in the third generation since these events occurred, it will be needful to explain that the Spencer here mentioned is the Rev.

The day of his landing, he formed one of Spencer's hearers in the evening, with little thought of himself, a stranger, being a trouble to the wearied minister. Writes Dr. Raffles, however (p. 238) :—

"The Rev. Mr. Wray, a missionary at Demerara, was then in Liverpool, and was at the chapel. A friend who saw Mr. Spencer in the vestry, after service, observed him to be much exhausted, and heard him say for the first time : ' Oh, I did not feel comfortable in seeing a brother minister in the congregation this evening !' Usually, he did not fear the face of man."

But the two soon became even more than acquainted, for (p. 242)—

"In the evening of the Saturday following, Spencer met the Rev. Messrs. Charrier, Lister, and Wray, the missionary, together with Mr. Laird, of Greenock, and others, at the house of a friend. It was a pleasant interview, and, in reflection, has afforded to the persons who composed that social party, the sincerest pleasure."

The labours of Sunday, 4th August, over, they again met, as Mr. Wray tells us, and as Dr. Raffles, more at length, details (p. 245) :—

"After the labours of the day Spencer went to the house of a friend to supper ; he did not appear to be unusually fatigued. With great fervour he led the devotions of the family. . . . . He

Thomas Spencer, the immediate predecessor of the Rev. Dr. Raffles, his biographer as well as successor. A youth of great piety, devotion, and gifts, he had, 3rd February, 1811, when just turned twenty, left Hoxton College, to become pastor of the church assembling in Newington Chapel, Liverpool. On the 15th of the following April, and in the presence of some 6000 persons, he laid the first stone of a new chapel, calculated to accommodate 2000 worshippers, the well-known Great George Street Chapel. On Thursday, 27th June, he was ordained ; and on the following Sabbath, 1st July, presided for the first time at the ministration of the Lord's Supper. After a few weeks of constant engagements in town and country, he returned, his biographer says, on Wednesday afternoon (31st July), much fatigued, to Liverpool, but preached in the evening with great animation.

was remarkably copious and earnest in prayer; commending especially to God the family, the Church, the members who had recently joined, the missionary who was present, and every object to which his holy and benevolent mind recurred. At supper the conversation was pure and spiritual. . . . The subject was 'sudden death.' The countenance of Spencer, always animated, was lighted up with holy joy as he discoursed upon the glory of departed saints. . . . He appeared to lose the memory of the day's fatigue in the interesting theme, and frequently observed that he had not, for a long time, felt himself so free from weariness. A little after eleven he parted with his friends for ever."

At the same hour, on the following morning, and about the turn of tide, Spencer left his lodgings to bathe, but chose, not without inquiries from bathers on the spot, a new and more retired place than formerly. Slipping, it is conjectured, from a ledge of rock, into water one or two feet deeper than that in which he had been swimming, a start and spasm are supposed to have rendered him helpless, and in less than an hour his body, bearing no indication of violence or struggle, the features of the face perfectly undisturbed, the countenance placid and serene, was found and landed on the beach.

Thus Mr. Wray and he did not meet again as they had hoped; but, as we think of the youthful pastor, so soon called hence, and of the older missionary brought through so many perils and spared for more than a quarter of a century longer through trials and dangers even greater and more numerous, and ask, "Why the difference?" or reverently suggest various and seemingly good reasons, we find it is the old question, best met by the thought and fact, "My times are in Thy hand;" by the word, "Work while it is day, for the night cometh when no man can work;" or by the sentiment of the well-known hymn of our well-known poet, himself so mysteriously and deeply tried, lines Spencer was reciting at the moment one of the family came to remind him that soon it would be high water:—

> "God moves in a mysterious way,
> His wonders to perform ;
> He plants His footsteps in the sea.
> And rides upon the storm."

Thirty ministers and four hundred laymen formed the funeral procession, which, eight days after, on 13th August, conveyed Spencer's remains to the grave, and which moved along midst a press of people and gaze of spectators numbered at 20,000.*

But Mr. Wray, to judge by the Missionary Register, which records him as " arriving 10th August, 1811," was not among them. "The king's business required haste," and he was already in London.

To resume his own narrative :—

"When I arrived in London I was received with great kindness by the Directors of the Missionary Society, who entered warmly into the object of my mission. I was very soon introduced to those excellent men, Messrs. Wilberforce and Stephens, who used all their influence to obtain a repeal of the persecuting law. I was delighted with their pious conversation and holy zeal in the cause of Christ. They entered into the case with all their hearts. Mr. Stephens prepared the memorial and documents necessary to be presented to His Majesty's Government. Lord Liverpool, who was then Minister for the Colonies, not only attentively perused the memorial presented to him, but was also pleased to confer with me and the secretaries of the Missionary Society on the subject."

As to what all this meant of toil, &c., to these friends of the slave and their colleagues, we obtain several glimpses in the eminent philanthropist's Life, &c., vol. iii. pp. 544-47.

"Writing to Babington, 22nd August, he says :—'At this moment I have three applications depending, concerning the poor slaves and the missionaries: Trinidad, Demerara, and the Cape.'" "The Cape and, above all, the West Indies, supplied the other subjects of this care. 'You are not aware,' he tells Mr.

* *Evangelical Magazine*, 1811, p. 370.

Hey, 'of all the claims on my time and thoughts which the West Indies have lately furnished.'" "We are working," says Mr. Stephens (21st August), "like negroes for the negroes of Berbice, Sierra Leone, Trinidad, and Africa at large."

"The reluctant conviction that their work was incomplete, was being forced upon the abolition leaders. The West Indies clung too fondly to the vices of the old system ; and though perhaps Mr. Wilberforce himself did not as yet look forward to those great attempts to which he was led on step by step by the gradual progress of events, yet the present vigilance and zeal of the protector of the negro were undoubtedly preparing for them." " 6th September.—His present object was to stop the 'persecution of the missionaries, or rather, to the forbidding religion to the slaves of Trinidad and Demerara.' For this purpose he appealed earnestly to Lord Liverpool, pointing out to him that it was 'a cause interesting not merely to the objects of the particular sect to which the missionaries belonged, but all religionists will make it their own. All will feel it deeply who believe in the truths of Christianity, and are capable of sympathizing with the injuries and sufferings of their fellow-creatures. In truth there is a peculiar call on our sensibility in the present instance, for in proportion as the lot of the slaves is hard in this world, we ought to rejoice in every opportunity of bringing them under the influence of principles which may cheer them under their present sufferings, and secure for them a rich compensation of reversionary happiness. . . . If no clergy, and the remark is of the first importance, it is only through the missionaries that the slaves can receive any religious instruction whatever. To silence them, therefore, is to bar out and close up the only passage through which the light of Divine truth might be conveyed to that deeply injured class of our fellow-creatures. It is not, therefore, injustice and cruelty towards the missionaries of which I would complain (though they are great and flagrant), so much as injustice and cruelty towards the slaves, in whose case this puts the finishing hand to the long catalogue of their wrongs.' There were many difficulties beset this application."

The result of which was, however, again to resume Mr. Wray,—

"that an official letter was transmitted to the Governor of

Demerara (copies of which were also sent to other Colonies), signifying the determination of His Majesty's Government that the slaves should be allowed to meet every Sunday for worship and instruction, from five in the morning to nine in the evening; and on other days from seven to nine in the evening, provided they had the permission of their respective masters." So "the following communication was received (at the Mission House) from the Colonial Office, 15th November, 1811 :—'In consequence of the instructions which have been transmitted by his lordship (Lord Liverpool), to the Governor of Demerara, the slaves in that Colony will be permitted to assemble for Divine worship and instruction on Sundays between the hours of five in the morning and nine at night, and on the other days of the week between the hours of seven and nine at night.

            "'(Signed) ROBERT PEEL.'

" This was just what we asked for."

Not to be enjoyed, however, so soon and so readily as it was enjoined. We shall see the Governor of Demerara attempting, though with less serious consequences, what another Governor a dozen years later attempted with terrible results all round. But leaving this subject a few moments, we observe Mr. Wray himself meanwhile diligently employed in other ways and with no little success.

"During my residence in England I visited many British Churches and endeavoured to excite their attention to the wants of the heathen. I was received everywhere with the greatest kindness. I believe it was on this occasion that the Rev. George Collison first suggested the propriety of missionaries occasionally visiting their native land to declare to the Churches what God was doing for the Gentiles."

Of course he visited Hull, and judging by the sums reported at the close of the year from that town among others, his pleas were met with considerable liberality. No wonder that the suggestion named, if not previously forthcoming, should then be made; or that it should since have come to be so largely acted upon, with what abounding good results any attempt would fail to tell.

His great object accomplished, anxious also as soon as possible to return to his family and station, and to tell of his success, he engaged a passage on board the *Russia Company*. But in those days missionaries were rare, and John Wray seems to have been taken for a sort of Jonah.

"When the owner was applied to, he said he did not much like to have missionaries in his ship, for the devil was against them, and he was the prince of the power of the air, and perhaps he would raise a storm at sea and the ship would be lost."

However, Mr. Wray was accepted, and "we sailed on 13th November, and landed on the 18th December, so I had been just six months absent."

The passage seems to have been without unusual incident, save one reminding us how hardly evil things are surrendered, and how little it seemed possible for Wray to be long out of contact with a horrid institution, shocking to his and to every humane heart.

"We fell in with a slave-ship, which had brought from the coast of Africa one hundred slaves; ten of whom had died and been thrown overboard. Three of the whites were also dead, the captain was very ill, the whole appearance of the vessel miserable, and in so leaky a state that it was thought she could not reach land. The captain, who came on board, pretended to be a Spaniard, and bound to Cuba, but we had every reason to believe he was either an Englishman or an American, and intended to smuggle the slaves into some American port. Our mate went on board the slave-ship, and two of the negroes on seeing him, and probably expecting he was going to release them, lifted up their shackled hands and exclaimed, 'O King George! King George!' Our captain gave this dealer in human flesh a few potatoes and fowls, and two or three bottles of wine, and he proceeded on his voyage with his miserable cargo, either to perish in the waves or to sell them like beasts in the market. Some of the black boys and girls were working at the pumps. The captain of the slave-ship swore in a most horrid manner. I prevailed upon him to take a few tracts."

On landing, Mr. Wray found his "dear wife and little girl quite well, and God had graciously given me another." This other was born on 24th October, was named Rebecca, after her mother, and became the intimate companion of her elder sister, not only through the days of infancy and youth, but throughout a long life, until death them did part, leaving Rebecca the survivor. Mrs. Tuckett writes of Elizabeth :— "With many tears we laid her to rest till the morning of the resurrection. . . . She was a great loss to me, for we had scarcely been separated through life."

The day after his arrival he "waited on his Excellency, Governor Bentinck." A very cordial reception would not be expected, but more reasons than at the moment appeared would afterwards account for the barely cold civility, if so much, shown to our law-abiding but courageous missionary.

"He did not receive me very politely ; but, after asking me some questions, told me to go to his office and have my name recorded."

The truth is that no recall of the proclamation had been made, and the Governor was secretly scheming to injure, if not to ruin the mission ; only, however, as frequently happens in such cases, to be caught in his own meshes.

Different was the missionary's reception elsewhere on the morning of the same day.

"A great number of the negroes came to see me and bid me welcome to Demerara again, praying earnestly that God would bless me. The first Sabbath I preached, the chapel was very full, and I rejoiced to hear that they had attended well during my absence." Mr. Davies had "preached every other Sabbath on Le Resouvenir as well as in town, which was attended with great fatigue in this oppressive climate. His meeting-house there, however, was generally crowded."

Affecting cases of sickness and death had occurred at Le Resouvenir, visited by Mrs. Wray or other Christian friends, one instance forming the occasion of a funeral sermon preached by Mr. Davies ; and it was whilst so fully occupied with work of teaching and preaching in town and country that an incident had occurred, frivolous in itself, but made to become vexatious to both missionaries, and troublesome to not a few besides. Mr. Wray has thus recorded it :—

"During my absence in England a circumstance of a very unpleasant nature occurred, and which showed the Governor was determined to do all in his power to bring us and our mission into disrepute with His Majesty's Government. A gentleman (a Mr. Gravesende) who had rendered considerable service to the mission, wrote to the Missionary Society to request they would forward to him a number of books. They sent his list to the bookseller, who, in packing the books, put in a quantity of waste paper, tracts, &c., to fill up the box. Among these was a tract called 'Cushoo.' When Mr. G. unpacked his box some of Mr. Davies's scholars were at his house playing with his children, and were busy in assisting him. One of them, probably attracted by the picture on the tract, requested to have it. Mr. G. of course gave it to the child. When the child went home, a member of the Court (of Policy) being at his father's house saw the tract in the boy's hand, and conceiving there was something in it injurious to the peace of the Colony took it to the Governor. Mr. Davies was then accused of distributing books containing sentiments of an evil tendency, and was summoned before the Governor and Court which was then sitting. The following is Mr. Davies's own account of it (in a letter to Mr. Wray) :—' I was ordered to appear before the Governor and Court of Policy. When I went the Governor charged me with the circulation of the tract "Cushoo." My reply was, "I am perfectly unconscious of the tract. I do not know that it was ever in my house ; I have never read it." The Governor said, "It was taken from one of the children of your school ; you are a very unfit person to educate children since you put books into their hands you know nothing of yourself ! I will take away your license." I again said, " I know nothing of the tract ; I never gave it to the child, nor have I ever seen it." His Excellency then inquired, "What books have you ?" I answered, "I have books on various subjects, but chiefly on theology." "Well," he said, "I will send a person to see

what books you have, and if I find you have any like this I shall
know what to do with you." I felt very happy at the thought
that my books should be examined, for I well knew that I had
no improper ones. A gentleman was sent with me to examine
my books, and take a specimen of them to the Governor. As
we passed through the schoolroom I called the child. "Who
gave you 'Cushoo'?" said the gentleman. "Mr. Gravesende, sir,"
he replied. "This clears up the whole circumstance," the person
said to me ; "it is useless for me to trouble you any further."
Yet for the greater satisfaction of the Governor and the Court he
looked over what tracts and school books I had, and took some of
L(indley) Murray's books which we use in the school, some tracts,
and your catechism.* After they had been informed what books
I possessed, and looked over those which we had brought as specimens, the Governor called me and said, "I am perfectly satisfied
with you, and as I accused you I now call you to tell you that
I am sorry for it." I replied, "I am glad that my innocency
appears, and I hope we shall always show that we are not the
promoters of rebellion, but of order." He said, "We never had
any other idea of you." Mr. Gravesende was then sent for ; but
as it appeared evident that he was perfectly ignorant of the contents of the tract, he was acquitted. All the tracts he had of the
kind were given to the Governor, who designed to send one to every
Governor in the West Indies. To prevent any unpleasant consequences to our missionary brethren in the islands, I wrote them
the particulars of the whole affair. Let us join to bless Him who
helpeth us in six troubles, yea, in seven. May the remembrance
of past mercies lead us to gratitude and animate us to proceed,
knowing that "goodness and mercy shall follow us all the days of
our life" while we are faithfully enabled to labour for God.—
I am, with much affection, your missionary brother,

JOHN DAVIES.'

"After the above candid explanation between the Governor
and the missionary," continues Mr. Wray, "we should hardly
suppose that 'Cushoo' would be made use of to prejudice the
minds of His Majesty's Government against the missionaries and

---

* For the use of negroes Mr. Wray had published a catechism on
the first principles of Christianity and on the duties of slaves to their
masters, &c.

the Missionary Society. It, however, was so. This pernicious paper, as it was called, was transmitted to Lord Liverpool by Governor Bentinck, and represented to his lordship as a plot intending to promote rebellion among the negroes. The Directors (of the Missionary Society) considered this representation as a very serious matter, and appointed a special committee to investigate the business and communicate their report to Lord Liverpool. The matter was fully investigated, and in the next communication (from the Directors), dated 12th of March, I received a letter containing the result of this application to Lord Liverpool respecting the pernicious tract he had received noted by the Governor. 'His Lordship does not view it in the same light as Governor Bentinck. From his Lordship's secretary, Mr. Peel, we (the Directors) received a very kind assurance by the direction of his Lordship that he saw clearly through the whole affair, and acquitted you and Mr. Davies and us and our bookseller of the least evil intention.'"

The packet that brought out copy of the report sent by the Directors to his Lordship, brought out the recall of Governor Bentinck.

1812.

General Depression—Growing Discouragements—Change of Governors— Proclamation by New Governor—His Favourable Views of Missions, and Ready Help—Obstacles to Marriage—Free Schools—Chapel in Town—Increasing Congregations—Serious Disputes—Missionaries' Aid Invited—New Preaching Station—Sad Effects of Licentious- ness and Colour-prejudice—Visitation of Sick—Sympathy with Oppressed—First School for Young Ladies—Cruelties to Slaves and Conduct of Missionaries—Abounding Sickness—Deaths—Second Owner of Le Resouvenir expires—Official Investigation there of Slaves' Complaints.

THIS copy came to hand in April, 1812, and it will be seen therefore that, to complete the story with Mr. Wray, we have been ante-dating a little. But what such a conclusion, so true and right, meant to the mission alone, cannot be con- ceived without a glance at the intervening months. For though some gleams of progress and brightness appear therein, discouragements multiply.

There were gleams of brightness; thus — what people could be got at, despite the proclamation, "make considerable progress in learning the catechism;" "Mr. Davies has purchased a piece of land and has got the frame of his house and chapel upon it;" Mr. and Mrs. Wray accompany the new owner of Le Resouvenir to the back of the estate to see the new additions for an increased growth of provisions (then very dear) which makes the entire depth upwards of five English miles; and, on 5th April, he and Mr. Davies exchanged, and "Mr. Davies baptized our little Rebecca"— the father's aspiration being, "Oh that God may early give His grace to her, and renew her heart, and make her such an one as He will love and bless!"—a wish which he lived to record as fulfilled when he beheld her, in 1834, "the wife of a useful missionary;" a wish and a record of which she has since proved only the more abundantly worthy.

But withal, discouragements multiplied. Under date of February, 1812, we read of the country as "in a depressed state," money very scarce, and that "coffee can hardly be sold. Provisions and other articles are very dear. We have paid five shillings per pound for candles." About the same time, the family were in town for a fortnight with Mr. and Mrs. Davies; Mr. Davies having recovered from an illness so severe that life was despaired of, and Mr. Wray, from the most severe attack of fever he had experienced in the Colony, Mrs. Wray having had a lighter attack, and the children being yet ill. In March, Mr. Wray became very lame from mosquito bites, of which pest he complains, "they attack me the same as a new comer;" and on the 26th of this month all felt a severe shock of an earthquake, the same, to be afterwards learnt, that in a neighbouring country had destroyed Caraccas and, with it, from ten to twelve thousand of its inhabitants. Then, since his return to Demerara, Mr. Wray had noticed that, despite the non-recall of the Governor's proclamation forbidding the assemblies of negroes after sunset except for the business of the estate, the people met for heathen night-dances as frequently as ever. Yet after three months had elapsed, and during the week preceding 5th April, he writes :—

"I went up the coast with an intention to preach, but was prevented by the attorney of the estate in consequence of Governor Bentinck's proclamation not being recalled. He said he had no objection against my preaching in the evening; but as long as that law existed, he was liable to the penalties. He advised me to go to the Governor on the subject. We know that instructions were sent out, last November, to rescind the persecuting law, but they have not been complied with."

Here was a crowning discouragement. Another such quickly followed; for on Monday, 6th April, the day after the exchange of pulpits and the baptism at Le Resouvenir of little Rebecca, arrived the packet, and by it

"I also received a letter, informing us that the tract 'Cushoo' had been transmitted to Lord Liverpool by Governor Bentinck, and had given the (Missionary) Society a great deal of trouble, and that they (the Directors) had forwarded to his Excellency, Governor Bentinck, a copy of their (special committee's) report to Lord Liverpool."

So "Mr Davies" (who apparently had remained at Le Resouvenir) "and I had much conversation respecting our present trials. We were exceedingly perplexed, and determined to wait on the Governor respecting 'Cushoo,' and to request a license to enable me to preach in the evenings of the week, according to the decision of Lord Liverpool; but it required some strength of mind to go to a Governor who was so much opposed to us."

Things indeed were now gloomy, but it was the dark before the dawn, the depth before the uprising. That mail, as has been told, brought something besides. "I will turn thee back by the way which thou camest," has been the word and work of God toward other opposers than ancient Sennacherib; and pen and press were already at work in a way little thought of by these troubled missionaries and ministers of Zion. Only close and copious quotations will convey a due sense of the relief as it came to them, and what a brighter day it promised. (Mr. Davies having returned to town,)

"*7th April.*—We know not what a day or an hour may bring forth. Yesterday and to-day we have been perplexed. 'How shall we wait upon the Governor?' But, about eleven o'clock at night, Mr. Davies sent a man on horseback with the *Royal Gazette*, containing the following Proclamation by Major-General Hugh Lyte Carmichael, Acting Governor in and over the Colonies of Essequibo and Demerara, &c., &c. :—

"'Whereas I have received instructions from His Royal Highness the Prince Regent to recall the Proclamation issued on the 25th of May, 1811, and to give every aid to missionaries in the instruction of religion, the Proclamation of the above date is hereby recalled, and the following regulations will take place from this date :—

"'*First.*—It is to be understood that no limitation or restraint can be enforced upon the right of instruction upon particular estates, provided the meetings for that purpose take place upon the estate, and with the consent and approbation of the proprietor and overseer of such estate.

"'*Secondly.*—(Hours of meeting on Sundays and other days to be as stated in the instructions sent out by the Home Government, already given.)

"'*Thirdly.*—All chapels and places for Divine worship or public resort shall be registered in the Colonial Secretary's Office, and the names of persons officiating in them shall be made known to the Governor; and the doors of the places shall remain open during the time of public worship or instruction.

"'Given under my hand and seal-at-arms at the Camp House, this 7th day of April, 1812, and in the 52nd year of His Majesty's Reign.   H. L. CARMICHAEL.

"'GOD SAVE THE KING.'"

Here, indeed, was a turn in affairs, which was met with corresponding emotions, response, and activity. Continues Mr. Wray :—

"*8th April.*—It is impossible to describe our feelings on the perusal of this Proclamation. Our hearts were filled with gratitude and love to our God, who 'had put it into the heart of the king to do this thing.' Myself and my dear partner were led to praise our heavenly Father for His goodness to us. I went early to town, and my dear brother-missionary, Mr. Davies, drew up an address to the Governor, expressive of our gratitude to His Royal Highness for what he had done for us ; and also to his Excellency for so promptly executing His Royal Highness's commands; for it was issued on the very day his Excellency assumed the government. On taking our address to Camp House we were immediately favoured with an interview, and had a long conversation with his Excellency on the subject of instruction. He assured us of his assistance and protection, and said that if we could suggest any plan for the furtherance of the Gospel he would communicate it to the Prince Regent. He gave us some very excellent advice, and observed that, to make ourselves as useful as possible, it would be well to meet the prejudices of the planters as far as we could ; 'For, you know, Paul,' his Excellency observed, 'became all things to all men, that he might gain some.' He told us that two of the King's negroes who attended Mr. Davies, behaved exceedingly well, and that he recommended the others to go to chapel also, that they might be reformed. Mr. Davies offered to teach all the soldiers' children gratis, with which his Excellency was much pleased, and said he would think on the subject, but that he had received instructions by this packet from His Royal Highness the Duke of York that they were to be educated by the chaplain."

Two days after came a written reply to their own written address. It and subsequent communications from the new Governor were all in harmony with his first and verbal profession. We give that of 10th April in full :—

"GENTLEMEN,—I received your letter expressive of your gratitude to His Royal Highness the Prince Regent for the interest taken on your behalf as engaged in the instruction of the negroes and others in the principles of Christianity. I promptly obeyed the commands of my Sovereign on this occasion, not only as my duty, but with the impression that the sacred office you have undertaken will be beneficial to the persons who may receive instruction. It is my opinion that your exertions, if properly directed, may be advantageous to that class of persons, both in religion and morality—as also to the political Government of the West India Colonies in general—by instilling the doctrines of Christ into the minds of all ranks of the community, to render to the King loyalty and his dues in all respects; and the Divine precepts (which) further enjoin governors, magistrates, masters, and servants, not only their respective duties to the public, but their reciprocal conduct to each other as explained in the Holy Scriptures, inculcating toleration and benevolence.

"I feel much satisfaction, gentlemen, in your assurance that it will be always your concern to perform your duty as missionaries so as to meet the approbation of His Royal Highness the Prince Regent. In which case you may rely on every assistance and support in my power. — I have the honour to be, gentlemen, your most obedient servant,

"(Signed)   Hu. Lyte Carmichael,
" Acting-Governor.

"To Messrs. Wray and Davies,

 " Missionaries, Demerara."

Stimulated afresh by this new prospect of things, the brethren exerted themselves in every way to forward the great work in which they were engaged. After a few weeks they were again in audience with his Excellency, who, approving their propositions, requested to have them in writing. They were : —

(1.) His patronage of the new chapel which was being built in town.

(2.) Grant of occupancy of a piece of Government land near Mahaica, upon which to build a place of worship ; and similar grants in other parts of the Colony for the same purpose.

(3.) Abolition of the great expenses of marriage as it respected the free coloured people and others, who could not afford to pay them, and made them an excuse for living in fornication.*

* Under the Dutch law, the act of Ondertrowing, or betrothing, was performed by civil commissaries. No objection was made to marriage being considered a "civil contract," but to the expense attending it, £16 to £20. As for slaves, they could not marry.

(4.) A free school on an extensive and liberal plan.

A reply came, dated from King's House, Georgetown, 15th May, 1812, and began as follows :—

"GENTLEMEN,—I have perused with attention your petition of this day, and from your character, which I have minutely inquired into, I have not any doubt that if the negroes will attend to your instructions it will be advantageous to them in the present life as well as in the future. Under this impression, and considering it my duty, I have enclosed some private pecuniary assistance towards building the chapel."

(1.) Heading the subscription list, the Governor contributed 10 joes (about £19) ; and also enclosed 6 joes (about 11 guineas) to Mr. Wray for the Missionary Society, " particularly with regard to the instruction of the lower orders of the population in these Colonies."

(2.) With respect to building sites—"Shall make your application known to His Majesty's Ministers ; meanwhile grant you occupancy of the ground near Mahaica."

(3.) Marriage licenses—" Requires time for consideration and inquiry previous to an answer."

(4.) Charity school—" I much approve of it, and shall attend to that important object. I have taken measures for the troops in garrison to avail themselves of Mr. Davies's kind offer of instruction for their children."

The whole closes with counsel of a tenor and spirit similar to that of his first letter ; advising also that " in a political point of view much prudence and precaution are necessary in addressing the persons of which your audience will be principally composed ;" but declaring "the state of the blacks may gradually be ameliorated by their loyalty and good conduct," of which his Excellency furnishes an instance from his own military experience in St. Domingo ; which, he goes on to say—

"And other equally honourable and disinterested traits of fidelity and courage in those black men have given me a most favourable impression what they may be brought to by persuasion and conciliatory measures ; and I anxiously pray and hope that your exertions may be blessed with every success, which I shall be happy to promote ; and I have the honour to be, &c.

 "The Revs. JOHN WRAY and JOHN DAVIES,
   "Missionaries."

In addition to the children of troops in garrison, all the little negro children belonging to Government were sent to Mr. Davies's school ; and before long a proclamation was issued respecting the marriage of poor free people who could not pay the expense of Ondertrowing, "that the publication of the banns of marriage in the *Gazette* and for three successive Sundays in St. George's Church, shall be equivalent to and answer the forms of Ondertrowing." The Rev. Mr. Straghan, chaplain, co-operated in promoting the welfare of this class of people, charging no marriage fees, and holding afternoon service for their instruction.

This measure, however, excited considerable opposition against both chaplain and Governor, and twelve years afterwards was rescinded ; marriages which had taken place under its provisions being nevertheless held valid. An effort, too, made by the Governor of his own good will, to obtain from the Duke of York, commander-in-chief, a small salary as payment to Mr. Davies who had attending his day-school about thirty children and young men from among the troops, came to nought ; and " for this labour of love," Mr. Wray remarks, " he never received any earthly reward."

On the other hand, very liberal was the response made by several gentlemen during a canvass by the two missionaries in the latter part of June, for donations toward the new chapel in town.

"One planter on the river told us candidly that he formerly prohibited his negroes from attending, but they wearied him out to go to chapel, and he at last gave them leave ; and instruction, he said, had done them much good. They had given over drinking and many other vices of which they were formerly guilty.

He thinks it would be a great blessing if marriage could be introduced among them.   He subscribed liberally."

Going to Mahaica on the same errand, they obtained about 60 joes (£115); and,—

"having heard that Governor Gordon of Berbice was on the coast, we waited on him, and he gave us 20 joes, upwards of £36 sterling. He requested a copy of Governor Carmichael's letter of 15th of May. We also called on a Mr. B., a Barbadian gentleman. He said he would give nothing except to the Church of England ; and, indeed, he said he had given nothing to St. George's Church, for it was in town, and he could not attend it.   He also observed that his negroes would now work for him on Sundays for a glass of rum, but if they had preaching they would not do so.   Hardly any on whom we have called have refused their assistance, and a few have contributed large sums.   For this we will praise God. There are, indeed, a number who oppose us, and do all they can to misrepresent our motives and conduct, but this we are to expect. The cause is God's, and it must prevail."

This effort was but a little of much and varied work that crowded upon them, and the success attending it but one item of prosperity which had set in along with a more liberal measure of freedom, and with the new Governor's favourable countenance of their proceedings. Preaching, 17th May, a funeral sermon on the death of Dr. Vanderkemp, of South Africa, Mr. Wray had the chapel on Le Resouvenir crowded to excess, with about 200 more round the open doors and windows, all anxious to hear about the great missionary. In connection with the same event, Mr. Davies, in town, addressed an audience of 600.   On the day following, being a holiday, Mr. Wray again held service, and baptized fourteen adults, who then brought their children to devote them to God.   Though a rainy morning, the chapel was full.   The whole service was very solemn and affecting.   Like numbers came on succeeding Sabbaths ; while in town, whither numbers of slaves came down the river in punts supplied by their masters, and many from the West Coast, the multiplied crowds made it needful to hold half-a-dozen services on the Sabbath. The plan adopted was :—Beginning at six in the morning with the first service, this congregation, after catechizing and a short sermon, went out on one side of the building, while a new congregation of 400 entered on the other ; half-past ten in the morning and five in the afternoon being reserved for service for the white and free people. The members of the church assisted the minister and his wife in catechizing the negroes, without which catechizing Mr. Davies deemed preaching to be useless ; and withal, found six times preaching in the day too much for him.

With their now tried character and growing influence, the services of the two missionary brethren came occasionally to be invited for remonstrance on behalf of master or slave, or to act as medium between them. Thus, on 23rd May, writes Mr. Wray :—

" I received a note from **Mr. W.** respecting the conduct of some of the negroes under his care. They would not take their rations, because there was only a common allowance, and it is customary to give more at holiday time. This caused a dispute between them and the manager, and they would not throw their grass in the evening as usual. Instead of inflicting corporal punishment, the attorney prohibited them coming to the chapel. I went to the estate at his request, and expostulated with them. This answered the purpose."

In August following, a dissipated character, named Scott, professing to be the son of a minister in Scotland, who himself had been a schoolmaster and was now insane, wandered up the river, telling the negroes that they were free, and that ships were coming from England to carry them away. This resulted in some unsettlement of the negroes on two or three estates about eight miles distant, and, as they sometimes attended Mr. Davies's preaching in town, instruction was blamed for it. The Governor, however, wrote to Mr. Davies, requesting him to visit those estates, speak to the negroes, and act as mediator. He consented, and, furnished with a letter of introduction given him by his Honour the Fiscal, he went and preached on two estates, and was invited to go again. On a second visit Mr. Wray accompanied him, and "preached Christ unto them. They were very attentive during my discourse. I also asked them several questions on religious subjects, which they answered aloud. This method of instruction keeps up their attention. The Governor furnished us with a tent-boat, and it was wise in him to send the Gospel instead of the whip. In returning, the moonlight was splendid, and we found it very pleasant; but, in viewing the banks of the beautiful river, we lamented that they were cultivated by slavery. Another place is open for preaching the Gospel, which would make an excellent missionary station."

This was in August, and the last remark savours of the pioneer. In September Mr. Wray attempted some extension on his own line of coast unsuccessfully; but the sequel shows the true man and father and Christian that he was.

"Having been for some time very desirous to obtain a place to preach in a few miles higher up the (East) Coast, and as there is a beacon in a suitable spot, I applied to the Governor for the use of the lower story. His Excellency gave me a letter to the burgher officer in favour of the object, which I presented to him, but found he discouraged it. He told me to my face that he had flogged two negroes for coming to chapel. This, of course, put an end to further application. The beacon stands on private property. While I was conversing with him on the subject, one of his own little coloured children came into the room. He swore tremendously at it, and told the child he would horsewhip it if it came among the buckras (white masters). These men are ashamed of the fruits of their wickedness, but not of the sin. This, however, gave me an opportunity of conversing with him on the evil of these abominable connections, which are so general and so pernicious both to parents and children, and to the public morals of any country. There is something exceedingly affecting to see a man ashamed of his own children, and who cannot introduce them to his table because they are of a different colour. I trust this system of licentiousness will soon fall before the Gospel."

Of course prejudice against colour alone had its share in this. It ran high in those days, bringing corresponding inconveniences ; how high sometimes, the missionary had an instance in his own house but a few days preceding.

"On the 7th (August) a white lady from town came to spend a few days with us on account of her health. Mrs. Wray has at school some children of colour whose parents and friends are rich planters, and who have put their children under her care to receive an education. This lady took Mrs. W. aside, and said if we were accustomed to have these children to sit at table with us, she would thank her to send her a little of something into her chamber, for she could not think of eating with them. She spoke of them in the most degrading language, considering them of a different species from us."

Not, however, as preacher and peacemaker, in public or by the master alone, were the services of Mr. Wray sought and willingly afforded ; as Christian pastor and as pleader for the wronged and the oppressed, he was often inquired for more privately and by persons of all ranks, both bond and free ; and himself and his excellent wife were at times much engaged in ministering to mind or body diseased, at the bed-side of suffering or death, in the planter's house or humbler cot ; or elsewhere listening to pleas for sympathy and counsel by the wronged bondman, or watching the course of justice as professedly administered. It was a varied and often perplexing business, *e.g.*—

"Lately (in May) I received a note from Mr. S. on the next estate requesting me to pray for his wife, who is very ill. Though so near the chapel, she has never visited it nor us. At the request of the doctor, Mrs. Wray went to see her, and to render what assistance she could ; also to speak to her about the concerns of her soul. This afternoon I visited her, and I trust spoke faithfully to her. I read John iii., asked her some questions about eternal life and faith in Jesus, and engaged in prayer."

It was a good pastoral visit, followed up by others on the part of Mr. and Mrs. Wray, all calculated to enlighten the ignorance, as to spiritual things, of her husband, and to correct mistakes on the part of his more enlightened but worldly wife. For this lady had been brought up by a father who, when she took leave of him, "solemnly entreated me to take care of my precious soul, not to throw away my soul; but I have neglected it." This poor woman, though in a deplorable state of body and mind, received benefit ; and, being restored, afterwards attended the chapel and also sent her little girl, their only child, to " Mrs. Wray for instruction."

It will have been seen, we may here remark in passing, that Mrs. Wray had already begun to devote some time each day to the instruction of children belonging to the wealthiest classes of the community. This she did afterwards and long years later on in Berbice ; numbering there, at one time, the then Governor's own child among her pupils ; and providing money wherewith, when the time came, some of her own daughters could be sent to England for a few years' instruction at a respectable boarding-school, and so become fitted, as they did, to return and themselves take up the work of tuition which the mother then committed to their hands. Thus Mrs. Wray, in Demerara or Berbice or both, began the first school in the Colony for the education of young ladies.*

A few days after the note from Mr. S., when in town and along with Mr. Davies about various business at the public offices, they attended the trial of a planter, James Jaffrey, who lived at Mahaicony, charged with the death of four of his slaves, one being his concubine whom he had treated so

* The Rev. E. H. Tuckett, August, 1888, writes :—" At that time there was no school open to the demands of many who had daughters to be instructed. Mrs. Wray opened one so that she might educate them with her own children, and this she did without interfering with the large share of aid which she rendered to her husband in the mission. She was greatly successful, and by this means her daughters were ultimately sent to England."

ill that she hung herself; and another, a man on whom he had inflicted two hundred lashes, then put him in the stocks, where he died. "The evidence against them was chiefly that of slaves, of whom eleven were examined and all agreed in their testimony." Found guilty, "he was condemned to be branded, which punishment was afterwards inflicted at the usual place of execution in Georgetown."

In June came "a large cotton pick, which," remarks Mr. Wray, "is a great blessing to the planters in these bad times." Unhappily with it came signs and sounds of cruel driving, and of incessant toil. Driver in the field, overseer, manager, attorney, and proprietor shared the responsibility; though infliction of stripes was generally by the first-named officials, and sometimes without the knowledge of the planter. Le Resouvenir had now become in many respects, if not altogether, like neighbouring estates. Mr. Vanderhaas was now its owner. He also had married Mrs. Post, widow of the late proprietor. Many of its bondmen, like great numbers of slaves elsewhere, not choosing to avail themselves of the means of Christian worship and instruction, were still but enslaved heathen. Both for these, however, and in some ways, for those who were learning better things, the yoke had been made heavier—the work more difficult, therefore, of the missionary, whose ears too were now constantly saluted with the crack of the whip and the cries of the sufferer, and whose eyes now and then witnessed the infliction. So we meet with such records as the following:—

"The negroes on Success picked the whole of yesterday (Sunday, the 14th). They came to ask my advice, but I found it difficult to give it them in their situation as slaves. I could only read to them the fourth commandment. Oh, what a curse is slavery!" "I hear the cart-whip every day on Le Resouvenir. Asia, the driver of the female gang, makes sad complaints, with tears in her eyes, of the treatment they meet with from the manager. Larger baskets than usual are given to them, and he flogs them severely if they are not full. It is in vain to deny this, because our own eyes see it, and our ears hear it. Our own senses cannot deceive us. Cursed slavery! We endeavoured to comfort Asia." "The whip is constantly sounding in our ears; this renders our situation uncomfortable, and we can do these poor people no good."

More good, however, even in this particular, and good in more ways than he thought, when speaking his word of comfort, or offering his counsel, or making his suggestion, apparently to fall fruitlessly to the ground; as shortly events showed when a crisis came.

Meanwhile he and his had their times of sickness; now one, now more of the family, and occasionally all being prostrate together; sometimes when sickness was rife, and in common with their neighbours.

" 28th July.—Mrs. Wray has lately been very ill; also one of our dear children. This afternoon I attended the funeral of a coloured woman. Many people attended, to whom I spake on the solemn subjects of death and eternity. All were attentive. I think it my duty to improve every opportunity afforded me of impressing upon the minds of the people the necessity of preparing to meet their God. In the evening many of the slaves came to learn their catechism. As Asia was returning home, I heard her repeating the answer as she went along—'Jesus Christ is the true God, who took upon Himself our nature, and became man.' I once did not think she would ever learn anything."

At length, with October, came a series of painful, solemn, and important events; one, however, bringing some relief to the smitten slaves on Le Resouvenir.

" Lord's Day, 4th October.—I preached a funeral sermon for the Rev. Mr. Ryle, the Dutch clergyman, who died last week. This is a loud call for the three surviving ministers (i.e., two missionaries and the military chaplain) to exert themselves for the spiritual benefit of the inhabitants. It is now a sickly time, and many are dying on every hand. Mrs. Wray is very ill. The negroes are much concerned about her. The doctor has prohibited them going to see her. She is very weak.

" 5th.—The weather is very fine, and the fields look beautiful.

We have had a great deal of thunder. I hear them flogging the negroes for not picking their quantity of coffee. They say the trees are not so full of ripe coffee, so they are not able to fill their baskets. When speaking to one, a driver, that all their sorrows would end with death if they loved and served Jesus Christ, she replied, 'There would be no flogging in heaven.'

"*6th.*—This morning, about three o'clock, the servant came to call me to see Mr. Vanderhaas, who was dying. Two doctors were with him, but had given up all hope of his recovery. I knelt down and prayed for him. It was a most awful morning of thunder and lightning. We had one of the loudest claps of thunder I ever heard ; I thought it would have split the roof of the house. At six, Mr. V. breathed his last. He was taken ill only last Thursday. This greatly affected Mrs. Wray, who is in a very weak state ; but her heart is fixed on Jesus. Our ears are almost daily saluted with the sound of death. In the afternoon I buried Mr. Vanderhaas, the second owner of Le Resouvenir. I do not remember ever seeing so many white people at a funeral. I enjoyed uncommon boldness and liberty of speech, and was enabled to exhort them with great earnestness to prepare to meet their God.

"*8th.*—To-night I hear them flogging the negroes. Only night before last their master was carried to the cold tomb. 'The small and the great are there ; and the servant is free from his master. They hear not the voice of the oppressor ;' nor the sound of the cart-whip."

Very different circumstances from those of three and a-half years ago, when the first owner fell on sleep. But some deliverance was at hand ; and this, as might be read between the lines were it not more plainly expressed, brought about by John Wray.

"*10th.*—This evening I received a note from his Honour the Fiscal, expressing a wish, in consequence of forty or fifty of the Le Resouvenir negroes going to complain to him of ill-treatment, to see me ; as he said these things could not happen without my knowledge. However unpleasant, it was now my duty to wait on his Honour, which I did as early as possible, and answered to the best of my knowledge all the questions put to me on the subject ; afterwards, at his request, committing to writing the substance of what I had said. Their complaints were chiefly of being severely cart-whipped, of being beaten very cruelly with a bamboo stick, and working on the Sundays. I gave him the names of several who had been very severely punished, and stated that I had almost daily heard the cart-whip, and often saw the stripes and bruises they received ; that I had made it my business to expostulate with the late proprietor, and also with Mrs. V., but the people got no redress ; and that I had even spoken to the manager on the subject. As soon as I returned from the Fiscal's office, I called on Mrs. V. and informed her of all that had passed, for I highly respected her and felt much for her.

"A few days after this, the Fiscal visited Le Resouvenir to inquire into the complaints. I was summoned to attend, and called upon to relate what I knew, the manager and his friends being present, and of course having full liberty to vindicate his own conduct. The medical gentleman of the estate was also present and several of the negroes were inspected. After much discussion, the Fiscal called upon any of the negroes to come forward and make their complaint."

This several did, one bringing in his hand a thick bamboo stick to show ; another, a doubled and knotted rope ; another stated the amount of daily work expected, and appealed to the Fiscal, as himself a planter, to judge whether or not it was more than could be done ; and said that in consequence of a beating with a bamboo, he had been six weeks in hospital.

"After all had said what they wished, his Honour told them that he would appoint another gentleman, whom he named, to be their master ; that the bamboo should not be used again ; that if they were further ill-treated they were to complain to the attorney, and if the attorney did not give them redress they were to apply to him and he would see that justice should be done them ; but that only one at a time was to go. They thanked him heartily. All was amicably settled, and the Fiscal said he hoped I should support what he had done. The negroes expressed their gratitude to me in the strongest terms for undertaking their cause, and though many evil reports were soon circulated about me, that I was the cause of the negroes going to the Fiscal, I do not regret what I have done. It is true that they could get no redress, and had determined to run into the woods as some of them did a few months ago. I entreated them by no means to do this, but rather go and lay their complaints before the Governor or Fiscal, who doubtless would investigate them, and do them justice. Surely it can be no crime to tell the oppressed to apply to the proper authorities for redress."

Without noticing in detail a run upon the Colony for provisions just occurrent, to supply Barbadoes, reduced, by a great catastrophe, to famine point, or the annoyance caused by an American privateer ravaging the coast, capturing estate-boats laden with produce, and ultimately a large ship at the entrance of the river, what has been given will serve to convey some idea, as a whole, of life and work in the mission during the critical eight months elapsed since Mr. Wray returned. Eight months more were still to be spent as resident on Le Resouvenir ; a period quite as trying, if for different reasons, as the preceding ; and dating from the 20th, perhaps the most critical day of this pregnant month of October, 1812.

<h3 style="text-align:center">1812—1813.</h3>

Visit from Agent of Berbice Crown Estates—Their History—Invitation to Labour there—Visit to Berbice—Prospects and Statistics—" Buckra No Know Preach from Pray "—Governor's Fear of a Mission—Request for Military Re-inforcement — Prosperity in Demerara—Individual Cases—Close of 1812—" One Drop of Bitter "—Long Illness—Encouragements—Captain Langley — Visit to " Swedenborgian Hermit "—Second Visit to Berbice—Death of Demerara Governor—Third Visit to Berbice—Painfulness of Deciding—Resolution to Settle there—Farewell to Le Resouvenir, &c.—Qualifications for Work in View.

" *20th October.*—I had a visit from A. A. De-la-Court, Esq., Crown Agent in Berbice. He brought a letter of introduction from Zach. Macaulay, Esq., Secretary to the Commissioners for Managing the Crown Property in South America. The purport of the letter was, 'to request me to afford all assistance in my power to establish a mission among the Crown slaves in Berbice;' and Mr. De-la-Court was authorised to make any arrangements with me he could to accomplish this object. Their number is 1143. They formerly belonged to a company of merchants and others in Holland, called the 'Berbice Association,' and became the property of the British Crown by the right of conquest, in 1803.*

"From that period to the end of 1811, they had been under the administration of the various Governors and their agents. In May, 1811, his Excellency Governor Gordon states, in answer to a communication of Lord Liverpool's :—'that these estates, from bad management, short crops, and low prices of produce, had never been productive of more revenue than what was sufficient to defray their annual expenses, that the negroes had been without clothing for nearly two years ; that by similar bad management the estates were destitute of provisions, and obliged to purchase at a very heavy expense ; and it would require twelve months before they would yield a supply for the negroes ; that they owed debts in the Colony amounting to £3200 sterling ; and that a large sum of money would be required to repair the buildings and works as well as to restore the cultivation.'† His Excellency strongly recommended Government either to lease or sell them on almost any terms ; and the estates were actually leased for fourteen years to a Mr. S., but in consequence of some observation of Mr. James Stephens, who was consulted as a legal adviser, the lease, by his advice, was cancelled. Government then determined not to barter away both the bodies and souls of these poor people, but to put them under the management of Commis-

---

* Berbice, Demerara, and Essequibo, because captured in war, are termed " Crown Colonies." Hence the enormous area of virgin soil is called " Crown Land," and none but the small remnants of roving Indian tribes may legally squat thereon. These particular estates of a public company, however, three in number, together with the Winkel village (now part of the present New Amsterdam), and all the company's slaves, were appropriated to the Crown, and are termed " Crown property," in a sense similar to the ancient Crown lands of our own country. Hence the personal oversight at first required from the Governor.

† Commissioners' Report, p. 6. Papers pp. 4, 5.

sioners, to ameliorate their state, and afford them religious instruction. The Commissioners were :—Mr. Wilberforce ; Mr. Stephen ; Mr. Long, afterwards Lord Farnborough ; Mr. Vansittart, afterwards Lord Bexley ; Mr. W. Smith ; and Mr. Gordon. Mr. Macaulay was appointed secretary to the Commissioners, a Col. Macalister was selected as their principal agent, and Mr. De-la-Court his assistant. I was introduced to the acquaintance of these gentlemen when I was in England in 1811, by Mr. Stephen, and had much conversation with this excellent man on the subject of the Commission. The estates were transferred to the Commissioners, 23rd December, 1811. Col. Macalister died very soon after his arrival in Berbice, and Mr. De-la-Court succeeded him in his agency.

"I considered the invitation to undertake the instruction of the Crown negroes as an opening by Divine Providence to introduce the Gospel into Berbice, and after due consideration, agreed to go if it should meet the approbation of the Missionary Society. I promised to visit Berbice, in the meantime, as soon as possible."

Which promise Mr. Wray, in a few days was able to perform, and both the occasion and the man—his object and his work, not to mention the difference in circumstances now as compared with those of travel, &c., then—claim that, with little omission, the account of these and several after proceedings should be in his own words.

"*2nd November.*—I left Le Resouvenir at four o'clock in the morning, breakfasted at Mahaica,* and changed my horse, dined

* The distance, he afterwards notes, between Georgetown and New Amsterdam is about seventy miles. There are four ferries to cross— viz., Mahaica, twenty-five miles from town ; Mahaicony, thirty-six ; Abary, forty-five ; and the River Berbice. Between Georgetown and Abary there are about 165 plantations, and between Abary and the Berbice River about forty-three in cultivation, chiefly cotton. This coast, so beautiful then, is now, he remarks in 1834, from the River Berbice to Mahaica, almost entirely abandoned, and the negroes removed to sugar estates. Frequent destruction of crop by blast and caterpillar, but chiefly the low price of cotton through competition, had led to the cessation of its cultivation in Guiana.

at Mahaicony ferry, crossed Abary ferry, which separates Berbice from Demerara, at dusk. I slept at an estate called Golden Fleece, belonging to James Fraser, Esq., where I met with politeness and accommodation. After taking coffee early next morning I rode sixteen miles and breakfasted with a planter, James Bennett, Esq., to whom I had a letter of introduction, who kindly lent me a horse as far as the ferry and assisted me over the Berbice River in his boat to New Amsterdam, the town of Berbice, which stands on the east side of the river, between it and the Canje Creek that here joins the river, a distance of three or four miles from the sea.

"On my arrival I called on his Honour the Fiscal, to whom I had a letter of introduction. He received me with great politeness, and offered me a horse to go to plantation Sandvoort, one of the Crown estates, on which Mr. De-la-Court resides; but a boat and four negroes having been provided by Wm. Scott, Esq., Crown Agent in town, I preferred going by water up the Canje. I was politely received by Mr. De-la-Court, who was just sitting down to dinner. A respectable coloured gentleman dined with us, and we spent the evening in interesting conversation.

"4th.—After a night during which the mosquitoes annoyed me so much in my hammock that I could not sleep, Mr. De-la-Court took me to see the buildings. Sandvoort is a coffee estate about five miles from town, and has 248 slaves. Owing to the heavy bush on the opposite side of the Canje, to windward, it must be unhealthy, and by sad experience we soon found it so to be. After breakfast we went to town in Mr. D.'s yacht, pulled by six strong negroes. I was introduced to a very respectable Dutch gentleman, owner of one plantation, and attorney of several, who seemed very favourable to instruction. He spoke much in favour of the Bible, of which I was glad to see a large family copy on his table. He freed two of his slaves because, after having purchased them, he found they had been baptized. They, however, would not leave his employ. As soon as tide suited, we went up the river about eight or nine miles to Dankbaarheid, a sugar estate, Crown property, situated on the West Bank of the river, and having 365 slaves. Plantation Dageraad, another sugar estate belonging to the Crown, is also on the West Bank, about a tide (or six hours' pull) higher, and has 166 slaves; but time would not permit us to visit it at present. The estates, including the slaves upon them (not including Crown slaves in town), were valued at £110,625 sterling.

"*5th.*—At 7 A.M. we returned to town and waited on his Excellency, Col. Murray,* Acting Governor. He promised his patronage and assistance in the instruction of the Crown slaves in town, and said that he would take care that those attached to Government House should attend; but that they were a bad set of people, and that he found it difficult to get them to go into a boat on a Sunday to pull him to church. He told us also that one of them had lately struck his white servant, and that the punishment which the law (Colonial) directs for this is that the right hand be cut off; but he would not permit this to be done, and had told the Fiscal not to exceed 100 lashes. The Crown slaves in town number 355, and are chiefly tradespeople, white-smiths, blacksmiths, coopers, carpenters, masons, &c. Many of them are excellent workmen, having been instructed by white artificers whom the Berbice Association used to send out for the purpose. Thirty were attached to Fort St. Andrew, and sixty-five, as servants, to Government House.†

"We can hardly conceive it possible that such properties should bring no revenue to the Crown; and that the very labourers should, for two years, have been destitute of clothing. It was certainly high time that some other mode of management should be adopted. All the negroes that I conversed with seemed highly pleased at the idea of having instruction introduced among them.

"After calling again upon his Honour the Fiscal, Mr. De-la-Court put me across the river, here about three miles wide, to the Ferry House on my return journey. Almost devoured with mosquitoes during the few minutes of my stay at the House, I was glad to get away and walked about three miles, but found the roads so bad and the sun so hot that I was obliged to stop at the first

* Afterwards Governor of Demerara.

† Six house boys; eight washerwomen; fourteen housemaids and seamstresses; three cooks; three ostlers; three gardeners; three stock keepers; four fishermen; two grass-cutters; two wood-cutters; and seventeen boatmen. This is the Governor's establishment of servants.

plantation and to send for my horse. Mr. and Mrs. Bennett, at whose house I had slept and left it, again kindly entertained me. I conversed with them on the plan of salvation, prayed with them, and supplied them with some tracts. The next morning I breakfasted at Golden Fleece, and had much conversation with Mr. Fraser on the instruction of the negroes. He has three or four estates, 500 slaves, and wishes much to have a missionary settlement in the neighbourhood; he will contribute towards its support as far as circumstances will admit. On the 7th I arrived at home to find my dear wife very poorly.

"During my journey to Berbice I met with the greatest hospitality wherever I called. There are no inns for travellers as in England, but in every house you find a welcome and entertainment both for yourself and horse. Commonly, travellers take their hammocks, and in almost every room are cleats on which to sling them. Rising in the morning often put me in mind of the words of Jesus, 'Take up thy bed and walk.' I have been pleased with my visit, and trust that a wide and effectual door is open for the preaching of the glorious Gospel of Jesus Christ to the slaves, and in various respects for ameliorating their state; also, that this will lead to the Gospel being more widely introduced among the other inhabitants. The population is:— Whites, about 600; Slaves, 25,000; besides a number of free coloured people.

"There are two clergymen—one, a Church of England minister, who preaches in a room under his dwelling,* and a Dutch clergyman living on his plantation up the river, but who, on the Sabbath, comes to town and preaches in a similar room. Mr. De-la-Court told me of a negro who, a few weeks before, had been severely flogged for preaching. The negroes had been teaching the Catechism and praying, as they are accustomed to do, and some of the masters called this 'preaching.' I had occasion to speak to some of the negroes on this matter. They replied that 'Buckra no know preach from pray; and when we pray, Buckra call it preaching.' Mr. De-la-Court very much disapproves of the negroes teaching and catechizing one another. I told him that the only way by which the Gospel could spread among them

---

* Houses there are commonly built on pillars, eight to twelve feet high.

was by the more intelligent teaching and assisting the ignorant to understand what the minister says, and that if this were prohibited I could not undertake the instruction of the Crown negroes.

"Many are considerably alarmed at the Commission, and think it will be very injurious to the Colony. Governor Gordon, in a letter to Lord Liverpool, expresses 'his opinion that the measure will be of very serious consequences to the security and tranquillity of the Settlement, and though the agents had not yet arrived, the tidings of the intended change had already occasioned sensations among the negroes that threatened insubordination, and requests his Lordship to send a *reinforcement of troops* to the garrison to ensure the tranquillity of the Colony, the present number of men being only 160.'* This shows with what jealousy every innovation upon the slave system was watched; but the alarm spread even to Demerara."

The last few sentences may create a smile, and, at some things they express, how heartily one could now laugh, did they not imply a measure of sin and sorrow, wrongs and fears, tyranny and cruelty unimaginable, but which, nevertheless, existed.

Arrived at Le Resouvenir again, however, Mr. Wray had returned to a station which continued to prosper, and to a colony not only much more populous than Berbice, but one in which new openings for mission work still continued to present themselves. These were utilised by the brethren as far as their limited strength and means would avail. The remaining few months spent by him as a resident here form a record, almost unbroken, of revival, success, and extension, including cases of individuals with most interesting details, and events of progress that were full of promise.

Failing, as we have seen, to secure a preaching room at the Beacon, people from that direction came to him to hear and to be catechized, numbers walking a dozen miles, and distance being not their only discouragement. Among others

* Report of the Commissioners.

from that direction was old Hannah, of whom many particulars are given. In Africa,

"when a little girl, one thief me, and put me upon his shoulders, and take me from my mammy, and sold me, and I was brought to Granada and baptized among the Roman Catholics ; but they teach me no good, only one little prayer, nothing about Jesus Christ,"—

was the account she gave of her childhood. Hannah, however, came to have a clear and heartfelt knowledge of the great truths of the Gospel. Old B. called to converse with the missionary, struck with the love of God manifested in the surrender of His only Son to die for men, and confessed "his whole heart to be put upon Christ."

Christmas day saw the chapel filled with negroes praising and blessing God, instead of joining in the old hideous heathen song and dance, a pleasing change indeed to the minister's mind, who again, on the day after, held service, when more than 700 attended, and when he baptized six adults and several children. He remarks :—"The service was very solemn, and all seemed deeply interested in it." One of the baptized, named Davy, had been a very wicked man, and a great thief, but now appeared a real penitent, whose changed conduct had stood the test both of time and investigation. Three of his children were baptized with him. A man named Philip was also to have been baptized, but he did not come forward, having just then some omission of duty on his conscience; about which, next day, deeply affected that he had refused baptism when offered him, he came to see the minister.

For some weeks there had been many inquirers, and now there seemed quite a revival among the people, the schoolroom being full every night of those "inquiring the way to Zion." An old man named Aaron, formerly an Obeah man, came to request baptism, expressing a wish now to serve God; also another named Jester, with a like request, confessing himself to have formerly been a great thief, and guilty of almost every sin, but now to be learning better things. At the sight and thought of these, how fittingly does the minister recall and record again the words of Paul:—"And such were some of you: but ye are washed, but ye are sanctified, but ye are justified in the name of the Lord Jesus, and by the Spirit of our God," 1 Cor. vi. 11. On the next day, 27th December, which was the last Lord's Day of 1812, the chapel was again crowded with attentive hearers; but these services of three successive days, Mr. Wray notes, "have been too much for my strength."

The last day of the year was spent by Mr. and Mrs. Wray "in a very comfortable manner, at the house of Mr. and Mrs. Semple, a respectable planter, where, on parting, we concluded the year with prayer and thanksgiving."

One drop of bitter, the last of 1812, was yet in waiting.

"On my return home I found a note from Mrs. Vanderhaas, charging me with the crime of teaching her negroes to write. I am sorry that I could not plead guilty, as neither my time nor strength will permit me to attend to this."

But a period of enforced leisure had now arrived; and, considering the missionary's recent journeys and exertions, to those who know the clime, it will be no surprise. 1813 was but two days old when Mr. Wray was taken with a fever, which so reduced him, that for five weeks he was unable to leave the house or do anything in the way of instruction. His devoted partner in life and ready helper was, also, during the period sometimes very ill. The negroes nightly visited him, and began at length to confess themselves hungry for want of preaching.

But the Word of God was not thus confined, nor elsewhere was the progress of the mission stayed. In the beginning of the year the new chapel in Georgetown had been opened, about 1000 negroes and a considerable number of free people attending the first services. It was named

"Providence Chapel," in consequence of the happy change which had taken place in favour of missions. Mr. Davies had also been able to introduce the Gospel on the West Coast of Demerara, on the road to Essequibo, among some thousands of negroes who could not come to town; and, during January, had further succeeded in forming at Georgetown, an Auxiliary Missionary Society, with a Juvenile Society, the subscriptions amounting to £80, 14s. 2d. Whilst an invalid, too, Mr. Wray was gratified with the receipt of a letter from James Fraser, Esq., Golden Fleece, Berbice, acknowledging a parcel of Reports of the Missionary Society, and tracts for religious instruction, offering a building on his estate for the purposes of such instruction, promising his mite towards the support of the work, and saying that, on Mr. Wray's removal to the Colony, he should be happy to converse further on the subject. Mr. Fraser was friendly to the establishment of schools, to which many objected.

It was on Lord's Day, 7th February, that Mr. Wray, though feeling very poorly, again attempted to preach, and "got better through than he expected." But during the week he and his co-workers experienced a sad shock in the sudden loss of a seafaring friend, one Captain Langley. The captain was a good man, with whom Mr. Davies had voyaged from England, and was very friendly to the mission, all the members of which were much affected by his death. Mrs. Wray was writing a note to him when a messenger arrived with the news that, on the 10th, whilst crossing the river in his boat, along with another gentleman and two of his sailors, all were drowned. Mr. Davies, with the mate, had recovered the body, and the day after attended the funeral. On Sabbath, the 14th, Mr. Wray preached again; this time a funeral sermon for him whose living presence had been expected there that day.

Improvement in health continued, and work resumed its greatly varied course; success also, its progress. On 7th

March, meeting for the first time in 1813 around the Table of the Lord, seventeen new members appeared, the Church now numbering fifty-nine, all slaves except two; but all, as the faithful and careful pastor hoped and believed, "were the Lord's freemen, who had been delivered from the slavery of sin and Satan."

On the 15th Mr. Wray had a long-cherished wish gratified in being able to visit an eccentric character, of whom he had heard soon after first arriving in Demerara, and how natural the wish of a pioneer in Christian missions to see such a recluse will appear from the account given of his call.

Old Mr. Glen is designated the "Swedenborgian Hermit." Many years before he had lived at the back of Le Resouvenir, and he and Mr. Post had been very great friends. He then went up the river for several years, living in a hut on little else than salt fish and plantains, and generally wearing only a checked shirt. Now he was living at the back of an estate neighbouring to Le Resouvenir. He employed himself in reading Swedenborg's works and the Bible, and in drawing pictures of the Indians, their houses, &c. Governor Nicholson had shown Mr. Wray a great number of these drawings, which the hermit had sent his Excellency as presents, and strongly recommended the missionary to pay him a visit, with the forewarning, however, that he did not like clergymen, and would not generally speak with people who did not understand Latin and Greek. A few days preceding Mr. Wray's visit to him, he had sent to borrow the memoir of Mr. Post, which copy, returned with marginal remarks, penned in English, Latin, Greek, and Hebrew, is before us as we write.

The missionary found him at the door of his hut, dressed in a checked shirt and an old pair of stockings.

"We sat down," says his visitor, "in the shade, under a large silk-cotton tree, and conversed some time on religious subjects. Saying he was much pleased with the missionary and Bible

Reports I had sent him, he told me to read the Bible by Swedenborg's works. After some conversation he said, ‘Do you read Greek ?’ ‘A little, sir,’ I replied, ‘but only the New Testament.’ He said, ‘I read that only.’ ‘Have you got a Greek Testament ?’ ‘Yes, sir ; I have got three.’ ‘Do you read Hebrew?’ ‘Yes, a little, sir.’ ‘Have you a Hebrew Bible ?’ ‘Yes, sir.’ I was now qualified to enter his hut. He made me a present of a very beautiful Hebrew Psalter, to read Hebrew with him. Possessing Parkhurst's Greek Lexicon, he requested me to lend him the Hebrew one, which he had not seen, and also Campbell's Translation of the New Testament. This eccentric character understood Latin, Greek, and Hebrew, English, French, Dutch, and German, and was familiar with Divinity, Law, Physic, and other subjects. He had an extensive acquaintance with the Indians.”

After a pleasant morning with him, a pressing invitation to visit him again, and the loan of Michaelis on the New Testament, Mr. Wray went home to send him the books he desired, and, in the evening, to be at the usual work of instructing and catechizing the negroes, aged ones and younger, but all so ignorant and so long uncared for.

In the afternoon of Tuesday, 20th April, the pioneer began a second journey to Berbice, arriving at New Amsterdam on Friday following. During his absence from home it rained almost every day, so that travelling was rendered very fatiguing and unpleasant. But the visit confirmed what already appeared favourable to the projected mission, and afforded some additional prospects of success.

Going to Sandvoort on Saturday, Mr. Wray spoke to several of the principal negroes, and on Sabbath morning, accompanied by the manager, he called at some of their houses, explaining the object of his visit, and speaking to them of God and Christ. All said it was their desire he should come and live in Berbice. The whole body of slaves were then called together and addressed, as plainly as the missionary could, on the subject of religion, with questions afterwards, an old driver named Jan acting as interpreter for those not understanding English. Jan had been much instructed in Scripture by a Dutch gentleman who formerly lived on the estate, and he became very useful to the missionary, in subsequent days, as an interpreter.

Returning to town, Mr. Wray spoke to the Crown slaves there, who expressed a great wish for instruction. He also had much conversation with a respectable planter from the East Coast, who invited him to visit his estate, and promised to assemble his negroes for him to preach to.

"His Excellency, Governor Gordon, received me politely, and promised his patronage and support, but objected to the negroes meeting together in the evening for Divine worship. I told his Excellency that the Sabbath was not sufficient to instruct ignorant negroes, but to make them understand, it was absolutely necessary to catechize them in the evening, after their work was done. He observed that the conduct of the whites would have an unhappy effect. I told him that I should not hold them up as examples for the negroes to follow, but the Christian character as described in the New Testament."

Mr. James Fraser on the West Coast introduced the missionary to Mr. Rader, another planter there who, like Mr. Fraser, was desirous to establish a mission in his neighbourhood; wishing to begin immediately, inviting the pioneer to his house, and requesting that he would always make it his home in visiting Berbice. Despite wet days and weary journeyings, Mr. Wray was preserved in health, and found his family well on arriving at home in time for the first Sunday of May.

On the 11th a great loss befel the mission and the Colony. Between eight and nine in the evening, Governor Carmichael died of apoplexy. He had been riding out the preceding day. In his death, Mr. Wray testifies,—

"the slaves and poor people have lost a kind friend. He was an advocate for the instruction of all classes, and rendered the missionaries all the assistance in his power. In his government he met with great opposition, as all must expect whose office it is to make great changes and rectify great abuses. Notwithstanding all, he has done much good in the Colony, where a monument was afterwards erected to his memory."

Before the end of May, Mr. Wray had paid a third visit to Berbice, whence he returned on the 31st, having "had an opportunity of preaching twice on the West Coast, on the estates of Messrs. Rader and Fraser, where the negroes were very attentive." On Sandvoort, coffee-picking had begun, and—

"I am happy to find they have not yet used the whip. I have recommended the agent to substitute the name of 'foreman' instead of 'driver' for the headmen, and to call the people together for their rations by ringing the bell instead of cracking the whip."

But a crisis and time for decision had now come, and there was another side which the pioneer did not and could not rightly overlook. To leave such a sphere as Le Resouvenir and Demerara had now become, was no light matter. Many things there were, not only to attach him and to claim his continuance, but, humanly speaking and humanly viewing, to make life and work easier. So we read on :—

"My mind is much exercised about moving to Berbice, as it will be neither so pleasant nor healthy as the East Coast of Demerara ; and the Crown estates being very distant one from another, very inconveniently situated, and in unhealthy spots, great labour will attend the undertaking. The negroes also are mostly unacquainted with English, and to be understood, it will be necessary to learn the Creole."

It must indeed have appeared a great sacrifice of self, and certainly for some years, proved to be.

But the sanction of the Directors of the Missionary Society had come to hand, who were also prepared to make arrangements for another to occupy Le Resouvenir ; so "believing it to be our duty to introduce the Gospel into Berbice, where so wide a door, under the express patronage of the Crown, is opened," Mr. Wray prepared to depart. As might be expected, it was a sorrowful business; how saddening let his own words tell :—

"*6th June*, 1813.—I preached my farewell sermon at Le Resouvenir from Acts xx. 16, and following verses, and afterwards administered the Lord's Supper. The time was solemn and affecting. Many of the people wept aloud. My voice was drowned by their sobs and tears. I could not go on, and was obliged to sit down. It was hard parting. Mrs. Wray was much affected. Next day, when we took our leave of several people who came to see us, they wept sore, and some of the aged females literally hung about Mrs. Wray's neck. I had some difficulty to get her from them. Some of the children ran after us along the road, saying, 'Good-bye, missy! poor missy! good-bye missy!' It is impossible to describe our feelings.

"At 5 P.M. on 16th June we sailed from (Georgetown) Demerara, in a Colony schooner, and arrived in Berbice river at half-past eight the next evening; considered a good passage, as we had to beat up against the wind. The sea was very rough at times, and a heavy rain coming on made it very unpleasant. It was quite dark when we landed, and Mrs. Wray had a narrow escape from serious injury on account of the wharf being full of holes, but the Lord preserved her from harm. Thus we bade farewell to Demerara, and to our beloved home and congregation at Le Resouvenir. During our residence there we had experienced many blessings, and though we had met with great opposition, yet we had many friends among the planters who had treated us with great kindness, and who expressed much sorrow at our leaving. I trust also the Lord has blessed our labours, and that many, by the preaching of the Gospel, have been called out of darkness into marvellous light, and have been turned from sin and Satan to serve the true and living God. We have entered on a new field of labour, which, by the grace of God, I trust we shall exert ourselves to cultivate. We shall now enjoy superior opportunities of doing good both to the bodies and souls of our fellow-creatures, and of ameliorating the state of the slave population; particularly of establishing schools among them, and of introducing marriage. We pray that the Lord may bless our labours."

We close this chapter with the words of a writer in the *Missionary Magazine* for 1861, who, speaking apparently from personal acquaintance, says of the pioneer at this juncture :—

"Mr. Wray was well qualified for commencing a mission in a country so peculiarly circumstanced as Berbice, in which slavery had long been one of the established and most cherished institutions of the land. He was kind and conciliatory. Where he thought he could act with advantage to the slave, he did so, and when he knew he could not, by his friendly advice and sympathy he assisted the oppressed bondman to endure patiently what he might deem to be most unjust, but at the time inevitable. By his upright and judicious conduct Mr. Wray soon gained the goodwill of the well-disposed among his fellow-colonists, and to some extent overcame the prejudices of those hostile to his mission. Thus, though for many (eighteen) years, single-handed, he was enabled to establish no fewer than eight stations in different parts of the Colony, it was not to be expected that he could efficiently superintend all the stations he was instrumental in commencing, and that, too, at a time when native assistance was not easily obtainable—but his great object was to prepare the way for the labours of others."

CHAPTER IV.

SETTLEMENT IN BERBICE TO SECOND RETURN
TO ENGLAND.

June 1813—December 1817.

House in New Amsterdam — Different Receptions — Commencement of Work — Sad state of Dageraad — Day Schools — Family Worship — Prohibition of Bell — Le Resouvenir : collapse of Arrangements — To Demerara — Trying Hour — Interviews with Governor Murray — Differences of Opinion — Prosperity — Extension of Schools — Up the Canje — Fourteenth Day obtained for Crown slaves — Limitation of Cart-whipping — Transgression thereof Investigated — Encouragements — To Dageraad — Singing by Mohammedan — Removal to Sandvoort — Obeah — Interview with Obeah man — To Demerara — Success there — Home an Hospital — Pioneer laid up — To Dageraad and Dankbaarheid — Inventory of Slaves — Children and Chigoes — Services at Christmas — Orderly Conduct of Crown Slaves — Prostrate again.

Such manner of persons then were John Wray and his estimable companion as now, with their little ones, they landed in Berbice, pioneer mission workers there. A slender hold they had upon the Colony, but they availed themselves of it—drawbacks came, more serious than any contemplated, still they held on ; former success seemed long in appearing, still they persevered.

Continuing associated with the London Missionary Society, they yet had entered into new relationships, having now become largely responsible to the Commissioners of the Crown estates as their agents of instruction, religious and moral, sacred and secular. So they began their work in their accustomed way, and with their accustomed diligence,

100

among the Crown slaves placed, as we have seen, partly in town and partly on three estates separated one from another by considerable distances; Dankbaarheid and Dageraad up the river, to be reached by water, and Sandvoort near to town, on the Canje creek, accessible more directly by land, though with a road so bad at times in the rainy season, that their horses' feet sank almost literally to stick fast.

At the outset, and for a little while, they dwelt in their own hired house in town. The best they could find, and rented, as exchange of money then was, at £10 per month ; it was a hot, leaky, filthy place. Formerly a butcher's shop, it had become infested with noxious vermin, rats, scorpions, centipedes, and, more serious still, "we do not enjoy that pure, delightful sea-breeze which we had on the Demerara coast." Entering into possession on 18th June, all, during the tenancy, were more or less ill.

On the next day, the new arrival called on Major Grant, acting for Governor Gordon, gone to the Islands seeking health. He was politely received by the Major, "who made many inquiries respecting the effects of instruction in Demerara, and promised me all the assistance in his power." Mr. Wray's object was becoming pretty well-known, and not all the first callers upon himself were so polite or promising. Writes Mrs. Tuckett :—

"Among them was an influential planter, Mr. K. 'Well Mr. Wray,' he said, ' come to Berbice to make your fortune? We all come here for that, you know.' My father replied that was not his object. He had come to Berbice to tell to all, white and black, that ' Jesus Christ came into the world to save sinners.' Mr. K. replied, 'That won't do, Mr. Wray ; we won't have the blacks taught. Now, we wish to be friendly, and if you will give up that nonsense we will soon put you in the way of making your fortune.' My father of course declined; the interview ended; Mr. K. left, politely telling my father he was either a fool or a madman."

On Lord's Day, the 20th, he began his missionary labours in New Amsterdam, when—

"the Crown negroes in town, with many others, assembled together to hear the Gospel. I preached to them 'Christ and Him crucified.' They were very attentive, and expressed a desire to be taught the things of God."

Many children were present, a great pleasure to the pioneer.

Before the end of the week he was on his way to Dageraad, thirty-five miles up the river. This estate occupies a prominent place in the history of the Colony, as it was here that a remaining handful of Dutch forces made and maintained their last stand during the slave insurrection, some fifty years before, when, for many months, the country was in the power of the insurgents. Solitary and very unhealthy, it was now sharing the mass of disease, bodily and mental, which, through long neglect and abuse, through the cruelty of slavery, the curse of heathen superstitions, and unbridled indulgence in vice, the Crown property was inheriting when taken over by the Commissioners ;* and which in effect led, before long, to the entire abandonment of Dageraad. On hearing from a gentleman well acquainted with the place a horrid account of the unhealthiness then existing there, the pioneer confesses he felt his spirits low. But he pursued his way, and arriving,

"the negroes were assembled, and I addressed them on the great subject of religion. Some of them understood English pretty well and interpreted what I said into the Creole. I also visited them in their houses. They expressed a wish for instruction and also their gratitude to the Commissioners for preventing them being cut up with the cart-whip as formerly, though it is yet used occasionally."

Returning they stopped at Dankbaarheid for Lord's Day, the 27th, and—

"I spoke to the people, for the first time, the words of eternal life ; when one of the drivers interpreted what I said. I also attempted to teach some of the children their alphabet."

* See their Report to the Lords of the Treasury.

Getting home the same evening, he was ready for the commencement of a day school in town on the following morning, to be conducted, as far as possible, upon the plan of mutual instruction; the plan, *i.e.*, upon which Joseph Lancaster had so successfully worked. At the end of the week, each day showed an attendance of forty to fifty children, some making good progress and appearing to come very willingly. Every evening, too, adults were welcome to unite with the missionary's household in family worship, when the Scriptures were explained to them. Thirty or forty free coloured people availed themselves of the opportunity, and "behaved with great seriousness and attention." One evening thirteen or fourteen white people put in an appearance, but they were so disorderly and rude that "we were obliged to show them the way out, and desire them to come no more except they set a better example. I suppose," Mr. Wray pertinently adds, "these are the people who cry out that we are going to make an insurrection among the negroes." It certainly was an earnest of many like instances of misconduct and interruption on the part of the whites, which the missionary for years had to put up with as best he could.

On Lord's Day, 4th July, after preaching in town, he went with Mrs. Wray to Sandvoort, inviting many negroes whom, riding along, they saw fishing in the trenches, to come and hear the Gospel; which many did. Here they remained some days, guests of Mr. De-la-Court's, and commenced the instruction of children and adults, just as at New Amsterdam in the previous week. A serious attack of illness seizing Mrs. Wray, sent them home.

Amid many and greater troubles the pioneer had a proportionately large share of those little annoyances which are all the more annoying because of their occurrence when most inconvenient. On Lord's Day, 18th July, one such came in the shape of a note from the Fiscal, prohibiting the ringing

of the Winkel bell for assembling the slaves to hear the
preaching. This belonged to the Crown, and would be used at
other times for calling the men to their work. The prohibition was on the ground of its being "contrary to law and
order." But, though it came through the Fiscal, the origina-
tor, Mr. Wray heard,—

"was the old Dutch clergyman, who, a slave-holder himself, and
opposed to the instruction of the slaves, came from his estate up
country to preach in town on the Sabbath, and claimed it as his
prerogative alone to have a bell rung for assembling people to
public worship."

John Wray, nevertheless, got his congregation; afterwards
had thirty adults remaining to read; and in the evening
preached in his own house to a great many of all colours who
attended, among whom was his Honour the Fiscal himself.

On Wednesday, the 21st, he returned to Demerara,
travelling by land; the first object being to visit his old
flock and see how they did. Here it may at once be briefly
explained that arrangements for another missionary to occupy
Le Resouvenir, eventually and to the deep regret of the
Directors, collapsed. Neither Mr. John Kempton, who went
out for the purpose, nor the Rev. Richard Elliot, who had
left Tobago, and whom Mr. K. had found in charge,
remained. The former returned again to England, and
Mr. E., after staying awhile, went to labour among the more
numerous population in Georgetown, and on the West Coast;
so that no suitable missionary, as permanent successor,
settled there, until 1817, when the Rev. John and Mrs.
Smith sailed for Demerara. Meanwhile, what help could be
afforded was rendered from Georgetown, and Mr. Wray
returned at intervals.

On this occasion he arrived about dark, the day after starting. A month had elapsed since manse and chapel and great
congregation and first friends had been left; the intervening
weeks had furnished opportunity for acquaintance with life

and work in the new sphere, with its sickly conditions and its scattered peoples, so lost, most of them, in darkness, disease, and death ; the lone hours on horseback would furnish time for reflection and questionings, such as the pioneer puts here and there in his diary pages, "Can these dry bones live ? O Lord God, Thou knowest." But, whatever the cause, Mr. Wray passed on to one of those affecting and solemn hours which occasionally surprise a faithful pilgrim or preacher.

"As soon as I turned up the road leading to the chapel, my mind was much affected with many things that had transpired during the last five and a-half years. Sending word of my arrival to the people, a large congregation soon assembled. I read, or tried to read, Eph. i., suitable both to them and to me, but found myself unable to proceed, and could not refrain from weeping. The people were affected, and wept aloud. Giving out a verse of a hymn, I then went on, and was enabled to explain the chapter ; but I think this was the most solemn time I ever experienced in the pulpit."

Matters had gone back with some of the slaves in the neighbourhood as to privileges allowed and permission to attend worship. This had discouraged them, and, with some cases of cruel punishment, rightly, however, reported to the Fiscal, was a subject of grief to Mr. Wray, who had never-theless to press on to Georgetown upon other important business. It was to see General Murray, who was acting as Governor of Demerara, but who had been appointed to the Governorship of Berbice.*

"We had a long conversation respecting the instruction of the negroes. His Excellency approves of their being orally instructed,

* John Wray, the pioneer, on his way from Le Resouvenir to see Governor Murray ; and John Smith, his successor, with Mrs. Smith, on their way, nine years afterwards, from the same Le Resouvenir, prisoners under military escort, after shameful arrest, to shameful imprisonment and trial under the same Governor, and one of them to virtually a martyr's death ! Those intimate with Demerara's intervening history will mark the contrast with peculiar and painful interest.

but says he will *set his face against teaching them to read*, whether adults or children. He thinks reading will endanger the peace of the Colony. He however promised me his patronage in communicating religious instruction when he assumed the government of Berbice."

Mr. Wray preached on Sabbath, 25th July, to a very full congregation, and arrived at home on Wednesday the 28th to find his eldest child just recovering from a serious attack of fever; continued thunder, lightning, and rain, and very bad roads, the latter greatly interfering with attendance at Divine worship.

On 16th August he travelled in a new direction—viz., up the Canje creek to visit some of the Crown slaves who were in the forest cutting timber. The opportunity was afforded by Mr. De-la-Court's having to go thither. The distance proved to be a pull of eight hours by six oarsmen, and necessitated a night from home. This was spent in a hut made of leaves, where the two had just room to sling their hammocks. To the pioneer it was a dreary passage, only however from the monotony, and evidently not from any lack of interest or of observation on his part. For here, as indeed constantly throughout his pages, are interesting details concerning his fellowmen, with descriptions of their employments and implements, or concerning the wonders met with in the animal and vegetable worlds; all which we omit, either for brevity's sake, or as being similar to what is now so readily accessible in the many excellent works on Natural History.

His Excellency, Governor Murray, took the reins of government in Berbice on 30th August, and Mr. Wray at once again waited on him, and again—

"We had a long conversation respecting teaching the slaves to read. He highly disapproves of it, and wishes me to desist. I told him I could not except he officially forbade me. He said, 'Very well.' I feel a little uncomfortable on this head, though

I am convinced the Commissioners will interfere and obtain permission from the Government."

The matter was an essential one in Mr. Wray's present position and work, and could not be allowed to remain thus, so—

" I returned home, and wrote his Excellency a long letter on the subject, to prove that teaching slaves to read could be attended with no evil consequences, but that we had reason to believe it would be (attended) with the happiest effects. What effect this had on his Excellency's mind I know not, but he did not interfere with me. He found I was determined to persevere except some official steps were taken on his part to prevent reading. But his prejudices appeared to be very strong, and I have no doubt that if I had not been under the direct patronage of His Majesty's Commissioners I should have been obliged to suspend the schools which by this time we had established."

Wray was right in his surmises, as is shown by this same General Murray's own words three years after, when, as Governor of Demerara, he threatened to expel the newly-arrived missionary, John Smith (not an agent of the Commissioners), from the Colony, if he ever heard of him teaching a slave to read. Withal then, Major-General John Murray kept on his way, a few months as Governor of Berbice, and afterwards some years Governor of Demerara, and John Wray went his way. The outcome was seen when the former, by his own disobedience to orders from home, caused what ultimately proved a terrific explosion in the Colony under his control; an explosion that also shook Berbice, saved, however, from like fearful results largely by the efforts and influence of the latter.

The pioneer, as we have said, went on his way—this was, to continue and, if possible, to increase the opportunities for giving the young people of the Crown slaves useful instruction. Very close upon our last quotation are the following entries :—

"Our school in New Amsterdam now consists of eighty scholars, a few of them free, but chiefly slaves. We are much pleased with their attention. They are very fine children, and come very decent and clean. Mrs. Wray proposes to establish a school of industry among the Crown girls under fourteen or fifteen years of age, and to employ them in making clothing for the Crown negroes; also to have some of the little girls from the estates to teach them to work at their needles."

All duly carried out. It was hoped that such a school would be of use in other ways—*e.g.*,

"in forming habits of virtue and industry; as many of these girls were hired out to people in town, and were exposed to great temptations."

On Tuesday and Friday evenings, Mr. Wray instructed adults in town, and on Wednesday evenings, preached in his own house; going to Sandvoort two or three times a-week to look after the instruction of old and young there.

Our friends were successful in another happy attempt, made about this time, to benefit their charge. Slaves, it must be explained, worked six days in the week; having Sabbath days only for any marketing they had to do or for the cultivation of their provision-grounds. A day in a fortnight was asked on their behalf, that they might have more time on the Sabbath for purposes of religious worship and instruction. The thing was opposed "by many planters on the ground that, if the Crown slaves were allowed this, it would create dissatisfaction among the slaves of others." The experiment, however, was made, and it proved a blessing to the people.

Translating parts of Watts' "Catechisms" into Creole, or writing a simple discourse in it, to read, when needful, what as yet he could not fluently speak, filled up intervals of time; as did visitation of the Crown slaves in their own houses and at opportune seasons. The last, specially if before worship or preaching, was followed by larger attendances; the numbers being swelled not by Crown slaves alone, but by relatives or friends from other neighbourhoods, met with during the call. Sadly, however, was it then visible, even in town where the people were healthiest and finest looking, how many because of feebleness and disease, age, leprosy, old sores, and such like, could not come. Much of it was the fruit of habitual neglect by others, or of a wilful defiance of the laws of health on their own part, which the risk of a cart-whipping did not always prevent; as was seen in cases that still, on the Crown estates, led occasionally to the shocking punishment. Thus, when the pioneer was up the Canje, a woodcutter was adjudged it, part of the charge being that he had brought a leprous woman to some of his company; and on Dageraad, a few weeks after, an old woman suffered, having neglected to take her sick child to the manager for treatment, on account of which neglect the child was said to have died.

Believing in other or milder methods, but powerless to prevent such penalties, Mr. Wray's unavoidable nearness or presence at the time of infliction was with peculiar pain to himself; some satisfaction, however, being felt that it was administered after a period of waiting for Mr. De-la-Court, and of due inquiry by him.

This was a step in advance which our pioneer could and did insist should be maintained. In his own neighbourhood ears were not seldom saluted by the crack of the formidable scourge and the cries or shrieks of the writhing sufferer tied or held naked on the ground as, with unmitigated frequency or in bursts of passion, the torture was inflicted by slave-owners or their underlings. But on the Crown estates it was not to be so; if otherwise, Mr. Wray might justly and would, in fact, complain.

A case of this kind occurred in September during Mr. De-la-Court's absence, for some days, in Demerara on business. Taking advantage of it, the manager on Sandvoort, a young man, spent most of his time in town visiting his friends; and the negroes, taking advantage of the manager's absence, neglected their work, with the result that several were cart-whipped and punished in other ways for not finishing their tasks. Much dissatisfaction ensued. It was the first section of an oft-told tale :—the proprietor or chief agent is away, under officials, &c., "will play"; such play, in the long run, leading to pilfering of substance, and persecution of helpless ones; ending in persons outraged, properties damaged, and proprietors ruined. Two of the offending negroes came, one after another, to beg for letters of intercession, which Mr. Wray eventually wrote; with no saving result however, and, on his visiting the hospital, other cases of shameful usage presented themselves. He, therefore, became anxious for Mr. De-la-Court's return, and all the more as the manager went on to censure the missionary and to misrepresent what he had done as an interference which prevented his own getting the negroes to do their work.

When the agent came back, the whole business was investigated, and ended in expressed disapproval of the young man's conduct, who, on his part, expressed great dissatisfaction with Mr. Wray's visiting the hospital, and was for resigning his situation at a day's notice which, however, did not come to pass. The position calmly taken by Mr. Wray is best expressed in his own words :—

"I am sorry the people come to me to complain, and will not encourage them; but, when I think they are ill-treated, I shall certainly plead their cause. Visiting the hospital I consider a part of my duty."

Encouragement was now afforded by the willinghood with which some would come long distances to attend worship and instruction; also by the manifestly growing impression made upon several individuals, such as Jas, the driver, and Amsterdam, the sick-nurse on Sandvoort, Heindrick, the sick-nurse on Dankbaarheid; and if, on the other hand, cast down for the moment, as on the first Lord's Day in October, when the thought of his large congregation at Le Resouvenir came up as the preacher stood to address but 150 hearers in New Amsterdam, still he was there a forlorn hope to " hold the fort; " and that was not the only part of his charge. Next Lord's Day he was at Dageraad, addressing another and different assembly, and afterwards holding classes both for children and adults.

The passage up on that occasion had been with Mr. De-la-Court, the preceding day; and the return was with him on Monday, the 12th; a short stay, but illustrative of the medley of persons and things amid which the pioneer had to move. They arrived towards evening, just as the slaves were carrying the remains of an old negress, with deep lamentations and superstitious rites, to burial — an affecting scene; and they departed just after being entertained with a song in Arabic, sung before the house by an aged negro Mohammedan, who, in his own country, had been a parson; and who, when desired, and allowed paper and pencil, furnished each visitor with a copy in Arabic of what, he said, were the first words of their sacred book. The nights had been sleepless, owing to both being compelled by the mosquitoes to leave their hammocks and walk about in the mill-house. Painful above all was the punishment of the old woman, already referred to, charged with the death of her child; and a case against two men on Dankbaarheid, for Mr. De-la-Court's investigation of which, on the way down, a stop was made at that estate, when the decision went against the accused, who were sentenced to a like punishment.

October did not close before the missionary's whole household had removed to Sandvoort. Mr. De-la-Court, purposing to visit England for health's sake, wished them to occupy his house until his return, a wish with which the poor condition of their own present tenement made them glad to comply.

The agent's house was large, in a solitary situation, however, specially as compared with town, having only one cultivated estate on the way, much land having been abandoned. It faced the Canje, on the opposite bank of which were the front and dwelling-house of another cultivated estate; on other sides it was almost surrounded with bush. The change took place on the 25th. Reserving the spacious hall for chapel and school-room, they made their abode in the rooms of the higher storey.

All in town at the time was slowly but surely progressing. Thither now, of course, the journeys had to be made; three, at least, each week, besides going for the Sabbath services, &c. But any loss the work in town sustained by the removal, was compensated in measure by the stimulus their coming gave to the work at Sandvoort. Many, old and young, came to greet them as residents; and the alteration was not made without, as was his habit, Mr. Wray's thoughtfully and devoutly reviewing the past, and renewing purposes and plans, in dependence on his God and Saviour, for the future.

If any readers have never consciously heard of the Obeah superstition, they may thus make acquaintance with it, and some of its connections, by reading 1 Sam. xxviii. For the woman there is a woman of Obi (Hebrew term); and Saul, in earlier days punishing such with death, in later days, as he wanders farther and farther from God, becoming himself entangled in the superstition; finding his use of it bringing him no good, but rather leaving him much worse than before; is an illustration of what has occurred times innumerable. We know not through how many ages the superstition had, in Saul's time, been growing; but we know that through Africa and, along with Africans, in the New World, the name and thing have long been known; known, however, with all the grosser delusion, the greater craft and cruelty, and therefore consequent misery—terrors, diseases, death—which ages of wandering from God, and of destitution as to the Light of Life ; of correspondingly increasing corruption and wickedness of every kind, could alone entail. Such is the mischief it makes that, if not at this hour, in very recent days, a public flogging with the "cat" was the penalty, in British Guiana, inflicted on any convicted of practising it ; the great difficulty, however, being, as always, to secure a conviction, so afraid and unwilling were the dupes and victims to inform. In 1810, by the Colonial Court, it was made there, as in Jamaica, a capital offence, punishable with the gallows, "or such other punishment as the exigency of the case shall appear to require." But all was without the desired effect. "Superstition and witchcraft will fall before light and knowledge," is Wray's expressed belief, as it was the opinion of the Commissioners of the Crown property, who wisely preferred instruction and milder penalties to the gallows.

For some time the superstition had been unusually rife on Dageraad, but at last a seizure was made of a negro called "Joe" as the culprit ; and on 2nd November he was sent down the river for Mr. Wray to see.

At the interview Joe professed not to be an Obeah man, but rather the possessor of supernatural powers, by which he counteracted the mischief of such ; and that a long while since, when the negroes on Dageraad had been practising their evil work to such an extent that all were going to die, he had undertaken to put an end to it, which, by certain rites and incantations that he detailed as gone through in the presence of them all, he said he had succeeded in doing, and had blessed the estate with health and prosperity. Had Joe stopped at this point, Mr. Wray might have been puzzled how to deal with his man ; but, unfortunately for his case, Joe went on professing "that he had intercourse with invisible powers, that from the 'good spirits' he learnt how to do these things."

I

Here was Wray's opportunity, who at once said :—

"I am desirous to see them. *Joe.* You will be afraid. *W.* No, show them to me. *Joe.* If we go to windward they will smell us and go away. *W.* Then let us go to leeward. *Joe.* They can only be seen in the night, and very far off ; you will be too weary. *W.* I am so desirous of seeing them that I will go anywhere and at any time. *Joe.* They do not appear every night, and my images and instruments for telling when have been taken from me. *W.* I will obtain them for you again. *Joe.* They have now been tumbled about so much that they are spoiled." *

Joe went on to declare himself a sufferer from the Obeah men, who, he said, in retaliation for the frustration of their purposes, and for his restoring health and prosperity to the estate, had put Obeah for him, conveying it in a glass of rum; ever since drinking which he had been ill. A negro, named Moses had given it to him, and, in consequence, the people, enraged against Moses, put Obeah upon him, of which he died.

Recently, one, Peter, had died from the effects of the superstition, and a negro named Class had become suspected. The people (it was thought at the instigation of Joe, who professed to have found Class's implements in the ground by means of one of his own little images) fixed upon Class as the instrument of Peter's death. Hence Class, who had formerly been flogged as an Obeah man, was again in danger. Joe's tale to Mr. Wray was that this and other discoveries he made not by images, which were only to frighten the people, but by some particular leaf of a tree, wherein the virtue and knowledge lay.

Wray came to the conclusion that Joe was at the bottom of the mischief, and that Class was perfectly innocent; at his request, therefore, Class was neither punished on the estate nor given up to the authorities. He adds, among other remarks, "It is impossible to describe the influence these men obtain over the minds of the negroes."

---

* They consisted of feathers, hair, and four little images, which had been discovered hid in the ground, and were in possession of the Crown Agent.

Schools and other work all being arranged in accord with the new circumstances of residence at Sandvoort, Mr. Wray went to Demerara for the last two Sundays in November; taking passage on the 18th, and preaching, &c., at Le Resouvenir, where the chapel was filled with attentive hearers, who rejoiced to see him and who, he was glad to find, were going on as well as could be expected. His lament was that, suffering from fever and the weather proving very rainy, he was unable during week-days to preach on the coast so often as he could have wished. But he could record the efforts of others, and rejoice in their success; noting the crowds that came to Georgetown for worship and instruction, no fewer than 5000 of whom were learning or teaching the Catechism, hundreds applying to Mr. Davies from Sabbath to Sabbath for copies, and a visible change coming over many; that Mr. Davies had been invited by the Protector of the Indians to go some 200 miles up the river and undertake their instruction, but, for want of help, had been obliged to decline; and that a visitor from the Islands about this period writes, "Demerara seems the most pleasing missionary station in the West Indies."

Preaching on the 28th was followed by illness in the night; but on Monday, the 29th, Mr. Wray left on horseback for Berbice, riding seventy miles in two days under a hot sun, and experiencing great thirst, as well as great fever pains in knees, legs, and head. He arrived at home on 1st December to find it literally an hospital; wife and servants ill, also a friend residing with them in a very dangerous state. By two successive and severe attacks of fever he himself was rendered helpless for work on the succeeding Sabbath; and another attack occurring on the 8th, his stomach so nauseated as to be at times unable to retain the medicine deemed absolutely necessary, he had to be content, on a second Sabbath, with assembling negroes and children in the house at Sandvoort for simple catechizing and instruction.

On Wednesday, 15th December, however, he was off again

for Dageraad, stopping in town and at Dankbaarheid on his way, and returning on the 18th, much pleased with the tokens of interest and progress at every place. On the 21st an "inventory" was taken of the Sandvoort people by the estate authorities, which afforded Mr. and Mrs. Wray an opportunity of seeing the whole array. They were painfully struck with the number of poor, emaciated people, full of sores. A number of children, too, beside others, were still infested with chigoes, the result of parental or personal neglect. This had already presented itself to notice in a very disagreeable way. After classes of children had been reading, the place where they stood was, in parts, powdered over as with flour; being, in reality, covered with nits from the nests of numerous chigoes allowed to remain in the scholars' feet. Accordingly, their instructors had given Amsterdam, the sick nurse, a dollar, to clean the feet of such. No one in the West Indies escapes the pest (here most accurately described by Mr. Wray), but a little attention detects the intruders and will prevent their spread. Sores and permanent lameness are the fruit of neglecting them.

Christmas brought holidays for the slaves, &c., in Berbice, as in Demerara; days hitherto generally spent by them " in dancing, drumming, rioting, and drunkenness." Mr. Wray became anxious as to the behaviour of those for whom he had wrought, and, though weak, did not spare efforts to interest them in better ways. Beginning with Saturday, Christmas Day, he held services both at Sandvoort and in town on each of the three days kept as holiday, travelling thirty miles and preaching eight times; his only disappointment being on Sunday evening, when an increase of fever prevented his preaching on Sandvoort. He had his reward. Where he lived the hall was filled, people of almost every age and description coming to hear the Word from his lips. In town, also, there were good congregations. During the night, much yelling and noise were heard on the opposite estate, but none on Sandvoort. So with the Crown people in town, and throughout the holidays; all was orderly. "We have been much pleased," he writes, "with their conduct." Mrs. Wray spent a good deal of time in conversing with the children and people; and, along with her husband, walking on Monday among the negro houses, they received many kind salutations from the people, and expressions of great gratitude from fathers and mothers for the pains they had taken with their children. "The Lord," concludes Mr. Wray, "has far exceeded our expectations, and we desire to praise His holy name for His great goodness." On the 28th, the holidays being over, numbers of people generally went into the hospital; on this occasion it rejoiced the pioneer to find that only two on Sandvoort had done so.

But the end of 1813 was at hand, and such efforts, by one so weak, led to his increased sickness. On the 29th, pains and poorliness, fever and thirst, returned. The next day, use of Peruvian bark was again attempted, but none could be retained, and the doctor sent for from town could not come. Mr. Wray became too weak for anything, and the year closed as it had begun, with himself a prostrate patient.

1814.

New Year's Greetings—With Family to Demerara—Ordination of Deacons—Many Baptisms—Fruit after many Days—Stay at Blankenburg—Report of Insurrection in Berbice: Sad Results—Proclamation—Le Resouvenir School examined by Chief Justice—Prosperity—Return to Berbice: Improvements there—Governor Bentinck—Opposing Influences—Long Affliction—Deaths of Children—With Family again to Demerara—Unfortunate Journey—Yellow Fever—Kindness of Planter Friends—Stay at Friendship—Death of Mrs. Tyson—Return again to Berbice—Increasing Opposition and Difficulties—Encouragements — Laundress kidnapped — Expeditions in search—Licentiousness of Whites—A Happy Christmas.

MANY came on New Year's day to greet their friends, offer their good wishes, and, in lengthy addresses, profess their desires to "cease doing evil and learn to do well," to be able to read their book, professing also their prayers to God that He would renew their hearts.

We pause to remark how strange the scene in that land; strange, as compared with past ages of neglect; strange, in view of to-day's diffusion of knowledge and religion. Mr. and Mrs. Wray were both "pleased and affected," and in response he read and explained the 103rd Psalm.

With return of strength during the first week of the year, and considering the weak state of the whole family, the resolution grew that all should try a change to Demerara. On Saturday the 8th, therefore, they left Sandvoort to voyage thither. It was a rough and uncomfortable passage to Georgetown, and much of the drive thence to Le Resouvenir was through pouring rain, which so softened the road, as almost to bring them to a standstill. Mr. Wray helping, however, their horse pulled them through; they met with a very kind reception, the negroes being delighted to see Mrs. Wray again.

On Sabbath, 16th January, though very unwell, Mr. Wray preached twice; he adds, "the Lord helped me, as He has often done in times that are past." During the week five candidates for Church fellowship were admitted, and a refreshing season at the table of the Lord followed on the 23rd. Most of January the little girls were ill, so ill at times that life was despaired of; Mrs. Wray, also, being often sick, and having constantly a sense of fatigue. They were left, therefore, at the house of a kind friend on the coast, Mrs. Tyson, to be cared for and entertained, whilst the pioneer, at the beginning of February, went over to Berbice. Going and returning by land this occupied nine days, Sunday, the 6th, being spent on Sandvoort and in town, holding meetings for worship, preaching, and teaching. As usual, much hospitality and kindness were shown the traveller wherever he called to lodge, and he gained all the information possible that he thought might be useful to the agents of the Crown property, or as preparatory for commencing mission work on the Berbice West Coast, where, between Abary creek and the river, were 5000 slaves entirely without means of instruction.

After services at Le Resouvenir on Lord's Day, 13th February, there came on the evening of the 14th a church-meeting, important and noticeable as involving an ordination of deacons, the first, whether as regards minister or people.

" Having read and explained the account which the apostles of Christ give of the office, and described the qualifications of a deacon, I set apart with prayer and laying on of hands, five of the members." " Among the number," afterwards writes Mr. Wray, " were two, Romeo and Jason, who became venerable men, full of faith and the Holy Spirit, and truly devoted to God."*

The Sabbath following was also a day of solemn joy, Mr. Wray baptizing twenty-five adults, and thirty children of believing parents. But the hearts of himself and his partner in life must have continually been filled with gratitude and gladness, for the tokens on every hand of the seed sown in past years now bearing precious fruit ; of " bread cast upon the waters, found after many days ; " as the record of these baptisms is followed by most interesting cases of such ; instances of change for the better in both planter and slave, oppressor and oppressed, young and old.

But on the 21st the pioneer and his family moved on to Demerara West Coast, still seeking restoration to health.

* Both these were witnesses on the occasion of the Rev. John Smith's shameful trial. Romeo, Mr. Wray informs us, " was a Mohammedan, and was one of the first he baptised in November, 1808 ; and was then registered by Mr. Post as fifty-two years old. At this age he learnt to read the Scriptures well, and when sixty, being exempted from labour, spent his last twenty years as a Scripture-reader and catechist, and proved a blessing to many. He died, March, 1835, and was buried near his master, Mr. Post, twenty-six years after he had assisted in bearing his mortal remains to the silent tomb—master and slave now possessing each an equal space of Le Resouvenir."

They were most hospitably entertained by their kind friends, Mr. and Mrs. Dardier of plantation Blankenburg, about eight miles from town. During their stay, the eldest child, Elizabeth, "became so ill as for several days to lose the use of hands, feet, and speech." Deeply affected, out of their distress her parents looked unto the Lord, and were rejoiced to receive her again as one alive from the dead, and gratefully to witness the gradual restoration of all her faculties.

It was a fine coast, and had at the time about 8000 slaves, though with no place of worship, or minister to direct them to the Saviour of sinners. But the truth of the last item was about to cease; missionary operations by Messrs. Davies and Eliott commencing there, and one of their best stations being founded shortly after the visit of Mr. Wray.

An alarming rumour, meanwhile, here reached him as it spread throughout the Colonies; a rumour which, whatever of truth or fact, little or none, might be at the foundation, gathering, as it went, size and gloom, and dust of slander, was calculated to make them all feel very unhappy. The report was that a slave insurrection had been discovered, having its centre on the Berbice West Coast, but extending right and left so as to include all the shore from the Corentyne Coast to Mahaica, about eighty miles; that the negroes had chosen a governor and other officers; that it was their intention to murder all the white men, and take possession of all the rest; that some of the Demerara East Coast negroes were leaders in the rebellion, especially Philip, a member of the church on Le Resouvenir; and that instruction of the negroes was to blame.

Mr. Wray at once wrote off to a gentleman of position and respectability, asking him to furnish any information he could on the matter; and received answer that he possessed no correct information; but, as showing how readily a report of insurrection was got up, he told what came under his notice only on the preceding December, when an official report was made to the Governor of Demerara, that some negroes on the Essequibo were about to revolt and kill all the white people, and take possession of the Colony—a report founded upon some declarations made by some Indians who had quarrelled with some negroes on one of the estates, and which had no connection whatever with the accused negroes, and missionary establishment or Christian meeting. This was some relief. However, it turned out that in Berbice the authorities had taken alarm; that some slaves on the West Coast had been seized; and private slander had been helping to do the rest, specially as regards Mr. Wray and his work causing the trouble.

A letter to hand from Mr. De-la-Court in Berbice, informed the pioneer that a neighbour had accused him (Mr. Wray) of this insurrectionary movement; that the Court had written to the Sandvoort manager for information as to the time allowed the Crown slaves, exclusive of the Sabbath; and that a planter on the West Coast had written him (Mr. De-la-Court) a letter upon the subject of the present plot, copy of which was furnished. It was from one who owned 1000 slaves, and who, abusing "Wray and all Wilberforce's party," expressed the opinion that, " We planters must stir to have some alteration,"—*i.e.*, as to Wray's and the Commissioners' work; also, "the hope that you will give your assistance in private;" in other words, whilst receiving pay, &c., from the Commissioners, exert, as Wray puts it, "his influence, *in private*, against their humane plans."

Now, not a single Crown negro was concerned in the plot (if plot there was), and not one who lived even in the neighbourhood of the Crown estates. What negroes were taken up belonged to the West Coast of Berbice, where no Crown estate or missionary establishment existed; but the slanders, and the spirit they manifest, show the bitter feelings which then existed against the humane plans of the British Government. According to report, a report afterwards confirmed by Mr. Wray's personal inquiry, the account which the negroes gave of the matter was, that there had been formed a society in imitation of the Freemasons, they wishing to have, as well as their buckras or masters, a society of that nature ; and that the money collected was to support the poor and defray the expense of their dances, &c.; just as it had been formerly very common for them to assume the names of their masters, or of the Governor or Fiscal, and send invitations to friends to supper or a dance, and appoint a captain of their own as president of the feast ; sometimes to put feathers in their hats at holiday time and parade the streets. "No one," as far as Mr. Wray could learn, "had been injured by them, neither was any property destroyed," yet on 12th April six of the unhappy people apprehended on the West Coast were executed in New Amsterdam as ringleaders, their heads cut off and fixed upon poles on the different estates to which they belonged ; one of them white with age, whose master, Mr. Rader, told Mr. Wray that he denied to the last having any bad intentions. Several others were flogged under the gallows, and some were transported.

A proclamation was subsequently issued to the effect that as "the privilege allowed the slaves of the Colony, of publicly or privately dancing on estates and other places at stated periods, had been perverted by them to purposes of the *most dangerous nature*, all dancing was forbidden until next year, 1815, or the further pleasure of the Court ;" but, notwithstanding the charges brought against the missionaries and instruction, assigning no blame to them. This was followed, late in the year, by another calling upon the colonists to pay their quota of the expenses incurred in crushing the plot and indemnifying the proprietors of the slaves capitally punished ; to raise which a tax of two guilders (2s. 8d.) per head, to be paid by the owners, was levied upon each and every slave they possessed, that was at the time liable to the ordinary capitation tax. Better still, the law concerning Sunday labour was amended in favour of the slave, forbidding field-work on that day, except in sudden emergencies; and further enactments were issued limiting and regulating the excessive use of the whip, and forbidding the burial of any slave dying suddenly or by suicide, or in consequence of punishment or hurt, without previously acquainting the authorities and procuring a certificate from the surgeon of the estate, who had inspected the body, as to the nature of the disease, or as to the cause from which the negro had died.

But we have been somewhat anticipating. As March drew towards a close, Mr. Wray and family prepared to return to Berbice. Before doing so, however, an event took place at Le Resouvenir so gratifying, specially in contrast with what has just been engaging attention, and with what came to pass there in later days, that we transcribe the account verbatim.

" 28th March.—This evening, according to promise, his Honour the President of the Court of Justice visited Le Resouvenir, and heard several of the negroes read the Bible. He was much pleased with them, and observed that they appeared by their tones and emphasis to understand what they read. I catechized them in his presence. We went nearly through the Catechism, and his Honour expressed his pleasure to hear them answer the questions with so much correctness and propriety, and observed that he thought they understood as well as many congregations in England. They sang 'Salvation : oh, the joyful sound !' and ' Let the Indian, let the Negro, &c.,' delightfully."

At this period Mr. Davies also reported that the Gospel was preached to a greater number than ever, and, he trusted, with greater success, hundreds inquiring the way of salvation ; and to judge from their moral conduct, from the pains they took in learning the Catechism, the distance many of them came to hear " Christ crucified " preached, and their liberal contributions toward the chapel building—if these were signs of a Christian, they had become such. More than £150 had been contributed to the Auxiliary Missionary Society.

Leaving Demerara with such signs of encouraging progress, on 1st April, Mr. Wray and his family crossed the river Berbice, and in the evening reached home again at Sandvoort, to find they were not without signs of encouraging progress there. Left in charge of a young man as catechist, the people and children had made improvement in reading, singing, cleanliness, attention to their gardens and houses; and went on doing so. Best of all, some of the adult negroes were manifesting more and more interest in the things of salvation; one of them in particular, who had been a profane, drunken, repulsive-looking man, forsaking his sins and showing a decided change. On Dageraad too, as on Sandvoort, the missionary was greatly pleased to see the cultivation of their gardens and the amount of provisions they had raised for themselves, utilizing every piece of ground available, since a day in fourteen had been allowed them for the purpose; nor less gratified to find a custom introduced by the managers on Dageraad and Dankbaarheid of daily making a large quantity of nutritious soup for the children, which they saw shared out to them at the door.

A new Governor, though an old acquaintance, had arrived in Berbice—Mr. Bentinck, recalled, as we have seen, from Demerara in 1812. The pioneer soon waited on him, and was received very politely. Much conversation on the old topic, the instruction of the slaves, ensued. "His Excellency disapproved of teaching them to read and write, but told me I was to go on agreeably to the wishes of the Commissioners of the Crown property." His visitor left, trusting "that past experience had taught him not to interfere with the religion of Jesus."

Before long the catechist, Mr. Meadowcroft, went to labour among the people and children on Dageraad, and a young black man named Lambert was engaged to teach the children on Dankbaarheid to read, so that on each Crown estate the work of instruction, &c., was better established ; Mr. Wray still continuing his visits to the different places as heretofore.

But with all these encouragements, and though able himself, in the middle of May, to pay a short visit again to Le Resouvenir, his consciousness of a stronger stream running in opposition to him and his Berbice work generally becomes evident. How things might have been had less personal and family affliction befallen him at this period, and had he not been compelled to spend another three months, July to October, on the Demerara coast, we cannot tell. Apart, however, from particular incidents and events which he details, expressions here and there imply a more than usual discountenancing and thwarting of his plans in Berbice, which troubled him greatly. It might be, probably was, a product of the alarm with which professedly the authorities and a number of the planters had just been seized, and which, if soothed, would not be sweetened by the punishments inflicted, the extra poll tax levied, and the privileges prohibited ; a prohibition which, as the year went on, was extended to any shout or song on the part of slaves travelling up and down the river, and to any going from one estate to another without a pass. But what with that which was tangible enough, and that which was not so easily accounted for, the pioneer was now entering a very distressful period of his life and labours.

First then, to notice the course of family affliction. In the former part of May, Mrs. Wray and several younger members of the household were again prostrate, so much so that thoughts of returning to reside in town were seriously entertained. As to Mrs Wray, indeed, the doctor so strongly urged a voyage to England as alone sufficient to re-establish her health, that, after serious deliberation, she consented to the proposal, and a passage was engaged for her. Before the ship sailed, however, finding herself somewhat better, she determined to try a little longer, which little, happily for her husband, the children, and the mission, lasted seventeen years.

Besides much interruption of instruction, &c., on Sandvoort caused by gathering, preparing, and exporting the coffee crop, parts of May and June proved very wet. It was during the third week of the latter month that, in addition to three negroes who had died, Mr. Wray lost one of his most promising school children, and within a day or two afterwards, his own infant son. The tender fatherly heart of the pioneer shows vividly in the details of sickness, death, and burial of these youthful ones. Flora, thirteen years old, had been at school on the preceding Sunday, saying her catechism and prayers and joining in the singing. She had been a very attentive scholar, and had learned Watts' First Catechism. Her mother sent, asking the missionary's prayers for her sick child who, in another day was gone ; and whose remains, on the succeeding day, were conveyed in an orderly and peaceful manner and consigned to the grave with Christian burial, Mr. and Mrs. Wray attending, also the school children, down whose black faces, whilst he was speaking, silent tears ran.

On 23rd June Mrs. Wray and children were again down in fever, the greatest sufferer being an infant boy, John Thompson Wray, nine months old. He was strongly convulsed, and suffered much. From seven in the evening until three the next morning, the struggle went on, they doing their best for the little sufferer ; no medical assistance, owing to the impassable state of the roads through heavy rains, arriving till too late ; and so in agony he expired.

"On the 25th, after a solemn night, a night of thunder, lightning, and rain, at 10 A.M., we committed the mortal remains of our dear boy to the cold tomb, under a large mango tree, until the resurrection day. I spoke to the people who attended. As I was following the corpse of my dear child, my mind was carried on to the world of spirits, and I was led to contemplate the happiness of heaven. The soul of our lovely boy, for such he was, has learned more of God, of Jesus Christ, and of heaven than is possible for me here to know. I cannot doubt of his happiness."

On the following day, Sabbath, 26th June, both Mr. and Mrs. Wray were too unwell to do more than attend to the children, &c., who came to their house. Mrs. Wray continuing in fever most of the week, thoughts of again spending some time on the Demerara East Coast, and instructing the people there, ripened to decision. So, after preaching, Lord's Day, 3rd July, on Sandvoort and in town, then visiting the negroes on Dankbaarheid and reaching home about eleven at night, preparations were made and, Tuesday 5th July, early in the morning, the family crossed the Berbice to journey overland to Demerara. Fine at the outset, and with some of their kindest friends to be found on the road, it nevertheless proved a most unfortunate journey.

The first night they slept at No. 22, Bel Air, Mr. Rader's estate; with whom, as a friend of instruction, we have already made acquaintance; and were hospitably entertained. Next day they dined at No. 29, Trafalgar, and Mrs. Fraser gave them a note to the manager on No. 47, Golden Fleece. Here, on account of heavy rains, they were obliged to remain two nights, mosquitoes and sand-flies, however, rendering it impossible to rest. Proceeding on the 8th, first their chaise broke down; next their horse was taken sick; but by the kindness of different managers they got over these troubles. On the 9th heavy rains fell, making the roads very bad, and necessitating Mr. Wray's getting out to lead the horse. Arrived at Mahaica, both parents with one of the children became very ill, and consequently remained here until the morning of the 13th, when they started for Bachelor's

Adventure, Jonathan Hopkinson, Esq., an opulent and hospitable gentleman, who had invited them to spend a few days at his house. He had been their sincere friend when they lived on Le Resouvenir, and some of his children had been educated by Mrs. Wray. Arrived there in the evening, Mr. Wray was attacked by yellow fever, a most fatal disease, which continued three days and nights. Brought very low, he knew not what passed, and his life was despaired of. Dr. Robson, their former attendant in Demerara, was summoned and was very attentive; remaining four nights with his patient and, by God's blessing, succeeding in bringing him round. Mr. Hopkinson did all he could for his guest's restoration and comfort, and when, taking leave of him, Mr. Wray thanked him for his kindness, replied that "he was very glad he had had it in his power to show us attention."

It was to another and like-minded friend that the family passed on, William Postlethwaite, Esq., proprietor of Plantation Friendship, who, hearing of their position and desires, had written the following letter, dated 25th July, 1814, which, as it should be, is given entire :—

"DEAR SIR,—I have directed my little manager to have a bed put up for you. In a few days the house will be better furnished, well cleaned out, and put to rights, so as to make you as comfortable as possible. My seine and fisherman and gamekeeper aback, will supply you with fish and pigeons, my gardens with what they afford, my cassava field with sweet cassava, and my plantain walk with *West Indian breadfruit*, and my cows with milk ; and you are welcome to anything else the estate affords except my breeding stock, which I don't kill for myself. And, with all, a hearty welcome, *free of expense*. The Logie, too, is at your service to teach your flock in, so that I hope you will be comfortable, and under that pleasing hope, I remain, dear sir, your humble servant,

"(Signed)   WM. POSTLETHWAITE.

"The Rev. Mr. WRAY."

Such an offer at such a time filled their hearts with gratitude to God for inclining their friend to proffer his house, so
well accommodated and in so healthy a spot. To Friendship
accordingly, only about three miles short of Le Resouvenir
Chapel, they moved on 6th August, and at once commenced
the work of instruction and preaching. Thirty to forty
people attended their family worship. On the first Sabbath
the Logie, a room 70 feet by 28, was filled with attentive
hearers, and every evening the large hall with scholars.

More than two months now elapsed before they returned
to Berbice. Meanwhile the cotton crop in the surrounding
neighbourhood was being gathered, but planters were often
in straits about providing animal food for the large numbers
dependent on them. Prices of cotton ruled very low, and
prices of salt provisions very high ; small supplies reached
the Colony because of the war; in all which things
Mr. Wray, as shown by his reading, by his descriptions, and
the details he gives, took a lively and sympathetic interest.
So the time passed, the family receiving, and doubtless con-
ferring, much benefit.

While in the vicinity, by the death of one of their best
friends, Mrs. Tyson, at the age of sixty-nine, they sustained
a loss that could not have been very unexpected. She was
next to Mr. Post in receiving the Gospel into her house,
which ever since had been a place for Christian worship and
instruction. Though a person of colour, she had been highly
respected by all the whites in the neighbourhood. Kind and
obliging to all the managers around, she always rendered
assistance in times of affliction. She appeared to love the
Lord Jesus Christ in sincerity, was a friend to His people,
always expressed an earnest desire to do His will, and to be
found in Him. For some time sick and blind, she died in
the first hour of 18th October, on which day, after seeing her
remains committed to the grave, the Wrays departed again
for home, travelling overland. Their journey was a pleasant

K

one, and they arrived at Sandvoort on Saturday, the 22nd.

The day following, Mr. Wray was too weary and poorly to extend his labours beyond Sandvoort, but when rested and refreshed, all had for the rest of the year, if we except a short period in November when some were again prostrate with fever, a course of comparative health and strength. He had not, however, to go far beyond either his first Sunday or Sandvoort to find how increased and varied were the adverse influences against which, in Berbice, he would have to contend. When guests, or callers for accommodation at the houses of the managers of the Crown estates, could be guilty, as occasionally they were, of the grossest violations of politeness and decency towards the pioneer, it may be taken as an indication that ill-will towards the plans and purposes of the Commissioners had, since the apprehended insurrection, become more general, certainly more loud-voiced.

E.g., one Sunday evening, company at the Sandvoort manager's set up loud song-singing, seemingly to outrival hymns being sung at worship; and later, when going home, the rowdy guests visited Mr. Wray's residence, rousing the retired inmates with indecent shouts and attempts to effect an entrance, all with apparent impunity. Sad to say, this manager in particular showed himself too much in sympathy with such like, and multiplied obstacles to the work and to the benefits of instruction; while the general agent, Mr. Dela-Court, neglected even the very things he had been specially charged to provide—provisions, clothing, houses, and common comforts for the negroes; whilst no exertion at all had been made to erect chapels, schoolrooms, &c. "Indeed, everything was done to discourage us, to render the negroes dissatisfied, and bring the plans of the Commissioners into disrepute."

The penalties of the new laws, too, were very severe, a slave leaving his estate without a pass being liable to lashes

up to 39 ; singing or shouting or uttering songs of certain
kinds to slaves on other estates when passing along river or
creek, liable to lashes up to 100 ; and a white person per-
mitting his slaves so to sing, &c., to a fine up to 100 guilders
(nearly £7).

So the very first Sabbath, as on after occasions, many,
having had only salt given them, went to catch the fish ;
whilst both on Sandvoort and in town, the day in fourteen
allowed to the Crown slaves having come to be very
irregularly given, Sunday was often much taken up with
their own work. None came from other estates to worship,
and Wray felt he could look for none, being persuaded that,
had they courage to ask for passes, these would be refused
them. A rumour, too, had got abroad that the Colonies
were about to be restored to the Dutch, and wherever the
Crown slaves went they were told that then those who had
learnt to read would be severely flogged. What surprised
the missionary was the perseverance with which, in face of
all and under trying circumstances, a number did continue
both their attendance at worship and instruction, and their
attempts at learning. Whatever the drawbacks, therefore,
Mr. and Mrs. Wray were as determined to persevere with
their work, hoping that in due time the Commissioners,
hearing and finding how things stood, would rectify all in
their power. So with those who came, whether older or
younger, they did what they could. Mr. Meadowcroft, the
catechist on Dageraad, however, was rendered so uncomfortable that he was obliged to leave.

Some encouragements, nevertheless, still remained. Visiting Dankbaarheid the first time after his return, the pioneer
was happy to find considerable improvement under Lambert;
and afterwards, on Sandvoort, was so impressed with the
diligence and demeanour of some, their constancy and confession, that he began to teach them a short catechism on
baptism. Mrs. Wray, too, succeeded in cutting out and

superintending the making, by the sewing school, of between 600 and 700 shirts for the negroes, besides the repairing of clothes brought for the purpose.

Lord's Day, 13th November, was a day of peculiar distress to the household; Antoinette, one of their laundresses, having, on the preceding night, been kidnapped by Bush negroes. Her family lived at the Winkel village, and she had left Sandvoort at a late hour on Saturday to go thither, having got the manager's man-servant to accompany her. On the way, two runaway negroes rushed out of the bush, one seizing Antoinette, and the other, with a cutlass, chasing and threatening death to her companion who, however, outran him and so escaped. Mrs. Tuckett remembers the event, and gives the additional particulars that Antoinette, at the time, was guilty of disobedience; she and Jenny, another laundress, having been forbidden to go to town and having been refused passes by Mrs. Wray, who had heard of a great dance coming off there, and who promised them Monday instead.

On hearing of the deed, Mr. Wray at once informed the manager and, as he treated it lightly, went to the authorities in town, agent, commissary, fiscal, to find all three from home. The Winkel negroes would have gone in pursuit, but had no white person to lead them. Not until the 15th did a Sandvoort overseer and some of the negroes go in search. They found the track and following it, sometimes having to creep on hands and knees, came at last to a place where the remains of provisions including those of an alligator, traps set to catch bush rats, and short, sharpened stakes fixed in the ground and covered with leaves to check pursuers, indicated a spot used for rest and refreshment. Bringing pieces of Antoinette's frock, torn off as she was being dragged along, the party returned; to be followed, in a few days, by an organised expedition commanded by Mr. Galley who, in addition to many of his own negroes, had some

Indians. They were absent about a mouth; often up to their knees in water, and sleeping in hammocks suspended between trees. Discovering a settlement of the Bush negroes, they pursued the men. Unable to overtake them, they shot two and brought away their right hands; together with four or five women that, at some distance of time or other, had likewise been kidnapped, and one of whom, attempting to run with the men, had thrown her child into the water that she might escape being caught. But nothing was seen of Antoinette, who must have been taken to some other camp, and who was destined to remain in the bush upwards of eleven years before she escaped, afterwards again to form part of the pioneer's charge and care.

Sad details these, and calculated to cast a gloom over the household; but not less so surely the following which, in the more concise of two parallel paragraphs recording them, we give as we find, written in December. Well might the pioneer feel as if in the very depths of discouragement.

"The licentiousness of some of the Whites is awful. We cannot keep a servant virtuous, for the manager takes a delight in prostituting those in our house. He obliges them to comply by threats and actual punishments. We have been constrained, by his base conduct, to part with four or five valuable servants, three of whom have each a child by this unnatural man."

Christmas day, this year, was on a Sunday, and was a day of solemn joy to the missionary who baptized nine adults and six children, first fruits in Berbice. The adults came forward two at once, a short prayer and hymn intervening between the couples, each and all making "a good confession before many witnesses." Afterwards they brought forward their children to present them to the Lord in baptism.

On Sandvoort, the holidays were again decently spent, and this notwithstanding incitements to do otherwise, even on the Sabbath day. Mr. Wray, though but poorly, held services on each day; the children attended school apparently with pleasure, and Mrs. Wray gave them a little treat. Some crossed over to the estate opposite where, from Saturday night to Tuesday morning, the negroes were dancing, bawling, singing songs, and drinking rum; their mistress, professedly Christian, and her friends cheering them on.

The last words of the pioneer, for 1814, are :—

"This has been a year of great persecution, affliction, fever and pain, and of great anxiety; but the Lord has delivered us, and He will deliver. Blessed be His holy name."

<h2 style="text-align:center">1815-1817.</h2>

Prospective New Opening—Opposition—Cart-whipping a Watchman— Consequent Inquiry—New Crown Agents—Improved Management— White Rowdies on Sandvoort—Cart-whipping a Plundered Slave—Case before Court—Planters' Opinions and Experiences—Removal to Town —Visit to Demerara—Arrival there of First Wesleyan Missionary— Return to Berbice—Work among Sailors—Visit to Indians—Improvement at Dankbaarheid—Entertainment—Unhealthy Time—Consequent Deaths—Increased Congregations—Subjects of Discourse—Class for Aged and Infirm—Various Events—Dageraad Abandoned—Auxiliary Bible Society—Journey to Corentyne—Cruelty to Innocent Negro— Encouragements and Hindrances—Arrival at Le Resouvenir of Rev. John and Mrs. Smith—Reasons for Second Return to England— Diabolical Cruelty.

EIGHTEEN hundred and fifteen opened with a Sabbath, with good congregations at Sandvoort, and with a month that, when half way through, saw Mr. Wray guest of a respectable planter on the Berbice East Coast, who was wishful to forward any plans for the instruction and improvement of his slaves. Of these he had taken particular care. Like-minded men had been met with on the West Coast, and, in Demerara, on the coasts both East and West. Here in another quarter was an additional encouraging sign.

But the condition of things on the Crown estates was

growingly such as to cause the pioneer increasing anxiety and unpleasantness. Himself and the nearest officials at variance, how could it be otherwise? With a now neglectful agent, who too could be having his Sunday ball in town on one side of the street, while the missionary was preaching in a building just opposite; and with a dissolute manager who, every few weeks, could make midnight at Sandvoort hideous with his companions' drunken revelry, how could they be at peace or pull together? It must have been during such period that one or both of these officials were intent upon getting rid of the missionary, as Mrs. Tuckett, when telling how the first chapel was raised, declares was the case :—

"The manager of the estate soon showed he did not approve of the work of instruction, but, as he could not prevent it, he did all in his power to make my parents as uncomfortable as he could. He would not pay him his salary, and so they were obliged to live as well as they could without it. He was mistaken if he thought to drive the Pioneer from the field. What they could not get in the way of food they did without. Plantains, yams, could be had for little money; fowls and ducks could be raised. They had a shelter over their heads; they could work on—this was enough. They had counted the cost, and were not disappointed."*

Happily the conclusion of all this was not very distant, though, meanwhile, the rupture went on and grew; the following event, which occurred in the latter part of January, tending to widen it.

On Monday, the 23rd, whilst at breakfast, the family were startled by the cracking of the cart-whip and the cries of a negro under their window. It proved to be the infliction of thirty-nine lashes upon a man held down by four others. He was sixty years old, a watchman over the plantain-walk,

---

* Mrs. Tuckett's first letter. Mr. Wray was afterwards paid what had been so maliciously withheld by these officials. The noble use he made of the money remains to be told.

but, being afflicted with spasms, and the weather being wet
and cold, he had gone to his house to sleep. What plantains
could be had were only half-grown, but plantains were scarce
on the estate, and several of the people had gone and taken
some. Mr. Wray went, therefore, and informed the Fiscal
both of the punishment and of the scarcity of provisions
which prevailed on the Crown estates.

In such a case the law authorized the Fiscal to visit the
estates, but, for some reason, his Honour said that he would
petition the Governor to authorize him. This coming to the
ears of Mr. De-la-Court, the agent began complaining and
soliciting on his own account, representing that the negroes
on the Crown estates, and particularly on Sandvoort and
Dankbaarheid, were very dissatisfied and impertinent, and
had been so for some months back, and requesting the
Governor that the Fiscal might be immediately sent. His
Honour appeared at Sandvoort, attended by another official,
to find the negroes when assembled behave in the most
respectful manner, whilst he carefully and impartially investigated matters, their request being that they might have a
sufficiency of plantains given them, and all inquiry showing
that this had not been the case, either as to quantity or ripe-
ness.

But the manager, he who could so frequently run off to
town from his own duties, had his complaint. This was
against a particular negro, Augustus, one of those who had
been baptized at Christmas; and it was, not that Augustus
did not work, but that since he was baptized he thought
himself too great a man to work, &c., and had said so to a
negro on the other side of the creek. Augustus, called forth
and called upon to answer for himself, explained that a
woman on the estate opposite had asked him why he did not
go to dance at Christmas as formerly, and that he replied he
used to go from one estate to another to dance and get
drunk, and was frequently engaged in quarrels, for which he

was put in the stocks and flogged the next day, but now that the Gospel had come, he had learned better things, and had given himself to Christ, &c.

This was all, and charges more unfortunate for those who made them could not well have been brought; since, in Mr. Wray's experience, the Sandvoort negroes were the quietest gang he had ever seen, and the most contented; the manager's leaving the estate so frequently showing that he had no fear of them. At the conclusion, the Fiscal expressed a wish that his own negroes were instructed and baptized, and reproved the manager, says Mr. Wray, "for carrying my name about the Colony as he had done."

Afterwards the Fiscal visited Dankbaarheid. Mr. Wray was not present, but learnt that he found the same scarcity of provisions prevailing, and that the negroes being clamorous while he was there, a charge, too, of spoiling some produce being made against them, his Honour punished two or three. That the management here was at fault, however, was afterwards shown by the voluntary return of some negroes who, having frequently complained to Mr. De-la-Court and got no redress, but rather punishment in the stocks, had betaken themselves to the woods, and lived there for months until they knew a different management had begun.

Had such variance continued, the evil results, both on the estates and in mission work, can hardly be conceived. But new agents to amend matters were already on their way. These were James Walker, Esq., of Edinburgh, formerly a planter in Tobago, who was appointed principal agent; and William Scott, Esq., formerly a planter in Berbice, and several years Commissary for the Winkel Department, thus well acquainted with the Crown estates and negroes, assistant agent. Arriving in the early part of February, they relieved Mr. De-la-Court of his official duties as agent of the Commissioners on the 15th.

It will be remembered that Mr. De-la-Court at first had

been but assistant agent to the more experienced and tried
Col. Macalister, who had died after five weeks' residence;
and, in justice to the Commissioners, it should be said that—
though Mr. De-la-Court, in his correspondence, displayed considerable talent and intelligence, and acted with great energy
in conducting the estates' affairs, and this amid great opposition from private individuals and some of the local authorities, also under great difficulties arising especially from past
neglect, from the almost impossibility of getting managers
willing to carry ameliorating plans into effect, and from capture, in the first year, of the *Sydney Smith*, laden with
£5000 worth of stores for the estates, by an American
privateer—the Commissioners would never have confirmed
him as their principal agent had they been prepared to send
out a successor whose age, experience, and tried moral principles and prudence entitled him more fully to their confidence.*   As it was, after being for some time deeply interested, to all appearance, in the views of the Commissioners,
he became one of the executors of a very rich old lady, into
whose family he had married, and hence his change of feeling
and conduct.   The Commissioners, judging from his later
communications, as well as some from other quarters, that
their own plans were not being carried into effect, asked for
distinct explanations on several points.   These proving
unsatisfactory, they resolved to supersede him.

Before actually taking over the duties of his office, Mr.
Walker visited Sandvoort, attended a religious meeting, himself, at Mr. Wray's request, closing it with prayer.   During
the week he had much conversation with Mr. and Mrs.
Wray on the management and instruction of the negroes;
and particularly respecting the provision of rooms as a
lying-in hospital, for which nothing had as yet been done,
and for want of which much misery and great mortality
existed among the negro infants.   Mrs. Wray was very

* Commissioners' Report, pp. 5, 7, 11.

urgent on this matter, and engaged to make all things needful in the way of garments, &c.

But the first act of the new agents was to plant 150 acres
of plantains and other provisions ; the plantains, cooked in
various ways, and especially as foofoo, being the staple and
favourite food of the negro. Encouraged by the new agents
to raise for themselves both pigs and fowls, a multiplication
of these soon began to appear among the negro dwellings.
So deficient, meanwhile, were the estates that £250 per
month had to be spent in provisions. The plans of Mrs.
Wray, however, for the welfare of mothers and infants, were
soon carried into effect, and with the happiest results. Every
needful comfort was afforded during the time of confinement;
a dollar was given to each on leaving the hospital, together
with two or three frocks for the little one ; and a dollar to
the nurse ; whilst Mrs. Wray constantly visited these rooms,
instructed the midwives in their duty both to mother and
infant, and, in fact, took the entire management.

More work, our devoted friends could hardly well have
undertaken ; but what a difference in the doing, the kind of
spirit makes ! With such men as had now come to superintend affairs, and, with a fair measure of health still
continued, they pursued their course, but manifestly with
more cheerful hearts ; hearts assured of some at hand able
and willing to sympathize with them in their toil, gratified
by an occasional addition to the number of such, also by
increasing tokens that renewed efforts were producing happy
results in various ways. Visits, therefore, to the more
distant estates ; reasoning with suspected agents of Obeah,
and especially with the victims of disease who were dejected
by superstitious fears and by dark suspicions of the designs
of such agents ; settling domestic quarrels ; seeking to get
persons living as man and wife to be faithful to the only
bond, their mutual promise, which as slaves could unite
them ; attending to critical cases connected with the new

hospital; reading the Scriptures; teaching the young; preaching the Word; visiting the sick; burying the dead; were constantly carried on.

Jas of Sandvoort, himself once a believer in Obi, informed Mr. Wray about the time (Good Friday, 24th March) that the two or three agents, living there, found their occupation gone, and had to visit other estates, seeking dupes. At the Easter holidays there was not a drunken negro on the estate. Several times towards midnight the missionary walked among the houses, but all was quiet. The Sunday and other services were very well attended. About two o'clock one Saturday morning indeed, the whole family were waked out of sleep to find the negroes roused and all in an uproar; but it was caused by the shouting and swearing of the manager and a companion who had both just arrived in a half-drunken condition—a like thing occurring about a month afterwards, when midnight was made hideous by a drunken party of his which included several managers, revelling, curs-ing, and shouting most indecent language. As houses are there, it would require no effort of Mr. Wray to hear himself, as he did, made the subject of their mockery and hate. Between the two dates, however, another most painful event had occurred, causing some stir in town as it did on Sandvoort.

On Easter-Tuesday morning, Mr. Wray saw two white gentlemen with the manager and a strange boat at the wharf; afterwards, while teaching some children, a white man in a blue jacket and, with a stick in his hand, driving a negro, who passed the window, but too far off to hear what was said between them. Soon drivers came, fixed some stakes in the ground just opposite, then brought the negro, stretched him all naked on the ground, and tied his hands and his feet to the stakes. Standing one on each side, they began to flog him with their cart-whips. About seventy lashes had been given when Mrs. Wray, who was looking out of another window, called to the white men for God's sake to have mercy on the sufferer; they, however, going on till the poor fellow had received one hundred.

Anxious to know what the man had done to deserve all this, Mr. Wray was told that it was for impertinence to a magistrate, himself a slaveholder, who had come to visit the provision grounds. It seems that one of this visitor's slaves had, some time before, stolen four guilders (5s. 6d.) from this negro on Sandvoort who, hearing that the thief's master was in the manager's house, came and pressed his request that the money should be refunded. The magistrate was angry, and told him to go.

"*N.* Massa, so long as me poor negro, massa no want for give me right; massa no tell me if the negro shall pay me or no.

M. If you do not go, I will flog you.

N. If we had come on massa's plantation and tieved, massa would come and flog all we, and our massa would make us pay the negro what we tieved from him.

M. (Strikes him on the head with a stick.)

N. Me come to beg massa for me right, and massa beat me upon the top of my right.

M. (Drives him forth and, becoming judge, jury, and virtual executioner in his own cause, inflicts the punishment narrated.)"

But the Crown agents had to be reckoned with, and under a sense of duty, they resolved to bring the case before the criminal court in town. Attempts were made to alter their decision, as afterwards a request made that the circumstances should not be written home. The agents, however, felt it right to let the prosecution take its course. Mr. and Mrs. Wray were amongst the witnesses summoned to testify what they could not help hearing and seeing, as all their windows were open. No oath was administered to any witness, and the court justified the punishment on the ground of impertinence—a conclusion worthy of the Colony, as it then was.

The pioneer had met with planters under various circumstances; here came in a word with one, almost novel. During this month alone, he had conversation with a planter from Essequibo, come to Berbice to buy slaves, strongly but ignorantly opposed to their instruction, but content to let the missionaries live and labour if only at a distance from his neighbourhood; again with another, after a six years' absence, just returned from England to a property that had been sold, since his return, for almost nothing; the estate having been so neglected by his agent that his negroes had diminished one-third, his fields were all desolate, and all was involved in debt; a tale echoed by a lady present, whose husband's property, during a short absence, had narrowly escaped a like condition. Now, however, after this semblance of a trial, it was a planter who came and said—

"that he was sorry anything unpleasant had taken place between him and me, and that he now believed it was all from false reports and tale-bearing; that if I would come to live in town, all his negroes should attend me, and that he would subscribe towards building a chapel and a house, and if I would draw up a subscription-paper he would hand it about himself."

A few more weeks and their return to live in town, whether anticipated or not, had become a fact. It seems likely to have been a change required by the re-arrangement of things under the new agents, as, in course of time, Mr. Scott became manager of Sandvoort as well as assistant-agent, and Mr. Walker would possibly require some accommodation for himself in the house formerly occupied by Mr. De-la-Court. The people were very sorry to lose their teachers as residents, but, of course, the work went on, not excepting Mrs. Wray's care for the women in their maternal experiences. Their efforts and the results had not been all they could have wished; some changes for the better had, however, been accomplished in people and things at Sandvoort. But in his review and prospect at the time Mr. Wray remarks:—

"We have seen enough of West Indian management, having lived seven years on estates. A person may reside many years in a West Indian town, and be in the habit of visiting plantations, and know very little of the treatment of the negroes. I am astonished that insurrections are not more common than they are."

On the evening of Thursday, 5th May, they were settled again at New Amsterdam; and on Whitsunday, the 14th, attendances at worship, both at Sandvoort and in town, filled the rooms, and, by express wish of the people, a meeting was held, and was well attended, both in the morning and evening of Whitmonday.

On Friday, 2nd June, he voyaged to Demerara, preaching at Le Resouvenir on the 4th. Generally in his visits to the Colony, our pioneer had the satisfaction of noting some advance. On this occasion it is an event well worth specifying — the first settlement there of the Wesleyan missionaries.

"On the evening of the 7th I preached for Mr. Talboys, a Wesleyan missionary who lately came from the Islands to establish a Mission in Georgetown. The place will hold 300 or 400 people. It was crowded chiefly with free coloured hearers, also a number of whites attended." "There are now three places of public worship in town (London Mission Chapel, St. George's Church, Wesleyan Mission Room), and all well attended."

Later on in the year he was happy in being able to place a gift of Scriptures at the service of the Wesleyans, forwarding them from Berbice. Instances of the good effect of former labours in Demerara, and of the circulation of the Scriptures there, were constantly coming to light. He rode back on the 12th.

Visiting some sailors dangerously ill, belonging to the ship *Antelope*, a vessel that lay some time in the river, was followed by his preaching occasionally on board; "a new field of labour," he says, "in which I hope to be useful."

With a few Indians, who now and then came down the river, Mr. Wray had already made some acquaintance; but, on Monday, 17th July, along with a Captain Ellis for his companion, he started on his first visit to their nearest villages, which lay about as far again up the Berbice as plantation Dageraad. Spending some time at each of the Crown estates on their way, as well as at one or two solitary houses higher up the river, they came on Thursday to two little settlements, and had some interesting converse with the dwellers, not the least so being with an old Indian, who professed himself a Christian, and who turned out to have been baptized long years before by the Moravians on the Corentyne river, prior to their enforced retirement. Wray was able to inform him of their return again, and subsequently to write a happy account of the week's excursion, with some particulars of good fruit that afterwards appeared growing out of his passing efforts at the houses of call.

August proved an unhealthy month. Spared themselves, and responding to signs of improvement and encouragement on Dankbaarheid, Mr. Wray in his visits was twice accompanied by his wife, on both occasions for a few days' stay. The opportunities were turned to good account by all parties. A further impetus was given to instruction, and additional arrangements made. In company with the agent, the sick and disabled were visited in their houses, and comforts furnished to the helpless and neglected ones. With one voice the people requested that, during their holidays at the end of the month, they might have their friends to instruct them, and not be left to themselves and their African dances. The request was complied with, and, holidays over, Mr. Walker was so well pleased with their conduct that—

"He had an ox killed to give them an entertainment, Mrs. Wray superintending the cooking. Eighty gallons of soup were made in one of the large sugar boilers, an abundance of beef was roasted and boiled, and a beverage made of lime juice and sugar. Old and young came neat and clean, and close upon 450 sat down at five long tables fitted up in a large building near the dwelling-house. Parts of the 100th Psalm served for grace before and after meat. The invalids in hospital and at home were then supplied, afterwards the assembled company. The negroes were very much delighted with the entertainment; and old Sampson came next morning to the agent with the thanks of the plantation, saying 'they had never spent such happy holidays.'"

The unhealthy weather that prevailed continued into September, and went on seriously to affect a great number of people and to become very fatal. In his own house, Mr. Wray had little Rebecca laid like a dead child; a young man who had brought a letter of introduction from Mr. Talboys, very unwell; and at Sandvoort Mr. Scott was laid up. Report said that five, out of eight passengers arrived by one ship a little while before, were dead. The missionary several times visited one young man, settled only a few weeks in the Colony, but seized with an illness which proved fatal. Gratified with the converse thus held, he accompanied his remains to the grave, trusting that the "early called" had been taken from "the evil to come." Happily, the lives of all in his own house and the life of the agent were spared. About the middle of the month they removed to another house in town, the ground floor of which made an excellent store for the Crown agents, the second storey was turned into a place of worship, and the third became their dwelling.

The congregation at New Amsterdam grew in numbers both of whites and free coloured people, as well as of negro slaves. Thus, 1st October, twenty whites were present at evening service, and on the 8th, twenty whites and from thirty to forty free people of colour. But of the twenty whites present on the 1st he notes that four were living in open and notorious adultery, another was a profane infidel, and most were living in fornication.

L

"It requires more resolution to be faithful than is generally supposed, and it is exceedingly difficult to keep from giving offence. I pray that I may have grace to be faithful in all things."

On the evening of the 8th his subject was "The reciprocal duties of masters and slaves." He was also going through a course of lectures on the Ten Commandments, which seemed to excite much interest, and on the evening of the 15th he had the largest attendance, particularly of whites, that had ever come to this service; a number, however, much diminished on the following Lord's Day evening, when the Seventh Commandment came to be considered.

"Such subjects as this strike at the very root of the customs of the country. I felt pleasure in quoting the sentiments of Archbishops Leighton, Secker, and Bishop Hopkins. They say all I wished to say, perhaps with much better effect."

Wednesday, 11th October, after visiting on the previous day among the sick and afflicted of the Winkel negroes and arranging with them, about thirty old and infirm people, some half blind, some hopping on crutches or sticks, but all very decent and clean, came to be instructed, being the first members of a class that continued for twenty years. Conducted first by Mrs. Wray, who could speak Creole fluently (and they understood none other), Mr. Wray afterwards shared the labour, the only other change being on the day of the week, from Wednesday to Friday. "It proved a blessing to many."

A visit to an adulterous and wicked driver on Dankbaarheid, who had attempted to hang himself; another to a very different character, a negro named Joest, on Sandvoort, who had embraced the Gospel, and who died in the faith of it, clinging to the Lord Jesus, his prayers and longing spirit-utterances deeply impressing all who visited him; and the departure, on the 19th, of Mr. Walker, principal Crown

Agent, for England on business, leaving meanwhile the whole management of the estates to Mr. Scott, are the chief events noted of this month.

In the first days of November, Mrs. Wray accompanied her husband and Mr. Scott to Dankbaarheid, also to Dageraad. Important changes in reference to the latter had been decided on, and already in large measure carried out. On account of its distance from the other properties, its very unhealthy situation, and the amount of nightwork which, owing to peculiar circumstances, was absolutely necessary, it had been resolved to abandon Dageraad. Houses on Dankbaarheid, therefore, were prepared for the younger and abler negroes, who willingly removed to be nearer town and the means of instruction. No separation of families took place, but a number of old people who had not as yet made up their minds to leave the home of their earlier days and the tombs of their friends, were let alone, though not left to themselves. On this occasion "Mr. Scott conveyed to them some tobacco and fish, rum and salt." Of course, all opportunities for preaching, teaching, visiting, were utilized; the would-be self-murderer of last month not forgotten, and found in a somewhat better mind.

Finding his stock of Bibles and Testaments, English and Dutch, becoming exhausted, the pioneer, Monday, 6th November, suggested the formation of an Auxiliary Bible Society; and on Wednesday night following, after Divine service, a gentleman asked if he had made any plans, as some other gentlemen had expressed their willingness to subscribe. In response, therefore, to an announcement on the next Sabbath, nine gentlemen met at Mr. Wray's house, on the evening of the 13th, to form an auxiliary. Committee, treasurer, and secretary were duly appointed, and it was resolved to request his Excellency, Governor Bentinck, to become the Patron, with which request the Governor kindly complied. Thus, amid the missionary's prayers, and long to be followed by

his efforts for its usefulness, came into existence the first
Bible Society in Berbice.

The river Corentyne, flowing northwards, separates British
from Dutch Guiana, having Berbice for its left bank, and up
this river the Moravian missionaries had returned to settle.
Naturally the pioneer wished to visit them, particularly as
he had a long-standing invitation from William Ross, Esq.,
Protector of the Berbice Indians, who resided on the Corentyne, to accompany him to their settlement.

5th December, therefore, Mr. Wray started in a light one-
horse chaise to carry out his cherished intention.   Travelling
on the East Coast road, he spent the 6th with a respectable
planter, whose wife, a pious, good woman, greatly lamented
that on all the coast there was neither minister nor school.
Leaving with early morning of the 7th, he breakfasted about
ten miles further on.   The coast lands between the Berbice
and Corentyne rivers had been laid out, about the beginning
of the century, in estates, chiefly cotton ; but, from several
causes, many of the planters had become involved, the slaves,
except where the cultivation was changed to sugar, were
being sold into Demerara, and the estates being fast abandoned.   An incident by the way is painfully significant.
As the pioneer journeyed, a solitary negro accosted him,
pointing behind to blood-covered marks of stripes—"See,
massa, what that buckra do me ! Me do nothing but call
for beg a drink of water, and me have pass from me massa."
Shortly before, he had been severely flogged with the cart-
whip—why, we shall presently see.

Coming to the mouth of the Corentyne :—

"I drove my chaise close to the water for five or six miles, on
a beautiful sand-beach, which was very pleasant.   I had seen
nothing like it in the country, for in general there is nothing but
mud along the water's edge."

Approaching a creek, he spent the night in a white man's
hut, and next morning, leaving horse and vehicle in his care,

crossed in a boat sent by his friend, by whom, soon after, he was politely received.

Spending the 8th there, he met with the master of the negro just mentioned, greatly enraged at the man who had committed the outrage, and saying that the negro was a very excellent and quiet man that had never been punished; in which he was corroborated by another gentleman present, under whose management the negro had been some time before. It seems that his master had met with a negro who had no pass, had taken and put him in the stocks for the night, and next day sent him home with a letter; home happening to be the estate where afterwards the drink of water had been begged; so, out of spite, the innocent caller had been cart-whipped. Any prosecution for the cruel injustice was deemed absurd, as no evidence but that of negroes, which would not be taken, could be got, and it would have been an easy matter to accuse the negro of impertinence.

On the 9th, the pioneer and protector, along with three Warrow Indians, and a boy Mr. Wray had brought, proceeded together up the river by an early tide, reaching Equevi creek, about forty miles up, where were two villages of Warrows, and where they breakfasted.

Unfortunately, the pioneer's own papers, for a considerable space, are now missing. But much may be learnt of the Moravian Missions in Dutch Guiana from their own records; and what has been said of himself and his devoted wife, of their labours and trials hitherto, will give some idea of the manner of persons and of life, their patience to endure, and their unwearied industry in active service, greatly varied; which we must carry along with us where we have more briefly to pass over seasons and events which concern them.

From a very brief history of the Berbice Mission, published in the *Evangelical Magazine* for 1835,* therefore during the pioneer's lifetime, we learn that in 1815 he

* Page 523.

baptized fourteen negroes, and, on the last day of the year, admitted eleven to the privilege of Christian communion— that many adults, as well as children, had learnt to read.

" In the following year he was gratified by seeing his place of worship filled on the Sabbath with well-behaved negroes, but suffered a severe trial in consequence of the British Government restoring a moiety of the Crown estates to the Dutch company, to whom they formerly belonged ; an arrangement fatal, for a time, to Mr. Wray's usefulness on the estates thus restored ; the managers being averse to the instruction of the negroes. This abridgment, however, of his labours, enabled him to give more of his time and attention to the Crown negroes in town, where, the attendance on his ministry continuing to increase, he formed the design of erecting a chapel."

Le Resouvenir would, of course, still have what help he could give it, and early in 1817 he had the pleasure of welcoming to it, as their sphere of labour, the Rev. John Smith and his devoted wife ; as afterwards of occasionally visiting them ; kindnesses duly acknowledged by Mr. Smith in his letters to the Society. Writing, 10th July — " Mr. Wray has been here and preached to the people. He has rendered me much help." Again, in December, concerning a baptism of twenty-eight persons in September —" The sermon was preached by Mr. Wray, who had unexpectedly come from Berbice," and who " during intervals gave out verses from Dr. Watts." *

" But serious impediments having been thrown in the way of his labours," says the brief account of 1835, " by individuals inimical to the instruction of the negroes, he was induced to visit England for the redress of these grievances."

What these impediments were, is not specified, any more than in the entry of the Missionary Register, which simply runs :—" Visited England for a purpose similar to the former, arriving early in 1818." Not unlikely, the humane

* *Evangelical Magazine*, 1817. 1818.

efforts to ameliorate his condition, put forth by the friends of the slave, and the professed fears of an insurrection, were rousing into activity the opposition of the more virulent and unscrupulous part of the slave-holders. It would seem, indeed, from expressions used on a later occasion and quoted by us in their place, that in connection with the Crown estates and the changes of ownership, &c., affecting them, Governor Bentinck was again troubling the missionary; and barbarous cruelty on one of them had certainly to do with his return. Reprimands, addressed by the Governor to the pioneer, were followed by disputes with his Excellency, who professed to derive his authority from Earl Bathurst, grounds of which profession Mr. Wray, not without reason or success, proceeded to test; and as in a subsequent diary he speaks of their ears, during the earlier days of residence at New Amsterdam, being constantly saluted with the cracking of the cart-whip and the cries of the sufferers, at what time more likely than after the passing of such enactments touching passes, singing, &c., as have been detailed. In particular, he incidentally refers to the circumstances of a case which seems to have been the climax that determined him.

"23rd *July*, 1835.—I buried poor old America on Sandvoort,* I suppose eighty years old. It is now nineteen years since that dreadful cruelty was committed upon her, which brought upon me great persecution and cost me a voyage to England; but I do not repent of the interest I took in it. The state of the negroes has improved ever since, and, blessed be God, slavery is now abolished by law, and I trust will soon be so in practice. Blessed be God for the great change which has taken place."

Mrs. Tuckett prevented the request for any explanation of the above, by furnishing an account in her second letter.

"I have remembered also the reason of this second visit to England. The account also, was in the Journal (the part missing). It was this. A most cruel punishment was inflicted on a woman—I think her name was America. She was in the last

* In 1817-8, Sandvoort was again in the hands of the Dutch Company.

stage of pregnancy. In that state, stripped of all clothing, she was fastened down to the ground and inhumanly flogged by the drivers within an inch of her life. The babe of course was killed, and she was for a long time at death's door. And what was her offence? The manager who witnessed the punishment had, as almost all the white men, his kept mistress, and she had, as her servants, as many negro girls as she chose. One of these girls was a daughter of America. This girl, for some trifling offence, was most severely flogged. Her mother, hearing of it, went to her mistress to inquire into the affair. When she saw her child had been so cruelly treated, she no doubt spoke her mind. Her offence was 'impudence' to this mistress. When my parents heard of it, and more too, my father could bear it no longer. The lashes inflicted on these poor creatures seemed to eat into his very soul. No redress could be got in the Colony, and he determined to go to England."*

This on an estate so recently a Crown estate, on which Mr. Wray had lived and laboured, on which but recently Crown agents had willingly fitted up rooms for the comfort and safety of women in their hour of pain and peril; and Mrs. Wray had so assiduously looked after all! But what matters the estate to which America belonged? The British Government was the supreme authority and, at some cost, helped to maintain a small army in British Guiana in case of servile insurrection. Berbice, too, like Demerara, was a Crown Colony, subject therefore to legislation by Orders in Council. Would His Majesty's Ministers then not interfere? At any rate the pioneer would go and see. So again they parted; he returning alone, and his self-denying wife remaining to watch over her own little ones, and, for others, to do what she could.

*A printed account since met with (*Evangelical Magazine*, 1818, p. 343), gives the girl as being a little daughter, and the mother as receiving 170 lashes; " the savage manager meanwhile deliberately smoking his pipe during the punishment. He was, however, tried for the offence, found guilty, and sentenced to a fine of about £25, and three months' imprisonment ;" whether before or after Wray started for England is not said.

CHAPTER V.

SECOND RETURN TO ENGLAND; TO INSURRECTION IN DEMERARA, AND DEATH OF JOHN SMITH.

December 1817—August 1823.

Departure for England—A Wonderful Deliverance—Position of Affairs: Work in England — Return to Berbice — Improved Prospects, &c.— First Chapel—" No me da Massa "—Auxiliary Mission Society—Ill Health: Stay in Georgetown—Change of Governors—New Schoolroom Enlargement of Chapel—Progress Generally.

In the brig *Cambrian* of Liverpool, Captain Watson Sheriff, and on the 6th December, 1817, Mr. Wray took his departure, landing safely toward the latter end of January following. During the voyage they were the happy instruments of a " wonderful deliverance," particulars of which appear in the news of the time.

When twenty-two days out, their ship hoisted English colours responsive to a small boat discerned about a mile away, and to the inexpressible joy of its occupants. These proved to be Captain Andrew Harraden and seven of eight, crew of the brig *Superb*, that on 29th November, had sailed from Salem, U.S., bound for Martinique. On 10th December, the *Superb* had capsized so suddenly as to cause the death of a seaman, drowned in its forecastle; ultimately it sank, and for nineteen days of a winter season, in a poor tub 16 ft. long by 6 feet beam, the men had been tossing about the Atlantic, subsisting each on a daily allowance of three gills of brackish water, and about six ounces of more solid food. Continually wet, with hands and feet swollen, their sufferings were extreme. For nine days the captain had been unable to feed himself; and when hauled up each by a rope on board the *Cambrian*, not one was able to stand. But they were most kindly received, and every possible assistance and comfort was administered to them; after all which,—

"The Rev. John Wray read and commented on part of the 107th Psalm, and then offered up with them thanksgiving to God for their wonderful deliverance." "Captain Harraden, who was an attendant on the ministry of the Rev. Dr. Worcester of Salem, and had a family living there, was deeply affected by these tokens of God's goodness to him and his."

It was during the night their boat and the ship had been brought so near, as at daybreak, on 28th December, to allow the mariners ready to perish the sight of a sail, for the first time apparently, and at only about six miles' distance; then, whilst with what feeble strength remained they did their utmost to lessen the distance, and attract the ship's attention, baffling and light winds checked the vessel's course, so that at length they succeeded, and were thus "brought out of their distresses."

If less deeply affected than the immediate sufferers, their spiritual friend would derive equal encouragement with them from the striking event. Out of the ocean of difficulties surrounding him and his work, could not the same Providence bring about deliverance, and ultimately great success? The Lord could and would, so Wray believed, though after many days, to all appearance, and through great toils and sufferings. Meanwhile, thus encouraged, as we may well suppose, he landed to labour on.

At this time his position, in more than one respect, was peculiar and critical; as was indeed the position of others with whom he had co-operated, not excepting that of the older and more influential friends of the African. His

business in England was more with these and with the
Government. Not so fully connected, as once and as afterwards, with the Missionary Society, his name barely appears
in their Chronicles. During the May meetings in London,
he gave an address at a communion service in Silver Street
Chapel. This would be but a few days before he sailed
again for Berbice, and is the only engagement connected with
the Society recorded of him. On the other hand, he
apparently obtained the redress, wholly or in part, which he
came to seek, for when he did return, it was with improved
prospects of usefulness. His appeal to Earl Bathurst was
answered by a denial that his Lordship had given the
authority asserted by Governor Bentinck, and a promise to
call for an explanation ; also the assurance that if Mr. Wray
"returned to Berbice he should receive protection from the
Colonial Government, and the respect due to a minister of
the Gospel."

An Official Report of the Commissioners for the Crown
Estates having been attacked, Mr. James Walker, in defence
of the Commissioners and of himself, was on the eve of
publishing his "Letters on the West Indies," which appeared
with a final note, furnished probably by Wray. An entry in
Mr. Wilberforce's diary, dated 13th February, runs :—

"Mr. Wray called and told me of the insurrection in Berbice.
Alas, this I fear will make against us, though it ought to have an
opposite effect." (Life, &c., vol. 4, p. 370.)

At page 365 of the same volume, we read :—

"The year 1818 was an important era in the West Indian
struggle ; for, though no ameliorating measure was actually
carried, the friends of the African were led into new counsels,
and assumed a new position. The opposition made to the Regis-
tration Act forced them to establish its necessity, by going into
an examination of the actual state of the slave population ; and
these inquiries revealed at once such an amount of crime and
cruelty, as proved there was no cure for the evils of the system,
short of its entire subversion."

One might well conjecture that, from the outset, Wray had a share in all this, as we find from his own journal of after years that he continued to have; a surmise which becomes a certainty in presence of the following testimony from Mrs. Tuckett's second letter :—

"He appealed to His Majesty's ministers, stirred up the anti-slavery party, and, wherever his voice could be heard, he denounced slavery. He pleaded that the flogging of women should be abolished, that the long hours of work should be curtailed ; and though it took some time, and though it brought great persecution on him after his return to Berbice, he eventually gained what he asked. He was in constant communication with Buxton, Wilberforce, and others, to whom he had personally appealed ; never let the matter rest, and though he did not live to see entire emancipation (repeal of the apprenticeship clauses), he had the settled conviction that it would come, that the negroes would receive it gratefully, and that not a hair of a white man would be injured."

After a safe voyage Mr. Wray arrived again in Berbice, 17th July, 1818, to find his family increased by the birth of a son, whom he named John Davies Wray. His improved prospects of usefulness did not disappoint him. Welcomed by the poor negroes, they again diligently attended his ministry, and many longed for Christian instruction. The work, centred henceforth in New Amsterdam, went on in its varied kinds, and on every side more encouragingly than ever. Applications for Testaments, catechisms, spelling-books, were made to him daily. On the West Coast too, numbers were learning to read, and like applications from that quarter were almost of weekly occurrence. A respectable planter, favourable to religious instruction, purchased what of the Crown estates had been restored to the Dutch Company, and invited the missionary to resume his labours there. This, Mr. Wray did ; arranging to go personally to Dankbaarheid every alternate Saturday, and to Sandvoort every alternate Sunday morning.

His immediate want was a commodious chapel in town. To get land, however, was the difficulty, since none would sell land for such a purpose. But God opened the way. For just at this time, a house and a large piece of ground upon which it stood were for sale, possessor of which, he could quietly pursue his object; and the pioneer was in receipt of money, which an investigation of the affairs of the Crown estates had shown to have been due to him, but wrongly withheld, as we have already seen, by an unprincipled official. The sum thus opportunely to hand became part of an amount with which Wray purchased the property for his own residence; then, reserving one half of the site for a garden (his only recreation), the other half, Mrs. Tuckett informs us, he made over to the London Missionary Society, whose agent he came again fully and finally to be. On that part, the first missionary chapel in Berbice was built.

Meanwhile, a gentleman lent a commodious building for purposes of worship, and subscribed 154 guilders (about £10) towards the chapel; another subscribed 566 guilders (about £37) and obtained several other subscriptions from his friends; £400 in all being contributed by residents, and £200 being voted by the Directors of the Missionary Society.

1818 did not close before another difficulty had been overcome, and the work had been more than commenced. This other difficulty was somewhat unique. Mr. Foreman mentions it in his "Echoes from Slave-time," so does Mrs. Tuckett, who well remembers the scene. On the site for the chapel, and exactly opposite the house, was a large silk-cotton tree, which stood in the way, and for some time Mr. Wray could get no one to venture upon cutting it down; for the negroes held the tree in great veneration, and feared to offend its spirit, who, they thought, could punish them. So at last Mr. Wray said:—"That tree has got to come down, and if you won't cut it down, I will," and taking off his coat he seized the axe and commenced the work, the men looking on for some minutes. But when, says Mrs. Tuckett, they saw my father was not afraid, and was the real transgressor, they took courage, came for the axe, and, receiving it, began cutting; at every stroke crying out, "No me da massa! No me da massa!" and levelled the tree to the ground. In February, 1819, the chapel was opened.

Premising that in town all was accompanied by a growth, more or less steady, in piety and desire for instruction, also in the numbers respectively of scholars, hearers, catechumens, and church members; here is a brief detail of little more than the unusual events of each year.

In August, about six months after opening the chapel, the Berbice Auxiliary Mission Society was formed. It was composed chiefly of free people of colour, about 100 becoming subscribers, and it raised during the first eight months about £35. In the former part of 1820, the labours, both of Mr. and Mrs. Wray, were interrupted by ill health, but a visit to Georgetown later on proved very beneficial. Governor Bentinck, whose health had long been declining, died; and was succeeded in March, 1821, by Henry Beard, Esq., who had arrived in Berbice in 1819, to be President of the Court of Justice, and who proved a true friend to Mr. Wray. During 1821 the debt on the chapel was liquidated, and the building of a new school-room, to accommodate 200 children, was commenced; while the inhabitants of New Amsterdam, generally speaking, manifested an increased attention to the means of religious instruction, and the improved behaviour of the negroes in the vicinity attracted common observation. Consequently, it is no surprise to read, under 1822, not only of the opening of the new school-room, but that an enlargement of the chapel was rendered necessary. And so on towards August of 1823, the prospects of the mission progressively improved, and Mr. Wray had entered into engagements to instruct the negroes on several additional estates, one of which contained upwards of 1600.

1808-1823.

Cares—Troubles of a Constant Kind—Difficulties of Marriage Question —Annoyances by Whites — Training of Family—Raising a Native Agency—With Illustrative Details.

PAUSING in the more continuous history, we here find a convenient opportunity of noting and illustrating several matters which, throughout his whole course as Missionary Pioneer, were constantly a source of anxiety, of toil and disappointment, or of annoyance and distress.

One of these was the marriage question, as it presented itself in the man with more wives than one; or in the pair sold far asunder; or in the people that were fickle in their attachments ; or in view of the illegality of slaves marrying.

What has been discussed in connection with missionary enterprise until well thrashed out, Wray had to settle pretty much for himself. Is it lawful for a man, having more than one wife, to retain more than one on his becoming professedly a Christian? As a condition of church membership, the pioneer decided that but one should be retained, and he held fast to his decision. Agreeing with him or not, we cannot but admire his self-denial; for there were occasions when to stand firm was at no small cost of time and feeling, if not of other temporal advantage.

Greater sacrifices still of time and effort had to be made in inducing parties at variance to be at peace, and companions, as man and wife, to be faithful one to the other. Pages are filled with such details ; and, considering the hard lot often to be borne and the atmosphere of selfishness and ignorance, well they may be.

But to proceed further was at the peril of accumulating risks. Nevertheless Wray did; and if it had been less than an almost imperative necessity, amid such a clime and people, for man to have a helpmeet, he would, as in the sight of God and of the congregation, with certain preliminaries and prayers, have a marriage service, even though it was illegal for slaves to be married. In his " Echoes from Slave-time,"* Mr. Foreman puts this pithily, with a glance at still existing awkward consequences.

"The Order in Council—the marriage law of the Colony to this day—was passed on the 7th day of September, 1838, and bears the name of Queen Victoria. In slave-time, the slaves could not be married. But slaves who had been taught somewhat of the Bible expressed a wish to be married. The Rev. John Wray, therefore, acted in the following manner. He read out their names three successive Sundays, as those of persons wishing to be married. At the close of the service on the following Sunday, he called them up to the front of the congregation and said :—'Thomas, will you have Susan to be your wife ?' 'Yes, massa.' 'And Susan, will you have Thomas to be your husband ?' 'Yes, massa.' 'And will you both promise to live good together ?' 'Yes, massa.' Mr. Wray then joined their hands together, and offered prayer to God on their behalf, when, as my informant said, 'the story was done.' A very simple and inexpensive matter, you see; yet the Rev. John Wray, I have been assured, was liable to fine and imprisonment for every couple he thus married.

"I had occasion to mention this on the West Coast of Berbice, when a man (I believe he is still alive) came up to me and said :—' Papa, how did you get to know how Mr. Wray married us ?' 'Never mind,' I said, 'was what I said right ?' He replied, 'If you had said Joe and Sarah, instead of Thomas and Susan, I should have thought you meant me and my wife.'

"Slaves had only one name, as may be seen above. At Freedom, very many took also their 'old massa's name.' About two years ago, amongst some other papers relating to some property which were brought me to look at, was a certificate of marriage signed by my predecessor, the late Rev. James Scott, of a marriage between William (I think) and Mary. What was wanted of me was that I would certify that the 'Mary' of that certificate, was *the* Mary then before me. That I could not do. I could certify the certificate was a correct copy of the Register, that it was in the handwriting of the late Rev. James Scott, and

* *Demerara Daily Chronicle*, 1st August, 1888.

that I had known that Mary, as Mary, for some years, but to certify that she was the Mary of the marriage certificate, I could not."

The behaviour of the whites was another such matter. If a Governor of Berbice could urge it as a reason for not attempting the mission at all; and if, at the outset, the missionary soon tasted its quality; it is little surprise that, failing improvement in legislation or in the social system, he should long have the odour and not seldom a draught of the bitter stream. Lines here and there in the diaries indicate, where they do no more, how it went on; milder or more virulent; ceasing awhile, then breaking out afresh. Anonymous letters or letters forged in his name, involving, when not of the viler kind, some practical joke; lying reports; interruptions of public worship or misbehaviour during its observance; such were the milder forms it took. But these were trying enough, and were met or overcome in various ways—by tact, patience, or, when things grew worse, by an appeal to some official in high civil authority for a letter of remonstrance to be addressed to such "gentlemen"; never forgetting, as opportunity offered, to return good for evil. Mrs. Tuckett writes (first letter):—

"The white young men used to amuse themselves by playing practical jokes on him. He thought silent forbearance was the best. Sometimes they were very annoying in the chapel, but mother used to keep her eye on them. I remember one Sunday evening in the first chapel we had (the chapel had only a few pews on each side of the pulpit, the body was filled with benches), mother, being in very delicate health, had an arm-chair. On this particular evening, about a dozen white young men came in, evidently brimful of fun. They commenced by repeating all that my father was reading or speaking; they interrupted the singing, and behaved in such a disgraceful manner that mother felt a stop must be put to it. So she rose, took up the chair on which she had sat, placed the chair in front of them, and so continued to the end of the service. The object was gained, they sat perfectly quiet. On rising to go, mother said, 'Gentlemen, I am sorry to find you require a governess to keep you in order.' 'O Mrs. Wray,' they replied, 'we are so sorry; it shall never occur again: only say you forgive us and, in token of it, shake hands.' Mother did so, and, with a word of advice to which they politely listened, they departed."

Mr. Foreman records the following (Echoes, &c.):—

"When that first chapel was built, the Sunday evening service was frequently disturbed in the following manner. I have already said there were, at that time, European soldiers stationed in the fort, where is now the lunatic asylum in Berbice; and the band, after playing whilst the officers dined, were then ordered to go and play round the town, and especially round 'old Wray's chapel.' I was told this by a European, who at that time had been a drummer in the band, and who added:—'I was a giddy young fellow then, and didn't mind it; indeed, I thought it was fine fun to bait old Wray.'"

The following is an instance of what was done, perhaps when the time was getting past for worse things to be attempted. It was told in the author's hearing by a successor of Mr. Wray at New Amsterdam, and as an illustration of the pioneer's adaptation in meeting his peculiar circumstances there.

"Mr. Wray was in the desk conducting some meeting, when four young men, sons of planters or managers, having edged their way to the corners of the pulpit, attempted by united and varying pressure to make it unsteady, pushing it about, or raising it from the floor. The movements were not wide nor high, but sufficient to tease and provoke. Wray knew well the secret of his safety, of his power, and of the way to victory. In fact, patience, in his case, must by this time have had its perfect work. If they could keep at it, so could he; and as for the negroes, they could sit it out at meeting with any man. The minister, laying hold on each side of the book-board, to steady himself, went on and on; the hearers, sitting still, listened on and on; the gay young fellows pushed and lifted on. But no! they wearied. The speaker does not stop, much less get into a passion; the meeting does not become a row, much less disperse. As they pause, the proceedings of the assembly continue, and at last the troublers slink away outside, defeated."*

Yet the chief butt of all this, cherishing no ill-will, but seeking to sow beside all waters, was, as Mrs. Tuckett on another page writes :—

"Ever ready to visit the sick among the careless white young men, who, perhaps, had often disturbed public worship, but when death stared them in the face would say, ' Oh, send for Mr. Wray, to pray for me.' He has even been aroused in the middle of the night to visit some who had praying parents in England, and who, at the eleventh hour, remembered what they had been taught in their early home. For such, his pity would be intense, and he ofttimes quoted Doddridge's hymn, ' Arise, my tenderest thoughts, arise '—the last two verses especially :—

> ' My God, I hate the mournful scene ;
> My bowels yearn o'er dying men :
> And fain my pity would reclaim,
> And snatch the firebrands from the flame.
> But feeble my compassion proves,
> And can but weep where most it loves, &c., &c.' "

* Such things, of course, were confined neither to Berbice nor to first years of the mission work, as the private diary of the Demerara martyr would alone serve to show. From the Rev. James Scott, who went out as missionary in 1831, and on the premises where it occurred, the author in conversation had the following incident :—"I was preaching one week-time to a few people, when in came two white 'gentlemen,' planters or managers, smoking cigars. They sat down on a bench just below, and in front of the desk, went on smoking, and looking up at me, began to puff their smoke toward my face. I looked at them steadily, and said :—'Gentlemen, put out those cigars ! I am surprised at you. You ought to be ashamed of yourselves, coming into the house of prayer, and acting in this manner, &c., &c.' " For so Mr. Scott went on, his searching remonstrances penetrating further than did the smoke of their cigars, as they became ill at ease and retired, upon which the minister resumed his former theme. Not for long, however. Noises convinced him and his hearers that the disappointed pair, after new mischief, had got entrance into the other storey of the building, which was the missionary's residence, to make disorder or do worse damage

The upbringing of his children was of course a care constantly present with the pioneer and his devoted wife; their thoughts of upbringing too, almost superfluous to remark, extending beyond health and growth of body or of mind, but including habits of virtue, and "nurture in the chastening and admonition of the Lord." And this in an atmosphere so void of useful learning, and socially corrupt; so godless, cruel, and profane, as to resemble the swamp reeking with rottenness, or its miasm filled with pestilence. Yet those out of a numerous offspring, who, struggling through the many sicknesses of infancy in that clime, attained maturity, grew up useful, virtuous, Christian characters. For Wray began at the outset. "If a man know not how to rule his own house, how shall he take care of the Church of God?" Discipling by baptism was no meaningless rite to him. His children were reminded of it, and taught accordingly. The home, in their younger days, was never left without a parent; and, as much as in them lay, was made the happiest place. Let Mrs. Tuckett give some particulars (second letter) :—

"When I now remember the state of morals then prevailing, I can only wonder at the unceasing care which guarded us from the contamination around us in early life. Our parents were our only companions, and our garden and the ground around our only recreation. We had no beautiful walks; no gathering sweet Spring flowers; though flowers we had in great variety, for my father was especially fond of his garden, and often, in the early morning, before the sun was hot, he was in it helping and directing the gardener. Nearly all the trees were planted by him. We were never allowed to slap, or in any way to behave to the number of little black girls about us but with strict propriety. For when my father had the Crown slaves at the Winkel village under his instruction, we always had numbers about to

there. "So out I had to turn, along with the stalwart negroes of my congregation, to protect my property, and to get rid of them, in which we at length succeeded."

wait on us, &c., but mother was very particular that we should not imbibe the spirit of slavery."

And in a later communication :—

"When Mr. Davies baptized me in those far-off years, he preached for my father, and took for his text, Ps. xcii. 13-15. These verses were taught to me by my mother as soon as I was capable of learning anything; and I always read them with great pleasure, thinking of those who are gone, and I can add, 'He is faithful to His promises.'"

(First Letter). "Almost from infancy we were engaged in teaching. I have often sat on the lap of some grandmother with perhaps some forty or fifty sitting around, it may be on the floor, and 'pegged away' with Dr. Watts' First Catechism and the texts of Scripture we had been taught or learnt during the week. We always had attentive scholars, and we often wearied before they did; for they could stand any amount of teaching. During this 'pegging away' with the old people, my father was engaged with those who desired baptism, &c. He was very cautious; he baptized none but those who he believed had experienced a change of heart. Mother also had her peculiar work, and so time went on."

A native agency again, Mr. Wray soon had in view, and early began and for years continued, as opportunity offered, to prepare such, meeting with varied success. This care and work had both negroes and Indians in prospect.

Mrs. Tuckett says (first letter) :—

"My father's great desire was to raise up native agency. To this end he selected the most promising of the young boys, and gave them extra attention of an evening. These boys, chiefly belonging to the Crown, he made monitors to assist him in the free school which was under the chapel; and he was anxious to fit them as catechists, who he hoped would be useful in that important part of missionary work. Of these were William Henry, a young man of colour, and Henry Rose, one of the Crown slaves." "Nor were the poor Indians forgotten. As often as possible he, accompanied by his faithful servant George, would go up the river to their settlement, swing their hammocks between two trees, and (sometimes), after waking, find that the vampire bat had been drawing blood from his feet. But it was enough for him if he could get their attention while he told them that God so loved them as to give His Son to die for them ; and whenever they came to town, they would come to our house to hear again and again that old, old story, and in some cases it was not heard in vain.

"My father was very fond of children ; he had often noticed a young boy, the son of one of the chiefs. The child would stand by his side and listen most attentively to what he was saying. One day as he was bidding good-bye to the Indians, this child came up to him with a smiling face also to say good-bye. My father said to him in Creole language, 'Well, my little friend, would you not like to come with me and learn to read this book ?' (he had his Bible in his hand). The little child immediately replied, 'Yes.' My father turned to his parents to hear what they would say ; but the idea was too sudden. They promised, however, that the next time they came to town, they would bring him, and if he still wished it, they might perhaps leave him with us for a little while. Time passed on, and as they did not come we thought they could not make up their minds to give up the child. But one day they arrived ; the boy had gained their consent ; he was to be left with the understanding that at any time, if the parents wished it, he was to be given up to them. They came to see him from time to time, but finding that he was happy and had no wish to leave, he remained with us. He was about my own age (seven). I remember him perfectly, though I have forgotten his name. He quickly learnt to read, and we used to tell him Bible stories. Mother taught him to sing. Of this he was very fond. He would sing softly to himself the doxology, 'Glory, honour, praise, and power ;' and the last line, 'Jesus Christ is our Redeemer, hallelujah ! hallelujah !' he was very partial to ; and 'Salvation, oh, the joyful sound !' (a great favourite with the negroes). He would sit by mother of an evening and say, 'Tell me about heaven.' We could never get him to sit down to table with us, and mother thought it best to let him do as he liked in such things, saying, 'it would come to him in time.' While we were at dinner, he would stand behind mother's chair and in a soft, sweet voice sing, 'Glory, honour, praise, and power.' It disturbed no one ; my parents loved to hear him. How long he remained with us I cannot remember, but he never returned to his tribe.   He was taken ill of fever, and in a few hours he 'was not, for God took him.'   God does indeed 'move in a mysterious way.'   My father had hoped to see him teaching his people in years to come that Jesus Christ is their Redeemer also."

A second disappointment of the kind, we may add ; the pioneer having, several years back, recorded in his diary the death of one in whom he had taken a like interest, and who died at the hut of his father, living near, and engaged for some estate as hunter.

Such were the circumstances and concerns, or some of them, constantly attending the pioneer's path.

1823.

Letter to Society's Treasurer—Progress in Demerara :
Extracts from Letters.

WE resume the thread of our narrative with an extract from a letter, confirmatory of the progress and state of the Berbice mission in the middle of 1823, as already briefly told.   The letter, it will be seen, is filled with bright hope, asks for a helper, and shows how the pioneer could look with gratification and interest on the success of other mission fields as well as on that which was peculiarly his own.   It is addressed to William Alers Hankey, Esq., Treasurer of the London Missionary Society, and is dated 17th July.   Will our readers please mark the date.

" I have lately taken a short journey on the Corentyne Coast. I had two objects in view in going up.   The first was to obtain subscriptions towards enlarging the chapel, in which I was successful to a certain degree.   I obtained nearly 300 guilders. One gentleman, a member of the Council, gave me five joes, and took me to see his little Creole children, with whom I was highly delighted ; they are the finest I have seen in the Colony.   In January last he had 130 under ten years.   He had them

altogether in a yard appropriated for them, with proper buildings
and nurses, where they are daily fed, cleaned, and taken care of.
As we walked among them, five or six at a time came around us ;
one taking hold of our hands, another of our coats, &c., so that we
could hardly pass along, saying " How de massa ? " " How de
massa ? " as fast as they could. They seemed as happy as the
days are long. I spoke to him about going up to catechize them ;
he said he would consider of it.

"Another object I had in view was, to prepare the way, if
possible, for the introduction of the Gospel; and I am happy to say
that I found the planters, in general, favourable to it, and
desirous of encouraging it, particularly the gentleman at whose
house I slept. He is putting his estate in sugar, and says that as
soon as his buildings are in order, I shall preach to his negroes.
Wherever I called, I was treated with the greatest politeness and
hospitality. A great part of this fine healthy coast is abandoned,
but I think in this neighbourhood a congregation of 500 would
be obtained.

" *Lord's day, 6th July.*—Last evening L. F. Galley, Esq., came
with his manager, to request me to preach to-morrow on plantation Wurtzburg, which he has lately bought, and which he took
over this week, with upwards of 80 slaves : more have been put
on since. This was a call to preach the Gospel which I could not
resist, and I promised to be there this morning at seven o'clock.
On my arrival, I found Mr. Galley waiting for me. He ordered
all the people into the coffee logie, a very large substantial building. They detained us some time by dressing, and came neat
and clean. They do not understand English, but I explained the
Ten Commandments in the Creole language, and pointed them to
Jesus, the Saviour of sinners, and told them how thankful they
ought to be that their master had introduced the book of God
among them, and that I hoped they would be obedient people.
They thanked me and him, and all expressed a wish for me to
visit them again. There are about 1500 slaves in the immediate
neighbourhood. The estate is about four miles from town.

" *Lord's day, 13th July.*—This morning at seven o'clock I
crossed the river, to preach on plantation Ithaca, belonging to
L. F. Galley, Esq., at his particular request. We were just twenty
minutes in crossing the river to it. I explained the Ten Com-

mandments in Creole, for they do not understand a word of
English. I, of course, also directed them to the Lamb of God,
who taketh away the sin of the world, and who is ' the end of the
law for righteousness, unto all who believe,' whether bond or free.
They seemed to understand well, and expressed a great wish for
me to go again, and some of them said they would try to come to
chapel in town. They also expressed their thankfulness that God
had given them a master who had sent the Word of God among
them. This is surely the best thing he could have done to secure
their affection and obedience ; and sixteen years' labour and
experience, and almost daily converse among them, have convinced me that the Gospel alone can eradicate Obeah, fornication,
theft, &c., and establish good order and contentment among them.
There are on Ithaca 117 slaves, and upwards of a thousand in
the neighbourhood.

"Mr. Galley made none of those objections against preaching
on the Sabbath morning which some do—viz., that the slaves are
employed in fetching wood and grass, and taking out their allowance of fish, plantains, &c. To teach them the nature and use of
the Sabbath is one of the first things to attend to. I informed
them that the Fourth Commandment not only teaches us to remember the Sabbath to keep it holy, but also that we are to attend to
our work on the six days of the week. Thus they are taught their
duty to God on the Sabbath, and their duty to their master in
the week. The glorious Gospel of the blessed God has been proclaimed on the two last Sabbaths in two parts of the Colony
where it was never preached before. Oh, that it may have free
course, run, and be glorified ! After I had done, they began to
explain to one another what I had said.

"I feel thankful to my heavenly Father that I have lived to
see the day when so many seemed inclined to permit the blessed
Gospel to be preached among their slaves. This richly repays us
for all our toil and opposition in years that are past. May God
help me to devote every moment to His service in pointing
sinners to the Saviour who died to redeem them from all
iniquity, and to purify unto Himself a peculiar people, zealous of
good works ! It will appear, however, to the Directors, that
without help it is impossible for me to carry on and extend this
blessed work. May some devoted missionary ' come forth and

help us!' Indeed, I have been thinking that till a missionary be obtained I must give up preaching one Sabbath in a month in town.

"We have been highly delighted in perusing the *Quarterly Chronicles*, &c., lately received. Oh, what a wonderful work is performing among the people in the South Sea Islands! I never read of them and the negroes in Sierra Leone without the greatest interest and delight. The Owhycean Chief brought to our minds some of the simple questions put to us by a few of the old negroes, 'Whether God can understand the Berbice Creoles when they pray, or whether they must learn English?' Blessed be God for what He is doing, and blessed be His glorious Name for ever, and let the whole earth be filled with His glory. Amen and Amen.—Believe me, dear and honoured sir, yours sincerely,

"JOHN WRAY."

As in Berbice, so at Le Resouvenir and in Demerara generally, Mission work had been progressing, and religious institutions, too, had been multiplying. In 1819, St. Andrew's Church, for professors of the Church of Scotland, was opened, and intended originally for the sole use of Scotch Colonists, as had been St. George's, of the Church of England, for English Colonists. The London Society's missionaries also, increased by the stay for several years of the Rev. James Mercer, who had been obliged to leave Trinidad for a time, had more than doubled the number of their chapels and preaching stations, and had extended their labours to the slaves in Essequibo. In 1822, Mr. Mercer returned to Trinidad, and Mr. Davies, accompanied by Mrs. Davies, visited England for the benefit of his health, not landing in Demerara again until October, 1823, so that the work, and at a critical juncture too, had to be carried on with a diminished staff. Nevertheless, up to that year, and during the earlier part of it, all went on prosperously. Mr. Wray, under date 22nd August, 1822, thus writes the Directors concerning a visit paid to his former congregation at Le Resouvenir :—

"On the 11th of last month I arrived at Le Resouvenir, spent two days with Mr. Smith, and preached to the people on Friday evening. I had great pleasure in seeing many of those who were the first-fruits of the Gospel there, walking in truth and rejoicing in the Lord Jesus; others have been taken to their heavenly rest. They manifest great zeal in the ways of religion, and adorn the doctrine of God their Saviour.

"On my return from Georgetown on Monday, Mr. Smith pressed me much to remain all night, and speak in the evening to his people. We visited many of the negro houses, just when they were leaving work, and conversed with a considerable number. I was much pleased with two young men, who were little boys when I lived there. They have been baptized and married, and are highly commended for their good conduct by Mr. Smith. They seconded the exhortation I gave to the people with great earnestness, especially one of them, who told the people that they must attend to what I said, turn to God, go to hear His word, and love and serve Him.

" In the evening a great many came together, with whom we conversed a long time. I rejoice that they have a minister so much interested in their spiritual welfare as Mr. Smith. I was also much pleased with some of his plans, particularly his dividing them into classes, according to the estates to which they belong, and examining their progress in the Catechism in rotation. He thinks the number under regular instruction is about 2000.

"I greatly lament that the missionaries in Demerara are not permitted to teach the slaves to read. Mr. Smith would willingly devote part of the day to this work; and yet, after all, many do acquire the art of reading. I met with a negro, halfway between New Amsterdam and Georgetown, who has no opportunity to attend chapel, learning to read, and studying Dr. Watts' Catechism. Indeed, all along the coast, which is about seventy miles, a desire for instruction prevails."

And, later on, in February, 1823, after having laboured six years at his station, Mr. Smith communicated to the Directors of the Missionary Society the following gratifying particulars. After stating that the number of marriages during the preceding year was 114; that the number admitted to the Lord's Table during the same period was 61; and that the total number of Church members was 203; he observes :—

"We have now many candidates for baptism and the Lord's Supper. Our average congregation is 800 persons. We have certainly much cause to be thankful to the great Head of the Church for the success that attends our labours. We behold every Sabbath an overflowing congregation, behaving with praiseworthy decorum; and we see them zealous for the spread of Christianity. They are fast abandoning their wicked practices for more regular habits of life, as is evident from the number of marriages, few of which (not one in fifty) have been hitherto violated. A great proportion of them are furnished with Bibles, Testaments, Dr. Watts' First or Second Catechism, and a hymn-book; and these, being their whole library, they usually bring to chapel on the Sabbath. All our congregation, young and old, bond and free, are catechized every Sunday, first individually in classes, and afterwards collectively."

The subsequent labours of Mr. Smith and those of his excellent wife, who was actively employed in instructing the female negroes, were attended with the most pleasing results.*

It might then seem that missionary operations, now well launched in both Colonies, had only to go on and prosper; especially as planter after planter, and manager after manager testified to the beneficial results, and in Berbice, a Governor friendly to Mr. Wray and his work had succeeded Mr. Bentinck. But there still existed in large numbers, persons of another stamp, planters, &c., whose language and spirit were bitterly inimical, the lives of many of them godless and profane, and their view of the pious missionary and his work one of malignant and cruel hatred. These, and their like in Britain, keenly opposed to any interference or attempt at improving the slave and his condition, had of late watched

<hr>

* "Demerara Martyr," pp. 55, 56.

such attempts with increasing excitement, which grew as 1823
went on, and culminated at last in words and deeds of such
brutality and cowardice, cruelty and crime, as to form one of
the darkest passages of our colonial history.   It is painful
writing, but the page cannot be avoided.   We would, however, pen it, overshadowed by the thought that those involved
have gone to the tribunal of Him who "sits in the throne,
judging right," and from whose sentence there is no appeal.

1818-1823.

*Revived Activity in England of African Institution—Wilberforce and
Burton—Petition and Motion in House of Commons — Canning's
Amendment—Negotiations with Government—Order in Council sent to
Colonies—Growth of Excitement—How Received in Berbice—Assault
on Wray's Children.*

For a few moments we must glance at the position and procedure of the friends of the slave in England.

The Anti-slavery Committee which saw its long years of
effort crowned with the abolition of the slave trade in 1807,
was then merged into the African Institution.   "There were
various reasons which prevented those who had effected the
abolition of the slave trade attempting also the emancipation
of such as were already slaves," although "in that year
(1807) the Earl of Percy, afterwards Duke of Northumber-
land, proposed the emancipation of their children, but without effect."   The African Institution, after seeking mainly to
get other European Powers, by persuasion or purchase, to
decree the slave trade unlawful, then became somewhat
inactive.   Difficulties were great, discouragements many, and
the position of its leader, who was at times almost worn
out in the struggle, one of no small delicacy and perplexity.
Such was the position during Wray's second return home.
Measures for protecting the slave and improving his position
were thwarted by the difficulty of securing, at such a distance,
legal proof.   A few extracts from the great philanthropist's
diary, &c., during the period covered by the present chapter,

will lead us into the working of his mind and heart, and of more besides.*

"*14th February*, 1818 (the day after Mr. Wray had called upon him).—Lieutenant Gordon at breakfast . . . generously offering to go out to the West Indies if he could thereby bring out the oppression and cruelty which is now veiled over. But Stephen says nothing can be brought to light. It is shocking that we now know of one of the most horrid murders ever perpetrated, and tried to be fastened on another, yet we cannot bring it out because we should ruin our informant."

"*11th March.*—Sadly distressed in mind about the proper course as to West Indian matters.

"*28th March.*—I still am in no little embarrassment what course to pursue as to the West Indian question. Denunciations not only against those who are guilty of the positive acts of oppression, but against those who connive at its continuance, are so strong that I am truly uneasy at my having permitted so much time to pass away without having done anything for relaxing the yoke of the most degrading and bitter bondage that ever ground down the human species.

"*13th March*, 1819.—General Hall, late governor of Mauritius, with us to breakfast. He opened a world of villainy in slave trade, peculation, &c.†

"*2nd April.*—Then to a meeting of the Berbice Commissioners.

"*June*, 1820.—I am often prompted, by the injustice and unfairness of men, to look upwards, and to say to myself—well, the time will come, when He will make thy righteousness as clear as the light, and thy just dealing as the noonday.

"*16th March*, 1821.—The rest of the week was occupied in opposing Maxwell's bill for removing his slaves from Antigua to Demerara.

"*2nd June*, 1822.—But it was not to spare himself that he consented to postpone another year his great attempt for the West Indian negroes. 'I think you are quite right,' was Mr. Stephen's judgment, 'as to this being an unfavourable occasion for bringing forward our case against the Colonies.

* Life, &c., Vol. iv. pp. 370, 374, 376.

† *Ibid.* Vol. v. pp. 15, 16, 65-6, 97, 128, 158, 168-9, 170.

They have quite overlaid us with their intrigues, and have got some of our real as well as nominal friends committed against us.'

"Near end of 1822. — Mr. Buxton informed me that he should be in town 'by the 10th of January,' and expressed his hope that the 'Congress on the subject would not be later. It is exceeding well for you, who have powder and ball—*i.e.*, knowledge of the whole subject, and the power of projecting it with force, to be primed and loaded of a morning, and fired off at night, but it won't do for me. I can do nothing in this rapid method.'

"But no counsel of war was needful to decide that the first steps in the new attempt must be taken by himself, and that the subject must be introduced to the parliament and to the nation by the long acknowledged patron of the negro race ; the duty of improving it, and of gradually emancipating them. Indeed 'my conscience reproaches me,' he says, 'with having suffered this horrible evil to go on. We must now call on all good men throughout the kingdom to join us in abolishing this wicked system, and striving to render the degraded race by degrees a free peasantry. Oh, may God bless our attempt !'

"Early in March, 1823, his Appeal was published.* He then speaks of himself as 'busy for the first time on' his 'slavery abolition work. My pamphlet is well liked, thank God !'

"No address was ever better qualified to produce that mighty effect which followed its publication. Its kindness and forbearance towards individuals rendered its earnest expostulations irresistible. Its perusal, a West Indian proprietor told him, 'has so affected me, that it cost me my whole property ; I surrendered it willingly, that my poor negroes might be brought, not only to the liberty of Europeans, but especially to the liberty of Christians.'

"But the nation was slow to be persuaded of the cruel and debasing nature of a system which it had so long maintained, and which was linked with innumerable private interests. Mr. Wilberforce had learnt too much in his thirty-five years' apprenticeship in African controversy, to expect the chains of slavery to crumble under a single blow. He did not dare anticipate so

* "An Appeal to the Religion, Justice, and Humanity of the Inhabitants of the British Empire, in behalf of the Negro Slaves in the West Indies."

speedy a result as the eager wishes of his friends besought ; that, 'though it seemed too great an honour for one man to effect the abolition of the trade in negroes, and their emancipation, he might yet live to see the fruit of his present labours.'

"The second act of the drama was now opening ; and on the 19th day of March (1823), he presented to the House of Commons a petition from the Quakers, who, having been the first to protest against the slave trade, now led the way in the attack on slavery."

This point, however, was not reached until men of fresh and younger blood had been enlisted and had become actively engaged in the cause. First among equals was Thomas Fowell Buxton, whom Wilberforce had persuaded to take the leadership, and who is the party referred to, when, asked by Mr. Canning " Whether it was his intention to found any motion upon it (the petition)?" Mr. Wilberforce replied, "It was not, but that such was the intention of an esteemed friend of his." How this came about can better be seen by another brief series of quotations, covering the same period, and drawn from the memoirs of that Baronet as edited by his son, Charles Buxton, Esq.*

"27th January, 1821.—I had spent the morning with Wilberforce, who was quite delightful. I begin to think that of all men he is the most subjected and controlled, and invariably in the right frame of temper. 30th.—I got notice of the meeting of the African Institution for to-day. In the course of the meeting an opportunity occurred, which I could not pass over, of declaring my mind, as to the inactivity and ineffectiveness of the society. I told them it was certain we once had the confidence of the country, and it was now certain the public knew little and cared less on the subject. I really felt, and still feel, exceedingly grateful that I did not shrink from the duty. My remonstrance was well received, and a meeting was appointed for Saturday next, at Lord Lansdowne's, of all the members of both houses interested in the subject, and perhaps it may be a means of great good."

"3rd February.—I was quite astonished at Wilberforce yesterday. I had not seen him since my vehement reprobation of the

* See pp. 92-120.

African Institution. Yesterday, he was warm to excess; over and over again 'thanked me for the boldness and openness of my remarks, and said they had penetrated deeply into his heart.'"

Terrible evils engaged the efforts of himself and other good men of the time—*e.g.*, the state of prison discipline and of the criminial code; the slave trade; Suttee in India; and all with an unreformed Parliament, and with slavery existing in most countries. Some hard work, and one of his most powerful speeches in favour of the abrogation of the punishment of death for forgery, had proved vain, so far as then passing the bill was concerned; but, "the evening after Mr. Buxton had delivered his speech on criminal law, he received a letter from Mr. Wilberforce, dated 24th May, 1821," announcing his choice of Mr. Buxton as his parliamentary successor, saying that :—

"Now, for many, many years, I have been longing to bring forward that great subject, the condition of the negro slaves in our trans-Atlantic colonies, and the best means of providing for their moral and social improvement, and ultimately, for their advancement to the rank of a free peasantry ; a cause this, recommended by me, or rather enforced on me, by every consideration of religion, justice, and humanity," and entreating him, "if I should be unable to commence the war—and still more if, when commenced, I should—be unable to finish it,—that you should continue to prosecute it."

Causes concurring to prepare Mr. Buxton for accepting this were many. The impressions of early training, his connection with the African Institution, a letter from his brother-in-law Mr. Wm. Forster, the dying charge of his much beloved sister-in-law Priscilla Gurney ; but it was not until after long and mature deliberation that he acquiesced. Many of his other friends encouraged him to accept, but he does not appear to have fully resolved till a year and a half after the receipt of Mr. Wilberforce's letter ; an interval spent by him, as far as other claims would permit, in closely studying the question in all its bearings. How serious and critical were some of the connected questions, may be judged from the fact that—

" What chiefly led him to hesitate in adopting this question as his own, was the fear that the discussion of it in England might lead to a servile insurrection in the West Indies. He deeply felt the weight of this responsibility, and it was the subject of long and anxious thought. 'If,' said he, 'a servile war should break out and 50,000 perish, how should I like that?' But even this extreme supposition he met by the consideration, that if 'I had two sons, I would rather choose to have one free and one dead, than both living enslaved."

It was autumn, 1822, before Mr. Buxton finally decided; in the course of which season he had Mr. Wilberforce and Mr. Zachary Macaulay visiting at Cromer Hall, "for the purpose of discussing the question with him, and also with Dr. Lushington and Lord Suffield; when was drawn the first outline of those plans, in which each, from this time, took his respective and important share."

A short time afterwards, Mr. Macaulay and Mr. Buxton were visiting Wilberforce at Marden Park to arrange their plan of operations for the ensuing session.

" I have often rejoiced of late years," wrote Mr. Wilberforce, when inviting Mr. Buxton, " in thinking of having you for an associate and successor, as indeed I told you. Now, my dear Buxton, my remorse is sometimes very great, from my consciousness that we have not been duly active in endeavouring to put an end to that system of cruel bondage, which, for two centuries, has prevailed in our West Indian Colonies; and my idea is, that a little before parliament meets, three or four of us should have a secret cabinet council, wherein we should deliberate to decide what course to pursue."

" Long and deep were their deliberations, how best to shape their measures, which were to change the structure of society throughout the Western World."

With how much of the spirit of Christ, of faith and prayer

for Divine guidance, will be well understood by any who are at all acquainted with the eminent and robust piety of these devoted men.

On the publication of Mr. Wilberforce's Appeal in March, 1823, public feeling was soon roused into activity, and petitions began to flow in. At about the same time the Anti-Slavery Society was formed, Mr. Buxton being appointed vice-president; and the lead was taken by the Society of Friends. After presenting their petition to the House, and answering, as we have seen, Mr. Canning's inquiry, Mr. Wilberforce's "esteemed friend," Mr. Buxton, then gave notice that on the 15th of May, "he should submit a motion that the House should take into consideration the state of slavery in the British Colonies."

A few weeks before this motion came on, Mr. Buxton communicated his intentions to the Government, stating his views. An urgent request for delay from the Government was declined as follows:—

"10th May.

"Your letter really gives me great pain. I do not like to refuse anything you ask. I do not like to appear obstinate, but the opinion of all the persons with whom I act is strongly opposed to any delay, in which opinion I as strongly concur. The more the subject opens upon me, the more do I think that I should be answerable for a great crime if I consented to let the session slip away without proposing something. In short, pray excuse me for saying that on Wednesday I *will* bring forward my motion."

On the 15th of May, he wrote to Mrs. Upcher:—

"In five minutes I start for the House. I hope to begin at five o'clock. I am in good health, in excellent spirits, with a noble cause, and without fear. If I am only given a nimble tongue, we shall do."

Then took place the first debate on the subject of negro slavery.

Mr. Buxton began by moving—

"That the state of slavery is repugnant to the principles of the

British Constitution and of the Christian religion ; and that it ought to be gradually abolished, with as much expedition as may be found consistent with a due regard to the well-being of the parties concerned."

In his speech, while he plainly declared that the object was the extinction of slavery, he explained that the method they desired was not by sudden emancipation, but by such preparatory steps, as first fitting and qualifying the slaves for it, shall gently conduct them to freedom. This, and the propositions beforehand submitted to the Government, ought to have shielded Mr. Buxton and his friends from the blame, long and severe, of having set the slaves free before they were fitted for it. It was the planters who, rejecting such preparatory measures, paved the way for a more immediate emancipation.

An animated debate ensued, Mr. Canning, on behalf of the Government, moving and carrying amendments which were :—

"1st. That it is expedient to adopt effectual and decisive measures for ameliorating the condition of the slave population in His Majesty's Colonies."

"2nd. That, through a determined and persevering, but at the same time judicious and temperate enforcement of such measures, this House looks forward to a progressive improvement in the character of the slave population, such as may prepare them for a participation in those civil rights and privileges which are enjoyed by other classes of His Majesty's subjects."

"3rd. That this House is anxious for the accomplishment of this purpose at the earliest period that shall be compatible with the well-being of the slaves themselves, with the safety of the Colonies, and with a fair and equitable consideration of the interests of private proprietors."

Various communications, and a long interview with Mr. Canning followed ; Mr. Canning's opinions on all points of the subject were thoroughly ascertained, and Mr. Buxton learned exactly what were the intentions of Ministers at this period.

In accordance with the Resolutions passed, circular letters were addressed by the Government to the various Colonial authorities, containing copies of the Resolutions, and recommending certain reforms. In the case of the Crown Colonies, regulations were sent in the shape of an Order in Council enjoining, among other salutary enactments, the limitation of the hours of daily labour to nine, and the abolition of the flogging of females at once and for ever.

On receipt of these in Berbice by Governor Beard, he communicated in due course with Mr. Wray, desiring him to explain the matter to the slaves from the pulpit. By the adoption of such like means *all was quiet*, in a way—*i.e.*, the slaves were informed and were peaceable. But with what had been going on in England, and with this as the outcome, there were not a few of the slaveholding party who were highly dissatisfied and growingly excited to insolence and injury, of which the missionary before long had painful experience. The following, told by Mrs. Tuckett as occurring in 1823, was perhaps a foretaste of what later on he was called to endure.

"The Winkel village was only a pleasant walk from our house. My mother was in the habit of sending us when we were children, accompanied by a servant, to the village to see the poor old people, and to convey to the sick some little comfort, such as wine, &c. They were always so glad to see us, and to hear us read or repeat Scripture or hymns to them. I remember them well, Daddy Tom, Daddy Gabriel, and a good many more. I remember on one occasion, in 1823, we were on our way from the village, Elizabeth, Robert, self, and servant, when we were rudely stopped by half-a-dozen white men, who tore off our bonnets, shook us violently, shoved us into the trench, using dreadful language. As soon as we could we hastened home, very much frightened, but rejoicing that our poor people had received the things we had brought for them before we met these '*gentle-men*' (?)."

The letter of marked date (17th July) to the Society's Treasurer, however, seems all oblivious of outrage, whether present or prospective; as does one of about a month later, addressed to the Rev. John Smith, Le Resouvenir, received by him on Saturday, 16th August, and which, to use John Smith's own description when surrendering it on the seizure of his papers,—

"contained pleasing information as to the manner in which the inhabitants of Berbice had met the views of the Government and of the people of England in ameliorating and improving the condition of the slaves." *

And such might have been the character of communications immediately following, but for the different action taken by the authorities of Demerara. There, within two days of the last-named letter being received, an explosion occurred which could not but make Berbice feel something of the shock.

1823-4.

Insurrection in Demerara—Stoppage there of Mission Work—
" The Missionary Smith's Case."

INSURRECTIONS of slaves in the West Indies were no uncommon things; but the rising of 18th August, 1823, on the East Coast of Demerara was an event of interest, of causes and issues more than common. For some months in that Colony, Governor Murray, himself a planter and slave holder it will be remembered, and still unchanged in his opposition to the instruction of the slaves and in his sympathy with the more vehement part of the slave owners, had begun a process of "stroking the cat's back the wrong way." Aware of what was proceeding in England, as well as of the growing acceptance and success of Mission work in the

* See London Missionary Society's full report of Smith's Trial, &c., p. 61.

Colony, these men set themselves more decidedly on the opposite tack. Not only did the Governor block the way to erecting a second Mission chapel, which parties were prepared to build farther up the East Coast, he also issued regulations calculated to hinder attendance at what means of instruction already existed, and to harass the people who still made use of them. The whip, which it was talked of abolishing to some extent, received, on one part of the coast, the addition of a cat-o'-nine-tails. At another part, and at the time when the news began to ooze out that something greatly good had come from England for the slaves' benefit, a large sale of bond-servants was impending, which would involve the forcible and final severance of the closest human ties. The Governor, in fact, on 7th July had duly received the Order in Council, but was keeping it back. Nevertheless he talked about it at his table, and was overheard by his servants. Other chief men likewise talked. On Success, the very next estate to Le Resouvenir, and from which, more than from Le Resouvenir itself, people attended the chapel, one of his Excellency's own servants had communicated to Jack Gladstone, head cooper, what, as he thought, he had heard talked of at dinner, that "freedom had come out." Managers knew something, and told the mistresses they kept; sailors knew, and talked to the slaves as they were taking in or discharging cargo. But weeks passed, and the Governor made no public sign. Twice had the Colonial Court of Policy met, but nothing had been proclaimed. So rumours got afloat; reports, more and more exaggerated, became rife; and it can well be supposed that, what the Governor afterwards termed, an " existing susceptibility," should not only be existing, as he and most other people were well aware, but that it must have been becoming keenly intensified. The idea, in fact, became prevalent that freedom, in some form, for the enslaved had indeed been ordered by the King, and that the Governor would not make it known. On more than one occasion Mr. Smith was appealed to by individuals, whom he assured to be mistaken as to " freedom having come out ; " but said that "something was come for their good ; and advised patience, therefore, until the Governor should see fit to make it known." Subsequently he expressed to two neighbouring gentlemen, both officials in the planting interest, an inclination he had, on account of the growing impatience, to make some such explanation from the pulpit ; but was cautioned " not to take anything of that sort upon himself, as it might be exaggerated to his own prejudice." Later on, the Rev. W. S. Austin, minister of St. George's Church, and chaplain to the Garrison, had been led to feel serious apprehension that something unpleasant might ensue, and spoke, accordingly, to the Governor.

Six weeks elapsed ; no change was made either in the long day of their unrequited toil, or in the cruel severity of their treatment ; so the idea of something like a present-day strike, which had secretly got abroad, came, on the East Coast especially, to be more talked about and earnestly thought of by those in bondage. A boat captain, named Paris, and Jack Gladstone, the head cooper already mentioned, neither of them more than a very occasional attend. ant at Le Resouvenir chapel, and the latter a gay, dissolute young fellow, were the two chief ringleaders in what eventually assumed some appearance of a revolt.

In the afternoon of Sunday, 17th August, when all services at the chapel were over for the day, a number of the last congregation went to a meeting of slaves on Success, whither they were followed by Quamina, chief deacon. Quamina lived there, was head carpenter, and father of Jack Gladstone ; but with two or three of his brethren had first gone for a few minutes to the manse, as was their custom, to say " goodbye " to the minister.

With minds naturally running on the object of the slaves'

meeting, conversation in a low tone had already begun between Quamina and another when they entered the dwelling. Mr. Smith, a little distance from them at the time, overhearing the words "manager" and "new law," spoke up about their talking of such things; to whom Quamina replied, "It is nothing particular, sir; we were only saying it would be good to send our managers to town to fetch up the new law;" on which the minister, after at once remarking the folly of saying anything to the managers about it, as they were not the law makers, added, "that if there was anything for them they would soon hear of it, but if they behaved insolently to their managers, they would lose their religious character, and would provoke the Governor here and the Government at home; to which Quamina again replied, "Very well, sir, we will say nothing about it, for we should be very sorry to vex the King and the people at home." Mr. Smith, who knew nothing of the meeting, and had not the least idea of any revolt, simply thought of the two men's talk as arising from that "existing susceptibility" with which nearly all the whites in the Colony, as well as the Governor himself, were well acquainted.

At the slaves' meeting, which did not last many minutes, various opinions were expressed. Some were for waiting; a simple cessation from work was most in favour by those disposed to take any step; whilst a proposition to seize any guns for the purpose of self-defence, which was urged by the leaders and some others, led a number who were only for milder action to hesitate altogether. Of these was Quamina. He had so far yielded to the growing impatience of waiting, and to the opinion more and more prevailing, that something should be done to bring out official information, as to say that they should "put down shovel, hoe, and cutlass,* and sit down." Disposed at the end of the meeting to draw

* A very common implement; a kind of broad and long-bladed knife with short haft, used in cutting grass, sugar-cane, &c.

back, and even, according to subsequent report, entreating afterwards his son, Jack Gladstone, with tears to refrain; eventually he may be said not to have gone beyond his own counsel, protecting his manager from hurt, and resting or rambling only on the estate or its immediate vicinity.

The people separated; part of them, including a few connected with the chapel, determined on something, and, more definitely still, on beginning about sundown of the next day; of course communicating this decision to others on various estates.

Long, however, before sundown of Monday, 18th August, the matter became known to the authorities. A militia captain, resident in the very centre of the disturbance, heard of it, but said and did nothing; afterwards, when charged with this negligence, being excused by a Court of Inquiry, on the ground of his not wishing to raise needless alarm. A planter and cavalry captain heard of it through his servant; by ten o'clock had informed the Governor, and by one o'clock, the manager himself of Le Resouvenir, whom he happened to meet in town. His Excellency ordered "the intelligence to be communicated to those in charge of the several estates along the coast, with directions to be on their guard and to secure their firearms." The manager remained in town to finish business, then to dine with a friend, not returning until after three o'clock, and not saying a word to his near neighbour, Mr. Smith. The missionary himself had been early in town, and, as yet all uninformed of any intended outbreak, had by this time probably made what proved to be the last entry in his strictly private diary :—

"*Monday, 18th August*, 1823.—Early this morning I went to town to consult Dr. Robson on the state of my health. It is ten months since I had his first advice, during which time pains and debility have been increasing. I have not indeed been obliged to take to my bed, nor to omit one public service, though it has been very difficult for me to keep about, and more difficult for me to preach. He says cupping and blistering may ease the pain in the side, and allay the cough, but that a thorough change of air, such as a voyage to Bermuda or England, would be preferable."

At four o'clock the work on places near had already begun, and the Governor, who had mustered a detachment of Colonial cavalry, and with some other Government officials had proceeded up the coast, met about forty armed negroes, to whom, in a parley, he then and for the first time communicated the chief particulars of what, in his own disobedience to the home Government, he had so long kept back. But the little crowd distrusted him; would not lay down their arms; one at last firing his musket at the Governor, who thereupon immediately began a return to town.

It was six o'clock when Mr. Smith got first intimation of the intended rising. As he and his devoted partner were preparing to take a short walk, a note was delivered which had been brought by one Guildford from Dochfour, an estate fourteen miles higher up the coast. It was written and signed by a fellow-slave, Jackey Reed, who, complaining of a note he had received from Jack Gladstone, and which he enclosed; that in it Jack Gladstone (Jack had assumed all to be of the same mind with himself) assumed that he (Jackey) had made an agreement and promises which, says Jackey, "I never did;" concluded with the hope "that you will see to it, and inquire of the members whatever it is they have in view, which I am ignorant of," adding, "the time is determined on for seven o'clock to-night."

These notes brought to mind what Mr. Smith had casually overheard on the preceding day, and caused him to suspect some hidden meaning, and to apprehend that the "existing susceptibility" was about to ripen into serious mischief. Inquiring of Guildford as to some particulars, the man appeared to know nothing about the matter. Mr. Smith thereupon told him to return with all possible haste, and tell Jackey Reed: "I am surprised, and vexed, and grieved to find the people are meditating mischief, and hope he will endeavour to keep the people quiet, and have nothing to do with the project, whatever it may be."

Just as Guildford was going away, however, it occurred to Mr. Smith that he would write, and so prevent mistake of any kind. Quickly, therefore, he pencilled in few words his ignorance of the affair; that it was too late for inquiry, and, referring to what had been overheard, that, without asking questions, he had begged them to be quiet; concluding, " I trust they will; hasty, violent, or concerted measures are quite contrary to the religion we profess, and I hope you will have nothing to do with them.—Yours, for Christ's sake, J. Smith."

The intended short walk, by this interruption and the consequent uneasiness, was happily made still shorter; for on returning at half-past six, they heard a great and an unusual noise, and Mr. Hamilton, the manager, in a hurried voice calling Mr. Smith to come to him. Proceeding, they found the great house besieged by forty or fifty men, all naked, armed with cutlasses, &c., looking very fierce, and about effecting an entrance by forcing the outer doors. Mr. Smith following, asked what they wanted, and was answered by brandishing of cutlasses. On repeating his question, they replied, "the guns and our rights." Entreating them to desist and to depart peaceably, they became furious and determined, behaving most rudely to him, but desiring him to return home, and saying, "they were not going to hurt any one, only they would have their rights." The guns they soon obtained, and the manager they were intent upon putting into the stocks. Prevailing upon them to refrain from this, thanked by Mr. Hamilton for his friendly interposition, and unable to do more in quelling the riotous proceeding, Mr. Smith returned to his own house, whither his wife, terrified and in tears, had already repaired.

On Success, the slaves had risen about an hour and a-half

before, and service like what the missionary rendered on Le Resouvenir had been rendered by Quamina; for, said the manager, Mr. Stewart, afterwards on oath, "I did not see Quamina do anything improper; he was keeping the rest of the people from hurting me," after which, neither as an armed man nor as a rebel, but simply as a man without work, or at last and worst as a runaway, Quamina continued on or near the estate. Similar scenes took place during the evening on a number of the estates, and several negroes connected with Le Resouvenir chapel were involved; but as on Le Resouvenir and Success scores, so on other properties hundreds, were simply the naked heathen, and the down-trodden, ignorant, and brutish slaves they had ever been. Twelve ringleaders lived on estates where none had been baptized by Mr. Smith, and the attornies of which were great enemies to the instruction of their slaves. The beneficial influence generally of mission work, however, was seen in the fact that, when they had the fairest opportunity of murdering every white person on the coast, the insurgents contented themselves with putting such in the stocks; these of course being released by the troops as they arrived. Opposed on one or two plantations with firearms, the like had been used in return, and thus a white or two was killed, and three or four were wounded. "We will take no life," said they, "for our pastors have taught us not to take that which we cannot give;"—"A memorable peculiarity," remarked Lord Brougham, "to be found in no other passage of negro warfare in the West Indian seas."

It was nine o'clock in the evening before the Governor again reached town. By midnight fresh troops were on their way up the coast, and at break of day the militia were called out, and martial law was proclaimed. The Scotch Church, its minister an earnest defender of slavery and a most bitter opponent of the missionaries, was turned into barracks, and all free people were put under arms. The Wesleyan minister presenting himself, his services were declined, the Governor politely hinting that he might do more good in his own line of things than by handling a musket. The Rev. W. S. Austin proposed that Mr. Smith and himself should go amongst the people and use their joint influence as ministers of the Gospel of peace in persuading them quietly to return to their accustomed employments, wise counsel which, remarks Mr. Wallbridge, "was madly rejected."

"An insane, unreasoning prejudice against Mr. Smith and the Missionary cause led the rulers of that day to set aside the interposition of one who might thus have rendered them the most valuable service."

Instead of this, "an immediate appeal was made to military force." During the 19th, further detachments of troops were despatched up the coast, and all united met with a large body of the negroes early on Wednesday morning at Bachelor's Adventure. A few of these had firearms, but by no means skill to use them; others, cutlasses or bayonets fixed on poles.

A parley ensued; the commander of the troops, Colonel Leahy, asking the slaves what they wanted; and they in reply, after details of hard usage, concluding, "and we hear for true that the great Buckra at home (the king) give us our freedom for true." Peremptorily refusing to lay down their arms unless certain requests for time in the week for themselves were at once granted, which requests the Colonel said he would communicate to the Governor; an hour was allowed them for consideration. As they still continued obstinate, the soldiers were ordered to fire; and a conflict ensued, fatal to nearly 200 of the negroes. Several other brief skirmishes on that and the two following days took place, much to the disadvantage of the slaves; and what of revolt existed, then ceased. Some fled into the bush, but the greater part had returned to their respective plantations and had resumed their labours.

Not a single white soldier lost his life, yet shocking slaughter of the negroes, and a display of horrible brutality accompanied and followed these events. Little mercy was shown. Many prisoners were wantonly shot by the militia for mere sport, and Colonel Leahy stood upon no ceremony as to trial, not less than twenty-three being put to death by his sole authority. Martial law was continued for five calendar months, and a Court Martial assembled to try prisoners, of whom there remained nearly 200. So, whilst the military were being honoured—Colonel Leahy by the Court of Policy with a vote of 200 guineas for a sword, and, jointly with the other officers of his regiment, with a vote of 500 guineas for the purchase of plate, besides a piece of plate of 350 guineas' value presented to the Colonel by people on the West Coast; the officers of another regiment by the Court of Policy with a vote of 200 guineas, and a Lieutenant with one of fifty guineas—trials, floggings, and executions were going on incessantly. Seventeen prisoners were sentenced to lashes numbering from 200 to 1000, and to work in chains; ten, within a week, receiving some 600 or 700, and five 1000 each, of which one received the whole, and two almost the whole, at once. More still were condemned to death, and before the end of September, forty-seven had been executed—*e.g.*, thus:—26th August, two; 27th, two; 28th, four; 6th September, six; 12th, nine, &c., &c., several being hung in chains along the East Coast road, others decapitated, and their heads stuck on poles. On 24th May, 1824, fifty prisoners still remained under sentence of death; but the British public who had now begun to learn and, though late, to believe the true state of the case, were becoming horrified, and the bloody proceedings were arrested by orders from home. The outbreak, caused really by disobedience to his Sovereign's commands of one who had taken oath and office both as a military General and a civil Governor, cost the Colony chest more than £50,000.

But our present concern is with its results, &c., upon the work commenced here and elsewhere by the pioneer, and continued and extended in Demerara by men of like spirit.

False reports and lying statements were soon afloat as to the extent to which the congregation of Le Resouvenir chapel were involved in the attempt, but a calm and minute investigation, made in the spring of 1824 by a writer whose account is given in Appendix I. of the "Martyr of Demerara," shows that, comparing the list of persons baptized by Mr. Smith, as those who were willing to put themselves under regular Christian instruction (Mr. Smith not admitting such to the Lord's Supper until evidence was afforded of repentance towards God and faith in our Lord Jesus Christ), a list kept by him with the greatest exactness, not more than five or six out of about 2000, and these of no note in the congregation, had been executed, and only one communicant out of about 200; whilst on estates where there was any considerable proportion of these, either no outbreak occurred, or they behaved well during its continuance. How little, nevertheless, this would avail to save either the property or the agents of the mission from the fierce malignity of its enemies, who now found their opportunity for perpetrating, in the most cowardly fashion, deeds of cruel and monstrous injustice, was soon seen in the fate of poor Quamina.

Leading deacon of the church, and universally respected among the members, his character is given by this investigator as that of, "in every sense of the word, a peacemaker, and a good father, husband, and servant." On the 18th, after endeavouring to keep his son Jack from commencing proceedings, and after protecting his manager from ill-usage, he left the buildings, but, as has been already said, not the estate or its near neighbourhood. Coming on Wednesday evening, the 20th, in his ramblings to Le Resouvenir buildings, he called at the manse, unexpectedly to Mr. Smith, when, without responding to his pastor's expression of great grief that the people had been so wicked and mad as to revolt; of hope that he was not concerned in it; or to the more direct inquiries that his silence produced, as to where he had been all the time and whence he had come; he turned round, and not having remained more than two or three minutes, he suddenly departed. In fact, his call had been made consequent upon a wish to see Quamina or Bristol (another deacon), incidentally expressed by Mrs. Smith on the previous day when conversing with a woman named Anchey, one of two or three persons left on Le Resouvenir, for whom she had sent to inquire of her what the people were doing, and if she thought they were going to return home. Anchey appeared to be as ignorant as Mrs. Smith herself; who then, thinking of Quamina and Bristol as deacons, naturally spoke as she did; not knowing any more than her husband that they were even reputed rebels, and not mentioning the casual utterance to Mr. Smith until, the caller come and gone, he began to wonder what had brought Quamina there. A day or two more, and a reward having been offered, Quamina was shot in the bush as a runaway by an Indian.

Buried then, of course? No! Despite his character and service rendered, his prayer-book and hymn-book still found in his pocket; such, one has well noted,

"was the wild savagery, called justice, then in Demerara, his dead body was dragged to the front of Success estate, and there, between two trees, he was gibbeted as a rebel, the corpse bound together with chains allowed to swing in the breeze for many months after, to the terror and disgust of every passer-by."

But already the manse of the minister was shut up and silent; private revenge having started the course which, carried on and crowned by monstrous public injustice, presented to the view of Britain and of the civilized world, what was then and for years afterwards notorious as "the case of the Missionary Smith."

No sleep came to Mrs. Smith after the disturbance on the evening of Monday the 18th, and not a soul to give any information had been near the house, when on the 19th, walking anxious and alone up and down the front part, or gallery as there called, it occurred to her to send for Anchey as we have seen; after which she tried to get some rest. Mr. Smith occupied himself, according as his weak state would permit, in reading or writing. On Wednesday, the 20th, he penned a letter to his friend Mr. Mercer, then at Trinidad, which, after telling of the outbreak, closes thus:—

"How all this will end I know not. I feel perfectly safe, not because we have so many soldiers patrolling about, but because I am conscious we have not wronged any one. Here I must come to a hasty close. You say, 'Write me a long letter.' I am too unwell to write much at a time. Dr. Robson advises me to take a trip to Bermuda, as it is too late in the season to go to England. Some remove I shall certainly make ere long, either into another climate or into the grave, and sometimes I feel indifferent as to which of the two. To leave the country just now does not appear desirable, though I shall be of little or no use here."

At night Quamina came, and after saying "how do" to Mrs. Smith, seeing Mr. Smith sitting in a room, passed on to speak to him, with the result just now told. Having heard from his wife her word to Anchey about seeing Quamina, Mr. Smith remarked—

"that she was very foolish for so doing, for that from the manner in which he (Quamina) had suddenly gone away, there was no saying but that he might be also engaged in the revolt, and if that was the case he (Mr. Smith) never wished to see him."

On Thursday Mr. Smith began a letter to the secretary of the Missionary Society, informing him of the condition and real causes of the sad affair. At three o'clock, however, and whilst writing, he and it received a check as final to the letter as it was amazing to the writer. Soldiers moving about in the name of peace and of protection, if to any in particular, specially to the whites, were the instruments of this rude interruption and wrong.

A file of militia infantry appeared, headed by a lieutenant who desired to speak with Mr. Smith. They had been sent by Mr. M'T——, a doctor residing near, and holding a superior command. This Dr. M'T—— is remembered as one who never forgot an insult, nor forgave an injury. Not that Mr. Smith had been guilty of either, but some years before a misunderstanding and consequent difference had arisen between them. The doctor was a determined enemy to the mission, and in dealing with some cases of small-pox on Le Resouvenir, had, in Mr. Smith's opinion, vexatiously prolonged his interference with slaves' attendance at chapel. Seemingly the doctor's opportunity had now come, and the errand of the soldiers was to require the missionary's presence at M'T——'s, and his enrolment there as a soldier.

All this, however, was, as soon appeared, a mere pretence. If the Governor's rebuff of the Wesleyan minister was not known, or John Smith's ailing condition, the revolt had begun to cease. But these facts were not needed to burst the bubble or to show the hollowness of the summons; for, as soon as Mr. Smith objected, pleading his profession as entitling him to legal exemption; the lieutenant, instead of marching off or taking the minister with him if he doubted the validity of the objection, proceeded to say that he had another command to execute—viz., *to seal up all the minister's papers.* Inquiring what authority he had for this, Mr. Smith was answered, "the order of Captain M'T——." Resistance was out of the question; all papers were surrendered, even to some class books which the minister requested might be left out, and the letter from Mr. Wray, received on the 16th, which Mr. Smith wished to answer. The officer and his men then went away.

Nothing tells us what the lone missionary and his poor wife, when left to themselves, thought of all this. Possibly

as time went on they were beginning to deem it only another
scheme of M‘T——'s to annoy them. And it might have
come to nothing more had not Mr S——n, a planter near,
who was another enemy to the slaves' instruction, and a
captain of cavalry, called just then at the doctor's. He could
not understand the sense of security felt by Mr. Smith and
his wife, "not so much because," as the missionary had
written, "we have so many soldiers patrolling about, but
because I am conscious we have not wronged any one." On
the contrary, when afterwards put upon his oath, S——n
said :—

"I stated to Captain M‘T—— that it had a very bad appearance, that the parson and his wife remained on an estate where
the negroes were all, to a man, in a state of revolt ; and that they
could not remain there, his wife especially, unless they were in
collusion with those negroes so revolted ; that it more properly
came under his department to have them removed from the
estate, but that if he would not do so, I would by my own
authority. Captain M‘T—— said he would do so."

Perhaps we can nowhere so well as in this place inter-
polate the conclusion, different and better, of another actor
in the scenes.

The Rev. W. S. Austin, Episcopal clergyman and chaplain,
had only heard of Mr. Smith's character and labours, and was
not personally acquainted with him when, at the outset, he
made the suggestion to the "powers that be," as we have
told. Within a day or so afterwards, from some reports that
were circulating, he began to fear that the missionary had
been taking part in promoting the insurrection. On Wednesday, the 20th, however, landing at six in the morning
from a schooner in which he had been sailing to a part of the
coast with the object of saving life, and meeting with a number
of the revolters, "in no one instance," he says, "among his
numerous inquiries, did it appear or was it stated that Mr.
Smith had been instrumental in the insurrection." Remark-

ing that little bloodshed had marked its progress, the answer was : " It is contrary to the religion we profess ; we cannot give life, and therefore we will not take it." Some weeks later, and after sitting on a Committee of Inquiry into the evidence got up against Mr. Smith, in a private letter to a friend, Mr. Austin thus writes :—

" I feel no hesitation in declaring, from the intimate knowledge which my most anxious inquiries have obtained, that nothing but those religious impressions which under Providence Mr. Smith has been instrumental in fixing, nothing but those principles of the Gospel of peace which he has been proclaiming could have prevented a dreadful effusion of blood here, and saved the lives of those very persons who are now (I shudder to write it) seeking his life."

Such was he who, not only at the mere whim of one neighbour, was removed from his house, but on the plea of non-compliance with the call made in pretence by another, removed to a prison, and in the following fashion :—

" In about three-quarters of an hour afterwards our house was again beset with soldiers, consisting of a troop of cavalry, under the command of Mr. S——n, and the company of infantry under the command of Mr. N——. Mr. S——n, in the foulest language and the fiercest manner, demanded why I had dared to disobey Captain M'T——'s orders. I told him that I was entitled to an exemption from military services. 'Damn your eyes, sir,' said he, ' if you give me any of your logic, I 'll sabre you in a minute ; if you don't know what martial law is, I 'll show you,' at the same time brandishing his sabre in my face, in a menacing manner, and swearing that I was the cause of all this disturbance. He then called for a file of men to seize me, while others ordered my chaise to be got ready, and Mr. N——, or some one by his order, I suppose, went upstairs and took away all my papers, some sealed up in a desk, and the others loose in a drawer which had been sealed. As they insisted on Mrs. Smith leaving the house, I requested Captain M'T—— to allow us five minutes to pack up some linen and lock up the place. But in less than three minutes, I apprehend, a file of soldiers came to the bottom of the stairs and said to me, 'If *you* don't fetch Mrs. Smith, by God, sir, *we* will.' In this manner we were hurried away from our house and property, without being allowed time to bring away a change of clothes, or to lock up our doors. After keeping us in the road about three-quarters of an hour, they escorted us to town under a military guard."

This, written the day after, and by official request for the information of Fiscal and Governor, did not save Mr. and Mrs. Smith from treatment worthy of such a commencement. Confined in a small room near a roof exposed to the burning rays of a tropical sun, with door open day and night, and Mr. Smith challenged every two hours by a sentry, at first with no needful change of apparel; for seven weeks they continued, denied pen, ink, the sight of any face except that of some prison official, or liberty to communicate in any way with the Society's Directors.

Meanwhile his enemies were at work, changing the charge into one of inciting to insurrection; raking up any word or deed of his, not under martial law merely, or during the few weeks preceding, but belonging to years past, and said or done elsewhere than in the Colony, that could be made to appear suspicious; and when at last, on 13th October, he was produced for trial before a Court Martial ordered by the Governor, not only was the opportunity for challenging the legality of such a court past, but he had to hear the charges against himself whilst still destitute of a legal adviser, and, at first, seemingly, of a single white face as his friend. But he could afterwards write, "Thanks be to God, I have not been left altogether without a friend." Asking for time to obtain legal assistance, it was allowed; and in Mr. William Arrindell, a gentleman of the Colonial bar, he found an able counsellor, also, as likewise in the Rev. W. S. Austin, a friend, both of them faithful even at the cost of present earthly prospects. Dr. Chapman too, his medical attendant in gaol, had a warm interest in his case; and Mr. Elliott, a brother missionary, himself in custody, after being released, put forth much effort on his behalf.

Here it may be remarked that for the lengthened existence of martial law there was no necessity, and there can be no question, as Mr. Wallbridge concisely writes,—

"That the erection of this military court at such a time, and for such a purpose, was most unconstitutional, illegal, and unjust, —a breach of the first principles of British law. It had no rightful jurisdiction in the case of Mr. Smith ; and had its proceedings been the most unexceptionable, instead of being as they were, the most unjustifiable, still its fundamentally illegal and unconstitutional character vitiates its every act. But the Governor having, by his own wrong-doing, set the Colony in a blaze, must now have been endeavouring to make the unoffending missionary the scapegoat of his crime."

But Mr. Smith had to conduct his own defence, a work which, with all his disadvantages, he did most efficiently. The trial occupied twenty-eight days, closing on the 24th of November. On the evidence, &c., adduced by the prosecution, we shall presently quote the highest human opinion ; but that much of it was wholly irrelevant, some of a kind (hearsay) such as Mr. Smith was not allowed to bring for the defence, that the animus of the Court was strongly against the accused, that things said on his behalf were received with ill-favour, that the official report to the Home Government was a garbled document, are plain matters of fact.

"'When we went into the Court we were daunted, there were so many people there, and the gentlemen kept making signs and threatening the witnesses,' is the unterrified testimony, twenty-two years after, of a principal witness, who also says—'On my conscience, I do not believe that Mr. Smith had anything to do with the rebellion.'"

Worse still, revolters under sentence of death were encouraged to utter falsehoods, which they voluntarily confessed to be such, when after all they found it availed them nothing.

But the evidence at the trial does not sustain even the

mitigated charge (misprision of treason)* on which at length
a verdict against the missionary was returned; nor, again,
was "misprision of treason" a capital offence.   Yet in his
prison-room, situate above the Court room, loud shoutings of
joy heard on 24th November, indicated to the persecuted
man that he was pronounced "guilty," and on the same day
he was sentenced

"to be hanged by the neck until dead.   But the Court, under all
the circumstances of the case, begs humbly to recommend the
prisoner, John Smith, to mercy."

Fortunately this decision had to be sent to the Home
Government before further action was taken.   But the
prisoner was now removed to the common gaol, put in a
room on the ground floor, having stagnant water underneath,
with apertures admitting its pernicious miasma, and where,
despite the loud complaints of his medical attendant, he was
kept for seven more weeks.   His disease, which all along
had been gaining ground, now advanced at a rapid pace, and
little hope of recovery was left when at last removal to a
more healthy part of the gaol was permitted.   Here, after a
short and slight improvement, came a final relapse.

During the time since the trial, communication with the
Society had been renewed, in fact his persecutors had compelled Mr. Smith to draw a bill upon its funds in order to
defray the expenses of trial.†   But early in December
Mrs. Smith and himself each wrote a letter to the secretary,
he another to his old friend and former employer in London,
and on 12th January, 1824, after one just to hand from the

* "Aiding the rebellion because he did not tell, what by the evidence given on the trial, it is seen *he did not know*, and because he did
not secure a man whom *he did not know to be a rebel*."—"Demerara
Martyr," p. 130.   Yet Captain Spencer, who really did know of the
intended outbreak hours before, and said nothing, was afterwards
excused by a Court of Inquiry.

† On a corner of this bill, years afterwards, the secretary found
written in very small hand, the reference, 2 Cor. iv. 8, 9.

Society's treasurer and secretary, dated 19th November, 1823, Mr. Smith acknowledged it by the last letter he ever wrote.

As the end drew near, Mrs. Elliott made an effort to gain admittance to the prison. Seven times had she to call at the Government office, and thirteen or fourteen days to wait before permission, and only for one day, was given. Now, however, the sufferer was so far gone that the strictness of prison rules in his case was relaxed, and Mrs. Elliott remained to render help. But all the constant care of his medical attendant, the great humanity of the keeper of the prison, the watchful nursing of the devoted women, could only alleviate pain and express sympathy; for on 6th February, 1824, just sixteen years after John Wray's first landing in the Colony to begin the work now apparently destroyed, and only three days before such news of deliverance by the Home Government reached Demerara as would at least have gratified the patient, John Smith sank, dying in great peace.

Within twenty-four hours his remains were in the grave; a short period, but not without acutely painful scenes. The First Fiscal and some members of the Government came to the room and held inquest. Difficulty arose with the doctor, who repeatedly refused to sign his deposition on the ground of its being so different from the answers he had given. Mrs. Smith's evidence also was only in part admitted; on which Mrs. Elliott, who had at first replied, "I do not consider this a legal meeting, and do not feel bound to answer any questions;" and had been answered by the Fiscal, "Do not you know that I have the arm of power, and can oblige you to speak? but I should be sorry to be put to the painful necessity of so doing;"* persisted in

---

* He afterwards became paralyzed, and that arm of power which, writes Mrs. Tuckett, the Fiscal stretched forth to intimidate them, was thus rendered useless. It is a fact too, explain it as men may, that several ready witnesses against Mr. Smith came before long to sad and strange deaths. These will be noted as they occur.

refusing, and would only assent to corroborate what Mrs. Smith had said as to dieting and nursing, also as to the conduct of the prison-keeper. Afterwards it was found that neither widow nor her friend was to be allowed to follow the coffin ; being the order of his Excellency, which they would not have observed had they not been told of further orders being issued to detain them until the burial was over, in case they attempted to follow.

At half-past three, therefore, on the morning of the 7th, the two left the gaol to meet the coffin at the grave-side. A free negro, carrying a lanthorn, went with them, as it was quite dark. At four a head-constable called for the corpse ; the Rev. W. S. Austin, who had dared to vindicate the character of the deceased, attended and read the service, and so "*somewhere* in the burial ground in the centre of which St. Philip's Church now stands," the remains were interred,* amid circumstances thus touchingly detailed by James Montgomery :—

> "Come down, in thy profoundest gloom,
> 　　Without one vagrant fire-fly's light,
> Beneath thine ebon arch entomb
> 　　Earth, from the gaze of heaven, O night !
> A deed of darkness must be done,
> Put out the moon ! hold back the sun !
>
> "Are these the criminals that flee
> 　　Like deeper shadows through the shade ?
> A flickering lamp, from tree to tree,
> 　　Betrays their path along the glade ;
> Led by a negro :—now they stand,
> Two trembling women hand in hand.
>
> "A grave, an open grave appears !
> 　　O'er this in agony they bend ;
> Wet the fresh earth with bitter tears,
> 　　Sighs following sighs their bosoms rend ;
> These are not murderers : they have known
> Grief more bereaving than their own.

---

* See "Martyr of Demerara," and "Echoes from Slave Time."

" Oft through the gloom, their streaming eyes
        Look forth for that they fear to meet :
    It comes ;—they catch a glimpse ;—it flies ;
        Quick glancing lights ;—now trampling feet
    Among the rank grass, seen, heard, gone !
    Return, and, in dead march, move on.

" A stern procession ! gleaming arms,
        And spectral countenances dart,
    By the red torch light, wild alarms
        And with'ring pangs through either heart ;
    A corpse amidst the group is borne :
    A prisoner's corpse, who died last morn.

" Not by the slave-lord's justice slain,
        That doom'd him to a traitor's death ;
    While royal mercy sped in vain
        O'er land and sea, to spare his breath ;
    But the frail life that warmed his clay,
    Man could not give, nor take away.

" His vengeance and his grace, alike,
        Were impotent to save or kill ;
    He may not lift his sword to strike,
        Nor turn it's edge aside at will :
    Here, by one Sovereign act and deed,
    God cancell'd all that man decreed.

" Ashes to ashes ! dust to dust !
        That corpse is to the grave consign'd ;
    The scene departs ;—this buried trust
        The Judge of quick and dead shall find,
    When things that time and death have seal'd
    Shall be in flaming fire reveal'd.

" The fire shall try thee, then, like gold,
        Prisoner of hope ! await the test ;
    And, oh ! when truth alone is told,
        Be thy clear innocence confest !
    The fire shall try thy foes : may they
    Find mercy in that dreadful day ! "

SHEFFIELD, 20*th* *July*, 1824.

A carpenter and a bricklayer, negroes and members of Mr. Smith's congregation, began to fence and brick over the grave ; work stopped by the First Fiscal, who "ordered the bricks to be taken up, the railing to be torn down, and the whole frail memorial of gratitude and piety to be destroyed." "As they began, so they concluded," afterwards remarked Sir James Macintosh, "and at least it must be owned that they were consistent in their treatment of the living and of the dead." Mr. Wray, who as we shall presently see, had his own share of trouble and danger in Berbice,

"afterwards saw the grave, and had a piece of board with the initials J. S. painted on it, hoping some day to be able to raise a better monument, but he died before that day came." "He entirely believed in Mr. Smith's innocence. The feeling against my father in Demerara was quite as bitter, nothwithstanding which, he would have gone and stood by Mr. Smith, but Governor Beard refused him a pass, without which no one could leave Berbice. The Governor told him his enemies were looking out, and had declared if they could only catch him 'they would tar and feather him.' When matters were quieted down he got leave and went, I think before Mr. Smith died, but was not permitted to see him. After his death my father went again and saw Mrs. Smith before she left the Colony. She gave my father Fox's 'Book of Martyrs.' I remember Mr. and Mrs. Smith, and have it now. We brought it to England as it was her gift." (Mrs. Tuckett's second and third letters.)

Mr. Elliott of the West Coast, after being detained prisoner, was compelled to leave the Colony. A letter which he had addressed to the Society's treasurer was taken from his person, and not until a copy of it was forwarded by circuitous means, had the Directors information of the real circumstances in which their agents were placed. His chapel, as also that on the East Coast, were arbitrarily appropriated by others. Mr. Davies who, returning from England, landed shortly after the revolt, was so discountenanced and opposed, deserted too by many of his flock, that he sank discouraged, and, after a short illness, died in April, 1826. Thus dealt the violent slavery party, in their hector and the heyday of their seeming triumph, with the missionary work. Like one of the country's pythons, fabulous in size and anew emerged from the bush; its head in the prison mouthing its victim, its enormous folds encircling the property, its tail sweeping away or scattering former attendants and friends, the monster stretched its huge length along the coast, to receive at last, however, its death-wound, though to remain for years in rottenness and decay, exhaling a fetid odour that nauseated every true free man who came nigh.

" Recommendation to mercy " was no small disappointment to the many who expected and desired speedy execution. But when the mail of 9th February arrived, remitting the sentence, requiring John Smith's transmission to England, and superseding Governor Murray by the appointment of Sir Benjamin D'Urban as Governor, amazing offence was given to these persecutors. Meetings were held; strong feelings of indignation were expressed ; a resolution to present the Governor with plate of 1200 guineas' value, "in memorial of the late happy suppression of the revolt," was passed; also a resolution "that the Court of Policy be forthwith petitioned to expel all missionaries from the Colony, and to pass a law prohibiting the admission of any missionary preachers for the future." The meeting at which this latter passed was held " under the approving sanction of Governor Murray," and the resolution, aimed more particularly at the London Missionary Society, was opposed by only four gentlemen present. But nothing could exceed the virulence of planters and press shown at that date towards missionary work, unless it were the virulence of their friends and party in Britain. To say the least, this did not come far short, and, preventing for months any word other than their own reaching this country, all had an opportunity much to their taste, of which they swiftly took full advantage.

Filling the land with assertions of Smith's guilt, and with abuse of missions and of the Missionary Society, a storm arose, and the Directors were without advice. The Society's November *Chronicle* could but entreat members to suspend judgment. December found them in the same plight, as only letters from Mr. Wray had been received, and these said nothing of Demerara. But the despotic faction in Berbice had evidently caught the fever, and Mr. Wray had been in peril through charges brought against himself, such and so brought as to lead to his being summoned before Governor Beard, who, at Mr. Wray's instance, ordered an official investigation. This resulted in a letter, written by his Excellency's command, entirely exonerating the missionary. The anxious Directors reasoned therefore that thus it may prove elsewhere. They had confidence in their men; and as John Smith at his trial was seeking to vindicate the Society whatever befell himself, so did they withhold vindicating the Society apart from the defence of their missionaries.

"They believed in a day when the vindication of the missionaries would wipe away all the opprobrium thrown upon the Society, and judged it their duty to wait with confidence and calmness till it came." *

Against the anti-slavery party the outcry was both longer and louder. With the exception of Granada, St. Vincent's, and St. Kitt's, all our West Indian possessions had received the despatches of Government with vehement indignation, shared largely by sympathizers on home shores; and as news from these Colonies would arrive at about one and the same time, the sadder tidings of revolt in Demerara, which followed in a few weeks, came as a climax, and produced an outburst before which even the Government quailed.

Great indeed were the disappointment and grief of the anti-slavery leaders.

* "Martyr of Demerara," p. 158.

"Their luke-warm partisans left them at once, and joined in the loud outcry. They were denounced as the causes of the disaffection of the Colonists, and the disorders among the slaves. The people at large did not remember how gentle a remedy was proposed by Mr. Buxton, that all parties in England had agreed as to its prudence, and that only the wilfulness and prejudice of the Colonists caused these unhappy results."

But to Mr. Buxton, angry reproaches were as nothing compared with the mortification experienced on finding that the Government were determined to forfeit the pledge which Mr. Canning had given.

Prospects were wretched. Difficulties abounded. The small party was furiously attacked on every side. Hardly more than half-a-dozen could be counted staunch friends in the Commons' House. The weight of business that ensued was overwhelming. But occasional messages from praying and true friends came to cheer; letters, too, began to arrive, casting a different light on matters. Mr. Buxton had never flinched; and now he and his party determined to move onwards, whatever came of it. So, with further tidings, determined also the Missionary Directors.

In a letter to his wife the former writes :—

"As to the Demerara insurrection, we have a capital case. Smith is innocent. I am in excellent spirits, and hold my head very high in the matter, and mean to be rather bold in my defence."

Again to J. J. Gurney :—

"I have been reading Smith's trial. If ever I speak on that subject, as I surely will, it will be without qualifying circumstances. He is as innocent as you are."

Replying to Mr. Canning in debate on 16th March, when Mr. Canning "informed the House that the Government was determined to compel the amelioration only in Trinidad," Mr. Buxton fearlessly attacked the Government for its vacillating conduct. He read over the resolutions of the year before, which he justly denominated "a distinct pledge given by Government that the condition of the slave population should be ameliorated." He added :—

"I well know the difficult situation in which I stand. No man is more aware than I am of my inability to follow the brilliant and able speech which has just been delivered. But I have a duty to perform, and I will perform it. I know well what I incur by this. I know how I call down upon myself the violent animosity of an exasperated and most powerful party. I know how reproaches have rung in my ears since that pledge was given, and how they will ring with tenfold fury now that I call for its fulfilment. Let them ring! I will not purchase for myself a base indemnity with such a sting as this on my conscience—You ventured to agitate the question ; a pledge was obtained ; you were therefore to be considered the holders of that pledge, to which the hopes of half-a-million of people were linked. And then, fearful of a little unpopularity, and confounded by the dazzling eloquence of the right honourable gentleman, you sat still, you held your peace, and were satisfied to see his pledge in favour of a whole archipelago reduced to a single island."

He concluded his speech, in which he laid bare a series of acts of atrocious cruelty in the treatment of the negroes, by stating distinctly,—

"What I have now said I have said from a sense of public duty. I have no hostility to the planters. Compensation to the planter, emancipation to the children of the negro—these are my desires, this is the consummation, the just and glorious consummation on which my hopes are planted, and to which, as long as I live, my most strenuous efforts shall be directed."*

He was well supported by Dr. Lushington, Mr. Evans, and Mr. Wilberforce.

But leaving the steps taken and measures proposed in connection with slave emancipation, we confine our present notice to action in defence and vindication of the missionary. A motion for the production of a copy of the minutes of the

* Life, &c., pp. 128, 129.

trial and other papers relating thereto, was agreed to in the House of Commons. Though but imperfect as compared with the copy furnished to the Missionary Society by the prisoner's counsel, Mr. Arrindell, the papers were sufficient to convince many of his innocence.

Fully convinced themselves, the Directors prepared a petition for revision of the proceedings of the Court Martial and repeal of the unjust sentence. This was presented to the House, 24th April, 1824. As correct information was spread throughout the country, its influence soon became apparent. The tide began to turn. Special donations were forwarded to the Missionary Society, as a sort of atonement for expressions of resentment against the supposed criminal. Meetings were held, resolutions published, and petitions agreed to in every part of England, 200 of which last were presented to Parliament in eleven days; all witnessed to the intense and favourable interest now awakened; and the discussion of the case in the House of Commons, a case which, Mr. Canning himself affirmed, "all parties agreed was the most painful ever discussed within these walls," was awaited with more than ordinary solicitude by the public at large.

On 1st June, therefore, the day appointed for Lord Brougham (then Henry Brougham, Esq.) to bring forward his motion respecting "the missionary Smith," the gallery of the House, opened at an unusually early hour, was instantly filled. Immense crowds unable to gain admission occupied avenues, and the House itself was more crowded than on any previous night of the session. The diminished band of Abolitionist members, eminent men however, held well together; Mr. Wilberforce, eight weeks confined to a sick chamber, leaving it to be present. A better case and cause they could not have had, painful as the subject and circumstances were, and skilful as needed to be the lawyer and advocate who should clearly disentangle the web of falsehood and sophistry, and then worthily display the whole with

its horrid accompaniment of brutality, to the gaze of
an astonished and growingly indignant people. But
Mr. Brougham, who, unsolicited, had undertaken the work,
proved quite equal to the occasion. His opening speech,
well on to four hours in length, and his final reply were
amongst his greatest and most successful efforts. Both are
published with an introduction written, it is believed, by
himself ;* and if nothing else of the history, trial, and debate
is perused, these should certainly be read. Here we can
give only short extracts on two or three points.

The case as a whole : result of an experiment :—

" It will be my duty to examine the charge preferred against
the late Mr. Smith, and the whole of the proceedings founded on
that charge. And in so doing, I have no hesitation in saying
that from the beginning of those proceedings to their fatal
termination, there has been committed more of illegality, more of
the violation of justice—violation of justice in substance as well
as in form—than in the whole history of modern times, I venture
to assert, was ever before witnessed in any inquiry that could be
called a judicial proceeding. I have tried the experiment upon
every person with whom I have had an opportunity of conversing
on the subject of these proceedings in Demerara, as well
members of the profession to which I have the honour of belonging, as others acquainted with the state of affairs in our Colonies,
and I have never met with one who did not declare to me that
the more the question was looked into, the greater attention was
given to its details, the more fully the whole mass was sifted ; the
more complete was his assent to the conviction that there was
never exhibited a greater breach of the law, a more daring
violation of justice, a more flagrant contempt of all those forms
by which law and justice were wont to be administered, and
under which the perpetrators of ordinary acts of judicial oppression are wont to hide the nakedness of their crimes."

After reviewing at length the nature of the court,
individuals composing it, kinds of evidence and manner of
proceeding, comes the summary :—

* A copy forms Appendix 5 to "The Martyr of Demerara."

"But, in truth, there is not a tittle of evidence that Mr. Smith knew of the revolt, while there is abundant proof that he took especial measures and watchful care to tell all he did know to the proper authorities, the managers of the estate. The Court, then, having no jurisdiction to sit at all in judgment upon this preacher of the Gospel—their own existence as a court of justice being wholly without the colour of lawful authority—tried him for things which, had they ever so lawful a title to try him, were wholly beyond their commission ; and of these things no evidence was produced upon which any man could even suspect his guilt, if the jurisdiction had been ever so unquestionable, and the accused had been undeniably within its range. But in spite of all the facts ; in spite of his well-known character and upright conduct ; it was necessary that he should be made an example for certain purposes; it was necessary that the missionaries should be taught in what an undertaking they had embarked ; that they should be warned that it was at their peril they preached the Gospel, that they should know it was at the hazard of their lives that they opened the Bible to their flocks; and therefore it was that the Court Martial deemed it expedient to convict Mr. Smith, and to sentence him to be hanged by the neck until he was dead."

What means the " recommendation to mercy " ?

" Who propagated those reports? Certainly not Mr. Smith. The negroes naturally flocked together to inquire whether the reports were true or not, and Mr. Smith immediately communicated to their masters his apprehensions of what he had always supposed possible, seeing the oppression under which the slaves laboured, and knowing that they were men. But, it is said, that at six o'clock on the Monday evening, one half hour before the rebellion broke out, he did not disclose what he could not have known before—namely, that a revolt was actually about to commence. Now, taking this fact for the sake of argument to be proved to its fullest extent,* I say that a man convicted of misprision cannot by the law be hanged. The utmost possible vengeance of the law, according to the wildest dream of the highest prerogative lawyer, could not amount to anything like a

---

* A point afterwards well examined and disposed of by Mr. Brougham in his closing speech.

sanction of this. Such I assert the law to be. I defy any man to contradict my assertion that, up to the present hour, no English lawyer ever heard of misprision of treason being treated as a capital offence, and that it would be just as legal to hang a man for a common assault. But if it be said that the punishment of death was awarded for having aided the revolt, I say the Court did not, could not, believe this ; and I produce the conduct of the judges themselves to confirm what I assert. They were bold enough in trying, and convicting, and condemning the victim whom they had lawlessly seized upon ; but they trembled to execute a sentence so prodigiously illegal and unjust; and having declared that in their consciences, and on their oaths, they deemed him guilty of the worst of crimes, they all in one voice add that they also deem him deserving of mercy in respect of his guilt ! Is it possible to draw any other inference from this marvellous recommendation than that they distrusted the sentence to which it was attached? When I see them affrighted by their own proceedings—starting back at the sight of what they had not scrupled to do—can I give them credit for any fear of doing injustice, they who from the beginning to the end of their course had done nothing else ? Can I believe that they paused upon the consummation of their work from any motive but a dread of its consequences to themselves ; a recollection, tardy indeed, but appalling, that 'Whoso sheddeth man's blood, by man shall his blood be shed ?' And not without reason, not without irrefragable reason did they take the alarm, for, verily, if they HAD perpetrated the last act—if they had DARED to take this innocent man's life (one hair of whose head they durst not touch), they must THEMSELVES have died the death of the murderer ! Monstrous as the whole proceedings were, and horrid as the sentence that closed them, there is nothing in the sentence from first to last so astounding as this recommendation to mercy, coming from persons who affected to believe him guilty of such enormous crimes. If he was proved to have committed the offence of exciting the slaves to acts of bloodshed, how unspeakably aggravated was his guilt compared with that of the poor untutored slaves ! How justly might all the blood that was shed be laid upon his head ! How fitly, if mercy was to prevail, might his deluded instruments be pardoned, and himself alone singled out for vengeance as the author of their crimes! Yet they are cut off in hundreds by the hand of justice, and he is deemed an object of compassion!

"By the negroes, indeed, little blood has been shed at any period of the revolt, and in its commencement none at all; altogether only one person was killed by them. In this remarkable circumstance, the insurrection stands distinguished from every other movement of this description in the history of Colonial society. The slaves, inflamed by false hopes of freedom, agitated by rumours, and irritated by the suspense and ignorance in which they were kept, exasperated by ancient as well as by more recent wrongs (for a sale of fifty or sixty of them had just been announced, and they were about to be violently separated and dispersed), were satisfied with combining not to work, and thus making their managers repair to the town, and ascertain the precise nature of the boon reported to have arrived from England. The calumniated minister had so far humanized his poor flock, his dangerous preaching had so enlightened them, the lessons of himself and his hated brethren had sank so deep in their minds, that, by the testimony of the clergyman, and even of the overseers, the maxims of the Gospel of peace were upon their lips in the midst of rebellion, and restrained their hands when no other force was present to resist them. 'We will take no life,' said they, 'for our pastors taught us not to take that which we cannot give;' a memorable peculiarity to be found in no other passage of negro warfare within the West Indian seas, and which drew from the truly pious minister of the Established Church the exclamation that 'He shuddered to write that they were seeking the life of the man whose teaching had saved theirs.' But it was deemed fitting to make tremendous examples of these unhappy creatures. Considerably above a hundred fell in the field, where *they* did not succeed in putting one soldier to death. A number of the prisoners also, it is said, were hastily drawn out at the close of the affray and instantly shot. How many in the whole have since perished by sentences of the Court does not appear; but up to a day in September, as I learn by the *Gazette* which I hold in my hand, forty-seven had been executed. A more horrid tale of blood yet remains to be told. Within the short space of a week, as appears by the same document, ten had been torn to pieces by the lash : some of these had been condemned to six or seven hundred lashes; five to one thousand each ; of which inhuman torture one had received the whole, and two almost the whole at once. Look now to the incredible inconsistency of the authorities by whom such retribution was dealt out, while they recommend *him* to mercy, whom in the same breath they pronounced a thousand times more guilty than the slaves. Can any man doubt for an instant that they knew him to be innocent, but were minded to condemn, stigmatize, and degrade him, because they durst not take his life, and yet were resolved to make an example of him as a preacher ? "

The great aim of Smith's opponents :—

"The whole proceedings demonstrate the hatred of his persecutors to be levelled at his calling and his ministry. Nay, for teaching obedience to the law which commands to keep holy the Sabbath, he is directly, and without any disguise, branded as the sower of sedition. Upon this overt act of rebellion, against all law, human and divine, a large portion of the prosecutor's invectives and of his evidence is bestowed? What though the reverend defendant showed clearly, out of the mouths of his adversary's witnesses, that he had uniformly taught the negroes to obey their masters, even if ordered by them to break the rest of the Sabbath ; that he had expressly inculcated the maxim, ' Nothing is wrong in you which your master commands ; and nothing amiss in him which necessity prescribes ? ' What though he reminded the Court that the seventh day, which he was charged with taking from the slaves, was not his to give or to withhold ; that it had been hallowed by the Divine Lawgiver to His own use, and exempted in terms from the work of slave as well as master, of beast as well as man ? He is arraigned as a promoter of discontent, because he, the religious instructor of the negroes, enjoins them to keep the Sabbath holy when their owners allow them no other day for working ; because he, a minister of the Gospel, preaches a duty prescribed by the laws of religion and by the laws of the land, while the planters live in the contempt of it. In short, no man can cast his eye upon this trial without perceiving that it was intended to bring on an issue between the system of the slave-law and the instruction of the negroes."

Sir James Macintosh followed on the same side, Government meeting the motion by a direct negative, and an adjournment was agreed to.

Such, however, was the effect already of the debate that the ministry again quailed, and on its resumption, finding they were in peril of a defeat; though to prevent an inconvenient rupture with the West India interest, opposition was not withdrawn, and a simple act of justice allowed to proceed; Mr. Canning substituted "the previous question." This was done after powerful speeches by Dr. Lushington, Mr. J. Williams,* Mr. Wilberforce, and Mr. T. Denman.† Dr. Lushington, after analyzing the evidence, remarked :—

"And yet on such evidence did they, after five days' deliberation, sentence him to the punishment of death ; on such evidence did the Governor of the Colony, to his eternal shame and everlasting disgrace, sanction the sentence. No honest jury ever pronounced such a sentence as that which the Court Martial at Demerara pronounced upon Mr. Smith, and it could have emanated from nothing but the most virulent spirit of prejudice. *They knowingly and wilfully gave a* FALSE VERDICT."

He then, reading extracts from the public journals, exposed the hateful spirit existing in Demerara.

Mr. Wilberforce rose amid loud and long-continued cheering, and made, in vindication of the missionary's character, an impressive address, his last speech in the House.

When Mr. Canning, with an eloquent attempt to soften down matters, had moved "the previous question"; Sir Joseph Yorke expressed his opinion that it was only an eloquent apology, but no defence. Mr. Brougham then closed with a most powerful and eloquent reply, involving a scathing exposure of the assumptions, speculations, suggestions offered in excuse ; and on a division 146 voted for his motion, 193 against.

* Afterwards a Judge in the Court of Queen's Bench.
† Afterwards Lord Chief Justice.

But though lost in outward form, it was felt that a victory of no ordinary value had been achieved.

"The discussion had an extreme and powerful effect in changing the current of public opinion. The nation which before had shared the consternation of the Government, began to awaken to the truth. Henceforth the religious public in England was strongly enlisted on behalf of the oppressed missionaries and their persecuted followers.* 'The Missionary Smith's Case' became a watch-word and a rallying cry with all the friends of religious liberty, as well as the enemies of West Indian slavery. The measures of the abolitionists all over the country became more bold and decided, as their principles commanded a more general and warmer concurrence. All saw that at the fetters of the slave a blow was at length struck which must, if followed up, make them fall off his limbs for ever." †

An earnest of this appeared only four days after the debate, when, 15th June, Mr. Wilberforce renewing the subject, a promise was wrested from the Government to uphold the Order in Council at St. Lucia and Demerara, as well as Trinidad.

It only remains to add that Mrs. Smith, on her arrival in England, was met with tokens of esteem and affection by Christians of every name. Provision was made for her support by a life-annuity, purchased with a sum generously contributed for the purpose. This, however, was not long needed, she surviving her husband but four years and four days, which were spent chiefly with highly esteemed friends in London. 31st January, 1828, in a very debilitated condition, she went to Rye on the Sussex coast, but had no sooner arrived than it became plain that the end could not be far off. On Lord's day, 10th February, in great peace and in the full faith of Christ as her Saviour and Lord, she passed away, being only in her thirty-fourth year.

The mission work checked in Demerara, had not even

* Life of Buxton, p. 131.
† "Martyr of Demerara," Appendix 5.

then been resumed ; 1828 about closing before this was done ;
but the sentence upon her devoted husband as a *felon* and to
a *felon's* death, though one of the best of men, and long now
universally accounted innocent, still remains UNREPEALED !—
"though unexecuted; sanctioned, nay, adopted by the
Government of this country, because suffered to remain
unrescinded" (Brougham).

CHAPTER VI.

INSURRECTION IN DEMERARA, TO VISIT OF MR.
AND MRS. WRAY TO ENGLAND.

August 1823—April 1831.

Effects upon Berbice and Mission there—Attitude of Whites—Governor Beard, a Friend—Wray a chief Sufferer—False Charge—Destruction of Mission Premises—Sympathetic Aid from England—Second False Charge—Letter to Mr. Brougham—Attempt to silence Wray—Memorial to Home Government—Base Slanders—Letters from Wray to Governor—Duplicity and Meanness of Whites—Interviews with Governor—Disfavour, &c., of Whites—Encouragements by Governor—Good News from Abroad—Adherence of Negroes, &c.—Pastor's Fidelity—Birth of Twelfth Child—Missionary's spiritual Condition—Virulence of Slavery Press—Memorial disapproved—Escape from Berbice Council—Happy Results of Labours—Pupils from High Places—Deaths among Persecutors—Signs of Progress—Use of Anniversary Days—Review of Doctrines held, and of Pulpit Work.

That Berbice should afterwards be the first to know and feel the shock of these events, goes without saying. Its sea coast a continuation of the Demerara East Coast, though the outburst itself did not extend beyond Mahaica Creek, intelligence thereof would in a few hours have reached the Abary, and as many minutes would suffice to bear the news across. Unhappily, the malignant spirit and violent reprisals of the slavery party found too large and continuous a sympathy in Berbice ; and the meanness of the whites generally for some time to come, towards the missionary and mission work, became almost incredible. They could not have been

218

exceeded unless it were by the fresh outburst of licentiousness and of heathen revellings which seems to have taken place. In these respects there was little to choose between the two Colonies; and nothing more likely to bring either to ruin or to cause fresh and far more widely-spread thoughts of insurrection. The language of the press, the bickerings of proprietors and officials, yet the almost complete unanimity with which they rejected the proposals of philanthropy, opposed the presence of missionaries, and repelled co-operation with any not their own colour; betokened ill for the settlement and peace of communities already in a state of panic, and in which the word "freedom" was not to be spoken. Had such beneficent agencies been completely withdrawn, and had the Home Legislature, whose Ordinances were so resented, recalled its regiments and ships of war, leaving the slave holders to themselves; where then, with all their bluster and bitterness, would these men have been?

Humanly speaking, but for the presence in Berbice of a Governor ready to respect the wishes of the Home Government, wise to carry them out, impartial to hear the accused as well as the accuser, and ever willing, as far as was right, to befriend the missionary; the mission there—notwithstanding years of labour by the agent, his high and long tested character, the many deeds of kindness shown by himself and his equally devoted partner in life, towards any in need, whether bond or free, and without respect to age or colour, rank or occupation — would have been made as desolate as that in the adjoining Colony. Even as it was, Mr. Wray, with his wife and growing family, could but hold on to what was immediately at hand; other work near having to remain in abeyance for awhile; and the work in Demerara for years to be let alone, until much quieter times. This, relying on an all-wise and gracious God, with strength vouchsafed according to his day, he succeeded in doing. Billow after billow, the effects of the storm, long continued to roll on. John Wray met each and surmounted it; not swamped, nor wrecked, nor driven from his moorings.

But among the sufferers from the sad events of 1823, we find a chief one in him who, amid his own perils and wrongs and losses, had to hear, from week to week and month to month, of cruel wrong to much-loved brethren, himself unable to render aid; then of their removal entirely, and of the destruction largely of the work, both his and theirs. He had to hear of all, as his copious private diary shows, with the sensitive heart of one who loved and cherished the mission as his own soul; and, with a tender affection long accustomed to sympathize with others, " in all their affliction himself to be afflicted;" whilst fully conscious of his own imperfections and frailties, the uprising within of " passion's storms both loud and high," that had to be controlled, happily were so, despite most grievous provocations. Thus several years passed; but, when gone, and happier opportunities had returned, how many, friends and foes alike, had been removed from the scene!

The first piece of mischief followed closely upon news received of Demerara doings. It consisted of the lying rumours and false charge referred to by the Directors, as we have seen, in their December *Chronicle*, and it exposed Mr. Wray to much unmerited reproach. At the Governor's request he had, weeks before, publicly in the chapel, explained to the slaves attending, all that concerned themselves in the Orders in Council that had been received. With some aggravating additions, the report and charge now were that he had been inviting such to a private meeting for the purpose of communicating important intelligence from England. His prompt response to the Governor's summons, and his request for a thorough investigation; the inquiry itself, with the resulting complete and official vindication of his character, were all over in time for their being reported to the Directors by a mail leaving early in September.

Not more than a fortnight then elapsed before the next blow fell. It was indeed a heavy one, and its effects were much less easily repaired.

On 22nd September, his twice-enlarged chapel and new school-house were consumed to ashes, and his dwelling-house, scarcely saved, received much damage. Mrs. Tuckett, then twelve years old, was a witness of the scene, and unhesitatingly affirms it to have been a piece of incendiarism : certainly the words and deeds of some present were worthy of such a crime. She writes in her first letter :—

"This chapel was burnt down at the time of the Insurrection in Demerara. It was no accident, for there was no dwelling-house near, only a small cottage, uninhabited, at some distance from the chapel. That was set on fire ; it was blazing hot sun, no water near, the white people rushing about, crying out, 'Down with chapel and the house ;' 'Seize his papers !' such a wild confusion I shall never forget. My poor father stood opposite the chapel with arms folded and lips firmly compressed until it was burnt out (for it did not take long) ; he said not a word ; it was no use seeking redress. This was a terrible time : I remember it well. Providentially the Governor (Beard) was his friend, also the Fiscal, whose wife mother had been kind to in sickness, and she was much attached to her.

"The under part of our house was again fitted up, and there the teaching went on. God blessed the words spoken, and this satisfied him ; but, like righteous Lot in Sodom, his soul was daily vexed at all he saw and heard of iniquity, oppression, and cruelty, heartrending cruelty."

The safety of his house must already have been seen to, as only by the most vigorous measures, including ejectment through the window of all his books and tracts, was it secured ; and not until nothing more could be done was John Wray a man thus to stand. But when, the fire out, no further fear of its spread remained, there would come enough to be done, and all the more upon himself now that he was so ignored, where not worse treated, by his white neighbours. Thankful then for the preservation of life, his own and that of wife and children, also for a dwelling spared in great measure ; he would, among his first works, have to plan accommodation of some sort for scholars and worshippers, and to see to its speedy execution. What arrangement was made, Mrs. Tuckett has already told us.

To send the sad intelligence home would be no second thing. The information arrived after the long and anxious suspense of waiting for word from their Demerara missionaries had been ended ; and it of course only deepened the Society's sympathy and the sympathy which had begun to spread throughout the country. Five hundred pounds promptly voted him by the Directors toward new buildings cheered him in return not a little, as did also the attitude of Christians and of the nation generally, now being roused to indignation at the tidings each mail brought from Guiana.

But as yet he had to pass on cautiously, content with much smaller things than had been his, and quietly doing the little he could as opportunity offered. For, diminished though they had become, neither he nor his remaining work were yet out of danger.

In common with the Demerara missionaries, Mr. Wray was slandered as having extorted money from the slaves in the sale of publications and in other ways. Strange as it may seem, the persecutors of Mr. Smith relied upon this as one means of helping on their case to a verdict of "guilty." Friends in England, preparing for their great attempt in Parliament to vindicate their martyred agent and themselves, needed all the reliable testimony that could be adduced. A letter dated 27th April, 1824, and addressed to Mr. B. (presumably Mr. Brougham) contains what the pioneer has to say. Part of it is here quoted almost verbatim.

" Along with the Catechisms, the Directors request I send you the plain Sermon on the Duties of Slaves, &c., preached on Sunday Evening, 7th October, 1815, in New Amsterdam. Notwithstanding the vile misrepresentations and false assertions of the anti-mission party, I can truly affirm that for the space of sixteen years I have taught no doctrines or principles contrary to those contained in the discourse, and that I have hundreds of times impressed the substance of them upon the attention of the slaves of these Colonies ; directing them, however, at all times to Jesus 'the Lamb of God who taketh away the sin of the world' ; and who alone can save them and enable them to perform these duties in a way which will be pleasing to God.

" As we have been charged with selling books to the negroes and extorting money from them, I would observe that I have distributed about 200 Common Prayer Books, a few of which have been sold at one guilder (1s. 4d.) each, while Prayer Books are sold at stores at six to twelve guilders each. I have also distributed a great number of Homily Tracts, perhaps as many as any clergyman in the West Indies. With respect to Bibles and Testaments, I have sold about 170, and distributed gratis about 240 : a large number in a country where so few can read. I have supplied bond and free ; sailors and soldiers ; prisoners and scholars with Bibles, Prayer Books, Homilies and Tracts. To the Bible Society I account for the Bibles I sell, and remit them the money. They have been sold much cheaper than Bibles can be purchased at a store ; at from three guilders to twelve, according to the size, value, and to the ability of the purchaser. I believe twenty-two guilders, or a Joe, is a common price for a Bible at a store. There is not one to be had at present. As to Spelling books I have generally had that of the Sunday School Union, which I think upon the whole is the best for the negroes. Besides what the Directors have sent, I have had about 1500 out on my own account, a few of which have been sold at one bit (4d.) a piece, the smallest money we have, to assist in paying for the rest : but hucksters and stores sell Spelling books for from six bits to three guilders. Catechisms, with very few exceptions, have been given by me ; also Watts's Divine Songs.

" Now, I know not how this can be called extorting money from the negroes.

"It appears from the Parliamentary Reports that many of the Clergy of the Islands, particularly Jamaica, have a dollar (4s. 2d.) a head for baptizing slaves, sometimes more, and that this is often paid out of the slaves' own pockets. I am not aware that Mr. Smith or any of the missionaries receive anything of the kind : what would be said of them if they did ?"

As instances, Mr. Wray adduces one clergyman in Jamaica who informs the Governor of having baptized 5000, and of expecting in about three months to baptize the rest of his parish, which numbers about 24,000 ; the fee being 2s. 6d. each, and the masters paying it : another who states he had baptized nearly 3000 in one year, the fee being 2s. 6d., paid sometimes by the master, sometimes by the slave : another who states that for twenty-three slaves baptized on estates, he had received two dollars each, paid by the master ; for forty-four baptized in church, four bits each ; and for five baptized in church, two bits each, paid by the slaves : a fourth case runs—2032 baptized in $3\frac{1}{2}$ years, fee 2s. 9d. or 2s. 6d. ; the clergyman stating that the fee is frequently paid by the slaves. "Such clergymen," adds Mr. Wray, "the good people in Demerara want."

Such clergymen, it may here be remarked, the people, or rather the whites of Demerara, in excuse for opposing and expelling the missionaries, soon obtained, as some years afterwards did those of Berbice ; paying them liberal stipends out of the Colony-chest ; clergymen, however, who, as a rule at that time, were of a character not particularly high, and who did little or nothing to instruct those in bondage ; whatever number might go through the form of baptism at their hands.

At the date of the letter just quoted, Mr. Wray was engaged in repelling an attack of another kind, which came to his knowledge about the beginning of April, but the result of which was not finally known until the 18th of August. It would seem as if, disappointed in not getting rid of the missionary by the burning of his chapel and in preventing all likelihood of its re-erection, his enemies were determined upon silencing the man himself. On 10th April, the entry is :—

"The people called Christians still imagine a vain thing and take counsel against the Lord and His blessed Gospel. It seems to me that many of them are like the Jews of old who are filling up their sins by forbidding us to speak to the poor Gentile Negroes that they may be saved. May God have mercy upon them!

"I find a memorial has been drawn up against me and signed by a great number of people—chiefly overseers, trades-people, managers, &c.; and is to be presented to the Governor in Council, to obtain, if possible, my suspension from preaching. I am well aware that the Governor will sanction no such thing, but I thought it proper to write him that he might be on his guard. In the evening he sent his servant to say that he had got my letter, that it was very good, and that I need not trouble myself. Though I do not fear these men, yet I certainly feel it much after labouring sixteen years in these Colonies, in some measure with a conscience void of offence to God and man, and then to meet with such treatment as this from those people whose good I am seeking, many of whom were schoolboys when I first arrived here, and others hardly able to speak. But the servant cannot expect to be above his Master. If they persecute Jesus, they will persecute His servant. O my God! do Thou change the hearts of mine enemies, and remove every obstacle out of the way of the preaching of Thy blessed Gospel."

Mr. Wray, who has preserved copies of his letter and subsequent short notes to the Governor, after referring to the signatures as being, some of persons quite ignorant of him, and other some of parties already convicted of slander or misconduct toward himself, proceeds in his letter of 8th April :—

"Ten years ago the Crown agent was called upon by a planter to give his private assistance in getting that fellow Wray out of the Colony who, he says, 'would not care one farthing if we

were all killed in a day*; but, after ten years, not an individual
has been injured by him. If I have broken the laws of the
Colony, I am liable to be punished by them ; but I solemnly
protest against such measures as I understand are now in agitation against me and to be submitted to your Excellency and the
honourable the Council of Government. I am sure indeed that
your Excellency, as a British Governor and as the representative
of our beloved King, who, like his venerable father, will maintain
the Toleration inviolable and suffer no persecution for conscience
sake, will never sanction such proceedings. It is not necessary
for me to state to your Excellency that the Toleration laws travel
with the British Flag into all the dependencies of the British
Crown, and that I am, as a British subject (a name in which
I glory), and as a Protestant minister, as much entitled by the
Toleration Act to preach the Gospel of Christ as the Archbishop
of Canterbury.

"As to the Directors of the Missionary Society consisting of
all denominations of Christians, they are in general men of as
exemplary piety, learning, talents, and respectability as Great
Britain has produced. As a Society they are entirely uncon-
nected with any political party whatever ; their whole object is
to spread the Gospel of Christ. It is true that sometimes, through
the opposition of 'unreasonable men,' they are obliged to lay
their complaints before the King and Parliament, and sometimes
before the British public, to obtain redress or liberty for their
Missionary to preach the Gospel in the Colonies ; and they have
never appealed in vain. It is only in this way that they have
any connection with political parties. Besides, in this Colony,
every man has absolute power over his slaves in a moral and
religious view, as no one can come to town without a written permission. This Law is sufficient to prevent slaves from being
instructed. With respect to the negroes obtaining any idea of
freedom, it is not from the Missionaries, but from the colonists
themselves. I need not inform your Excellency that it was at a
meeting of the Inhabitants that the Negroes of this Colony
imbibed the idea."

Of course Mr. Wray made diligent inquiries on what
ground, new or old, the request to be conveyed in the

memorial was based; and, by the end of the month, had not only been notified by the Governor of its reception, and, in response to a consequent summons, had attended upon his Excellency, but had furnished the Directors with full particulars—forwarding to them, as he had to the Governor, specimens of publications both for their own examination and, if thought needful, for submitting to Earl Bathurst; to whom, as Secretary for the Colonies, the memorial was to be referred.

The alleged grounds were—first, that the negroes attending Bethel chapel (Le Resouvenir), Demerara, had been the chief leaders in the revolt; and next, that pernicious doctrines were contained in the *Missionary Hymn Book.* Mr. Wray, happily, was already in a position to disprove the former assertion, and to show exactly, as he does in his letter to the Governor, the very small proportion of such negroes to the whole body of leaders and insurgents. As to the latter, he not only turned the tables on his assailants, but exposed a piece of theft and forgery, of duplicity and slander, worthy of characters so mean and vile as many of them were.

What about the books of Common Prayer, is his argument in brief, disposed of by himself, or on sale at the stores; and the hymn books of Watts and Wesley that are articles of merchandise in the town, from which books a number of the Hymns in the *Missionary Hymn Book* had been selected? Yet, so far were these thought otherwise than dangerous that Watts's Hymns had been used by an Episcopalian clergyman in the town. If again, a line or two here and there might be picked out and severed from the connection, how all might stand condemned as dangerous in the hands of slaves !

Lines thus picked out and severed, were being adduced as illustrations in support of the memorial; and a copy of the Hymn Book in the little book-bag of a school-boy, about eight years of age, after being pilfered and inscribed on the title-page as if given by John Wray, was forwarded to the Governor. In the boy's bag was also the " Catechism on the Duties of Slaves," drawn up by the pioneer, but it, for plain reasons, had been left.

Now, it so happened that the Hymn Book was not a child's book, and Mr. Wray, careful in the distribution of literature as in other departments of his work (who had even returned to the Tract Society publications containing expressions which, in such a social state as then existed, might have laid him under suspicion), had never given a copy to a child. His conjecture is that the boy, if he had not received the book as a gift from his father, a free man, or from one of the free people, had picked it up during the fire ; as several children afterwards returned books which, at that time thrown out of the window, they had taken away.

The memorial was confined to the whites, who in it state also their wish for established clergy ; * and was not to be shown to any coloured person, lest, the missionary further conjectures, they should inform himself. A white lad, presenting it to a doctor for signature, then asked a young man present, so nearly white as at first to be mistaken for such, to sign it. The young man took it and began to read ; when it was snatched out of his hand by the impudent lad, with the exclamation : " You are a mulatto ! " The missionary, some weeks later, calling on a gentleman who could speak little English, to pay him a small account, he candidly informed Mr. Wray in the course of conversation that he had signed the memorial. Mr. Wray found that he had been completely imposed upon. Expressions from a paraphrase

* Upon which Mr. Wray remarks that they do not employ the one they have ; and that the Rev. —— Austin, Senior, who was zealous for the instruction of the negroes, was as much persecuted as any missionary, and at last left the Colony in disgust ; like treatment being at that moment experienced by his son, the Rev. W. T. Austin, in Demerara.

of the 45th Psalm, quoted as if standing alone in the book in which the entire paraphrase was given, he had been made to believe as having been picked out by the African Society and then sent to the missionaries for distribution among the negroes. Of course he was informed that the picking out had been done in Berbice, and by whom. Declaring himself astonished, and remarking that the Bible itself if so treated might, most of it, be made revolutionary, he told his visitor that had he known he would not have signed.

"27th April, the Governor sent for me. On my arrival at his office he put the memorial into my hand. After having read it, he gave me the Hymn Book to look at with my name written on the title page. I returned it and said it was not my writing. His Excellency observed, he thought not, for he had compared it with my signature in my letters. He asked me if he should call Col. Innes, the (Berbice) Colonial Secretary, as a witness that I denied the signature to be mine. I, of course, agreed; Colonel Innes examined and compared it with my signature, and gave it as his opinion that it was not my writing. The Governor looked at the printer's name, and observed it could be bought in London by any one. His Excellency said that he should inform Earl Bathurst that I had seen it.

"The signature had evidently been written but two or three months, though dated 1st April, 1822; and I never write a name on the title page between the letters as this is written, nor in the way it is written."

Having done what he could in the matter, the pioneer left it and pursued his work. Occasional incidents did not let him forget the more than disfavour with which generally the whites now regarded him. None came near his religious meetings, and some of the other people who attended were threatened with loss of custom for so doing. His horse takes off and, followed by an old man, its keeper, turns into the timber yard of a merchant, where caught, it is being led out, but is seized by a clerk, sent to the Pound, and a charge of £2 made, professedly for the consumption of the mer-

chant's guinea grass. Cases long employed in conveying
Bible and Tract Societies' publications, passed at the Customs
heretofore without question, are now opened and searched :
a circumstance reported to the Governor, whose inquiries
into the matter proves vain. It reaches the missionary's
ear also, that some captains fear to bring him freight on
account of the clamour against him and the mission. Meanwhile there is shocking impiety around, and often, for so
small a community, some shocking event of suicide or other
violence, the outcome of such sin ; all sadly painful to the
pious mind.

But again, there were things to cheer. Meeting one day
with the Governor, he has his Excellency's opinion that
nothing will come of the memorial ; and is told that he (the
Governor) had written Earl Bathurst to the effect that he
had nothing to say against Mr. Wray. At another interview,
by a liberal private gift and promises of further aid, his
Excellency readily seconded Mr. Wray's efforts to relieve
two widows in sore distress. When in Demerara, the
pioneer had expressed to Governor Murray his opinion that,
notwithstanding the sentence of the Court Martial upon Mr.
Smith, the home country would take means for bringing to
view the righteousness of the departed missionary ; and now,
mail after mail contained news of efforts and speeches all
tending to this end ; very cheering, though to him very
affecting also, in their details. His meeting-room was sometimes filled to its utmost capacity with hearers of the Word,
and often had smaller companies of devout worshippers,
believers in Jesus, and steadfast adherents of His tried
minister ; who "declared their determination to go on in the
ways of religion, notwithstanding the persecutions they met
with." Yet Mr. Wray continued the same Pastor he had been ;
faithful and sound-minded ; caring not to purchase numbers
by the sacrifice of principles. One who expressed her intention to give up business and to become religious, he

sought to convince that she could be religious in her business.
Two old negro women, waiting admission to Church-fellowship, he deferred as yet too noisy among their neighbours.
Sickness or sudden seizure appeared now and then in' his
family; but on 26th May "God was graciously pleased," he
writes, "to deliver Mrs. Wray of her twelfth child, a little
girl"; received with thanksgiving and prayers; named Emily
Thompson Wray, and baptized on 11th June. The following
extract speaks what must frequently have been the conflict
within, and the varied emotions of the missionary's soul
during this period :—

"*Saturday, 5th June.*—I feel my heart deeply affected with all
the wonderful things that have taken place in the course of the
last eight months. My mind is continually led to think upon
them. I feel my thoughts wander too much from my God and
fix upon the troubles which have befallen us. Oh, that I could
stay my mind upon Him and take comfort in this time of darkness
and distress ! Oh, my God ! gather in all my wandering, roving
thoughts, and help me to 'set my affection on things above';
help me to trust under the shadow of Thy wings until these
troubles are overpast. I bless Thee, O my God ! that Thou art
in some measure bringing forth the righteousness of Thy departed
servant. I rejoice at the verdict that appears to be passed upon
him by his country, at least the best part of it.

"I have read with much pleasure the account of him and
Quamina in the British and Colonial Register. They reprobate
the conduct of the Colonists in hanging a man in chains merely
for advising the people to lay down their tools—for nothing else
can be proved against him. When he was shot, he had his prayer-
book and hymn-book in his pocket, but no arms in his hands.*
There can be no doubt now, that the whole blame is to be
thrown on the Governor and Court for keeping back the instructions of Government in July."

* On 22nd August a free woman and member of the church at Le
Resouvenir coming to Berbice, informed Mr. Wray that the people said
Quamina begged his son Jack, with tears on his face, the night before
to have nothing to do with the affair, and Jack told his father that "he
was an old man, but that he himself was young."

The following may serve also as introductory to what of good news comes immediately after :—

"16th August.—I have been much affected with reading some of the speeches delivered at the Anti-Slavery Society (meeting), respecting the Demerara business ; and the motion of Lord Calthorpe in vindication of Mr. Smith. But the speech of Mr. (Zech.) Macaulay's son * is wonderful. I could not read it without shedding many tears. Blessed be God that he is treading in the steps of his father, and that the young ones are now pledging themselves to carry on this glorious work. I was much struck with his remark on the Demerara Court Martial:—'That the plea of the vindicators of it was, that a Court formed of Planters would have acted with far more injustice ; and yet this Court none of them would defend—a Court which has not found a single lawyer to stake his professional character on its legality. What then must a Court, formed of Planters, be ? It must be bad indeed.'"—*British and Colonial Register*, 26th June.

"'The newspapers of this Colony (Demerara) continue to pour out the most infamous abuse on the subject of the late Missionary. The character of Mr. Smith is bitterly assailed ; he is branded with the epithets of wretch, murderer, and is compared to Thistlewood, Holloway, &c. The Court Martial is censured for recommending him to mercy ; the Governor, for not executing him in spite of that recommendation ; and the Ministers, for presuming to make him an object of royal mercy. Even His Majesty does not escape licentious reflection. We are not sorry to see this display of these extravagances, brutal and disgusting as they are. They plainly show what Demerara is.'"—*Ibid.*

So 18th August again came round ; a day not to be forgotten by the Mission ; a time, the recurrence of which was always felt by the pioneer, and made this year still more memorable for reasons thus reported :—

"18th August.—This is indeed a memorable day ; a year since all the troubles in Demerara began ; a day on which we ought to humble ourselves before our God for all our sins, and, at the same time, to praise Him for the difficulties He has enabled us to overcome.

* The late Lord Macaulay.

"His Excellency the Governor sent to say he wished to see me at two o'clock. He informed me that Earl Bathurst highly disapproved of the memorial sent against me ; that he said the book was printed for the Society in England and not for the slaves ; that the meaning (of passages adduced) was spiritual and so to be understood ; that I did not appear to have been in the habit of giving copies to slaves ; that the masters who did not wish their slaves to attend me had power to prevent them, but that nothing was to be put in the way of those slaves whose masters wished them to attend ; that a church would be provided, and that they could attend which their masters thought proper.

"His Excellency also mentioned that the Council (*i.e.*, of the Berbice Colony) at the time of the revolt (in Demerara) had wished him to seize all my papers, but he would not comply with them."

From this time, things seem gradually to become a little more settled, though not without an occasional reminder of the storm that was passing away. In short, the returning self-respect of the Home Government and consequent firmness in maintaining that their instructions should have some measure of observance, began to produce their due effect ; and officials and society in general, both in the Colonies and at Home, would be led to feel that dominion in the West Indies was not to be left altogether in the hands of blustering bullies and cruel brutes.

Mr. Wray was encouraged with tokens of deeper earnestness in prayer and life shown by a number who regularly met for worship ; and illustrations, in other ways, of good resulting from his labours, with instances of it in particular individuals, now and then came to his knowledge.

A visitor of the prisoners in gaol, he remarks the absence, as a rule, of any there who have been under instruction ; whilst a free man informs him of the happy change on an estate where instruction and religion had for some years been cherished, how that thieving and Obeah had ceased. Distributing tracts on board vessels, Mr. Wray left "The End of Time" on a ship. Afterwards, from the captain of another vessel, he learnt what had been the result. On his way home the captain of that ship cursed wind and weather and Him that made them. Shocked at his own language, he went down into his cabin, took up the tract, and read it. The reading brought his sins to remembrance and deepened his convictions. To divert his mind he took a quadrant and went on deck for an observation, but the sun at that moment becoming obscured, caused his utterance of Watts's lines :—

> " Well might the sun in darkness hide ;
>   And shut His glories in,
>   When God, the mighty Maker, died
>   For man the creature's sin ; "

and such a change followed in himself that he was led with deep emotion to address all his men on the subject of religion ; and he had become a Christian character. "This," notes Mr. Wray, after he had looked out a large bundle of tracts for his informant with the prayer that God would bless them to all readers, "encourages me to go on distributing."

When, therefore, from among soldiers of the 60th regiment newly arrived from Bermuda, one with his wife appeared at the mission-room, and were found to be very pious and excellent people—the man glad not only to read the offered tracts himself, but to convey them to his fellow-soldiers, from whom he had numerous applications, and who read them with great attention—we naturally find the entry closes with the remark :—"I gave him a large supply to-day."

And if white colonists at present could in general shun the pioneer, it was otherwise with his white countrymen, or with white officials of Government. Here is an entry not to be omitted :—

"*3rd November.*—The Governor sent for me to ask if Mrs. Wray would undertake to teach his little girl an hour a-day."

"Mr. Morris, the Governor's secretary, requested if I would undertake the education of a little white orphan boy, left very destitute, whom he had kindly taken under his care out of mere pity."

But if the face of a white friend here and there showed itself, that of some faltering one, or of some foe, disappeared altogether from among men, under circumstances sadly painful—*e.g.*,

"Mr. S——, manager of ——, from whom at Smith's trial it was with the greatest difficulty truth could be elicited, in some cases only by producing his own signature, soon after Mr. Smith's death, was obliged to leave for England, on account of his health, and died on the way." "*August.*—George M——, late a member of Council, gone to England for his health, died as soon as he landed. One of his last acts was to sign the memorial against me ; also one of those who before lodged a complaint against me founded on a slanderous report. He is now gone to answer for his stewardship." "*4th September.*—Mr. J——, the searcher and waiter (Customs'), who interfered with my parcels, taken ill at the beginning of the week, resolutely refused to take any medicine, in an awful passion saying, 'I will be d——d to hell if I will take it,' died. Poor man ! this is an awful state to die in. His interference with my parcels will not profit him now." "*23rd December.* — Last night heard that one of the R——'s, who so much persecuted Mr. Smith and the negroes, on his way to England, jumped out of the cabin window and was drowned." "I hear that Mr. H——, one of the agents of the Berbice Association, who joined in so dreadfully persecuting the poor slaves after the British Government had returned (part of) the estates, became mad soon after he went to Europe, and died."

Towards the end of September occurs the entry :—

"As for the whip, I seldom hear it. Formerly it was almost daily sounding in our ears, and sometimes often in a day. Blessed be God for it."

And the following has some promise of progress, though it closes with a not inappropriate question :—

"Sunday afternoon I went to church. Only four or five adults there. Mr. W—— was catechizing some little slave children belonging to the Crown. He did not hesitate to make them say the preface to the Ten Commandments: 'I am the Lord thy God, who brought thee out of the land of Egypt, out of the house of bondage.' This, in a missionary, would have been looked upon as treason. The children have been taught to read by me, but were never taught that. Mr. Smith, in publishing the Ten Commandments for slaves, left out these words. Suppose, as they grow up, they should interpret that passage of Scripture as meaning they were to be delivered from slavery, are the missionaries to be blamed for it?"

Mr. Wray not only distributed Books of Common Prayer, but himself at times employed its petitions, and also encouraged members of his congregation who were so disposed, to commit portions to memory for their own use. Important anniversary days in his own life and work he did not let pass without corresponding reflection, humiliation, praise or prayer; now and then especially utilizing them in some such way. This year, the anniversary of his landing in Guiana, seventeen years ago, was preceded by reviewing and recopying his Confession of Faith made at Ordination, and says he :—

"I am more than ever confirmed in those truths which I have so long preached, and which I believed to be contained in the Bible. I have also compared them with the doctrinal Articles of the Church of England, and find they are conformable thereunto."

Also when again another Christmas and the end of another year came to pass, he reviews his preparation for pulpit work; noting his increased pleasure and profit, upon the whole, in studying his sermon, and that though "some discourses were what I may call 'second editions,' as at first they were written either at Gosport or in Demerara," still they were carefully revised; some had been made very useful; and though "all my preparation is very imperfect, and needs pardon, without due preparation my heart is greatly condemned," and though he took pains to write his sermons correctly, in delivering them he used no notes, but "I have also in general found much liberty in the delivery, and I desire to bless God for the assistance He has given me."

With the closing year one or more meetings were daily held in their only place of assembly, several days in succession. Small had been the increase in numbers during the eventful period which was terminating, but not a few were the tokens of growth in grace and knowledge shown by those who remained faithful, and of the Church's deepening piety amid the affliction which the year now past had seen. So all were ushered into the year

1825.

Commissioners of Legal Enquiry — Freed Slaves and Field Work — English Peasant and Negro Bondman — Dedication of Chapel-Site—Governor's Departure for England: Missionary's Daughters' Ditto—Travels of Latter—Opening of New Chapel—Beginning of Long Bodily Disorder—The Ten Commandments—Shock of Earthquake—Winkel Village: Official Inquiry and Change of Managers—Wray Examined—Return of Antoinette—Illness of Mrs. Wray—Misconduct of Whites: of a Military Officer—Climax in the Conflict—Court Martial—Officer Sentenced—Peaceful Results and Cheering Tokens.

USUAL congratulations and good wishes of negro and coloured Christian friends, if of none other, greeted him and his on Saturday, 1st January; which day and the following were much occupied with conference and preaching, praise and prayer. The cheer of another year thus entered seems to have stimulated enterprise, for, on the third day, the determination shortly to commence erecting a new chapel became settled, though not without feelings of anxiety on the subject. The year had its important events in the history both of missionary and mission, which will be detailed as they occur ; and there was gradual improvement. But all went on, we should never forget, amid a shocking state of morals around and in every class, noticed, as are also the shocking consequences of such living, here and there in the diary ; and amid serious sickness in the manse, or sad misbehaviour of whites, who began again to appear at the religious meetings, that must have been sore trials to patience. Much of these we leave with this brief mention, as we must leave the cases of earnest inquirers after truth who came from far and near, and the notes of catechumen classes, baptisms, admissions to fellowship, and of impressions at particular services, which are the usual experience of the faithful preacher of Christ and Church-pastor in such a sphere. What, too, befell bitter opponents of the work in Demerara must here be dismissed with Mr. Wray's own remark, penned in November, on hearing of the seizure of a newspaper there by the Governor, and the reported arrest of its new editor ; that editor's predecessor of 1823, on the way to England, being lost with the ship and all on board, and never more heard of :—

"God seems in a very awful and striking way to have marked His abhorrence of this (Mr. Smith's) persecution, even in this world, in His judgments upon individuals."

His Majesty's Commissioners of Legal Inquiry having lately arrived in Berbice, on 16th January, Mr. Wray called upon them to pay his respects. Many questions respecting the instruction and amelioration of the slaves were asked, and a request was made that he would write them on the subject ; a request, in a few days, duly complied with. One Commissioner, inquiring how it was that no slaves, made free, went to labour in the field ; was answered that such, in general, had never been accustomed to field-work, for rarely was it a field-negro that was freed. "This seemed to strike their minds," but, adds Mr. Wray in his private notes, "other reasons may be given which arise from slavery itself."

And these, in brief, are all founded on the degradation which healthy honest labour suffers from being always done by slaves, associated ever with bondage and its cruel accompaniments. It comes to be thought too degrading for a free person ; and a slave, made free, thinks himself far superior to a slave. Besides, a free man or two labouring in the field, would be followed by a driver with a whip in his hand, and it was not likely they would submit to this, and so not astonishing that—" I am not aware that any planters have ever offered to hire free people to perform field labour." How such a system seems to degrade all it touches !

Mr. Wray was not anxious to say much on topics other than religion and instruction. He was in a colony long and thoroughly permeated with the atmosphere of slavery ; the Commissioners themselves, or some of them, do not seem to have been free from its influence; and events of the past eighteen months showed how a missionary's utterances, the most simple or innocent, could be perverted by his enemies. One of the Commissioners, therefore, expressing the thought that, —" we should teach them (the slaves) that they are better off than the poor in England,"—his visitor remarks : " I did not make a direct reply, but this is a doctrine not found in the Bible."

The slave better off than the free man ! We should think not. Was it not enough that the pioneer was there to teach those in bonds to make the best, and how to make the best of their circumstances, as the Bible would have him, and, as he says, " I hope we do " ? But that he should teach them they were better off than those without the bonds, would have been to teach what, we need not say, is not only wanting in the Bible, but is utterly opposed to it, and, in fact, what was a plain falsehood, such as it should have shamed at least a Briton to utter. To have thus answered the Commissioner, however, would have been to invite as plain an intimation that he and his must prepare to leave the

Colony finally and for ever. But in his diary Wray waxes lengthy on the subject, running the risk of what it, if ever seized and used against him as his younger brother-missionary Smith's strictly-private journal had been against its owner, might say. John Wray well knew what country life and labourers in England were. Had he not spent his years up to manhood in the Yorkshire East Riding, with some years afterwards in the South? And now he had spent most of his missionary life on estates. So he is led on to compare the two, in substance thus :—

"(1). Unceasing reports of slaves run away to gain freedom : none of free people running away to become slaves.

"(2). Testimonies to the preciousness of liberty by slaves made free : none to the preciousness of bondage, by men made slaves.

"(3). (a) A pass, often tedious or difficult or impossible to obtain, required before a slave can go to a neighbouring estate, to worship in town, to market there, or be out after 8 P.M. without risks of stocks, flogging, gaol, seizure of market basket—a thing unheard of in England.

"(b) As is also the requirement of a master's consent to labourer's marriage, attendance at worship, child's baptism, or its going to school.

"(c) Or again, as is a change of masters—e.g., a bad for a better, being beyond the labourer's power ; the labourer's liability to be sold and forcibly separated from wife and children ; liability, for a trivial neglect, to be laid down, male or female, and cruelly whipped ; to have wife outraged by whites and no legal redress, often none at all ; to be without house as one's own, and liable to be searched at any moment :"

all so different with the free peasantry at home ; not to mention the lack of independence and openness, and of the ease with which neighbours visit one another, chat of politics or read the newspaper, or of the freedom with which a clergyman can visit the poorest of his flock without interruption, degradation, or suspicion ; more than enough, surely, to give the lie to such teaching, even without a vision of the man of Tarsus lifting his chained hands before his judges ; and, personification of Scripture truth, saying, " except these bonds."

In the afternoon of Lord's Day, 13th March, a company assembled on the site intended for the new chapel, and held a dedication service which consisted of Scripture-reading, prayer, and praise ; all seemly and sacred ; brought, however, into stronger relief by the occasional remark of some passing white, shocking as it was shameful.

During the same week Mr. Wray called on the Governor, who was shortly to depart for England on leave of absence, and who then promised him an introduction and recommendation to Sir Benjamin D'Urban, Governor of Demerara, meanwhile to be also Acting Governor of Berbice. The promise was fulfilled on the 21st, when Sir Benjamin told the missionary he would give him all that protection and patronage which the Governor himself had afforded. When, therefore, on the 23rd, amid all the honours of martial parade and music and salute of cannon that Berbice could furnish, Governor Beard took his departure, without misgiving Mr. Wray witnessed the scene, "pleased to see so much honour paid to one who has been my sincere friend and patron for about six years."

Less than two months and there came another departure to England, trying to the parental heart.

" *Friday*, 13*th May.*—Elizabeth and Rebecca went to Demerara to go on board the *Cecilia* for England, Captain Hepburn, who has kindly offered to give up his part of the passage-money. Mrs. Wray went with them. They took leave of me with many tears. We have long wished to send them for a short time to our native land that they may see something of a land of freedom, and of moral and religious society. They have made considerable improvement in writing, arithmetic, &c., &c. It is hard parting from them now that they have become, as it were, companions, especially to Mrs. Wray, but it is our indispensable duty for their benefit and usefulness. They have taught many poor heathen to read the Word of God, and instructed them in the Catechism

Oh, that they may feel the influence of religion on their own souls !"

No Blackheath or Walthamstow "Schools for Missionaries' Children" then existed. To meet the expense, a school for young ladies, kept by Mrs. Wray, helped in large measure ; but—

" My good friend, Mr. Thompson, who has been a father to me, and, indeed, to my father also, has kindly provided a school for them, and promises to render them any assistance in his power. In him, I know, they will find a friend. What reason have I to bless God for His goodness to me in raising up such a friend, and continuing him for more than twenty years !"

And so with the prayers of their loving father and of Christian friends in the church, they went and, with their mother, were nine days on board the *Cecilia* before the vessel sailed, when, bidding them farewell, Mrs. Wray returned to Berbice. The rest must be told in the words of Rebecca, now Mrs. Tuckett, as penned at the age of seventy-eight, in her first letter to the author :—

" We were sent to England together, I think in 1824 or 1825. Captain Hepburn, a friend of my parents, had the care of us. He took us to his home in Greenock. From that place we were sent on to Glasgow, where a family named Semple lived, who formerly resided in Berbice, and to whom mother had been very kind in sicknesses, and who were very pleased to do her a kindness in return. Mrs. Semple took us to Leith, put us on board a steamer bound for London, but which took passengers to a certain point near Scarborough, and sent them ashore. It was arranged that Mr. and Mrs. Thompson (the life-long friends of our father) should go to Scarborough (they lived in Hull) to meet us. I shall never forget the feeling of awe as we were put in the boat with two sailors all alone (it was quite dark), and rowed to the appointed place where Mr. Thompson had promised we should be met. Oh ! what should we do if no one met us ? But the God of our parents took care of us, and as we neared the place of landing—O joyful sound!—a voice out of the darkness was heard, ' Have you on board two young ladies from Berbice for Mr. Thompson ?' Our fears were dispelled : we were kindly received. Mr. Thompson was unable to come himself, for he was an old man, but trusty friends had supplied his place ; and we were soon at his lodgings and in bed, thankful to feel that for a time our wanderings had ceased.

"We soon went to Hull, and, after a time of rest, we were again on our travels to Wakefield, where was a school for ministers' daughters, though not exclusively so, but ministers paid less than the others. We spent three or four years there, only going to Hull for the midsummer holidays."

On 12th June, the new chapel was opened. Like all structures there, it was built of wood. Attentive hearers filled it when, in the forenoon, Mr. Wray preached from Isaiah lvi. 5, " My house shall be called a house of prayer for all people " ; and he remarks :—

" People of every colour and in every situation shall have free access to it, without respect of persons. Nothing of a sectarian principle shall ever enter its door as far as I can hinder it."

In the evening, the sermon was from Romans xv. 29 : " And I am sure that, when I come unto you, I shall come in the fulness of the blessing of the Gospel of Christ." After solemn prayers for himself and the work, he writes :—

" We have called it ' Protestant Mission Chapel,' because I hope and trust the great doctrines of the Reformation, and no other, will always be preached in it. I am well persuaded that they are the doctrines of the Bible, and that they alone will prove effectual to the conversion of sinners. They are despised doctrines, but they always have been so."

In July came the first tokens of a long and trying complaint, which ultimately necessitated a visit to England. The effects of a moist tropical climate on the liver are well known, and on Lord's Day, the 10th, Mr. Wray notes :—

" I have experienced such severe pains in my back that I have scarcely been able to move and to attend to the duties of the day.

On the next day sent for the doctor ; found it arose from bile, and that a large dose of medicine was needed to prevent a severe attack of illness."

Successful in this, the mischief, nevertheless, upon the intestines went on until, after years of gradual advance, and, at times, of much suffering, only an operation would serve to meet the case. Meantime, with what relief he could otherwise obtain, the pioneer remained at his post.

Continuing his faithful ministry, the attendance of free people, as also the number of baptisms and marriages, slowly increased. Expounding again the Ten Commandments, the preacher found it difficult work, and—

"sometimes felt almost ashamed of being so pointed as I must necessarily be in this place, particularly on the 4th, 7th, 9th, and 10th. I have, however, reason to believe they have been useful, and many of the people have been very attentive. I have written the substance, but have often been led with earnestness to apply the subject in language not committed to paper, and in all my discourses have endeavoured to lead the people to Jesus."

Shocks of earthquakes, so terrible and fatal on some of the neighbouring islands and countries, are but seldom and slightly felt in Guiana. About ten o'clock on the night of 20th September, however, the mission household and the whole town were roused by a severe shock which lasted two or three minutes. Mr. Wray woke to find all the house rocking like a cradle or a ship at sea. Happily no buildings fell, and, beyond the fright, no persons suffered.

The Commissioners of Legal Inquiry, as part of their labours, held an investigation into the management of the Crown people at the Winkel Village. This had been in the hands of Mr. Walker, formerly agent for the Crown estates, and then friendly and helpful to Mr. Wray. But about 1823, a difference arose between him and the missionary, who, not able to approve a course proposed by the agent, consequently withdrew from any day-school instruction of the children; and Mr. Walker, besides further opposing its minister, stopped the children's attendance at the mission chapel. During the inquiry Mr. Wray was before the Commissioners three times examined on oath; and though the first time he refrained as far as he could involving Mr. Walker, since the latter in a communication to the Commissioners blamed Mr. Wray for his failure, the pioneer was obliged afterwards to say many things in his own vindication which otherwise he would not have done—

"for God, my heavenly Father, knows that I did not wish to injure him, and all that I have written and said has been in self-defence. I freely forgive Mr. Walker for all the injury he has tried to do me."

On 8th October Mr. Walker was dismissed by the Home Government, and Mr. Kyte appointed in his place; and on the 16th, the new agent allowing it, as many of the Crown children as their parents wished, began again their attendance at chapel.

November saw another return; for on Wednesday, the 8th, Antoinette, the laundress kidnapped by Bush negroes eleven years before, was brought back to town by two of them who had themselves been eighteen years away, and who, put in gaol, escaped during the night and set off again. On the 10th Mr. Wray went to see her. She knew him and, throwing herself at his feet, exclaimed, " O, my massa, my massa ! " She looked very wild, and had forgotten some parts of the Creole language, but made inquiries after Mrs. Wray, and two daughters each by name. The man who stole her was killed a fortnight afterwards in a quarrel about her. Often wishing to escape, she could not. She tried to get into the hands of the white people who formed an expedition into the bush in 1818, but was dreadfully beaten for attempting, and, with hands and feet tied, carried along by the runaways. The only daughter of an old respectable negro attending the mission chapel, the aged man was almost overcome with joy at having found her who had been so long lost to him.

For some weeks Mrs. Wray had been seriously unwell, and for many more, until far into February following, continued so. A fall some time before, was thought, at least in part, to have induced a condition of body which several times seemed beyond the possibility of cure, and to threaten speedy dissolution. Happily the support and stay of the Christian were her's and her husband's, else, indeed, heart must have failed in view of the many claims of family, school, and pastoral duty which had to be met. However, the pioneer did what he could ; notwithstanding all, succeeding on 24th November in re-organising the Sunday School, and the improvement of the Mission went on.

But as if Satan, by his children amongst men, must make one more effort to check the work or destroy it, the gross misconduct of some whites about this time caused considerable annoyance, if nothing worse, and several months' unpleasantness.

On Lord's Day, 13th November, some whites at chapel behaved so ill that several of the congregation sent afterwards to the missionary to say that, unless a stop was put to it, they could not attend ; which led to Mr. Wray's addressing a letter to the Fiscal on the subject. This grosser ill-conduct may have been connected with a previous piece of behaviour on the part of a military official, so scandalous and dangerous that Mr. Wray had taken a very determined course.

"*Friday, 4th November.*—I was much disturbed and annoyed by Mr. Sherburne. I was obliged to engage in writing unpleasant letters instead of preparation for the Sabbath."

This led in the long run to the arrest of the offender, his trial by Court Martial, a verdict against him on some of the charges, and to the sentence that, in presence of the troops assembled on parade, he should be publicly and severely reprimanded; the Court Martial being induced, as they expressly assert,—

"to award so lenient a sentence from its appearing that on his feeling convinced of the great impropriety of his conduct towards Mr. Wray, he made the only reparation in his power, by tendering his apology on his honour, and expressing his sincere concern that he should so far have forgotten himself as to address that gentleman in the manner he did."

Pulteney J. Poole Sherburne was Lieutenant and Barrack Master. "He had put himself," says Mr. Wray,

"at the head of the anti-mission faction, and had become bolder in the attack than any before him, at least openly."

In addition to addressing "certain scurrilous, abusive, and improper letters and papers to the Rev. John Wray," he is charged with threatening violence to him and Mrs. Wray, " to the terror and injury of the latter, she being in a very weak state of health." The whole proceeding, in fact, besides the toil and fatigue in which they involved her husband, were calculated to have anything but a favourable effect upon her health, distressed as she became as to what would happen to the accused, " who, according to common report, began much to fear the issue," and at the thought of having to give evidence, " which was much against her (recovery)."

The Court Martial met on 2nd January, 1826, and sat for nine days. Mr. Wray thought the members composing it, " just and conscientious men, desirous to find out the truth." On Saturday, 7th January, they attended at the manse to take Mrs. Wray's evidence, when fourteen or fifteen officers were there most of the day. " They behaved in the most gentlemanly and polite manner, as they have done through the whole affair."

"Mr. Sherburne seems to have taken considerable pains to scrape up all the idle tales about town that have been propagated

against me for the last twelve years, and even applied to the
Secretary's office for papers containing the reprimands addressed
to me by Governor Bentinck in 1817 respecting the late Crown
estates, and the disputes I had with him (Bentinck) on that
account ; but I protested against it, and produced the Minutes of
the Council myself, and my correspondence with Earl Bathurst
on my appeal to him from the ill-treatment I received from the
Governor, who professed to have derived his authority from the
Earl, but which his Lordship denies, promises to call for an
explanation, and also writes me that if I return to Berbice I may
be assured of receiving protection from the Colonial government,
and the respect due to a minister of the Gospel. The correspondence was read in open court. Mr. Sherburne had also a long list
of witnesses from whom he evidently intended to draw all the
scandal against me he could, for they knew not a word of the
matter that was before the Court (one of them was at Gibraltar
at the time). The two or three that he did examine were as
much in my favour as his. It is evident the poor man had been
deceived by the false reports he had heard from time to time, and
that he had eagerly listened to all the scandal of the town.
I pity him, and pray that God may give him true repentance.
I hope and trust that this affair will have a good effect in giving
us peace and rest "

Which hope was realized, for this seems to have been the
end of such troubles. The proceedings and finding of the
Court Martial were approved by the Home authorities, and
about the 1st of March, 1826, Mr. Wray received from head-
quarters an official report of the charges, finding, and
sentence, which is still preserved. Doubtless he and his
suffering partner refrained from expressing their utmost,
and the accused may well have thought himself happy in
escaping with so light a sentence; but the object was gained;
that was enough for the pioneer.

With all these clouds about, the change of years was not
without several cheering tokens. 1825 closed with a
fellowship of fifty-three members, a Sunday school of 125
attendants ; the mission had begun to re-assume its former

progressive character, and by the time March, 1826, was reached, the health of Mrs. Wray had begun to revive.

1826.

Busy Life—Sad Death of Mission Enemies: Cohen, McWatt—Mysteries Solved—Mrs. D——th: Sad End of a Strange Course—Prosperity of Mission — Beginning at Lonsdale — Farewell to Pious Soldiers — Indifference of Clergyman—Return of Governor—Dismissal of Council —Kindness of Governor—Occasions of Dreary, &c., Work—Arrival of Slave-Protector—Transport of Chapel to Missionary Society— Protector's Approval—New Code of Slave Law: Consequent Stir— Chapel Broken into—Legal Slave Marriages—First Arrival of Steamboat and Bishop—Kindness of a Commissioner—Tokens of Progress.

In addition to Mrs. Wray's more private and select ladies' school, and a day school conducted on the plan of the British and Foreign School Society, three or four week-day religious meetings were held, besides three, sometimes four public services and a meeting of the Sunday School on the Lord's Day. These, with family claims, and constant visits from slaves and others living at a distance, when such came to town ; with calls to converse with persons under spiritual concern, to visit the sick or to bury the dead ; and with a growing correspondence ; kept all occupied. Numbers more rapidly grew, and a spurt occasionally was given by some event foreshadowing the passing away of the old and the coming in of something new. Now it was the departure of some notorious opposer, then the arrival of some new friend or some order from the Home Government, begun, at last, in earnest to amend the lot of the slave.

"26*th January.*—I hear that Cohen, who threatened to burn down the chapel, leaving the Colony for the benefit of his health, *died at sea.* He looked miserable as he passed in the street. The unhappy white woman, who lived in fornication with him, left him some time ago."

"19*th February.*—About three weeks ago Mr. William McWatt, a witness against Mr. Smith, went on horseback into the bush on the Berbice East Coast, and has never been heard of since. Negroes sent in search could not find him. His brother, with the postholder and a party of Indians, spent some days searching, but not the smallest vestige of him or his horse could be discovered. A suspicion that the negroes of the estate, upon whom he was reported to be very severe, had had some concern in making away with him, was, after inquiry on the spot by the Fiscal, I believe thought groundless. It is now supposed that some of the runaway negroes have captured him."

Accordingly in March another expedition, including several of Mr. Wray's Sunday School Teachers, entered the bush, and, after about ten day's absence, returned, but without any account of McWatt. Another month passed without a clue, and then and therefore, about 16th April,

"a proclamation by the Governor stating that strong suspicion is entertained of McWatt's having been murdered, offers 100 Joes reward for the discovery of the perpetrators."

All in vain, and the matter remained a mystery. In truth William McWatt never entered the bush, and Mr. Wray, and something like a generation, were to pass before the mystery was solved. This solution, taken from Mr. Foreman's "Echoes from Slave-Time," we append in a note,* as

---

* "Years rolled on. The estate changed hands. Many of the slaves had died or been removed to other estates, when, on the new proprietor having one of the trenches on the estate deepened, the shovelmen came on some bones and the stirrup of a saddle. The master having been informed of the circumstance, he had these remains carefully removed, when the conviction fastened on himself and also on others, that these bones were those of the missing horse and its rider of so many years before. But how came they there? That was the puzzle. Some of the old slaves were sought out, and promised that nothing should be done to them if they would only tell all they knew about it. And this was their story. That one morning the Massa rode into the field where they were hoeing the cotton plants, with the big whip in his hands he always carried ; that, without a word he gave a severe cut with this whip across the back of a tall and powerful slave, who, in the anguish of the moment, swung round and dealt his assailant a blow on the back of the head with the hoe he had in his hand. The

also, from the same paper, the solution of a similar mystery connected with an estate often passed by the present author. The two will serve to illustrate the condition of things under that Slavery which was so cherished and defended by some as a happy institution both for master and man. We here proceed with the following, similarly illustrative, but

master fell from his horse and never recovered consciousness ; in fact, in a few moments he ceased to live. Great was the consternation of the slaves when they found the master was dead. They secured the horse, and held a consultation as to what was to be done. At length it was decided to kill the horse, and bury it together with the saddle, bridle, and whip, and their dead master's body all together at the bottom of the trench nigh at hand, and in which there was not very much water, Two 'stop-offs' were put in the trench, the water baled out of the space between them, and a huge pit dug, into which the man and the horse with the saddle, bridle, and whip were laid. This being done, the bottom of the trench was carefully levelled, the 'stop-offs' as carefully removed, so as to leave no trace of their existence, and the water flowed over the grave of the dead. The driving of the herd of cattle, and the flock of sheep, for a day or two along the road from the house, past the field where the slaves had been at work, effectually destroyed all traces of the marks of the feet of the horse thereon. So that at the time the master was missed—beyond the fact that the master had been seen to ride out of the house-yard —no trace of him could be found. The slave who struck the fatal blow had been dead some years when the remains of the horse and its rider were found."

"There was an estate with a long Dutch name up the Berbice river, but to which the name of Egypt got attached. I have heard it spoken of as Egypt by persons who had no idea how it got that name. It became noted for the cruelty with which the slaves were treated on it ; and when the slaves in Berbice came to know a little of Bible history, some of them gave to it the name of Egypt. One of the modes of punishment adopted there was to put the slaves into an old boiler or old iron chest, and to set others of them to beat the outside of it with hammers, by means of which some, so punished, lost entirely the sense of hearing. Near to the buildings was a long row of tombs of managers and overseers who had died there. One result of the cruelty practised on the slaves was that they bound themselves together by what they deemed an oath of the most solemn and terrible character, that no selected as indicative also of the changes and the often strange events going on around the pastor, which not seldom called for his presence and effort in some form or other.

"*25th February.*—This evening I attended the funeral of a Mrs. D——th. About seven years ago she was brought from Barbadoes by a Berbice merchant as his kept mistress. Soon after her arrival she suffered three months' imprisonment for cruelty, he also paid a heavy fine ; and for this cruelty her name is in the tract lately published by the Anti-Slavery Society. Two or three years ago the man who kept her went to England. She soon followed him. Making over to her his property in town (New Amsterdam), which he valued at 30,000 dollars (£6250),

manager or overseer should live more than six months on the estate. This came to my knowledge in the following manner. When my dear friend, the late Rev. John Dalgliesh, had been about a year in the Colony, he was sent for to see an old woman who was very ill. He was asked to go at once, as she said, 'She could not die till she had seen him.' He went, and after she had ordered all other persons out of the room, she told Mr. Dalgliesh what I have narrated above, and a great deal more. The burden on her mind was this : she had been one of the slaves in the house, and hence on her devolved the work of putting into the gurglets that which acted as a slow poison. She told Mr. Dalgliesh what this was, but for very obvious reasons I shall not mention it here. She also told from how many persons she had thus taken away their life, giving their names, or the names by which they were known to her, or a description of some personal peculiarity they possessed ; and now, as she said, 'She could not die,' because all these murders were on her soul. ' Yet,' said she, ' had I not done it, the other slaves would have killed me.' There was one overseer who escaped. He was a young man, who treated the slaves on that estate with such exceptional kindness that they did not like to carry out on him their oath of vengeance. Yet, what were they to do ? ' How could they let him off ? They must kill him for their oath's sake,' said some. Others, that this woman should try and frighten him away by the awful stories she could tell him, or manage that he should hear. Apparently the plan succeeded, for he shortly after left the estate, and went back, the woman said, to his own country. There seems to have existed in slave-time a great dread of being poisoned—and probably not without cause—on the part of slaveowners, or those who managed the estates."

he got married. Where she lived in London, she represented herself as under the guardianship of Mr. A., and that the property was left her by her mother. She appeared so very modest and virtuous that a simple-hearted young man fell in love with her, and married her as a virtuous young lady of property. She left England to settle her property and then return; but the young man came after her. Not until this morning, when it was discovered to him by her papers, and by a young friend, as he assured me, had he found that she had kept him entirely in the dark; and he knew not a word of her former conduct, or that she came by her property in the way she did. He asked me many particulars about her, and told me he had been completely taken in. He believes she died of a broken heart, for having so deceived him; but, afraid to discover her own character, keeping everything perfectly secret. Poor, unhappy woman! She is gone to render an account of her conduct and deception to the Judge of all. A few days ago he wished to have a pew in the chapel; but behold, instead of a pew, a coffin. It was a very large funeral, and I felt much earnestness in speaking to the people. The poor young man is much distressed. He opened his mind freely, and I endeavoured to comfort him."

Accompanying the many and now more unfettered labours of the mission, amid the changes around, there appeared tokens of general improvement in the manners of the town, and cases of decided renewal in the hearts and lives of individual sinners. Prayers for the presence and work of the Holy Spirit were not without marked response. "Paul planted, Apollos watered, and God gave the increase." On Lord's Day, 23rd April, Mr. Wray notes with joy, not only the cheering numbers, and the aspect of things in town, but, pioneer-like, the first sign of extension.

"Whatever may be the feelings and sentiments of individuals and lukewarm Christians on the subject of missions, I rejoice greatly in God's great goodness to-day. Baptized a woman from the country, the wife of Bernard, whom I baptized last holidays. Two or three came for books. They have now a small society on Lonsdale. May God help them to look to Him for His blessing!"

Which was vouchsafed, and the small society became, before long, the Lonsdale Mission Church and Station.

Soldiers and soldiers' wives, among whom a good work had been going on, had, about this time, to say farewell, being under orders to leave. The parting was with deep, mutual regret. They had been blest and made a blessing. As if in mitigation of the loss, a pious American sea-captain arrived, who remained a-while, helping and being himself helped in Divine things. The following is indicative of a difference in more respects than one :—

"*Lord's Day*, 25*th June*.—Mr. W—— (the clergyman) absent some time previously in the Islands, after an absence of about nine months in England, I believe on private business, has returned and preached to-day. Had it not been for our Chapel, the people would have been destitute of any worship in the English language. But such ministers are the most approved by a large majority."

On the evening of 9th July, Governor Beard had returned again, and Mr. Wray was amongst the many who, Monday, the 10th, called on him to pay their respects. Soon after, important changes were announced.

"I see by the Wednesday paper that the old council who have been opposed to religion and amelioration, the very men who were opposed to me as well as to the Governor, are dismissed by His Majesty and another council appointed. Lately a very strong party of the leading people presented a strong memorial against him (the Governor), the council taking the lead ; but God has completely confounded their devices. I have full confidence in God that He will accomplish His own purposes in His own time in the conversion and salvation of poor sinners."

Toward the end of the month, Mr. Wray called again on his Excellency, and had a longer interview than was possible just after landing ; found him as affable and kind as ever ; "promising, when time permitted, to come and see the new chapel." His Excellency, some weeks later, contributed

£20 towards the cost, and, later still, informed the missionary of donations obtained from the Fiscal and several members of the Council, and of others he hoped to obtain, as opportunity offered for commending the work to the rest of the members. And the end of July was not reached without further news of intended attacks on mission work by bitter enemies, editors of the press, being thwarted through the death or discomfiture of the assailants.

With an increasing flow of engagements, it is not strange to read occasionally of some work as dreary, trying, or weary —*e.g.*,

"18*th July.*—This evening, a funeral of the poor person I have visited a few times in her sickness, but saw no change in her. Have lately visited another person in the same state. But it is indeed dreary work to speak to people who know nothing of God or of Christ. Felt very different in visiting another person who has been accustomed to attend religious instruction and whose heart has been affected with it."

"12*th August.*—This week, have been much tried by some of the children in the school. Sometimes I think my lot among them is a hard one, and I long to have more time for study, but yet I hope it will in the end prove useful to many, particularly here, where education is in so low a state."

"*Lord's Day, 13th August.*—(After recording numerous engagements.) Both myself and Mrs. Wray have spent the whole of this day in the active service of our blessed Redeemer. At night, we felt very weary in the work, but not of it, for it is blessed work to labour for Jesus. Oh that I may live and die in His service, and reign with Him for ever in heaven!"

The following are red-letter days :—

"*Wednesday, 30th August.*—Called on a gentleman (David Power, Esq.) who has arrived as Protector of the slaves. Find he was acquainted with Dr. Milne in the East, and that Mr. Hastie, in Madagascar, was a friend of his. He seems an excellent man, and very zealous. I bless God that I have lived to see such a day as this. I certainly did not think it would take place in my time."

"*2nd October.*—Have been able to take out a transport conveying the chapel to the Missionary Society. Much distressed lest I should meet with opposition, but I bless God that I have been able to accomplish it. Evident, however, from questions asked, that there had been a wish in some to stop it on the pretext that the land was purchased with the subscriptions raised in the Colony and was consequently public property. Was able to show that the land was not so purchased, that they were applied entirely to the erection of the chapel destroyed by fire ; and, had it been otherwise, the money, as appears by the wording at the head of the paper, was given to the Society to erect a chapel. Blessed be God, it is now secured to the Society, and I hope and trust it will prove a blessing to multitudes."

"*29th October, Sabbath.*—Just before Sunday-School commenced, the Protector called and expressed his high gratification with the Winkel people and their improvement. He also expressed in very flattering terms his high approbation of our poor labours and of the benefit the Colony had received from them."

"*Wednesday, 1st November.*—A morning long to be remembered in the Colony of Berbice. This day the new Negro Code commences. Blessed be God that I have lived to see the day. Ten years ago, when we were labouring under such persecution, and when, in New Amsterdam, we could hear the whip daily in almost every direction, and the screams of the punished negroes, both male and female, we had not the most distant idea of such a change. But, blessed be God, it has gradually decreased and for the last three or four years we have hardly heard it at all."

Among chief points in the Code were—considerable modifications of punishment by the whip, and its abolition in the case of females. Another point was : Admission of slave evidence in Courts of Justice, if the witness understood the obligation of an oath. Consequent on this, the Protector, on 1st November, sent to the three ministers of religion belonging to New Amsterdam—viz., the Lutheran, the Missionary, and the Church of England clergyman, for a return of all the slaves sufficiently instructed in the Christian religion to understand the nature of an oath. The pioneer would be able to meet the requirement " with confidence and not be ashamed." But the Lutheran minister is reported as answering that he had not instructed any, but he would now begin ; whilst the English clergyman, two days after, gave in his resignation. "I suppose," remarks Mr. Wray, " he was not able to stand the test, but there is another day fast approaching when he and I must stand before the judgment seat of Christ."

Certainly the new Code must have made plenty of stir in men's minds ; but one way of expressing opinion upon it, if the pioneer's conjecture be right, was not polite, much less reverential ; characteristic, however, of foul slavery.

" *Saturday*, *4th*.—Last night some person or persons broke into the yard, entered the Chapel, took out the Ten Commandments which were pasted on a board with another Scripture lesson, daubed them over with mud, and hung them up as a sign upon the gate, I suppose to signify their contempt of the laws just come into force. Fiscal came to see the mischief done. In to-night's paper Governor and Fiscal offer twenty Joes reward for the detection of the offenders."

Another chief point was the Legalization of Slaves' Marriages. Hence :—

" *19th November*.—A day long to be remembered. The first two legal marriages of slaves under the New Laws, by Licence from the Protector, took place ; and, by the consent of the parties, before the whole congregation. Everything was conducted with the greatest order. One of them was also baptized. The chapel was crowded with slaves from the country. I preached on the subject of marriage. The Protector and Mr. Kinchela, who is one of His Majesty's Commissioners, attended chapel."

Sunday, 3rd December, was another day of mark. Steam vessels had come into use for coasting voyages, and the first to appear in Berbice now arrived. Further, she had on board the first Bishop to put in an appearance. It was his lordship of Barbadoes, one of the two appointed under the new laws, which included State Establishments for religious instruction in the West Indies ; the other Bishop being his lordship of Jamaica. Many Episcopalians as well as others, will share John Wray's sentiments at the sight.

"Steamer arrived from Demerara with the Bishop of Barbadoes. They excited great curiosity ; the Bishop as well as the steamboat being a new sight here. In the forenoon the bugle sounded for the militia to turn out and receive the Bishop. I am sorry his Lordship did not dispense with this honorary Sabbath-breaking. He did not preach, but confirmed six persons. 4*th*.—In the forenoon the Bishop took his departure. The militia were turned out and a number of troops from the Fort came to honour his Lordship's departure. A salute was fired from the Fort. I went with my little boy to see the steam-boat. I wished him also to see that the Bishop was only a man. To me, so much military parade to honour a minister of Jesus Christ, particularly on the holy Sabbath, seemed strange ; and I could not help contrasting it with the circumstances related of Paul, Acts xx.*

"8*th*.—I certainly count it a greater honour to have been the instrument, unworthy as I am, of establishing the first Christian churches among the heathen in these Colonies, and introducing education and marriage among them, than all the worldly honours bestowed upon the Bishop in the beginning of the week."

"12*th December*.—His Majesty's Commissioners of Colonial Inquiry left Berbice. One of them, J. Kinchela, expressed to the Protector his high approbation as to the improvement the

---

* Happily much of this state parade is a thing of the past. It would have gratified the venerable Wilberforce as well as the pioneer, could they have foreseen that one of the first to discard so much ostentation was Samuel, son of the philanthropist, when made Bishop of Oxford. " I recollect," said one, who is now almost, if not quite, the senior member of the University, " I recollect when a Bishop of Oxford never drove into Oxford without four horses and two powdered footmen ; and what does Sam do ? He gets upon a horse and rides in by himself, without so much as a groom behind him ! I met him myself to-day." *Life of the Right Reverend Samuel Wilberforce, D.D.*, vol. i. p. 353.

Crown slaves have made, and desired him to say that at any time he should be willing to give his testimony to the beneficial effects of moral and religious instruction among them. He left 44 guilders with the Protector towards the cost of the chapel."

Though "sorry to see so little fruit of my labours among the free people, and to see them lead such a useless life, and manifest so much indifference to Christianity;" and though his little daughter Jane had lately been long and very unwell, the year closed with many encouraging signs of progress. The *Gazette* of 27th December says :—

"A most favourable and visible change has taken place in the customs of the slaves at holidays. We no longer behold them indulging in those disgusting practices which used to be considered indispensable to the celebration of their festivals. In town, during the Christmas holidays, every respect was paid to sobriety, decency, and good order. We have not seen or heard of a single instance of intoxication among them."

The congregation had considerably increased : forty-one adults had been baptized, and twelve admitted to communion. The Sunday School numbered 230, being considerably more than one-fourth of the children in town; lack of a better room and a better supply of good teachers beginning now to be much felt. Marriages of slaves grew more numerous, and "almost daily applications for books evinced the thirst of the negroes for knowledge, and their desire to be taught to read."

1827.

Uninterrupted Prosperity — Terrible Accident — Opposition to Manumission-Clause — Protector's Courage and Success — Death of Mr. Davies — Arrangements for Work in Demerara — Shocking Sights — Protector's Departure for England — Also of Mr. Wray's Son, Robert — Economical Management.

AMID customary salutations, therefore, 1827 was entered with brighter hope and more of cheer than several Januarys of late. His record is :—

"In peace, as far as I know, with all around ; myself, my dear wife, and our children are in health, and we have a brighter prospect of extending the kingdom of our blessed Saviour than at any former period. 'Bless the Lord, O my soul, and all that is within me ; bless His holy name.'"

And his aspiration naturally—

"Oh that this may be the best year we have ever enjoyed !"

It was not unrealized. Of course he was occasionally cognizant of some painful event such as came from old slavery or in other ways ; and though a few who began to run well grew weary, or one now and then openly went back, the number attending instruction and worship continued to grow, and persons from far and near seeking the missionary's guidance or the means of learning, gradually and, as years followed, more uninterruptedly multiplied ; so that 1827 may be viewed as the period when, shallows and rapids passed, the current ran a safer, deeper, quieter, larger stream, that thus continued until life and labours on earth came to an end.

Not a small gratification was it to discover in those who came, sometimes the child of years ago that had been taught and then lost sight of ; or adults first seen, who yet had been taught by some such former scholar, or had themselves picked up the knowledge of reading and religion from some stray manual. But, whether with old attendants or new comers, religion was his chief concern ; and pages of particulars, many concerning individuals expressed by name, testify his patient, faithful, tender care, both as a minister of the Word and a pastor of the flock.

The year was but seventeen days old when a terrible accident shocked the neighbourhood. The Crown slaves were engaged in erecting a steam saw-mill for Government, the chimney of which had reached a height of eighty feet, when the scaffolding gave way and one fine young man of twenty years, a mason, highly esteemed by his manager, fell from the top. Others in imminent danger escaped unhurt. The poor fellow, alive when picked up, died in a few hours ; and on the next day, amid many tokens of respect and the lamentations of a multitude that followed the remains, was buried by the missionary, who conducted a short and suitable service both in the Winkel village and at the grave side.

13th February was an important day in Berbice, as touching the new Slave-Code. Opposition was made to the manumission of a female and her child according to the compulsory manumission clause. The Protector and the parties could not agree about appraisers, and the Court was applied to. Mr. Wray, in common with many of the whites, including most of the members of the old Council, with the principal planters and merchants, attended the Court-House. The opposition was by the attorneys of the child's uncle, then absent in Holland, and was based upon the assertion that the money offered was not honestly and honourably obtained. But, says Mr. Wray—

"Their whole address was rather an indirect attack on the clause of the law than anything else. The Protector, however, completely confuted all that was said, reading a letter from the Fiscal in favour of the woman, and maintaining that the state in which she lived with the child's father was to be charged rather upon the whites than upon the slaves. He observed, ' As for the scurrility of this small community he had heard enough, but he attended only to authentic facts.' The word ' cant ' was never more strikingly applied than by him to the speech just delivered, and to the idle conversation so general among us. The opposition being made by the agents of the child's uncle, he also dwelt, with considerable energy and feeling, on that avarice which makes men traffic in their own blood." "Such plain truths had not been delivered before in their hearing with such boldness and energy. He spake as one that cared not for the face of man. The Governor presided with great dignity, prudence, and impartiality ; and as the other party refused to comply with the law in appointing an appraiser, the Court did it for them. The father had lived for years with the mother of the child. The discussion was considered as very important to the whole Colony. I rejoice that the Protector was so pointed on the reception that scurrility and scandal meet with in the Colony, particularly of any one who may appear to be friendly to amelioration and instruction. For my part, I have suffered a martyrdom of feeling from base and false reports, and I thank God the time has come when a man is not afraid to stand up in the Court-House and tell them the truth. Not long ago he dined at the Governor's, in company with President Wray* and Colonel Goodman (both members of the Court Martial that tried Mr. Smith), and boldly told them his opinion of their treatment of Mr. Smith."

Some weeks later the Protector, having, along with the Governor, been attacked through the press by several ex-Councillors, again replied vigorously and fearlessly; helping thus to clear the air, and make it possible for friends of humanity more easily to live and breathe.

23rd April brought sad tidings of Mr. Davies, Demerara. The first missionary to follow the pioneer, he had, since the insurrection, struggled on, but now sank. A letter, telling of his serious illness, came to hand but a little while before a messenger arrived to say he was dead. In half-an-hour Mr. Wray was sailing thither to see if he could render any assistance; "weather very rainy and disagreeable, and I was as wet all night as I possibly could be." Friends, however, had done all that was required, and the disappointment in not seeing his old friend and fellow-worker once more before death, was modified by the information that an earlier arrival would have only found the patient unable to recognize him. After other reflections, naturally comes the following :—

"I earnestly hope the Directors will send out a steady, pious, and affectionate minister to his people. I doubt not a large church and congregation will soon be gathered, and that many of the East Coast negroes and members will join with them. A few of these now live in town, and have repeatedly requested

* No relation to the pioneer.

my advice respecting what church they should join, and if another missionary would come among them. It would be a pity to give up this promising missionory field, where the labours of the Society have been so abundantly blessed, and especially when a large chapel is ready for their hands."

Returning on the 26th, Mr. Wray reached home on the 28th, with face so dreadfully burnt through exposure to the hot sun, "that I was rendered almost incapable of doing anything."

Demerara was now destitute, indeed, of its first missionaries. More than three years had elapsed since the blow fell which followed the disturbance, and nothing had been done to repair the ruin. But the pioneer hoped on, not only in wish but in work, doing his utmost to stay further declension, and to give a turn to affairs. Despite, therefore, his many engagements and much toil in Berbice, he voyaged to Georgetown at intervals of two or three months, to spend ten days or a fortnight in unceasing preaching, catechizing, administration of ordinances, converse with candidates for fellowship, or any who wished an interview; until at last, after a further twenty months' interval, his request and wishes were gratified by the arrival at Demerara, in 1828, of another brother who was long to labour, and under whom, by God's great blessing, another happy and prosperous course of the mission was inaugurated.

Yet on went the work in Berbice, steadily growing, notwithstanding the follies and sins of a few of the baptized, or an occasional reminder of what had been a frequent experience, now happily to prove only a relic of receding institutions.

"12th June.—Called to see the Protector. While engaged in conversation he was called out to two negroes, who presented a most disgusting and shocking appearance. Their fleshy parts were cut into large furrows with the cart whip, blood dropping or standing upon their lacerated parts, or, as one walked along

stooping, oozing out of the wounds. The very sight made the
Protector quite faint. Their owner is in England. I was in
hopes such barbarous punishments had ceased, but it would
seem not."

" *Lord's Day, 17th June.*—After morning service, between
eight and nine o'clock, found a boy about eleven years old in our
passage waiting for me. He had a chain upon him, fast locked
with two or three padlocks, and a large weight hanging down
his thigh in the shape of a window-weight. Found he was a
boy Mr. Sherburn hired, and had put in chains. The boy had
worn them about a week, and Mr. Sherburn had frequently
beaten him severely. Sent to fetch beef, the boy took the
opportunity of calling to inquire if it were proper for him to go
to the Protector. I of course told him the Protector was here
on purpose to inquire into the complaints of slaves, and directed
him to go to him."

With such an official, many beside the missionary, would
be sorry to part ; but,

" Mr. Power, His Majesty's Protector of Slaves, on 7th July,
sailed for England. In the morning he called to take his leave
of us. We parted from him with great regret. He has boldly
advocated both humanity and religious instruction, and has paid
high compliments to our feeble labours."

Another parting was at hand :—

" *16th July.*—Our dear Robert went to England. We hope
and trust our God will go with him. Many of every colour,
bond and free, from the Fiscal to the slave in the field, showed
their respect by making him presents. In very delicate health,
it is necessary to send him home ; also on account of his religious
and moral improvement. Oh that God may provide for him
and bless him, and carry him in safety to the land of our
nativity ! He goes under the care of a kind lady ; also Lindoe,
a member of the church, and a person of an excellent character."

Robert arrived safely with letters to Mr. Thompson (Hull),

to his sisters, and their teacher, Miss Arnold, Westgate, Wakefield; and himself entered Silcoates School, near that town, to continue his education. Postage in those days was costly, and many were the business letters Mr. Wray had to write; but several cherished epistles to his daughters at school or elsewhere, chiefly folio sheets well filled, convey the words of an intelligent, affectionate, Christian father's heart and mind. One or two sentences from that of which their brother was the bearer, will show, among other things, the economy that had to be practised.

"We have received Elizabeth's letter of 26th March, and were happy to hear you were well, and diligently engaged in your studies. We also rejoice that you wish to remain another year at school, and gladly comply with your desires. We hope and trust that you will endeavour to make all the improvement you can, and store your minds with useful knowledge. Pray to God for the direction of His Holy Spirit, and He will bestow upon you the blessings you seek."

"Captain H. kindly offers to forward a box to you from London. In it you will find contained two French Bibles and the other books you request. Some of them want binding, which you can have done in Hull. Your mother has also sent a small sum to Mrs. Thompson to assist in purchasing you any clothes you may want. We hope you will be careful of your clothes. Remember that we feel it very difficult to support you at school, but we hope by your good conduct and attention you will give us every satisfaction."

The hope was not disappointed.

In his notes of 31st December he is able to record:—

"God has been very gracious to us as a church through this year. Thirty adults and twenty-two children have been baptized, nine admitted to the Lord's Table, and a number added to the list of Catechumens. Blessed be God for His goodness!"

1 8 2 8 - 9.

Painful Pastoral Cares — New School-Room — Dandy Fever — Awful Event—Letter to Daughters—Their Return—Antoinette's Marriage, &c.—Desperadoes in Prison—Pioneer re Religious Equality—Letters from England—Arrival of Rev. Joseph and Mrs. Ketley—Arrival of Pioneer's Daughters—Visit to Demerara—Governor's Restoration of Chapel there : New and Prosperous Course—Crown Slaves : Testimony of Military Official — Interesting Pastoral Cases—Free School—Crown Slaves : Earnest of Freedom.

THE new year began as usual with an early meeting for praise and prayer. But its opening day had hours of pain to the pastor's mind.

"Visited one of the baptized who is full of leprosy. He is in a most awful state, but says he trusts in Jesus for salvation." "Much pained to find one of the members, a free person of colour, had gone from our solemn meeting last evening and acted inconsistently, setting a pernicious example to the more ignorant members of the Church."

Mrs. G., who had always been a consistent useful member until this time, confessed she had felt very unhappy, and promised an acknowledgment of her fault. But she had attended her last meeting. Neither to that of the Church nor to the Supper of the Lord did she come. Another Sabbath, she was very unwell; before a third, and after being unable for two or three days to speak, she had passed away. Her pastor visited her, and on Lord's Day, 20th January, preached her funeral sermon, the event making a deep impression on the Church.

The mission still grew ; work also. At times, when—*e.g.*, "my dear wife has been very poorly, and confined to her room two or three weeks," the burden and continued strain told heavily, and would have been too much as a permanent thing. Of course, the private school had to go on, and in March—

"The school lies heavy upon me, so that I have little time left for study, reading, meditation, and prayer. My whole life is indeed a life of hurry. I long for more time to devote to reading and study. God, however, abundantly sustains me in my public labours."

1st June, the new Sunday School was opened. It had been fitted up under the new chapel, which, like most structures there, being erected on pillars, was some feet above the ground. On the 11th Mr. Wray was gratified by a liberal grant of 1000 guilders towards the cost, voted by the Governor and Council, a sort of gift in aid of education.

"The Governor himself called to inform me as he rode by. He said it was done with excellent feelings on the part of the members. Who would have thought this a few years ago, for the express purpose of teaching all conditions to read? I lament that I am so little acquainted with the best method of conducting Sunday Schools; but I trust my God will enable me to superintend this blessed work in the way which is pleasing in His sight. We labour under great disadvantages in having so few efficient teachers; but God can also raise up these, as well as put it into the hearts of men to make us so liberal a grant of pecuniary assistance."

For the forthcoming of which helpers he offers fervent prayer.

It is well established that the so-called "Russian Influenza," or La Grippe, of 1889-90, is no new epidemic, though of rare occurrence. Was this a visit thereof to the West Indian tropics during the summer of 1828?

"*Lord's Day, 6th July.*—A rheumatic fever very prevalent in the country. In town hardly a family escapes, or an individual in a family; sometimes four or five members are down at once. It is attended with very severe pains and stiffness, and leaves great debility, but only lasts a few days. They call it the 'Dandy Fever,' on account of the stiffness which attends it. Gone through several parts of the West Indies, it is said to have proved fatal to several in Demerara and Barbadoes, but I have heard of no death here."

In common with his neighbours, Mr. Wray's family suffered from the strange malady. Beginning with little Emily, who had it very severely, in a fortnight it had successively and not less severely attacked each member.

"*22nd July (Tuesday)*.—I was unable to preach last Sabbath, and to attend Sunday School, and was very poorly yesterday. My ankles were very painful, so that I could hardly walk, and I felt very low. My dear wife is very ill of the fever ; her legs very much swelled, and she has pains all over her."

During this period a most awful event occurred in high quarters. On Saturday evening, the 12th, Mr. M., the Governor's nephew, formerly Government Secretary, shot himself through the heart while sitting at the Governor's dinner table.

"Some disagreement existed between him and his uncle. His mind seems to have been greatly oppressed, and I understand infidel authors formed his principal reading. He died instantly."

He was not unknown to the missionary's daughters in England, who were now shortly to return, and to whom, on the 16th, their father communicates this among other intelligence, all with affectionate and pious counsel, and in glad hope of shortly seeing their faces and having their help :—

"I suppose you are now with your friends at Southampton, who I am sure, will do all they can to make you happy, and will introduce you to many pious and excellent people. You will also have the opportunity of hearing the Rev. Mr. Adkins, and I trust you will pray to God to help you to profit by what you hear. Remember that He sees you in the midst of all your friends and amusements, and that you can hide nothing from Him. Pray to Him daily that He would bestow upon you His blessing, and that it may accompany you wherever you go ; and be kind and affectionate one to another. Remember the words of Joseph to his brethren : 'See that ye fall not out by the way ;'

and also the advice of Paul, Phil. ii. 3: 'Let nothing be done through strife or vain glory; but in lowliness of mind let each esteem other better than themselves.' One excels in one thing, and another in another thing, but the best have nothing to boast of, and those who possess the least gift have much to be thankful for. God has not given to all, gifts alike; and He requires us to improve to His glory and to each other's good, the gifts He has been pleased to bestow.

"We long much to see you, and I trust you will try to make yourselves as useful as you can in our schools. You know our situation, and also that you are coming to an unfriendly soil as it respects spiritual improvement and society of your own age and complexion; but I hope you will be happy in yourselves, in your books, and in your own amusements. Last Saturday evening we had an awful instance of depravity and the ill effects of angry passions. You will remember Mr. M., the Governor's secretary (formerly), and also his nephew. He shot himself through the heart at the dinner table at the Governor's, and died instantly without a groan. We should learn to bear the disappointments of life with Divine resignation to the will of God, and in every change and adverse scene, to put our trust and confidence in Him, also to mortify all jealous and angry passions. Pray to God to sanctify you wholly, and make you His."

Correspondingly, we read in Mrs. Tuckett's first letter:—

"When we finally left school, we went to London to visit some of our mother's relatives; and then to Southampton, where aunts, and uncles, and cousins kindly entertained us for some months. On 8th November, 1828, we went on board the *Highbury*, Captain Cook, bound for Berbice. We had dreadful weather, being detained in the Channel by contrary winds for some time, but at last we landed safely in Berbice, and were once more at home. My sister and self soon found plenty of work. Our mother had kept up her school, through the means of which our expenses to England had been met; but she was worn out, and gladly gave it up to us; so, what with school keeping and mission work we were fully employed."

Antoinette, the kidnapped laundress, will not have been

forgotten by the reader. Brought back three years ago, after eleven years' captivity among the Bush negroes, she at length married, and on Lord's Day, 7th September, she and Dominic, her husband, were baptized by Mr. Wray. They belonged to the Crown. He had long been a very wild fellow, but an affliction with which he had lately been visited, seems to have had a very happy effect.

"He now regularly attends the ordinances of religion. I do think him truly penitent, and rejoice in the change which has taken place. May it be real and lasting! We were very thankful to our God to see A. married and baptized, and pray that God may bless and teach her."

Very different place and service were his when, a month later, he visited several sailors in prison, two or three of whom, in a drunken fit on the previous Sabbath, had nearly killed one of the constables and the Fiscal's son; and another who, having stabbed his captain in Demerara, afterwards broke out of jail, and had been caught in Berbice; but all these events were turned to account in a sermon preached on a subsequent evening.

The following casts some light on the pioneer, re "Religious Equality." It comes before the November dates.

"In reading the Parliamentary Reports, I find they have published my letter to the Protector, on Toleration; and I could not help observing the similarity of sentiments expressed in Mr. Huskisson's celebrated letter to Jamaica. Indeed, Mr. Power said he thought it was founded on it. My letter, dated 9th November, 1826, on Article 35 of the New Code (says):—'Every Protestant Dissenter from the National Church, on receiving a licence, is obliged to swear that he "abhors and detests popery from the heart;" but here, in this Protestant Colony, the Roman priest and the foreigner are admitted to privileges of which the English Protestant is deprived. He must take out a licence merely to qualify himself to give a certificate of the character of a slave, though he may have been a preacher of the Gospel for twenty years by the laws of his country: for it is expressly provided that "no licensed teacher of religion, except of the sects there specified, shall be competent to grant any such certificate." ' Mr. Huskisson, 22nd September, 1827, in his letter to the Governor of Jamaica, observes :—' It is impossible to pass over without remark the invidious distinction which is made, not only between Protestant Dissenters and Roman Catholics, but even between Protestant Dissenters and Jews.' Page 2."

Little Emily and her mother had been and were very poorly, but on 11th November Mr. Wray left them for a week's work, his last in Demerara, returning to find them much the same; and on 14th December the parents were "anxiously looking out for our dear children; we are expecting them every day." The next day brought letters, but the daughters themselves, detained by rough weather and contrary winds, did not arrive till more than a month later. One letter from his friend, Mr. J. Thompson (Hull),—

"informs me that Mr. T. Thompson (brother) is dead. He was a truly excellent man ; spent large sums in promoting the cause of Christ and in acts of charity ; and a long life in the service of Jesus. My beloved friend is also drawing near the eternal world. Blessed be God for giving me such a friend, and for continuing him to be a friend also to my beloved children. He speaks highly of the disposition of Robert. Oh that God may bless the lad and give him His grace ! "

17th December brought a letter from the Rev. Joseph Ketley,

" to state that he had arrived in Demerara to minister to Mr. Davies's congregation and to request me to go down. He arrived on the 7th and he wrote on the 8th. I rejoice that the poor people are again supplied with the Gospel, and pray that Mr. K. may be a pious, devoted, prudent missionary of Jesus Christ. I wrote him to-day (18th)."

The burden was now lightened a good degree, and Mr. Ketley, spared to a ripe old age, proved himself such a minister as the prayer desires ; and after thus serving, it may be said, two generations according to the will of God, left a son in the ministry who has long held the father's position, and is following in the father's steps.

The rainy season was more than, as sometimes, such in name; but on Lord's Day, 28th December, though roads were bad at New Amsterdam,—

"a very large congregation crowded the chapel, and numbers could not get in. I never saw so many before. The service was very solemn and the people were very attentive."

The year closed amid the usual services. During 1828 there had been twenty-two adults baptized, and twenty-four admitted to church-fellowship.

1829-1831.

Arrival of Daughters—Visit to Demerara—Governor's Restoration of Chapel there: New and Prosperous Course—Crown Slaves: Testimony of Military Official—Pioneer's Age: Fifty Years: Retrospect and Prospect—Deaths of Friends, &c.—Free School—Agnes, or a "Select Incident of Slavery"—Further Improvement in Slave Laws—Improved Methods in Catechizing—Unhealthy Season—Rev. Michael Lewis, a Helper—Jane sent to England — Shocking Death of Planter—An Historical Character — Increasing Disability — Kind Letters from Directors—Enlargement of Chapel—Return, with Mrs. Wray, to England.

24TH JANUARY of the new year, brought a further alleviation of the burden, not to say a cessation of anxious looks seawards, and a return of joy to the home.

"Our eldest daughters arrived from our native country, when we received them with great joy, and are much pleased with the improvement they have made both in body and mind. We trust that God will bless them with His rich grace and lead them into the way everlasting. May He pour His spirit upon them and bless them!"

These able now to help in the private school and to take more responsible duties in the home life, their father went on 9th February to see Mr. and Mrs. Ketley.

"They are young," he writes, "but they appear very pious, and truly devoted to God and His cause ; and are much pleased with the people. I thank God that I have accomplished the object. May He bless His minister and the people ! Some of them thanked me for getting them a minister. I was much pleased with the plans Mr. K. is adopting." "14*th*.—Went with Mr. K. to see the West Coast chapel. The Governor has ordered it to be given up to us. It is a fine situation in the centre of a large population of slaves. May God again revive His work in those Stations and give His blessing to the exertions of His servants ! *Lord's Day*, 15*th*.—Preached at Providence Chapel in the morning and the Methodist in the evening. It is a very spacious building and was crowded to excess. The female who used to begin the singing for me more than twenty years ago, led the singing this evening. 18*th*.—Left Demerara this morning in the steamboat and arrived at home this evening."

Which last would be a new experience, as compared with the voyages made in the small coasting schooners ; and would be truly a symbol of the new course of mission work just inaugurated, which now in Demerara, after and despite all and such attempts to crush and destroy or displace the work, was to have as rapid and unchecked a progress during the next five or ten years, as that in Berbice itself.

The following is a fit conclusion to the entries of this month.

"28*th February*. — Captain Gipps of the Royal Engineers communicated to me a plan laid before Government for the amelioration and ultimate freedom of the Winkel negroes. He states respecting them :—'that having had the most effective part of them under his superintendence for three years, and also a number of other negroes from a variety of proprietors, he can with great satisfaction say—that they are decidedly superior to any other in intelligence and cheerful obedience,—that they are decidedly in a state which calls for some further amendment, and that he had learnt to entertain for many of them respect and esteem ; that they have a desire for comfort in their houses, for furniture and good clothing; that they will work for wages when wages are regularly paid to them ; that many of them are married ; the younger ones can read and some can write ; whilst under the laudable exertions of a Missionary from the London Society that they have all attained a greater degree of religious and moral instruction than perhaps any other of their unfortunate race in the world.' "

Relieved then of some duties by the recent arrivals, Mr. Wray was able to give more time to pastoral care and private reading. His journals, therefore, for this and the following year, have much of their fewer pages taken up with details of his visits to the sick, or of his dealings with catechumens. Cases, entered at some length, are indeed interesting as showing in various ways the power of Divine grace and truth ; and must have been great encouragements to the faithful but now, through depressing weakness and sickness, often languid pastor.*

* *E.g.*, Good old Mary Ann Scott, who died 6th May, at the age of eighty-two ; and who, years before, was among the first-fruits of mission work in Demerara ; having entered into fellowship there, and preceded Mr. Wray to Berbice. She was an ornament to her Christian profession, and "I never knew her act inconsistently with it." By the younger members of the family to which she belonged, she was looked on rather as a mother and a friend than as a servant, frequently receiving kind and affectionate letters from her young mistresses in Scotland. She was highly esteemed by the members of the church, and was on all occasions a peacemaker. Happy in the ways of religion, she acknow-ledged the support afforded by her heavenly Father under all the trials and difficulties through which for many years she had been called to pass ; and was very fervent in prayer on the behalf of her children, her minister, the members of the church, and for the spread of the Gospel. A truly humble, pious disciple of Jesus, always ascribing her salvation to the free grace of God ; she died as she had lived. Unable to speak in response to her pastor's utterance :—

> "There shall we see His face,
>   And never, never sin ;
>   There from the rivers of His grace,
>   Drink endless pleasures in ; "

she expressed her approbation by the motion of her hand and a sweet

Of the Free School which had the pioneer's sympathy, he writes :—

"*Lord's Day, 20th December.*—I preached two sermons for the benefit of the Berbice Free School. Very rainy weather and the roads almost impassable. The congregation was very small both morning and evening. The Governor honoured us with his attendance, also the Fiscal. I trust the Free School will be a blessing to many poor children, but at present it is not well managed. Many children are admitted whose parents are well able to pay for them. The Governor is very anxious about its prosperity."

The last half of 1829 proved, both in its earlier and later part, very wet, and the months from June to September very

smile on her countenance. Her remains were conveyed to the silent tomb, amid the tears of many, both bond and free.

Poor Andries the leper, growingly afflicted with leprosy until he was one mass of sores, and full of pain, knew well both his Bible and Hymn Book ; but had all the more realized the truth of the Gospel since his affliction began ; and now, borne up in faith, praying without ceasing, with hope of better things beyond, was, on these accounts, a wonder to his minister, who visited his hut to the very last.

Among learners, fine intelligent men who in increasing numbers had begun to punt themselves across the river to attend a Bible class, &c., Toby was especially interesting. As a boy in his own country (Houssa) he had been taught the Koran, and had never seen a white man. Brought over when a big lad and sold into slavery, he had formed a very low but true estimate as to the amount of religious knowledge among the whites with whom he had hitherto met. Acquainted now with Mr. Wray, and having opportunity, he and his companions were "greedy" of knowledge, particularly that of the Holy Scriptures. Shown in succession Hebrew characters, Chinese, Bengalee, &c., &c., Toby shook his head. But Arabic he recognised as an old acquaintance, and afterwards wrote some passages of what he could remember as having learnt long ago from the Mohammedan parson. Toby will reappear in these pages. Meanwhile he would be drinking in Christian truth, and at present was learning to read his Bible in English ; answering also the occasional inquiries of the pioneer as to the probability, were a Station established on his side the river, of the slaves there helping and attending.

hot and unhealthy. The ill effects were fully shared both by the missionary himself and by his household.

Thirty-nine adults and forty-three children were baptized during the year, and thirteen persons admitted to the Lord's Table. Another item of consequence is unique, a drop of the shower not far away, which again, as the little cloud, was harbinger of abundance of rain. The Crown slaves were not yet to be freed as a whole, much less were slaves generally ; but

"four slaves, belonging to the Crown, who are members of the mission church, another not yet a member, but very useful to the chapel, and for several years our faithful servant, and another young man who attends occasionally, have been freed by the express command of His Majesty's Government ; having been previously commended for their industry and good behaviour by his Excellency, Governor Beard. Their names are Louis, George, Daniel, David, Jacob, and James. May God preserve them and help them to persevere in well-doing, that Government may be encouraged to grant the same boon to others !"

With 12th January, 1830, the date of his baptism, Mr. Wray pauses to reflect upon his having attained the age of fifty years, twenty-two of which had now been spent as a missionary. Gratefully he recounts past and present mercies, particularly in his calling, his family ; the church and the work. His elder children were proving very useful, intent on improving their minds by reading, very diligent in the private school, and giving considerable assistance in the schools and classes held on Sunday or on week-day evenings ; cheerfully declining invitations, even from the highest quarters, to receptions or assemblies, attendance on which would then have been the almost sure precursor of a life of frivolity, if not of dissipation. His prayer, not unanswered, was that indeed they may choose and possess the one thing needful, even God as their portion, from their youth giving up their hearts to Him.

"Many of the members too have given me much satisfaction and some rendered themselves particularly useful ; Miss Grimes, Gabriel and Tom, and Thomas and Henery of Lonsdale." He adds :—" I am now going down the hill and cannot expect to be very long, but I desire to devote myself to my God and Saviour, this day, that my few remaining days or years, as God shall see fit, may be to the promotion of His glory. I love His work and I love His people. I feel my own deficiencies and imperfections, and the plague of my own heart ; and I daily lament these things ; but I cast myself on my Saviour ' whose blood cleanseth from all sin.' O my God, take my poor sinful heart ; cleanse it from every sin, and fit me for Thy heavenly Kingdom."

The impressions recorded at the outset of this last quotation, were intensified by the growth of his disease, and the passing away of former friends both in the old country and in the circle immediately around. As the year passed on, he could neither relish nor perform work at his desk, as he had done. In other ways he toiled on, and progress was maintained. Whites, including ladies and sometimes officers from the garrison, were again regular in attendance at the chapel services ; and happy results still appeared. But to the unbroken continuance of these efforts he at length proved unequal, and the year had but half gone when additional help was peremptorily needed. Fortunately this was forthcoming in the person of the Rev. Michael Lewis, who, having been sent out to take charge of the restored chapel on the Demerara West Coast, landed there with Mrs. Lewis, a sister of the Rev. J. Ketley, 3rd April. But we have been anticipating.

23rd January, news arrived of the death of his long attached friend, Mr. J. Thompson, of Hull ; of whom the pioneer now writes what has already been given in Chapter I. of this memoir. Another death, 6th February, nearer at hand, was a sad close of a short and sad course. About three years previously, on a Wednesday evening, Mr. Wray noticed at chapel the minister of the old Dutch Lutheran church and one of his people; who, after service, spent an hour with the missionary. Wrote Mr. Wray at the time :—

"He has been represented as very wild, but I found him to be quite agreeable, and intelligent on religious subjects. He is young and surrounded with temptations, but I think there is something good in him and I shall try to cultivate his acquaintance."

More promising at first sight perhaps than some clergymen of that period, there was, alas, no root; and there is no further mention of him until 4th January of this year :—

"Visited some sick people, among them the late Lutheran clergyman, who is in a most miserable state brought on by licentiousness and drunkenness. He wept much while I spoke to him. He seems to be in want of necessaries. What is man when left to himself and his wicked companions !"

6th February, the end had come :—

"The Rev. Mr. Vos, late Minister of the Lutheran Church, died this evening, aged about 30. He has been a most awful instance of human depravity; ruined his character and constitution by whoredom, drunkenness, and extravagance. Since his dismission he has been in distress and want. Two or three ladies to whom I spoke, kindly sent him nourishment daily, and lately the Lutherans have allowed him something. He seems to have possessed good talents, and might have been useful, but was led away by dissipated companions, chiefly Lutherans, who were living in fornication and given to intoxication. At last he was forsaken by them and dismissed. An awful warning to those who enter the ministry without due preparation and without experiencing the regenerating influences of the Spirit of God. During my visits to him, he expressed his regret for his conduct in general terms; but nothing like true and sincere repentance. In the evening of the 7th, I buried him."

The prospects of the Berbice Free School, still an anxious care, somewhat brightened; and on the 22nd March,—

"Attended the Committee. The Governor, chosen president at the annual meeting last week, as well as patron, took his seat among us to-day. Two or three resolutions were passed, which I think will prove beneficial; and the subscriptions have greatly increased. I trust that education will be greatly promoted by it. If we could obtain a person well instructed in the British system it would prove a great blessing."

Funerals, more numerous than usual during the last days of March, were followed by one on 1st April, eight or ten miles from town, which was the finish of what might be termed a "Select Incident of Slavery." The hearts of the humane missionary, his partner, and household, must have exclaimed,—"How long, O Lord?"

" *Thursday, 1st April.*—Heard of the death of Agnes, a young mulatto girl, who was formerly with us for upwards of a year. She was the daughter of a former attorney of plantation 'Profit' by a slave-woman. Her father died some years ago. It was intended that she and her mother should be emancipated, and Agnes therefore was sent to Mrs. Wray for three years. She was a cheerful and well disposed girl, and was making considerable progress in reading. At the end of last year, the 'Profit' gang were advertised to be sold, and were purchased by the proprietor of the 'Friends' estate up the river; and through the neglect of her friends, Agnes was sold among them. In consequence of this, we received an order to send her to the estate. It was like a thunderbolt to the poor girl. Some attempts were made to purchase her, but in vain. She, of course, after the expectation of freedom, was reduced to slavery. Last Tuesday, taken with a fit, she never came round till about half-an-hour before her death on Wednesday evening, but she never spoke again. I doubt not it broke her heart. Her friends sent for me at five o'clock to bury her. The distance is eight or ten miles, and, in consequence of rain, the roads were bad. I buried her by candle light. It was an affecting scene. Her poor mother and friends wept bitterly. Thus men die and leave their blood in slavery, and they are bought and sold like cattle. About twelve o'clock before I reached home."

Easter Sunday, Whitsunday, as well as Christmas Day, even when on a Sunday, had long been legally proclaimed dancing days for the slaves; Mr. Wray had frequently represented to the Governor the importance of changing the day to some other in the week, and his Excellency had always seemed to favour the idea. The effort at length bore fruit, for under date 11th April (Easter Sunday) is the record:—

"In my return to the Protector last August, I particularly enlarged on the evil of legally setting two or three Sabbaths in the year (as dancing days) and of holding the public market on the Sabbath. I find Sir George Murray has been pleased to notice with approbation my statement respecting the dancing days, and has requested that they shall be removed from the Sabbath; and in new laws by the King in Council which came out a few weeks since, the Sabbath markets and compulsory working (of the slaves) on the Sabbath are for ever abolished. Also the compulsory manumission clause is established, and there are several other beneficial regulations for the slave. Blessed be God for putting it into the hearts of our great men to do these things."

With improved circumstances, the pioneer wisely adopted improved and suitable methods, even though, so far, apparently new in Berbice. On Whitsunday of this year, according to previous announcement, he held a public examination in Scripture knowledge, of all children who had been baptized and taught; also addressing them along with their parents and others who presented them: following all up, on the succeeding Sunday afternoon, by a further examination and by the distribution, to the most deserving, of medals from the British and Foreign School Society, and of Bibles, Testaments, Hymn and other books from the Bible and Tract Societies.

He still did what he could, though increasingly disabled by his personal affliction. But with July came another time of sickness throughout the whole town, continuing to the end of September. Doctors said they never had so much. Mr. Wray, for several weeks, was quite unable to preach, and members of his family and inmates of his house were frequently stricken with fever. Several church-members died very suddenly, and a most promising youth of nineteen, a Crown slave employed at the sawmill, baptized when a little boy and in whom the missionary took a deep interest, passed away in the faith of the Gospel.

The Rev. M. Lewis, hearing of Mr. Wray's prostration, arrived early on Sunday, 11th July, and stayed until the 29th, conducting public worship and preaching. His services proved very acceptable, the chapel being crowded by persons of all colours. " He seems," the pastor writes, " an excellent, pious young man, and I trust will be very useful."

Young Jane, who, after being seriously unwell, had somewhat recovered, it was decided, should go to England ; and all alone, but in charge of their friend Captain Cook of the *Highbury*, who kindly gave her a free passage, the child, in September, took her departure. Though most affectionate, " the dear girl went willingly and manifested much decision and firmness." Happily all went well, and like her elder sisters, Jane lived to become a useful Christian lady and to attain a good old age.*

One awful event in July, shocking to the Colony, was particularly so to the two missionaries. Going on the 12th with Mr. Lewis to introduce him to the Governor and the Fiscal, at the house of the latter Mr. Wray met a Mr. Kewley, owner of estate No. 49, on the East or Corentyne Coast, who, it is remarked, quite shocked Mr. Lewis by his profane swearing. This Mr. K. had hired some slaves who had long lived on the West Coast, and who, having heard their mistress was hiring them out to go so far off, ran away. The Fiscal, however, had succeeded in getting them back, had brought them over the river and put them in gaol until the schooner was ready to take them. On the 14th, they and Mr. K., with some other whites, about thirty souls altogether,

* In later days she became Mrs. Goss, Exeter ; surviving her husband until the close of 1890.

set sail. It was customary to hail vessels passing the fort and, if they did not answer, to bring them to.

"I never heard of any accident or injury done before," writes Mr. Wray, "but as these were passing the fort a gun was fired to bring them to, and whether obeyed or not I cannot say ; but a second was fired and, by accident or mismanagement, the shot struck the vessel. Some on board narrowly escaped, but none received hurt except Mr. K., whom the ball struck dead on the spot, rending his body almost in twain."

In a few hours, the shattered remains were buried, "a very great number of people attending."

As the year drew to a close, the pioneer again became very weak, disposed also to write bitter things against himself.

"I am very low ; I have indeed need of patience, yet my temper is very irritable and I manifest great impatience. Oh that my God would be with me and help me to bear my affliction with patience and resignation !"

But again Mr. Lewis, coming over with Mrs. Lewis, was able to render help. Forty adults and twenty-five children had been baptized during the year ; eighteen persons admitted to the Lord's Table, all slaves, except one ; and there had been seventeen legal marriages of slaves.

The new year, 1831, was begun, as usual, with a service at 7 A.M , which consisted of prayer and praise.

"Thus far the Lord has led us on," Mr. Wray notes, "I trust from the prospects before us that the increase will be far greater this year as the people are advancing in knowledge, and there is a growing desire among the slaves for improvement."

Its opening day saw the last of a very aged and somewhat historical character.

"1st *January*.—Buried old Frederick. He was past ninety-nine years of age. For the services he rendered to the Whites in the dreadful insurrection of the slaves in 1763, he was freed, and has received an annual pension ever since."

The growing attendance at the chapel services, advancing

beyond the capacity of the building to accommodate it, demanded an enlargement of the edifice, which was now planned and put into execution. Besides this, land had been obtained on the other side of the river, and people were subscribing weekly and monthly sums for a place of worship there. Also a few miles higher up the river, on the East Bank, a favourable opening for work was presenting itself. Mr. Wray's increasing affliction seemed the only drawback. This more frequently rendered him helpless. Then, " I see my dear wife and daughters constantly engaged, while I do nothing but moan and groan."

In January, however, he was cheered, not only by hearing of the safe arrival of young Jane, her good health and that of his son Robert, but by " a very kind and sympathetic letter from the Society, promising another to take his place and to arrange for himself and Mrs. Wray returning to England for a short time." All which was very grateful to the heart of the tried but devoted pioneer.

February brought further communications to the effect " that myself and Mrs. Wray are at liberty to return to England as soon as we wish, and authorize me to invite Mr. Lewis to take care of the congregation in my absence."

This arrangement was ultimately adopted. Propped up a few weeks until the work of enlarging the chapel was about completed, then leaving the Rev. Mr. Lewis in charge of the mission, and the two eldest daughters in charge of the private school and of the home; the suffering minister and his dear wife embarked on board the *Highbury*, Captain Cook, amid the most affectionate attentions of their poor people, and assurances of unceasing prayers on their behalf; also amid the politest attentions shown by the white and coloured inhabitants. In three days the *Highbury* left the bar, and on 14th April, just twenty-two years since Mrs. Wray had arrived in Guiana, and which had been spent by her without intermission there, the voyage home was fairly begun.

CHAPTER VII

VISIT WITH MRS. WRAY TO ENGLAND; TO NEGRO EMANCIPATION.

APRIL, 1831—AUGUST, 1834.

Reception in England—History of Mission—Early Return—Death of Rev. M. Lewis—Reception in Berbice—In Harness Again—William O. Ramsey—Coming Changes—Berbice Colony : Union with Demerara, &c.—Lonsdale Chapel : Liberality of New Governor, &c. : Sudden Death of Builder—Town Chapel : Third Enlargement—Rev. James and Mrs. Scott—Lonsdale Chapel : Opening—Increase, 1832—Reported Schism.

THE voyage to England, also that back again to Berbice, seem to have been without particular incident, Mr. Wray making no note upon either. Of the interval, about seven months, we have the following memorandum, here slightly condensed :—

"*6th June.*—This day myself and Mrs. Wray landed in England. We were received with great kindness by our nephew. On the Monday evening following I was introduced by Mr. Hankey to the Board of Directors, in the most affectionate and flattering manner, so much so that I felt quite ashamed. They have manifested the greatest kindness to me. I have always attended their Monday evening committee, when in London ; and have been treated with great respect. I also generally attended the Committee meeting of the Tract Society on Tuesday morning ; felt much interest in it, and was always edified. The Committees of the Bible Society and the School Society also I had the pleasure of attending, and was kindly received. On the 5th

Rev. JOHN WRAY.

July I underwent a surgical operation, performed by Dr. Kay, and was confined about a fortnight to the house.*   From the end of August to the end of October I was travelling for the Society in the shires of Warwick, Stafford, Norfolk, and Lincoln, and preached and spoke twice almost every day.   I was received everywhere with the greatest kindness ; and I trust the missionary spirit is increasing.   They often brought me on my journey after a godly sort.   We received our dear Emily, who had been very ill, and (was) sent over (to us in charge of) Captain Cook, much improved by the voyage.   (Rev.) Mr. Clayton, in particular, treated us with great kindness ; also did Mrs. Clayton.   We got quite attached to them.   (Rev.) Mr. and Mrs. Collison, and (Rev.) Mr. and Mrs. Arundell showed us kindness.   Blessed be God for His great goodness to us.   Having recovered, it is our wish to return to our field of labour."

The Directors would have had him prolong his stay, and even write a History of the Mission before returning ; other considerations too were not wanting to delay their return. Like Emily, their youngest, a most interesting child, would, it was thought, have to be left behind, as also young Jane, who had preceded them to this country ; while their son Robert, who had now left Silcoates and for whom some suitable situation had been sought but not obtained, would have no further opportunity here of personal inquiry, as it was concluded he should return with them.   But the now rapid growth of the mission ; the promise of further openings ; and the march of events in Britain, specially the tokens of some great changes as to negro slavery in our colonies, presented by a long-forbearing but growingly aroused and indignant people, would doubtless weigh heavily in the scale which decided them to return as soon as they did.

It was fortunate, for, had they deferred, another event, when known, would alone have hastened their departure. This was the decease, on 22nd January, 1832, of the Rev.

* Later on, Mr. Wray sat for the portrait whence our engraving is taken.

M. Lewis after three days' illness. But the pioneer and Mrs. Wray were then on their way : of course, therefore, did not hear the sad news until they landed.

"*4th January*, 1832.—We went on board the *Rosanna*, Captain Foster. Mr. Arundell accompanied us to the ship. We sailed from the Downs on the 13th, reached Berbice on 20th February, and were received by a number of people on the stelling, who all kindly welcomed our return. We found our dear children much better than we expected, and from all classes had testimony to their good conduct. They have been diligently employed in their school from eight to four : and in the Sunday School on the Sabbath. Mr. Lewis has made one of them Superintendent, and admitted both to the Lord's Table. I hope and trust God, by His Spirit, has wrought a change in their hearts, and that they will grow in grace and in the knowledge of our Lord Jesus Christ. We were much shocked to hear of the death of Mr. Lewis on 22nd January. Only three days ill, he was cut down in the midst of usefulness. He was indefatigable in his missionary labours, as well as for the promotion of the Divine glory. He died in a most happy state of mind, 'rejoicing in hope of the glory of God.' He is gone to his Father and his crown. May God prepare me for the rest which remains for His people !

" For the first three or four days after our arrival we had a number of visitors ; sometimes the house almost full."

Work of necessity, and in all its usual forms, then began forthwith.

"*Lord's Day*, 26th *February*.—The chapel was full notwith-standing its enlargement. A great number of negroes from the country. I improved the death of Mr. Lewis. All lament it."

"*Lord's Day*, 4th *March*.—I had the happiness of meeting again with the dear people of Berbice at the Table of the Lord, my beloved girls among them. May they be the Lord's for ever, and devote themselves entirely to His service ! Preached from 3 John 4. ' I have no greater joy than to hear that my children walk in truth.' As well as my own beloved children, I found all my spiritual children also walking in the truth of the Gospel of our blessed Saviour, and others added to their number. Thanks be to God, none had been excluded. Two aged members had been removed from the church below to the church above. Mr. Lewis wrote me that they both died in a very happy state."

"*Friday, 23rd March.*—Nearly every day since my arrival I have visited a young man, aged 23, born at Perth, in Scotland, and named William Orme Ramsey. Baptized by the late Mr. Orme, and named after him, his father and mother seem to be very pious people, members of the church over which Mr. Orme was pastor. Since leaving Scotland, the young man has been in (North) America, Demerara, then came to Berbice, where he was working on an estate as a plumber, when he and one of the white people having had a quarrel he had been beaten by his fellow, had come to town, and been taken ill at the house of a poor woman near the chapel. She sent to request me to visit him. He received my instructions with the greatest thankfulness, and was exceedingly anxious for them. I have reason to believe that he died a sincere penitent, and that the kind instruction of Mr. Orme, and of his father and mother, were 'not in vain in the Lord.'"

After details of visits to the sufferer, the missionary takes this as one,—

"among other instances, which afford encouragement to pious parents to persevere in educating their children in the fear of the Lord, and in training them up in the ways of true religion."

We cease further quotation here. Enough has been given to indicate the reception met with, and Mr. Wray's full re-entrance at once upon preaching and pastoral work. A few weeks were sufficient to show the influence of current events, as these tended to a relaxation of the bonds of slavery and pointed to their speedy dissolution. In a last letter written to his daughters before his return, Mr. Wray had said :—

"New laws have been sent out. I suppose they will create considerable commotion in the Colonies. The prejudices existing against the West Indies are very great. I should be glad if some great measure were adopted to satisfy all parties. Twenty years ago I did not expect to live to see the progress which has been made. I trust that the time is not far distant when 'the knowledge of the Lord shall cover the earth as the waters cover the sea ;' and that in Berbice the Gospel will spread through the Colony."

Berbice, as we shall see, seems to have received the new laws more wisely than some other colonies, particularly Jamaica, where the violence of the planting interest was such as to hasten, rather than retard, the day of emancipation. On the part both of many slaves and their owners or managers, in Berbice there appeared a disposition to utilize the means of instruction which the Mission had at hand.* It may here be noted, too, that during the Missionary's absence an important change had taken place in the civil government of the Colony. For, July, 1831, Berbice ceased to be an independent colony; Governor Beard returning to England, and Sir Benjamin D'Urban taking the governorship in union with that already held of Demerara and Essequibo. Henceforth the three colonies had their one seat of Government in Georgetown.

The first sign of what were to prove rapidly increasing numbers in attendance at the Mission, appeared on Good Friday, 20th April, under the new Order in Council now become a holiday for the slaves. A good number from an estate high up the river, with a letter from the manager, came to worship, &c., and a great many from other plantations. On Easter Sunday and Monday they came in still larger numbers, and from all directions, many neatly dressed, and all behaving well; a sight constraining the audible repetition at times, by Mrs. Wray, of Watts's lines :—

* The course of events in the Slave-Colonies cannot be fully appreciated without a knowledge of the course of events touching slave-amelioration and emancipation in the Mother country. No volume, probably, gives the latter at this period, so concisely yet so well, as the Life of the great leader of emancipation, Sir Thomas Fowell Buxton ; a work which, for this reason, were there none other, should be in every English Library.

> "That day shall show Thy power is great,
>   When saints shall flock with willing minds,
> And sinners crowd Thy temple gates,
>   Where holiness in beauty shines."

Succeeding Sabbath days and other opportunities only tended to augment these numbers, despite loss of friends or the missionary's sickness; for toward the end of May, Mr. Power died, of whom says Mr. Wray:—"I am afraid we shall not obtain a man of humanity and amelioration like-minded in the negro cause." And in the middle of June, the pioneer himself had attacks of fever severe enough to lay him aside from work. But on 6th May seventeen new members were admitted to the Table of the Lord, chiefly, however, of those who from childhood had been instructed in the faith of Christ; and on 29th June,—

"had the pleasure to lay the foundation of a new chapel on plantation 'Lonsdale,' and to entreat that God would be pleased to bless this new undertaking." "*Lord's Day, 1st July.*—There is now a large pick of coffee. The people are tired on the Sabbath and cannot come so well; yet the chapel is always full. I often feel very poorly; but God enables me to preach His holy word, and to attend to the duties of my calling."

31st July, he is further cheered :—

"Last week Governor D'Urban visited Berbice. His Excellency sent me a donation of 10 Joes (about £18) towards the new chapel. I have had far more encouragement to go on than I expected. During the month I have been very successful in obtaining donations. Several respectable planters have subscribed liberally, and most with whom I have conversed seem pleased with the undertaking. Some of the white gentlemen in the neighbourhood have told me that they will regularly attend. One planter wished for a pew for the white people on his estate, and said he would have no objection for all his little slaves to attend Sunday School."

Wednesday, 15th August, brought a sad interruption to the work :—

"The poor man, Mr. M'Kinsie, whom I employed to put up the chapel on Lonsdale, died this evening. Last Wednesday he went out of the manager's house without his hat, and received a stroke from the sun. He lay in a state of unconsciousness for two or three days. I went to see him on Friday, and found him quite insensible. He afterwards became quite mad, and died. I was deeply affected with this awful dispensation. He seemed to be a very quiet, inoffensive, industrious man; had only been about eighteen months in the Colony, and was very little known."

In town, the chapel, on Sabbath days crowded in every part, witnessed in September such further increase in numbers both of adults and children, that manse, schoolroom and chapel were all utilized for meetings of one kind or another, which, beginning early in the morning, continued almost uninterruptedly until night; not less than 700 being in actual attendance and 1000 under instruction. Many of those who came were from the country, some travelling ten or fifteen miles; and great numbers of such, after service, applying for catechisms and spelling books to convey back to their distant homes.

Though assisted by a number of willing helpers, so closely did one assembly of learners succeed another, the missionary says of his family:—"we had hardly time to take any refreshment"—and though, in addition to former enlargement, a gallery for the children had, during the pioneer's absence in England, been put up, he now writes:—"it has become absolutely necessary to make another addition to the chapel."

This crowding, due, of course, in part to the abolition of Sunday labour by the new code, and its securing the right of public Divine worship to the slaves, went on; the people from the country districts, however, becoming increasingly wishful to have places of worship in their respective neighbourhoods, and Mr. Wray longing for "an assistant who would labour humbly and affectionately for Christ among them." Letters informing friends and the Society of what was coming to pass, and earnestly entreating help, were accordingly sent home. Meanwhile all did what they could, and in December welcomed the company and help of the Rev. James and Mrs. Scott who, occupying the sphere in Demerara left vacant by the death of Mr. Lewis, now paid a fortnight's visit to Berbice. They were gratified with the prospects presented by the mission, and, arriving on the 4th, took part in a glad and important event; the first of several such shortly to be brought about correspondently with extension of the work—the opening of the chapel on Lonsdale.

"*Lord's Day, 9th December.*—The new chapel on Lonsdale was opened. It was crowded to excess and numbers could not gain admittance. The day was very fine. It was delightful to see the groups of people along the road from town and the different plantations, returning from the interesting scene. All seemed pleased. Such a sight had not before been seen in Berbice. I opened the service by a short address, reading the Scriptures, singing hymns, and earnest prayer. The Rev. James Scott from Demerara, preached an appropriate sermon from Ps. xxvi. ver. 8 ('*Lord, I have loved the habitation of Thy house, and the place where Thine honour dwelleth*'). To me it was a most interesting day. I bless God that the desire of my heart has at length been fulfilled in the erection of a place of worship in this populous district. May thousands be born in it for eternity!"

A new gallery in the town chapel, holding between eighty and 100 persons, was also finished before the end of the year. As this drew on, during Christmas week and closing days, crowded services, both at Lonsdale and in town, were held. The Crown slaves had all been emancipated during the year, and since his return from England, Mr. Wray had baptized sixty-five adults and nineteen children. Forty-two had been admitted to the Table of the Lord, half of them slaves, and nine from among the newly emancipated Crown negroes. Thirty-six couples of slaves had been married. Forty-one boys and ninety-six girls of the town children had been admitted to the Sunday School, which now numbered 317 scholars, under the care of twenty-seven teachers. In addition, great numbers of adults and children from the country were taught in a separate building.

But on the last night of 1832, business of an unpleasant nature occupied the attention of pastor and church. That schism should exist, was no new thing in the history of Christian churches, whatever be their constitution; but that it should be appearing in that under his charge, was news to the pioneer. However, no circumstances perhaps were more likely to favour its appearance than those of the church during the closing year; and no fellowship more than this mixture of nationalities and colours, of bond and free; a few of them taught, but the mass uneducated. Certainly, if not rightly met and checked, in none can it so easily spread or work mischief as in churches of the Congregational order. The freedom they enjoy is great, but correspondingly so are the perils. Mr. Wray was no bigot in the matter of church government; he was, nevertheless, as we have seen, a Congregationalist; continued such, and continued therefore to organize churches on the Independent or Congregational principle. We have him now meeting a crisis in an intelligent, faithful, open, and candid manner—meeting it successfully too, as the event proved.

It was from friends in Demerara, about a month previously, that a report reached him of a division in the church, and during December he had been endeavouring to ascertain if indeed this was the case. He had not succeeded; yet, says he,—

"there are a few of whom I am suspicious, and as a little leaven leaveneth the whole lump, and as with such suspicions in my mind I could not administer the Lord's Supper with comfort, I thought it best to call the church together and tell them what I had heard. This I did; explaining to them, in the first place, the right all had to attend where they could receive the most benefit ; that if they could not profit by their own minister, it was their duty to tell him, and if it was their wish to separate, to do it openly and honourably ; but that for any one in a secret, underhand manner to form a division in the church, unknown to the minister and members in general, was a sin of heinous nature. This I proved from Scripture, reading also some passages on the subject from Mr. (John Angell) James's 'Church Fellowship.' Telling them that I had tried to find out who the people were, but in vain, and that consequently I was not able to speak to them in private, I charged any who were thus trying to undermine my character and to make a division in this Jesuitical manner, not, with such sentiments in their hearts against me, to approach the Lord's Table."

The individuals suspected turned out to be the real parties. They were a Mr. A—— and some sergeants from the fort. Mr. Wray thought they had tried to inflame some coloured young men and women against him ; but not that they had gone amongst the people in general. During his absence in England they had begun a kind of meeting which the pastor could not sanction, as neither could he Mr. A.'s wish, after leaving the fort, to be ordained a missionary, or to gain the hand of a Miss G—— in marriage. In this last Mr. A. ultimately succeeded, but in nothing else.

" He must blame me for not being received as a missionary— but I should not have done my duty to the Society had I, after becoming more acquainted with him, recommended him."

Less than another year, and his connection with the church came to an end.

1833.

Impressive Communion — Sad Character of Clergyman — Arrival of Rev. James and Mrs. Mirams—Lonsdale: Church Formed—Slaves' Need of Instruction — Contrast — Bishop's Testimony — Remarkable Conversion—Difficulties of Transition-State—Renewed Protest—Passing of Emancipation Act —Preparations for Change—New Governor—His Visit to Berbice: the Mission, &c.—Arrival of Rev. James Howe—Fly in Ointment—Hanover Chapel: Opening: Church Formed—Grain of Mustard-Seed—Death of Troubler—Missionary Meeting: Chairman's Candid Confession.

" *Lord's Day, 6th January.*—About 120 assembled around the Table of the Lord. Many seemed deeply affected. Five new members sat down with us. Two of them were scholars with us, are yet very young, but they give every proof that they have the root of the matter in them."

Little need for such a fellowship to be divided or set against such a pastor; a fact emphasized by the sad conduct of other professed ministers of Christ, of which here is a further specimen :—

"The Rev. Mr. R—— has left for England. He has so long been in the habit of drinking that he seems to be irreclaimable. For the last five or six months he appears to have been almost always in a state of intoxication. He has drunk himself mad ; set fire to his house one night, and it is of the mercy of God that he and his house were not burnt together. He is said to swear dreadfully, has left two children behind him by two women, the fruits of fornication, and one of them a slave. The people have really had ministers according to their own hearts. In 1824, they petitioned to have our Mission suspended, and to have a minister of the Church of England. He was given in answer to their petition. Sometimes he sent for me to visit him, and would weep like a child when I have talked and read to him. But I have not seen him for some weeks. The bishop is expected here, and Mr. R—— gave notice in the newspapers for all who wished to be confirmed to apply to him for Certificates ; but, by strong drink, was rendered incapable of attending to them. Including his pay at the fort, he has had a large annual salary (a £1000 a year). Ours is again the only place of worship, as, during the last fourteen years, has frequently, sometimes too for long periods, been the case."

January was not out before the first instalment of the long-wished-for help arrived. It appeared in the persons of the Rev. James and Mrs. Mirams, who entered the river on Tuesday, the 22nd, and landed the day after. On the following Lord's Day he accompanied the pioneer to Lonsdale, of which station he took charge; for the first sixteen months, however, residing in town. In the afternoon of Lord's Day, 10th March, Mr. and Mrs. Wray

"went up to Lonsdale to give over to him the members living in that neighbourhood, and form them into a separate church. Here for the first time we had the Supper of the Lord. We felt it to be a time of refreshment from His holy presence; Mr. Mirams concluding with a very suitable address and prayer. We trust the little one will become a thousand. There are seventeen members, and about twenty adults baptized, not yet admitted to the Lord's Table."

What need of instruction, &c., existed, was being illustrated, at the time of Mr. and Mrs. M.'s landing, by a case before the courts which lasted some days and in which the pioneer took a deep interest. It was a matter of divorce between a Mr. and Mrs. K——. Decided in her favour, he, an opulent man, was to allow her £1000 a year. Evident that the poor young woman had been sacrificed to the ambition of her father, the judge, when passing sentence, remarked very severely upon him, and

"some of the slaves called as witnesses, as on other trials, manifested the greatest ignorance. They had not even heard of a God, much less of a Saviour, and seemed not to have the smallest idea of the obligation of an oath or of the sin of lying. Some of the people laughing at their ignorance, one of the judges remarked that it would have been much more to their credit to have instructed them than to laugh at their ignorance. The Protector assured me that, in consequence of the extreme ignorance of the people, he lost almost every case he had."

But what of those who had had opportunities of instruction, *e.g.*, the Crown slaves in town, numbering about 330, and already emancipated? The contrast is wide, while the observation and language of a Bishop and stranger, such as the following, must have been very gratifying to him who had so laboured and suffered in the cause of religion and instruction.

"18*th February.*—A few days ago the Bishop of Barbadoes visited Berbice and held a confirmation. He took an opportunity of visiting the Winkel negro houses, going into many of them, conversing very particularly with the people, inquiring what place of worship they attended, who taught them to read, hearing some of the little children repeat a hymn and Watts's catechism, and expressed his pleasure at what he saw and heard. A report had reached Barbadoes that they were abandoning the village, would not work, and were allowing their houses to go to ruin ; but he told Mr. Scott, the late Crown agent, that he saw anything but deterioration, and that he would write His Majesty's Government in their favour, lest the same unfounded reports should reach their ears. Mr. S. told him that a few of the young people had gone to Demerara and other places because they could get better wages ; that one of them (whose name his lordship recognized), was even engaged in painting the cathedral in Barbadoes ; that it was true they would not engage in field labour because they had never been accustomed to it, but were in general excellent mechanics ; that as to their houses, many of them had been in a state of dilapidation because Government, undecided for some years what to do, would not go to the expense of repairing them ; but that, since emancipation, most were improving their houses, and some were building excellent ones. That there are a few drunken, idle people amongst them," adds Mr. Wray, "is certain, but chiefly among those who were at the fort. Forty of them are communicants with us."

From present incidents of pastoral experience, the following must not be left unquoted :—

" *Lord's Day*, 3*rd February.*—Yesterday buried one of our members, a person of colour, aged 108 years or upwards. A native of St. Kitt's, she had spent 40 years, at different periods, in England,

and had been in Berbice about nineteen years.   Yet only in 1828 had she embraced the Gospel.   She saw no need of a Saviour, was one of the most self-righteous persons I have met with, and though her daughter, upwards of seventy, has long been a member with us, the old mother rejected the Gospel.   One morning I was riding by, stopped my horse under her window and called out to her, 'Granny!'   She said, 'I do not know you, sir.'   I told her who I was; that I had come to invite her to chapel and that she must come.   I got her promise.   Though so old, she became a regular attendant and her mind soon affected with the Gospel. Before long, she requested admittance to the Table of the Lord, and from that time to her death gave every evidence that she was born of God; often blessing Him for His great goodness in calling her out of darkness into His marvellous light.   She got up on Friday morning, the 1st, drank about half a cup of tea, fell down and died.   How wonderful are the ways of God!"

The transition state of the Colony, in common with that of the British West Indies, had its difficulties.   Some, serious and widespread, will presently engage our attention more at length; at this date, perplexities in cases of family relation-ship arising from past polygamy, and scandals connected with a too partial modification of the marriage-code, claimed the pioneer's attention, who records interesting but painful instances.   The former, after giving his careful and con-scientious opinion, he had to leave with the parties themselves, their households and owners or estate-managers to carry out or settle.   Against the latter he still protests, as he had already done to the Home Government, and, more lately, in a letter to the Colonial Governor, D'Urban.   With a clergyman often, through drink, incapable, and a Lutheran minister that could understand or speak hardly any English, frequently with long periods when neither was there; a British subject and minister of the Gospel was deprived of the power of performing marriage by the new law, merely because he dissented from the Episcopal Church.   "These things ought not so to be," says Mr. Wray.   Under the old slave law, all licensed teachers had the power, though then slave-marriages were illegal. Why now, when such marriages are legalized, should there be this exception?

Such business amid his usual engagements, with the lapses of health and strength which sometimes occurred, might of themselves account for a few months' silence here in the diary, specially if he had already begun his attempt to fulfil the wish expressed by the Directors that he would write a History of the Mission. The erection of a third chapel, however, was on its way, in anticipation, too, of another missionary arriving to work on the West Bank; besides which, events in Britain now moving rapidly on to the Act of Emancipation passed in the present year, were being watched with keen interest though very opposite feelings, both by abolitionists and by the whole West Indian party; not least so by him who, on 28th October, again breaks silence thus:—

"Since I last wrote in this journal (4th May), several important events have transpired worthy of notice;" putting foremost "the Act of Parliament for the Abolition of Slavery which received the Royal Assent, 28th August, and was published last week in the Colony."

We must give his remarks upon this grand success the friends of abolition had attained, and several following entries, virtually without abbreviation. The first will serve to show how well John Wray had studied and watched the question of abolition; and how correct, as events proved, were his surmises in respect to the working of the Apprenticeship clauses, &c.

"Though the friends of freedom have not obtained all that could be desired; they have done what they could, perhaps all that could be expected. Indeed, a few years ago, I never could have contemplated such a great and glorious change; and whatever feelings may exist in the minds of the enemies of emancipation, yet I have seen far greater outward agitation and fermentation manifested over a mere speech in Parliament than during the whole discussion of this important question.

"I do not think the system of Apprenticeship will answer. There will be constant disputes between the master and the apprentice respecting their respective rights : besides it will compel the Labourer to work for the cruel and severe Manager. They should have established compulsory labour with the choice of masters ; then the kind and humane would have obtained a sufficient number of labourers, while the cruel and severe would have had to cultivate their own fields. The apprentices, however, may annoy their masters very much by refusing to labour for them in the master's own time.

"It is nevertheless a glorious victory, for which I desire to bless and praise God. I would also adore His great goodness that I have been permitted to take a part, for so many years, in forwarding this blessed work. I feel grateful to my Heavenly Father that he ever brought me into connection with the Commissioners of the Crown property. The plans adopted on the late Crown estates, were similar to all the Orders in Council, since issued. I bless God that I should have been spared to see so much accomplished. A few years ago I should have been torn out of the pulpit, if I had attempted to read such a proclamation as I read a fortnight ago."

The Act coming into force 1st August of the following year, preparations were meanwhile made for its administration. All felt the importance of the crisis. Governor D'Urban having left the colony to be promoted; on 26th June, Major-General Sir James Carmichael Smyth took office. He was the last civil Governor whom the pioneer lived to see ; and his accession at so critical and important a juncture, with his consequent first visit to Berbice, are other particulars noticed as having occurred during the periods of journalistic silence. It may be remarked that Mr. Wray's first impressions of the new Governor's character and manner were fully borne out by his Excellency's after-administration, as they have also been corroborated by subsequent writers.

"The appointment of Sir James Carmichael Smyth to be Governor of British Guiana, appears to be a most happy circumstance for furthering the great work of humanity and emancipation. He seems to be a man of great decision of character, and determined to carry the plans of His Majesty's Government into execution.

"Last week (preceding 28th October), his Excellency paid a visit to Berbice. On my introduction to him at the Committee of the Free School, he told me that he had heard of my name and character; and also asked me several questions respecting schools in the district. I mentioned to him the Winkel School, on which he expressed a wish to see it, and promised to visit it in the afternoon. Mr. Mirams who was with me, soon had the children called; and, after visiting the gaol, his Excellency came to the school, heard some very little children read in the New Testament, asked them several questions, and expressed himself as highly pleased with them. He observed that we wanted a better and larger schoolroom. We mentioned that our plan was, if possible, to make the school support itself, by inducing each parent to pay a Bitt (4d.) per week; of which his Excellency expressed his approbation, and said he would bring the children some medals the next time. In the former part of Friday, we attended his levee, after which the Committee of the Berbice Free School, of which we are members, presented an address to his Excellency, praying him to become its patron. He said he would not merely give his name, but would promote its benefit in every way he could, and put it on such a footing as to afford education to the poor children of New Amsterdam. We then had a private interview, and brought before him some particulars respecting our Mission. He conversed with us in a most affable manner, and requested us to write him on the points mentioned. Later in the day, he visited the Infant school at the chapel. 150 were present, but half of them belonged to the Sunday school and came merely to look on. Mr. Mirams exercised the children in several pieces; and a very little black boy repeated the first six lines of the multiplication table exceedingly well; with which the Governor and his Aide-de-Camp were much pleased and amused. Remaining about half-an-hour, his Excellency then requested to see the chapel. I went with him. He made several inquiries about the attendance of the people, and when told that it was crowded on the Sabbath, he observed:—'It is very gratifying.' He also made some inquiries respecting our other chapel; and on his departure, he gave me a most cordial shake of the hand.

"The coloured people presenting a petition for civil rights equal to those of the white inhabitants in the Colony, his Excellency assured them there would be no distinction from that day on account of colour, for people would be dealt with not on account of colour, but on account of education, character, or property.

"When visiting the gaol his Excellency asked every prisoner if he had any complaint to make. One of the *Highbury* people, very severely flogged some months ago and condemned to a month on the treadmill, entered into a full and particular detail of the cruelties he had experienced, and of the ill treatment of the people on the estate, to which his Excellency gave the greatest attention. Going to the treadmill, he examined the 'cats' with which females as well as males were flogged (some poor women of late dreadfully so), and, quite shocked with those instruments of punishment, ordered them to be discontinued; these and other circumstances ending in the suspension of both Fiscal and gaol-surgeon.

"On Saturday, as his Excellency was descending the steps of the court-house, a negro from the West Coast, cartwhipped by his manager, presented himself with his stripes. The Governor sent him to the Protector with an order to take down the complaint and then forward it. The invalids among those lately belonging to the Crown, applying to his Excellency for clothing, his Aide-de-Camp was ordered to attend to them and report; with the result that a supply of new and proper clothing was directed to be given them, and that the Aide-de-Camp declared he had never in his life had so many blessings poured upon him as by those people.

"The same day, his Excellency returned to Georgetown. His condescension, affability, attention to business and to all classes, must have left a most favourable impression on all except those interested in the abuses which it is his determination to do away with."

One more particular of the period follows, given almost in

a line, the pioneer little thinking what more than a missionary he was welcoming.

"On the 11th of this month (October), arrived the Rev. James Howe to assist in this mission. I pray that God may bless him with every spiritual blessing."

These were cheering events, even though the brighter things appear all the more to deepen that awful darkness and those terrible cruelties which had so long and universally prevailed. Nearer at hand, too, was a fly in the pot of ointment, long borne with, but soon now to be removed.

" I have lately had a great deal of trouble with Mr. and Mrs. A——. He seems determined to annoy me in every way he can ; for about six months absenting himself from the teachers' meetings, which is contrary to the rules, and she doing the same since their marriage. Proposing that they should be called to account for their conduct, it was agreed to write them on the subject."

In vain, unless to bring out the unamiableness of Mr. and Mrs. A.'s spirit and the unreasonableness of their thoughts. In the church he had endeavoured to form a party against the pastor, and as neither amendment nor withdrawal were forthcoming, exclusion became a painful necessity. This took place after particularly explaining to the church (Rom. xvi. 17), reading Mr. James on the subject, whose opinions Mr. Wray shared, and informing any who might be of Mr. A.'s party that they were at full liberty to go with them. None did this but one female, a particular friend of Mrs. A.'s, who however soon returned ; and the church continued to flourish.

Lord's Day, 10th November, the new chapel on the West Bank, afterwards known as " Hanover Chapel," was dedicated. Built to seat about 350, from 800 to 1000 people assembled for the opening service ; a number at half past two, coming from town and from estates on the East Bank.

" Myself and my daughters crossed the river and entered the

chapel about ten. It was then crowded and great numbers could not get in." Marriages, baptisms, conversation, singing hymns, reading and explaining the Scriptures, occupied the time until the other missionaries arrived. "Mr. Mirams read suitable passages of Scripture and offered prayer ; I preached from Ps. xxii. ver. 27. 'All the ends of the world shall remember and turn unto the Lord : and all the kindreds of the nations shall worship before Thee ;' Mr. Howe giving out the hymns and concluding with prayer. It was to me a most solemn and interesting occasion, and appeared to be so to all."

As many from the West side had been accustomed to cross to town for instruction and worship, classes of varied grade and for adults or children would be the more easily arranged when, on the following Sunday, along with Mrs. Wray, he went to take the services and commence the school. The chapel was again more than filled, and during the day many were baptized, six admitted to fellowship, about as many couples married; but all was made ready for Mr. Howe who was to take charge, and who, going over on Sabbath, the 24th, was quite gratified to find, not only the place full, but all set so in order. The joy of none was diminished to find that, notwithstanding the number now ceasing to cross the river, the town chapel, such was the constant growth, was, on 1st December again well filled.

Lord's Day, 15th December, accompanied by Mrs. Wray and followed in the afternoon by his daughters and Mr. Howe—

"I formed the members who live on the West side of the river, forty-four in number, into a separate church, and gave them over to Mr. Howe as their future pastor. To us, a very interesting day. We rejoiced to see a third Christian church formed in Berbice. The place was crowded to excess, and many could not get in."

The negroes of this neighbourhood, Mr Wray describes as a fine, intelligent, and interesting people, every way fitted for the full enjoyment of freedom. Many, under great difficulties, and some, under great persecutions, had learnt to read; and the history of the whole movement here is a striking realization of the parable of the mustard-seed, and illustration of the service of little things, or of what a young person may do.

Some years before, a boy-scholar in Mr. Wray's school, who, as he grew up, became a well-disposed youth, and a helper in the Sunday School, was bound apprentice to a carpenter, and, in the course of business, went with his master to work on one of Mr. Blair's plantations. He soon began to teach some of the negroes there to read and to say catechism, in which they made considerable progress. The attorney, hearing of it, instantly turned him off the estate, and forbade his ever going on it again; insisting also on all the negroes bringing their books to him, which they did. Writing his own name in each, he however returned them; just as in after days, when a member of the Council, he would not consent to a grant of land for the chapel, and still would not oppose. But the desire of instruction had been begotten, and grew so that nothing could quench it. Spreading down the coast, a pious corporal stationed at Fort Wellington taught the negroes, until one of the managers complained of him to the commanding officer, and the good man was, for some time, confined to the barracks. Every opportunity however, such as holidays, &c., was seized for crossing the river to attend worship, if there should be a service, and to spend all time else in school or chapel receiving instruction.

Warmly attached to the missionaries, who first laboured and cared for them, it was natural for such, and for their fellows in sympathy, to crowd to their new chapel, some walking thither a mile or two more than the six, for which, according to the slave law, it was legal to give a pass for worship. This last circumstance soon seemed likely to beget trouble; for, though the day of Emancipation was drawing so near, one attorney of several estates was disposed, taking advantage of the distance, to prohibit their attendance ; and even punished some with several days' confinement in the dark hole. But his death on Christmas Day, after a week's illness, led to the cessation of such interference, also of anxiety in the minds of the missionaries to whom the sufferers had made known their cruel usage.

On Christmas Day, sermons were preached at all three chapels for the benefit of the Berbice Missionary Society, and on the 26th December, Mr. Wray writes :—

"This day we held our public missionary meeting. The chapel was crowded, and though it lasted three hours and a half, attention was kept up to the last. It and the collection far exceeded my most sanguine expectations. Several respectable gentlemen were on the platform, and the Honourable Simon Fraser, who took the chair, in a very suitable address given at the conclusion, acknowledged that he had been much prejudiced against us in years that were past, but his opinions now were entirely changed ; that he was happy to see so many there, and that he congratulated me on having outlived the prejudices of people. Blessed be God that I have lived to see so glorious a day !"

During this most encouraging year, besides many he had baptized or united in marriage at other stations, in town the pioneer baptized 167 adults, 94 children, and married 167 couples. Sixty-two persons had been admitted to the fellowship of the church ; and apart from a great number of adults and children not included in the Sunday School, this contained 363 scholars, instructed by 27 teachers. A respectable clergyman also had come to New Amsterdam, and had established another Sunday School. No marvel that, praising God, he adds :—"This has been a blessed year."

1834.

*Eventful Year—Interest Excited—Wray on the Watch—Preparations—
Preaching, &c., in Upper and Canje Districts—Private Flogging
Abolished: Governor's Address — Great Encouragements — Offer of
Fearn—Prospecting on West Coast—Perils, &c., of Travel— Lindoe—
Bible Society Meeting—Marriage in Family—Fearn Chapel: Opening
—Growth of Work—AUGUST FIRST—New Marriage Act—Brunswick
Chapel: Opening—Friends at Home—Wilberforce: Dying Words—
Buxton: Great Exertions—Abolitionists' Dinner—Anxious Suspense—
Buxton: Receipt of Colonial Letters—GOOD NEWS—James Mont-
gomery's Lines.*

A.D. 1834, the eventful year, on *1st August* of which that
Act of Emancipation, passed at a cost of £20,000,000 to the
British people, would come into force, was entered, on both
sides of the Atlantic, amid the deep interest which such a
measure, unique in the world's history, and generous beyond
all former human precedent, was calculated to inspire.
Hopeful expectations or fearful apprehensions, feelings of
admiration or anxiety, everywhere mingled or prevailed.
The struggle of years, a struggle waxing in severity until at
last culminating in noble victory, still left all parties to wait
awhile the great event ; and it seems hardly possible now to
realize the tension which grew as the months moved on
towards the time of accomplishment.

In his place and work, interested as any well could be,
John Wray was on the watch-tower. As usual, he met his
people at an early hour to begin the year with God ; feeling
that, as he expresses it,—

"the great change which is to take place among the slaves
concerns us all, and it should be our duty to use every means
that it may take place in a peaceable manner."

In the disposition of the negroes everywhere to seek after
religious knowledge, he saw a most favourable sign ; and
confesses himself without doubt that,—

"should the proprietors and managers act with prudence, the change will be attended with the most beneficial results."

As obstacles long in the way of instructing the young would be removed, his thoughts ran on the training of such, and his hopes were to establish Infant schools for the children under six years, who were at once to be made free, and Night schools and Sunday schools, for any above that age who would still have to labour; and in the forenoon of the first Sabbath, 5th January, preaching from the 15th ver. of P's. xxxi.—"My times are in Thy hand":—

"I made some remarks on the important changes to take place, and exhorted the people to pray earnestly to God for wisdom to direct."

But praying and working went hand in hand; attentive still, therefore, to his pastoral work in town, he was speedily on the move, availing himself of doors that now, in prospect of what was to come, began to be thrown open; proprietors, attornies, and managers, one here and another there, offering him opportunities of addressing the people on their estates, and belonging to their neighbourhood. So, before another Sabbath came round, the pioneer had visited and returned from an upper part of the river.

"*Saturday, 11th January.*—Went up to Bloemhoff, the highest cultivated estate on this side the river, five hours' pull from Town, to preach in that neighbourhood for the first time, Mr. Prass the attorney having offered me his Logie, and Mr. Forsyth, one on Schepmoed, about the centre of the estates there. As they do not understand much English, I spoke Creole to them. At the first place about 230 attended; and on Schepmoed, at eleven o'clock, about 500 came. All were very attentive, and expressed the greatest desire for instruction. Several had learnt the first catechism. A very long and dreary pull, but a fine situation for a Missionary station. Arrived at home about twelve at night."

A similar visit was paid on Lord's Day afternoon, 19th

January, to Bleyendaal, about five miles up the Canje, where P. Van Holst, Esq.,

"offered us his Logic. Between 400 and 500 people attended, all expressing a most ardent desire to hear the Word of Life. Several attend in town and have learnt the first catechism. Mr. Van H. wishes us to establish a school among his little negro children. He will find the place and give them time, but the estate cannot afford any pecuniary assistance."

The two younger missionaries accordingly established a school, beginning with about thirty children, and meeting on two days a week ; one or another, at times, going thither also, or up to Bloemhoff, &c., to preach.

February brought a further sign of the new times coming.

"The Governor and Court have passed a Law that on the first of March, all private flogging of slaves shall cease, and that slaves shall not be whipped except by order of a magistrate given after due examination of both parties ; the evidence to be taken down in writing. The Governor, in a printed address to the slaves, calls them his friends ; entreats them in the most kindly manner to conduct themselves peaceably and quietly, telling them that he shall always consider the day on which he signed that Law as the happiest day of his life."

The numbers attending school and worship continued to grow, and the Berbice Agricultural Association passed a resolution to establish Sunday and other schools on all their plantations. 1000 first spelling books, lately to hand at the pioneer's, were all disposed of in three or four weeks, the demand still continuing ; and on 17th March, letters from the Missionary Society were received, containing the intelligence, most pleasing to the recipients, that the Directors were about to send fourteen missionaries to the West Indies, and a promise that the mission in Berbice should be placed on an efficient footing.

The stimulus for Mr. Wray to occupy new ground thus grew to a flood, and assuredly he was not unwilling to be borne along. On Saturday, 22nd March, going to the upper district to preach, he was kindly entertained there by H. C. Mittelholzer, Esq.,—

"who requested me to preach in his Logie, saying it should be at our service till the coffee crop came in. 120 feet long, 21 wide, and without seats, the place nevertheless was full, the negroes standing thick together; several white gentlemen of the neighbourhood also attended. The former were clamorous for books. Returning and waiting at Herstelling for the tide, I dined there, then proceeded to Rossfield, where I slept."

Rossfield, in the middle district on the West Bank, was owned by John Ross, Esq., a respectable gentleman, and magistrate for the district; between whom and the pioneer not only did conversation pass, but before they parted, important business was entered on and settled.

"Mr. R. has already introduced the plans to be adopted when Emancipation commences, allowing his people that time which is then to be secured to them, and intends to divide a plot of land into half acre squares for each one. He is very anxious to introduce instruction among them. This morning (24th) we went to look at the dwelling-house on Vraw Johanna, now Fearn, which belongs to him, a spacious building but out of repair. This, on condition of our putting it in repair, he has agreed to secure to us for the six years of the apprenticeship, free of other expense, and should he, at the end of the time again require the house, what expenses we have been at, he will refund. It is in the centre of the district. The bottom storey, which is a store, will make a fine school room; the second, which was the dwelling, will make a large chapel, and the chambers will serve as a temporary residence, when we go up to preach. Blessed be God! we have now got a firm footing on the river in three most populous parts. Reached home about the middle of the day."

Soon however to be off again, for on the next day, 25th March—

"Mr. Howe and I went over the river to take a journey a few miles down the coast to see if we could fix upon a suitable spot for another place of worship. Borrowing a horse and chaise from

J. M'Dougal, Esq., we proceeded to No. 11, M. S. Bennett, Esq., breakfasted and changed our horse; then went on as far as No. 30, and were politely received by L. Cameron, Esq., and his lady, both very desirous to have a place of worship in the neighbourhood, but without accommodation on the estate. He thinks however, a spot may be obtained on No. 27, for a temporary building. Many of the estates here have been abandoned and the inhabitants, about 3000, are scattered on an extent of frontier land, about twenty-five miles long, so that it is impossible almost to find a central spot that could be obtained. Two or three places of worship and another missionary would be needful. Returning, slept at No. 11, reaching home at mid-day of the 26th."

Multiplied journeys meant multiplied perils and discomforts. The last was amid heat astonishing even to the inured pioneer, whilst Mrs. Wray, at home, was only just recovered from a hurt in the back, received a month before, through a fall from the chaise when returning from the West Bank chapel. A much more serious peril to Mr. Wray on 30th March, the Sabbath after his return, happily ended with little more than a fright.

"In the afternoon I went to Bleyendaal. Passing through a narrow gateway, I was thrown out of the chaise, and in the most imminent danger. By some means or other I was just able to extricate my head from being run over by the wheel. A little bruised, not I trust materially hurt, I was able to preach; also in Town in the evening. Blessed be God for His goodness!"

And the plague of mosquitoes, so bad in the middle months of this year, that

"in the evening it is almost impossible to sit; reading, writing, working, or doing anything but brushing them away is out of the question; smoke, the common remedy, not succeeding,"

was found even worse in the upper district, which of course was constantly visited.

Now and then too, amidst all the preparation and anticipation, would pass away from the church in town, after a consistent Christian course maintained for years, some aged one who, having shared darker days with its pastor, rejoiced with him in the brighter times; and, if not spared to see the consummation of these, departed thankful for the near prospect, and to a still happier state. A chief of such was Lindoe, deacon and Sunday School teacher, who died just after Mr. Wray returned from the West Coast on 26th March. An African, a tailor by trade, and, before his conversion, a very gay fellow; but a most faithful servant to his master, with whom he had several times visited England; he became a devoted Christian, of good understanding in the Scriptures; liberally supporting, according to his power, the ministry of the Gospel, and highly esteemed by his fellow-members and fellow-teachers. His pastor spent much time with him during the last few days of illness, cheering the dying sufferer; and was himself cheered by the departing one's manner of spirit and pious utterances, of which, as in other cases, he makes memoranda.

But the work went on. After efforts to interest some of the whites in the matter, on 31st March a Bible Society meeting in town crowded the chapel to excess. The Parent Committee were arranging for a gift of New Testaments and Psalms to every one freed on 1st August, who was able to read. The meeting was addressed by the two new missionaries: gentlemen moved and seconded the resolutions, or gave their names as annual subscribers, and the Protector, who was in the chair, concluded with a very appropriate address, which was followed by a very respectable collection.

Accessions to the congregation and church in New Amsterdam still continued, almost every month having new guests at the Table of the Lord; visitation of the sick, &c., being kept up, and prisoners in gaol not forgotten. Among the last, a poor soldier, under sentence of death for the murder of his comrade whilst both were intoxicated, was about this time the object of Mr. Wray's special concern.

Happier changes in prospect were not limited to the social state around; within the pioneer's own domestic circle, some were in process. For the Rev. James Howe, in pure affection for Rebecca, the second daughter, having early in the year made proposals of marriage, these, after prayerful consideration, had been accepted. But betrothment there and at that time, was a public as well as a private matter; and on 8th April, this "Undertrow," as the Dutch term it, was performed, the marriage taking place on Tuesday, 6th May, when the legal part of the ceremony was conducted by the Rev. Mr. Junius, minister of the Lutheran church, and at his request, as he himself understood very little English, the devotional part of the proceedings by Mr. Wray. Several Dutch friends, ladies and gentlemen, were present, together with Mr. and Mrs. Mirams, and Mr. and Mrs. Scott from Demerara; who, after the service, partook of a friendly breakfast. The union thus formed was a most suitable and happy one; the prayers and hopes of the parents being fully realized, as already in their daughter, so in the Rev. James Howe, who proved a worthy son of a worthy sire; the two working happily together, little thinking as yet, that together they would die.

On 27th May, whilst in the upper district,—

" we had the pleasure of erecting the frame of another chapel on a piece of Crown land; a building measuring 69 feet by 31 and 13 feet high. Of about 1600 slaves, almost all attend."

The brethren in Berbice had been favoured with occasional assistance from Mr. and Mrs. Scott, but the rapidly extending work made very welcome the arrivals, on 3rd June, of the Rev. John Ross and the Rev. Samuel and Mrs. Haywood; and, on the 5th, of the Rev. Charles D. and Mrs. Watt, the last on their way to Demerara. On the 10th, too, a further supply of books was landed, "and the negroes begin again to flock for them."

From John Ross, Esq., of Rossfield, very encouraging

REV. JAMES HOWE.

accounts of the behaviour of the negroes in the middle district were received; and on Lord's Day, 29th June, at three o'clock in the afternoon, the building fitted up on Fearn as a chapel, &c., was opened. Leaving the Revs. Ross and Mirams to follow, Mr. Wray was there much earlier in the day, meeting and conversing, &c., with the people. When he began the service, the chapel, fifty feet by twenty-nine, was quite full, not a single white person, except the missionaries, among them. After the devotions, Mr. Mirams and Mr. Ross addressed them in a very appropriate way; then came the collection, singing and prayer concluding the whole. The return, against tide as far as Lonsdale, proved long and weary; the pioneer alone going on with the tide to town, where he arrived between two and three next morning, weary and stiff, but thankful for the encouragement God was vouchsafing the missionaries.

In July the work grew immensely, and the strain of feeling, here and everywhere concerned, became most intense. Little abbreviated, the following are the pioneer's entries of the later days, and of the ever-memorable 1st of August, &c.

"*Sabbath*, 20th.—Chapel in town very crowded. Preached from Phil. i. chap. 27 ver., and addressing the people on the approaching change, earnestly entreated them to act as became the Gospel of Christ in the new position on which they were about to enter; pointed out the necessity of industry, and mentioned the noble resolution of the Bible Society to put into the hands of every one about to be freed, and found able to read, a copy of the Scriptures (New Testament and Psalms). All were very attentive. Preached at Bleyendaal in the afternoon to about 300. Do hope a church will be built up in this place.

"22nd.—Sent letters to the Bible and Missionary Societies. The Governor has directed that Friday, the 1st August, shall be set apart as a day of worship and thanksgiving. Blessed be God for the near approach of that day when the chains of Slavery shall be broken and the blessing of Liberty bestowed!

"*Lord's Day*, 27th.—A day of great labour, but blessed be God for strength vouchsafed according to my day. Mr. Haywood taken very ill, which imposed upon me additional work. Addressed my own people at seven A.M. At eight, went to Overwinning and preached to a goodly number. At half-past ten, went into the vestry; married several couples, and conversed with many on the subject of baptism. At eleven the chapel was crowded with people. Preached from 1 Peter i. chap. 18 ver. Illustrated the text by their redemption from slavery with a large sum of silver and gold by the people of England, and showed them the duty, &c., of giving themselves up to Christ, from the wonderful price He had paid for them; their duty to behave as good subjects of the King, and of becoming an industrious class of people, for which they were being redeemed from slavery. At one o'clock went to Bleyendaal. Found several managers waiting, one of whom had been in the Logie teaching the people. He expressed great pleasure at finding so many able to read, including two or three from the estate of which he is manager, and on which, he said, he will now establish a school, and would be very glad to see me there to assist him. More than 300 attended worship. Delightful, in riding along, to see the provision grounds, which belong exclusively to the people, and which they had during the whole dry season, when many in the Colony could hardly get food. A respectable attorney has frequently observed that every estate might be well supplied, by a little management; that it is far better to cultivate less coffee and sugar than to be without provisions, for which, in a dry season, high price has to be paid. Indeed, anxiety for large crops, leading to the neglect of provision grounds, has always appeared to myself bad policy. In the evening preached in town again. Mr. Howe had his chapel crowded, and married twenty-eight couples.

"28th.—A delightful morning. Much fatigued; but looking forward with unspeakable delight to the first of August. Yesterday was the last Sabbath of slavery. Not that I can approve of the Apprenticeship, which will be liable to great abuse, especially as we have (at present) no stipendiary magistrates from England; yet a new system will be introduced, and the power of managers greatly checked, particularly in the extortion of labour. About 8000 children in British Guiana, under six years of age, we hope to have an opportunity of educating. Certain that the Demerara persecution would prove a death-blow of slavery, how or when I could not possibly conceive ; little did I think that so soon I should have the happiness of writing slavery abolished for ever. Blessed be God that it has hitherto been accomplished in so peaceable a manner!

"*1st August.*—This glorious day is now past. Slavery has ceased for ever, at least in name. About one million men and women who were slaves yesterday, are free to-day. The complicated Apprenticeship will, I trust, soon abolish itself, and the master will find it, I doubt not, more profitable to employ free labour than compulsory.*

"This being set apart by the Governor as a day of thanksgiving, I proposed services in my chapel. At seven A.M. between 600 and 700 attended, chiefly from the country. We began with, 'Blow ye the trumpet, blow !' &c., and I addressed the congregation from Ezra vii. 27, 'Blessed be the Lord God of our fathers which hath put such a thing as this in the king's heart.' At eleven, we assembled again. It is impossible to give any description of the congregation. The people were so crowded together in every seat, in every aisle, in all the doors and steps and pulpit stairs and vestry, that we could not press in and were obliged to take some gentlemen and others by a backway through the vestry. I think we could not have fewer than 1200 or 1300 people inside, and hundreds could not gain admittance. We again began the solemn service with, 'Blow ye the trumpet, blow !' &c., and after prayer and reading suitable portions of Scripture, we sang :—'O'er the gloomy hills of darkness,' &c. Preached from Psalm cxxvi. 3, 'The Lord hath done great things for us, whereof we are glad ;' noticing some of the great things done for us, for which we are met to return thanks to Almighty God ; the effects they should have upon us ; lessons of instruction we should learn from this subject. We concluded by singing :— 'Except the Lord conduct the plan.'

" After service, great numbers of the country people came to us with smiling faces to express their gratitude to God for the great boon which had been conferred upon them. Particularly, many

* In Antigua, the legislature dispensed with the Apprenticeship.

of the women brought their little free children in their arms to
Mrs. Wray and my daughters with joy pictured in their faces.
It was indeed a most delightful day, and all passed in the most
pleasing manner; all the people behaved with the greatest
propriety.

"In the evening, the chapel was full. I preached from
1 Peter ii. 15, 16. Our chapels on the West Bank, Lonsdale, and
Fearn were also crammed with people, and hundreds could not
gain admittance. The first of August will be one of the most
glorious days recorded in British history. Praise ye the Lord.
Praise ye the name of the Lord. Praise Him all ye servants
of the Lord. Let Britain praise the Lord for His goodness that slavery has ceased this day through the British
empire. Britons never shall be slaves.

"This day too the new Marriage Act took place. It extends
to Christian ministers of every denomination who have been duly
ordained according to the usage of the persuasion to which they
belong, and who have been duly licensed in the Colony as
ministers of the Gospel. All marriages are to be registered in
the Colonial Secretary's office. Last October, we spoke to the
Governor, when in Berbice, respecting it; also wrote him last
January. We are under great obligation to the Hon. Simon
Fraser, member of the Court of Policy. He proposed it, the
Governor seconded, and not an individual objected."

As closely connected with what precedes, we here add the
following :—

"*Lord's Day, 3rd August.*—The chapel was crowded to excess.

"*Lord's Day, 10th August.*—Preached on Bleyendaal, and
addressed the people particularly on the necessity of labour and
of obeying the new Laws. Am convinced that they are all willing
to labour the time appointed by the Act, and that, by good
management on the part of the whites, everything would go
on in the most pleasing manner.

"*Lord's Day, 17th August.*—Opened the new chapel in the
upper district. At eight o'clock, it was two thirds full. Some
of the Winkel people had come up to help in the singing, and we
began with the 72nd Psalm; 'Jesus shall reign where'er the
sun,' &c., which I then read and explained; spoke also on other

religious subjects, and prayed. They were very attentive. Telling them that we should not begin public service until 11 o'clock, they chose to remain in the chapel, rather than go home to breakfast; and long before the time appointed, the large building was crowded with negroes from every part of the district, numbers outside gathering about the windows and doors. When the people stood up, they appeared to form one mass. Again beginning with the 72nd Psalm, after reading and prayer, we sang, 'How beauteous are their feet, Who stand on Zion's hill!' &c.; and I preached from Psalm cxxvi. 3, 'The Lord hath done great things for us whereof we are glad.' During the service, I asked them several questions which they answered publicly, and so that I was convinced they perfectly understood. I could not help telling them that twenty years ago, as some of them might remember, I used to go along the river to Dageraad, a few miles higher, to instruct the Crown slaves; that then my heart often yearned over the poor negroes of the estates on each side the river, and longed to speak to them about Jesus, but I dare not put a foot there nor speak to one of them; but now God had removed the difficulties and we had three chapels on the banks of the river where the negroes could attend without any interruption, and in the district where they had long been sitting in darkness and in the shadow of death, the light of the Gospel was now shining. I think from 1000 to 1200 attended. Many earnestly entreated that a teacher should be sent up. It is a most interesting field of labour, the chapel standing amid eleven estates; all, except one, coffee estates, and three of which belonging to Dutch gentlemen — viz., La Prudence, Waak-zamheid, and Mara—have contributed in labour towards its erection. We have called it 'Brunswick Chapel.'* The district is reckoned very unhealthy for whites,† who number only about twenty. Almost all the managers were away attending a Court

---

* The pioneer was accustomed to call it his "youngest daughter."

† Not altogether otherwise for negroes, a dwarfed and a diminishing people here as compared with those on the coast. Only three or four estates remain under cultivation; the rest, as with Dageraad years before, having been abandoned. Like remarks apply to Fearn. The present Brunswick Chapel stands a little lower down the river, upon L'Enterprise estate.

Martial in town; an unfortunate circumstance at this important juncture, as the negroes were left entirely to themselves. Blessed be God that another house is erected in Berbice for the worship of Jehovah!"

A glance at the home country and friends there, will appropriately close this chapter.

The venerable philanthropist, Wilberforce, had passed away, not, however, without a knowledge and pledge of the crowning triumph that was at hand; for "the last public information he received was, that his country was willing to redeem itself from the national disgrace at any sacrifice." * "Thank God," said he, "that I should have lived to witness a day in which England is willing to give twenty millions sterling for the abolition of slavery." His remains, intended for private interment, had, by request of members of both Houses of Parliament—where once he and his measures were the objects of intensest virulence—been laid in Westminster Abbey, followed thither by royalty, peers, and commoners.

His successor in the leadership, Mr. Buxton, not forgetting, either in private or in public, to give God the glory of the triumph won, spent the

"spring and summer of 1834 chiefly in active exertions for the benefit of those so soon to be liberated; watching the regulations adopted in different islands; carefully investigating the appointment of stipendiary magistrates; and especially endeavouring to provide for the education and religious instruction of the Negroes. He was in constant communication on this subject with Mr. Stanley, and corresponded largely with the secretaries of various benevolent societies."

The important scheme of the Mico Trust which after much expense and trouble had been successfully established, occupied then a deal of his time and attention in seeing to the proper and most efficient application of the money.

* Life, &c., vol. v. p. 370.

" He spared no labour in the endeavour to establish schools,
and to procure schoolmasters of ability and piety." All
such work was of course shared by other officials and many
friends.

" When the anxiously expected first of August at length
arrived, it was kept very generally throughout England as a day
of rejoicing. To Mr. Buxton, it was rendered memorable not
only by the consummation of that great work to which his heart
had so ardently been given, but also because on this day, his
eldest daughter was married ;" Priscilla, who had been his chief
secretary.

" In the evening, the leading abolitionists dined together at the
Freemasons' Tavern ; the Earl of Mulgrave, the late Governor of
Jamaica, in the chair. But many of those who shared in the
festivities of the day could not divest themselves of the feeling of
uneasiness, when they thought of what might, at that very time,
be passing in the West Indies. The period that intervened
between August, 1833, when Mr. Stanley's motion became law,
and 1st August, 1834, when it was to take effect, had indeed passed
away in unexampled tranquillity. But, would not the gloomy
predictions of the West Indians be now fulfilled ? The bloodshed, the rioting, the drunkenness, the confusion they had so
often foretold—would not these tarnish the lustre of this glorious
deed of the British people ?

" It was, therefore, with feelings of deep solicitude, that Mr.
Buxton and his friends awaited the news from the Colonies. He
was at Northrepps Hall, when, on the 10th of September, a large
pile of letters came in with the Colonial stamps upon them.
Well-knowing that they would contain the long-looked-for
intelligence, he took them, still sealed, in his hand, and
walked out into the wood ; desiring no witness but One of
the emotion and anxiety he experienced. He opened them ; and
deep indeed was his joy and gratitude to God, when he found
that one letter after another was filled with accounts of the
admirable conduct of the Negroes on the great day of freedom.
Throughout the Colonies the churches and chapels had been
thrown open, and the slaves had crowded into them on the
evening of the 31st of July. As the hour of midnight approached,

they fell upon their knees, and awaited the solemn moment, all hushed in silent prayer. When twelve sounded from the chapel bells, they sprang upon their feet, and through every island rang the glad sound of thanksgiving to the Father of all; for the chains were broken, and the slaves were free." *

Many were the beautiful verses which the occasion called forth. Those by James Montgomery stand, it is said, pre-eminent. Placed side by side with the same author's lines on the burial of the " Missionary Smith," already given, they form a striking monument of change and many things that had gone on during the ten years between. Are not the two pieces worthy of a more frequent place in our young people's reading or recitation books than they seem to have?

> " Hie to the mountains afar,
>   All in the cool of the even,
>   Led by yon beautiful star,
>   First of the daughters of heaven :
> Sweet to the slave is the season of rest:
>   Something far sweeter he looks for to-night,
> His heart lies awake in the depth of his breast,
>   And listens till God shall say, ' Let there be light ! '
>
> " Climb we the mountain, and stand
>   High in mid-air, to inhale,
>   Fresh from our old fatherland,
>   Balm in the ocean-borne gale.
> Darkness yet covers the face of the deep :
>   Spirit of freedom ! go forth in thy might,
> To break up our bondage, like infancy's sleep,
>   The moment when God shall say, ' Let there be light ! '
>
> " Gaze we awhile from this peak,
>   Praying in thought while we gaze ;
>   Watch for the dawning's first streak,—
>   Prayer then be turned into praise.
> Shout to the valleys, ' Behold ye the morn,
>   Long, long desired, but denied to our sight ! '
> Lo ! myriads of slaves into men are new-born,
>   The word was omnipotent—' Let there be light ! '

* Life of Buxton, pp. 291-297.

" Hear it and hail it ;—the call
        Island to island prolong ;—
      Liberty ! liberty ! all
        Join in that jubilee song.
Hark, 'tis the children's hosannahs that ring !
  Hark, they are freemen, whose voices unite !
While England, the Indies, and Africa sing,
  'Amen ! hallelujah !' to 'Let there be light !' "

CHAPTER VIII.

NEGRO EMANCIPATION TO PIONEER'S DEATH.

AUGUST, 1834—JUNE, 1837.

THE work of the Mission, of instruction and amelioration, now went on with more than redoubled speed; while heathen dances, drunkenness, rowdyism, and revelling proportionately ceased. As was foreseen by the pioneer, there arose, through the abuse of the apprenticeship clauses, a serious and widespread hitch in the carrying out of the Emancipation Act, which Berbice did not escape; and which, as will presently be told more at length, involved Mr. Wray among others in a considerable expenditure of time and trouble. But if, like boulders in the stream-course, it caused a noise, yet it could not stop the flow; and, as sometimes in their case, the current at length swept the clauses clean away.

The willingness of individual planters or managers as they came forward here and there with sympathetic help, was no less encouraging than the aid furnished by societies at home in sending out men and material—ministers, teachers, books, &c.—or the eager desire for instruction shown by thousands of the emancipated.

On 9th September, the pioneer went up the East or Corentyne coast, greatly lamenting as he rode along, the many estates which, cotton not paying, had then long been out of cultivation ; but stopping at "Albion," still in cotton, to marry five couples (which ceremony, for want of a chapel, was performed in the hall of the manager's house, who "assisted me and was very polite indeed ;") and to find there "the negroes exceedingly anxious for religious instruction, earnestly entreating us to send them a minister." He rode on to "Port Mourant," where again was cultivation and a population scattered in the neighbourhood, but amounting to many hundreds. In less than nine months he had welcomed the Rev. Daniel and Mrs. Kenyon, who arrived to commence the Albion Chapel, or Fyrish Station, &c., on this coast. In fewer months still, at Bleyendaal, up the Canje, where he had often ministered hoping for a chapel, &c., Mr. Wray had his wish gratified in the opening of Orange* Chapel, with the presence and work of Mr. and Mrs. Haywood there. And if the coast to the west of Hanover Chapel, already prospected, had to wait a while for a missionary, it was not only served well, and as far as lay in his power, by Mr. Howe, but "Hanover" had already been enlarged so as to contain upwards of 800 ; and, as we shall see, in less than two years after emancipation the coast had its own large chapel on "Waterloo," built by the negroes

---

* In a quiet way, if in no other, Mr. Wray indicated his political sentiments by the names given to some of the stations he founded : "Hanover," "Brunswick," "Orange ;" intimating principles very different from the absolutism of the Stuarts and of slaveholders.

themselves. Also, even before 1834 closed, two members of the church in town had been appointed as catechists and teachers—viz., Mr. Rose, a negro native, with Mrs. Rose to Brunswick, and Mr. Henery, a coloured native, to Fearn. As 1834 drew to an end, during Mr. and Mrs. Ketley's presence in Berbice, anniversary mission services were held at the different chapels and attended by large numbers, the assemblies at Brunswick, Hanover, and in town, being each estimated at about 1000 persons. Some of these meetings were again attended or presided over by whites, chief men in the country; that at Hanover being made the opportunity for two of the neighbouring proprietors, Mr. Bennett and Mr. L. Van Rossum, to move and second a vote of thanks to the Rev. James Howe, acknowledging his zealous exertions and conciliatory conduct on the West Coast.

In 1835, principal stations had become 6; communicants were 604; baptisms numbered 359; and 6000 were under instruction. Failing the possession, in many cases, of other teachers, the people had for the time to utilize whom they could get. But so desirous were they of acquiring particularly the art of reading, that instances are recorded of some young schoolboy being carried two or three miles in an evening, for the sake of what instruction even such could afford to adults that had never been allowed to learn, and that now met in some house for the purpose.

One stimulus to this at the outset, would be the offer, by the Bible Society, of a copy of the New Testament and Psalms as a gift to every one who came under the Act of Emancipation, and was found able to read on 1st August, 1835, the time having been extended to the latter date.

In this matter Mr. Wray naturally took a great interest. Long a willing helper and correspondent of that Society, he became the agent through whom the distribution in Berbice was effected. During March, he was staying in Demerara, where, in addition to missionary brethren, his son Robert, engaged in a large mercantile establishment, now lived ; and whilst there, addressing a letter to his beloved Mr. and Mrs. Howe, full of wise counsel and fatherly tenderness, he gives also, among other items of business information, some account of a gratifying interview with the Governor, and of the demand there of the proffered boon of Scriptures. A beautifully written copy of his letter to the Society, dated 15th December, 1835, giving details of the distribution, &c., in Berbice, is also preserved. From this are taken the following :—

"I feel much pleasure in informing you that on the recommendation of Sir James Carmichael Smyth, the Court of Policy have remitted the import duty of £2½ per cent. on the Testaments and Psalms sent by the Society for the emancipated Negroes. We are making considerable progress in distributing the last consignment of the 3000 copies forwarded to us.

"The Rev. Mr. Bernau, Church Missionary on the Corentyne Coast, requested to have a supply, so we forwarded to him one of the boxes. The Rev. T. R. Reaum, Rector of New Amsterdam, also requested to have fifty copies for his people, and the Rev. Mr. Junius, fifty copies for the Emancipated Negroes on Augsburg, the estate belonging to the Lutheran Church. The Rev. J. Anderson, minister of the Scotch Church, has had a supply, and has become a member of the committee.

" You would learn from the newspaper I sent you that we had passed a resolution that a collection should be made on 1st August (1835), in all the chapels in Berbice belonging to the London Missionary Society, and sent to the Bible Society as a freewill offering of the Negroes, and a token of gratitude for the magnificent gift of upwards of 4000 copies of the New Testament bound up with the Book of Psalms, in commemoration of the 1st August, 1834, when Slavery ceased for ever throughout the British empire. ' Praise ye the Lord.'"

Additional to money sent earlier in the year, Mr. Wray had, with this letter, the further pleasure of forwarding the thankoffering thus gathered, amounting to £38, 0s. 10d. ; along with £26, 19s. 3d., the amount of subscriptions and anniversary collections in June, &c., which the committee voted should go to the fund for supplying the emancipated with their gifts.

Improvements in the Colony were such as to call forth "a most excellent speech from the Governor to the Court of Policy." A considerable increase in the amount of produce exported had taken place; and on 15th December, in the one gaol of Berbice, besides a soldier of the 86th, sentenced by Court Martial, were only three, out of 25,000 apprenticed labourers, confined.

The rains of December, 1835, and during an early and a large portion of 1836, were excessive, beyond what had been witnessed for many years, or almost what had been remembered. Portions of the coast were quite inundated, and the roads out of town and elsewhere, under water. Considerable damage was done in certain ways, and attendance at Divine ordinances was much hindered. What he could do, Mr. Wray did. A fine Sabbath, now and then, brought crowded assemblies, and intervals of sunshine were seized for visitation of the sick, &c. : though both he and his dear partner in life had occasional attacks of sickness, and were both getting more infirm.

Lord's Day, 14th February, 1836, though very poorly and the day rainy, he "crossed the river to assist Mr. Howe in the setting apart, by prayer and the imposition of hands, of nine deacons, belonging to various estates from which the people come;" a service which they also, notwithstanding the wet, attended in sufficient numbers to crowd the chapel.

1st April, when the Rev. Giles and Mrs. Forward landed, bringing with them an encouraging letter from the Society, was fair; as was the Sabbath, 3rd April, when Mr. Forward first preached; and the 4th inst., when he with his host and Mr. Howe went to open the new chapel at Waterloo; but for the rest of the month, except occasionally, of which occasions Mr. Forward availed himself to go on horseback and preach somewhere, the newcomers were detained prisoners at the mission house in town.

The chapel at Waterloo, on the West Coast, was built wholly by the people in their own time. Dividing the work amongst themselves, some cutting the timber, others grass for the thatch; the women undertaking the mud-plastering, which they did with great neatness; the whole structure, says Mr. Wray,—

"80 feet long by 25 feet, does much credit to the people. When we came near, a great number were on the road to receive us. They had hoisted a flag made of two strips of printed calico, with a strip of white between, and fired a salute of four guns as we entered the chapel. Inside and out there were not fewer than 1000 persons, all decently dressed, chiefly in white. Most of the white gentlemen of the neighbourhood also attended, and the collection to pay for the boarding and nails used, amounted to about £20."

Short and simple annals, these, of the poor; but not a small advance upon the brutality, ignorance, and degradation in their late condition under slavery, and an early lesson and example in that independence of State aid, which has so long and so honourably distinguished the Mission Churches of British Guiana.

The History of the Mission, promised to the Directors, was on the way,—

"engaging a great deal of my attention, and fills my mind with far too much anxiety. I fear sometimes it interferes with my preparation for the pulpit and visiting the sick, though I try to guard against it."

Throughout June and July heavy rains still occurred; the roads were in a terrible state, and the town in a most neglected condition, arousing fears that when dry weather returned and the trenches became stagnant, great sickness would ensue. They were not groundless; even already his daughter Jane, and afterwards her father, having a serious attack of illness.

"On 23rd July I buried three old people, two in town, and poor old America on Sandvoort ; I suppose eighty years old." *

August brought Mr. Wheeler, an agent of the Bible Society. Arriving on the 9th, he remained until the 31st. His object was to visit all the missionary stations, &c., and, wherever deemed advisable, to form associations in furtherance of the Society's work. A plan of proceedings was accordingly arranged, which himself and Mr. Wray, on Tuesday the 14th, began to carry out by then visiting Hanover Chapel. It was during the time allotted to this business that the pioneer and his household met with a loss, the greatest they had been called to sustain.

On Monday the 15th, Mr. Haywood returning from Demerara brought news that Robert, the previous Wednesday out in the sun all day receiving a cargo, had then been taken very ill with what proved to be sunstroke ; that strong remedies had been employed ; and that, though for some time deranged in mind, the means used being effectual, the patient was on Saturday in a fair way to speedy recovery.

Mr. Wray at once sought for a vessel going to Georgetown that he might fetch his son home. None, however, could be found, and as he was engaged to go up the river with Mr. Wheeler on Wednesday the 17th, he got Mr. Gereauld, a long known and trustworthy helper, to go by the first boat and bring Robert as soon as he could well be removed. Then, along with Mr. Howe, Mr. Wray proceeded to accompany the agent to Brunswick, returning on the 18th to Fearn, and reaching home about midnight ; on after days also attending meetings with Mr. Wheeler in town or at places near. All the more readily was this done, since, from one after another, reliable intelligence of the son's improvement began to be received, and though left, at the end of the week, some time in suspense, the household were hoping to receive the convalescent on Monday evening, the 22nd.

<hr>

* See page 151 of this work.

About eight o'clock, Mr. Gereauld arrived without Robert, but with the sad news of his death and funeral, the former on Friday evening, the latter on the evening of Saturday.

It was a blow indeed; "like a thunderstroke," writes Mr. Wray, "to our anxious minds, and particularly to Mrs. Wray; and his sisters, whom he tenderly loved, were deeply affected." Mr. Gereauld had reached Georgetown on Thursday evening, and was with deceased twenty-four hours before death; but the relapse had then gone so far that, though accustomed to him from a child, the sufferer did not know him, and kept wandering much on business. Every care possible, however, had been taken of the stricken one, whose employer had done all in his power. Mr. Ketley and other ministers had visited him, and several old friends, people of colour, had watched over him.

"In lucid moments, especially on Wednesday night, he frequently spoke of his father and mother; wished much to see them; said that they had taught him from his infancy about Jesus Christ, and that he believed through Jesus he should be saved; that though he could not see us here we should meet again at the last day. He prayed for pardon for the sake of Jesus Christ."

But Robert seems to have been an engaging youth, at school or wherever he went, obtaining the goodwill of all. Their old friend, Mr. John Thompson, of Hull, formed such an opinion of him when in England as to remember him with a legacy of £500, to be paid on his coming of age.* Diligent in business, he gave great satisfaction to Mr. Christy and all his employers, and had every prospect of doing well. He was but a few weeks beyond the completion of his twentieth year, and was not without thoughts of entering the Christian ministry.

The smitten family bowed in submission to the Divine

---

* Additional to £500 bequeathed to Mr. Wray by this generous and faithful friend.

will, believing in the higher reasons for such a loss ; and on
the Sabbath following the news, the pioneer's text was
Ps. xxxix. ver. 9, "I was dumb, I opened not my mouth,
because Thou didst it."

They would have much sympathy, and in September the
Governor, coming to Berbice, made it one of his first duties
to condole with Mr. Wray, and show his interest in the mission premises and work.

"The morning after his arrival, his Excellency kindly and con-
descendingly called on us, to personally sympathize with Mrs.
Wray on the death of our beloved Robert. His Excellency also
requested me to accompany him the next morning to the Winkel
village, but I was taken ill with fever, and not able to go. On
the Sabbath, accompanied by the Sheriff and his Secretary, he
visited the Sunday School, expressed great pleasure in seeing so
many children, and requested that a hymn might be sung. He
also asked to see the chapel. It is a mercy when God inclines the
great and mighty to be favourable to His cause, which, I sincerely
believe, Sir James is."

It had been agreed by the brethren that Mr. Mirams,
with his wife and children, should go to England, and in
October, having suffered much in health, they took their
departure, not to return ; Mr. and Mrs. Forward occupying
Lonsdale. Mr. and Mrs. Howe's going, about the same
time, to the Islands to recruit, "left the work with few
labourers indeed." But, depending on God, Mr. Wray went
on doing all he could at the chapels, both on the West side
and also up the river. On 14th March of the following
year (1837), died Mr. George Gereauld, who has just been
mentioned.

"When a boy he was our faithful servant, till he went to learn
the carpenter's work. Since then, I may say, he has been our
friend. In all our difficulties he stood by us, and in all our
affliction he was our friend. Almost always he travelled with
me, and he superintended the building of most of our chapels."

Another loss, in March, 1837, came in the death of Mrs. Rose, wife of the teacher at Brunswick, a very quiet, inoffensive, unassuming woman, to whose usefulness, and steady, consistent, Christian character, Mr. Wray bears strong testimony. She was in town at the time, and her husband, sent for as soon as danger appeared, did not arrive till a few minutes after her death.

"Poor man! he is deeply affected; and well he may be, for she was a very kind, prudent, affectionate wife."

On the other hand, Mr. and Mrs. Parish landed at New Amsterdam, 4th February, to labour there as schoolmaster and mistress; and,—

"on Lord's Day, 16th April, in the afternoon, all the Sunday School children, with many of their parents, assembled in the new schoolroom, called the British School; a very neat, substantial, and spacious building, fitted on the British system, as completely as we are able, under the superintendence of Mr. Parish. It will be for the reception of all, without regard to sects and parties. I trust it will prove a blessing to many."

1834–1837.

Abuse of Apprenticeship Clauses—Want of Preparation—Danger Consequent—Slander of Missionaries—Firmness of Governor—Colony's Indebtedness to Mission—"King's Law"—Injustice and Cruelty—Wray's Action: Suggestions—English Deputation of Inquiry: Arrival—Letter from Mr. Howe—Visit of Wray and Howe to Demerara—Return: Sicknesses and Deaths—Funeral of Pioneer—A Phrenological Resurrectionist—Great Lamentations—Tombs: Tablets: Inscriptions.

WE have thus given, in brief detail, varied items of event and work during these last years of the pioneer's life. They are items suggestive, still more than declarative, of the scenes amid which, and of the unceasing toils with which he, his son-in-law, and the other brethren, had to labour in meeting the calls made upon them by the new circumstances and rapid changes in the social state which had come, and which were coming.

In addition, however, to all these, running along with all, though as yet unmentioned, were other events which caused John Wray, as they did many besides, not a little either of pain and grief, or of anxious thought and work.

This arose chiefly in the operation of the Apprenticeship clauses of the Emancipation Act, or, rather, the abuse of those clauses by avaricious, unprincipled, unfeeling proprietors.

Berbice, if it did not suffer so much as other slave colonies, had its cases of this kind; but complaints to their friends, to Wray amongst the rest, soon began to accumulate, and the outcry from our West Indian possessions waxed long and loud.

It was more than the British people could brook. And rightly so. Had they not paid the slave owners £20,000,000 compensation, of which, by the way, more than £4,000,000, or one-fifth part, went to British Guiana alone? and was the last state of a number thus redeemed to become even worse than the first? Not so, if they could help it. At any rate it was resolved that inquiry should be made, and this having been done, the Apprenticeship was altogether terminated, 1st August, 1838.*

* Mr. Buxton, unwilling at first either to relieve his friends' anxiety over his broken health by retiring from Parliament, or to agree to the abolition of the Apprenticeship clauses, at length did both. His reasons, at the outset, for declining to retire, are given or suggested by the following, written in a reply to a pressing letter on the subject :— " I have received very encouraging accounts from the West Indies of the conduct of the Negroes, and this, I am sure, will please you. Three years ago (1833), it appeared, by official reports, that in Jamaica there were 300,000 floggings with the cart whip in a year. Last year, the number was reduced nine-tenths—from 300,000 to 30,000. The result being such, I grudge neither the time nor the money, nor the labour, nor the health even, spent on this object; and I hope this considera-

In one or two of the colonies, the days immediately following Emancipation had been attended with considerable danger. Due preparations for the change had not been made—*e.g.*, the emancipated had not been informed or instructed as to the Apprenticeship clauses; when, therefore, called to resume work under the new and temporary arrangements, they could not understand, and would not, for a little while, accept the conditions. Such was the case in Guiana or parts of it, and the voice of slander, ascribing this to the missionaries, began to rise. These devoted men were not unaccustomed to the glaring falsehoods that could be cherished in the West Indies, nor to absurd charges brought against themselves. But this was so palpably false that, though under circumstances of former days and particularly under such Governors as Bentinck or Murray, it might have been turned to advantage in silencing, banishing, or hanging the entire company; under so impartial and firm a Governor and friend as Sir James Carmichael Smyth, it soon proved a failure. Mr. Mirams, at Lonsdale, did indeed receive a prohibition from his Excellency as to public speaking; but in three days, and before his answer reached Sir James, it was withdrawn. For the worst of the disturbance or strike was in Essequibo, where no missionaries had lived; in less measure it affected Demerara, where missionaries had, as we have seen, been shamefully interfered with; and but little or none of it was felt in Berbice. The Governor proved just the man for the occasion, as well as for the critical years of transition now upon the Colony; and, though grossly abused by sections of

tion will make you better satisfied with my having been in Parliament. Can I, as an honest man, retire now, when I know for a certainty that the effect of my motion in the House last year, and the year before, has been to frighten the magistrates, and to save the backs of thousands of poor fellows from unmerciful floggings?"—"Life, &c.," p. 323.

the planting interest, outlived what, as a rule, he treated
with cool indifference or silent contempt, so that when he
fell, in 1838, victim to a few days' fever, he was mourned
alike by all classes ; a monument to his memory, from the
hand of Sir F. Chantrey, being afterwards erected by the
colonists in the Georgetown Cathedral.

But if Berbice, especially, was more tranquil than the rest
of the country, it was not for lack of excitement that the
discontent did not more openly show itself ; and instead of
accepting the blame sought by some to be put upon the
missionaries, Mr. Wray claims that it was to the missionaries
they were indebted for the measure of peace, as compared
with some parts, which there prevailed.

"They (the missionaries) have indeed used their utmost
endeavours to pacify the people, when complaining that their
masters had given them no time or have laid heavier tasks on
them than before ; and have entreated them to wait until very
soon when all would go well with them, and the Governor would
see that they got their right ; assuring them they need not be
afraid the laws are too strict." "We have used great pains to
quiet and calm their minds, and are sure that we have succeeded
in keeping them in that peaceable state in Berbice in which they
have been kept." "My opinion is that the whole disturbance
has arisen from want of proper arrangements before the 1st of
August," or, as expressed by others, "a want of union of purpose
and conduct on the part of our magistrates, proprietors, attorneys,
and managers."

These sentences were written in September, 1834, after
some very anxious and troublesome weeks in August. The
jubilation on the 1st over, on many estates the negroes had
been sent into the field neither with any explanation of the
Apprenticeship nor any agreement as to the distribution of
working hours. Where these had been made, all went on in
good order. Elsewhere there was ignorance, &c., and in
many cases advantage was taken of that ignorance ; for the
old spirit was not exorcised in a day. Dissatisfaction,

therefore, soon arose, and a few struck work; were tried, condemned, and sent to the treadmill; not, unfortunately, by a stipendiary magistrate, but by planters appointed as Justices. This increased the dissatisfaction, the opinion being formed that "they (the Justices) will help one another, but not us."*

Seven and a-half hours a-day, six days a week, was the working time, and the negroes called it, "King's law." But different estates wanted different arrangements; some, nine hours a-day, five days a-week, and, in Demerara, with the further provision that Saturday should be free only if the work on the preceding five days had been duly performed, and conduct had been good and orderly; not otherwise. Other estates wanted to divide the hours of labour, distributing them over the day. A scheme of work published by the Governor, 31st July, and taken by some as Law, became the occasion of other complaints, and was acknowledged to be more than many could accomplish; all which, however, was corrected by a proclamation from his Excellency, showing that it was neither Law nor intended for any but the most effective negroes.

The labourers in general stuck to the "King's law," and to taking the seven and a-half hours at one stretch; some fearing that any deviation might be viewed as a rejection of the law, and be followed by a prolongation of their tied condition; most, because of the present advantage to themselves. To go a distance on an estate, fulfil the required task, return home or to their own little plots, was to them better than any other plan. They were willing accordingly; there were estates where this was the rule, and little if any loss came of it. Elsewhere, the propositions were such as to make common the expression :—

* One negro, so condemned, being told, when at the mill, that the magistrates were now put to protect them; asked his informant, "If he ever knew people put the cat to watch the meat?"

"When the King's law came before and brought hand stock and dark hole, the managers took it and did not want to change; but now that a good law is come, they want to change it."

Some of the special Justices, proprietors themselves, to their honour refused to convict in such cases—*e.g.*, Mr. Ross of Port Mourant on the Corentyne Coast, and Mr. Fraser, another magistrate, who received an angry letter from one proprietor because they declined punishing negroes simply for refusing to rest two hours in the middle of the seven and a-half required by law to be spent each day on estate work.

Such troubles, judging from the emptiness of the gaol in December, 1835, they had either got settled or had to settle among themselves. Stipendiary magistrates also, one or more, appeared. But, despite all, worse abuses were at hand, if not already begun.

Work on a sugar estate was the more arduous toil, but sugar was the best paying crop; and to make money by it, what or whoever else suffered, seemed to become the object of some owners of these properties. The growth of provisions was neglected, and all the time of labour they could command under the Act, was devoted to the making of sugar. Worse still: a sugar planter would purchase, say, a coffee estate with its Apprenticed labourers, then insist upon removing the labourers to his sugar estate, frequently selling the mere land again. This meant more than the likelihood, or certainty of such land going out of cultivation. The Apprenticed labourers, though just redeemed from slavery, were not consulted in the matter; very many were strongly attached to the place where they had been born or had long lived; they had huts and gardens there, relatives and friends in the neighbourhood, some a wife or a husband, Apprenticed labourer on a near estate, now, in many cases, to be placed thirty miles apart; all besides the work being new and more arduous to them, and the British people having already paid the price of their redemption on the understanding they should be apprenticed where they were for a few years, preparatory to their becoming free as English labourers.*

This, of course, met with stubborn resistance. In one case (not specified below), that of Vryheid, near town, the owner of which had died, October, 1835, and the people of which his executors proposed to remove to Philadelphia, about nine miles up the Canje, known then as a most sickly and fatal spot, the labourers protested they would not go.

"*Lord's Day, 26th February.*—They have called them up several times, and on several Sabbaths, to propose their removal, and have also had Mr. MacLeod, the (stipendiary) magistrate several times, but the negroes still resist, and say they will not move a foot ; that they and their children will soon die there, and then what use will 'Freedom' be to them? The manager came to request my influence with them, of which they heard, and came to beg me not to say anything to them on the subject, for they would be sorry to refuse me anything, but they were determined not to go ; that if they brought soldiers they would not resist, but retire on their master's grave and fall there ; that they may as well die there as go to die on Philadelphia from the unhealthiness of the place, and the hard work of the sugar cultivation ; that if tied like hogs, and put in a punt, they will not resist, but they will not live on Philadelphia, or turn New Negroes again ; that they are Apprenticed labourers to Vryheid, and they will stay there till the apprentice term is out." "Their distress is very great."

At Waakzamheid, not until two were flogged ; at Vryburg, two; at Overwinning, some imprisoned; and those at Golden Grove had been starved into it, did the Apprenticed ones yield.

Had the pioneer wished, he could not wholly have escaped

* Thus Vryburg and L'Enterprise, both in the upper district, were purchased, and the labourers removed ; those of the former to Providence, near town, and those of the latter to Canefields on the Canje ; Waakzamheid was purchased, and the people removed to Mara ; Zorgenhoop, to Friends ; Overwinning, to Lochaber ; Golden Grove, to Hope and Experiment ; No. 22, to Smithson's Place.

being involved in the contentions thus raised.   Most of the estates named were close upon one or other of the mission stations; numbers therefrom were attendants at school and chapel; and to whom should the burdened ones go so readily, as to the men who had first taught and cared for them, especially to him who had, for so many years, been their steady and sympathizing friend?

But true as ever, and without needless meddling, Mr. Wray would not shut his ears to the complaint of wrong advantage now being taken, yet of which the Courts could not take cognizance.   Leaving acts of barbarous cruelty, or cases of gross neglect, which still at times occurred, to be dealt with by the law; on cases of doubtful legality he would get an opinion, also redress if possible; and wrong, to prevent which law was wanting, he would report.

In Demerara, during 1835, he took the opportunity of laying before the Governor the case of an Apprenticed labourer on the Berbice West Coast, flogged for declining to be a driver, which his Excellency at once pronounced could not be allowed, and promised to direct the magistrate to report upon the matter.   Women that could show marriage certificates he sent to the Stipendiary, who wrote letters directing they should be returned to the districts respectively in which the husbands still lived.   Else, he could only report to the friends of Emancipation in England; and there remains copy of a paper thus sent, under date 10th February, 1836, which, with particulars of such illustrations as have been specified touching the sale of estates, consequent separations, &c., contains also the following suggestions:—

"(1) Passing of a law to prevent planters purchasing estates on purpose to remove the labourers to their sugar estates.

"(2) The authorized amount of labour should be confined between the hours of six and six, all labour performed after that hour at night to be paid for.

"(3) If not a legal Protector of the Apprenticed appointed to each Colony, suitable persons as representatives of their friends, coming out to watch over their interests, would be a great blessing.

"(4) Establishment of a regular fixed price at which an Apprentice can purchase his time, and not be left to the precarious appraisements of planters.

"(5) Such warning as is contained in the information (a) that some apprentices were threatened with the withdrawal of medical attendance should they send their free children to school, a less evil than which would be the refusal of food, as food the parents might be able to find, but not medical skill, &c. (b) The neglect of the cultivation of provisions in consequence of the absorption of labour in sugar cultivation, which might lead to scarcity if not famine, and against which the Government ought to be on their guard."

But enough was coming to the knowledge of friends in England as to lead at length to several gentlemen visiting the West Indies, personally to observe and inquire. These, at the end of 1837, published a work describing the condition of the Apprentices, which caused such indignation, that, in the beginning of 1838, delegates from all parts of the country were sent to London to urge the discontinuance of the system. Success ultimately crowned their efforts, for on the evening of 22nd May, Sir Eardley Wilmot gained, by a majority of *three*, a motion in the House of Commons against the Apprenticeship; and the planters afterwards agreed to surrender it on the 1st of August, 1838.

The time when these visitors arrived in the West Indies was November, 1836. Mr. and Mrs. Howe, as already remarked, were then recruiting in the Islands, and it was from his son-in-law that Mr. Wray received intelligence of their coming.

" BARBADOES, 14th Nov., 1836.

" MY DEAR FATHER,—In the postscript of Rebecca's letter I named the arrival of four gentlemen from England. I have just returned from my interview with them. I have only time to state their names and object by the mail-boat—Mr. Joseph

Sturge, Mr. Thomas Harvey, Mr. Loyd (all members of the Society of Friends), and Mr. John Scoble. Their names will convey to you an idea of their object. Their great object is to obtain correct information respecting the working of the *Apprenticeship system* and the progress of education generally.

"Mr. Scoble and Mr. Loyd are coming on to Demerara and Berbice in a few days. They have a letter of *introduction* to you from Mr. Arundel. Mr. Buxton's Committee will resume its inquiries next session of Parliament, and the above gentlemen are come out to collect all the facts and evidence they may be able to obtain on the working of the Apprenticeship. They have heard of the court of inquiry on B——,* but neither of these gentlemen has been able to gain a sight of the document I sent home. I shall write home to Mr. ——, on the subject, and beg him to cause it to be placed in the hands of Mr. Buxton as early as possible.

"I have introduced Dr. H.'s name to the gentlemen, also B. C.'s, as individuals able to give them some information on the points of inquiry. If you see the Doctor, you can name the subject to him, with a request that he will not make it the subject of common conversation—although they are not ashamed to avow their object.

"They are very anxious that I should be in Berbice, but I am afraid I shall not. Were I to consult my feelings on the subject, I should accompany them to Guiana. My heart is in their benevolent object; and I should not be surprised to find myself in Berbice in a few weeks. They are delighted with the idea of being able to obtain information direct from the Negroes themselves. I fear this can only be done by my presence among the B—— Negroes. C—— and M—— can now tell their stories to advantage. I feel that I can scarcely remain in Barbadoes under these circumstances.

"I am to have a second interview with Mr. Scoble to-morrow.

---

* On the Berbice West Bank; an investigation ordered by the Governor after receiving a letter from the medical attendant, Dr. H., who, failing to get attention paid by the attorney to his complaints of cruelty exercised and of the shocking state of the hospital there, wrote to his Excellency. The inquiry was the means of bringing to light several atrocious deeds on this and connected estates.

The boat is now about to sail, so I must conclude this hasty scrawl. I will write again in a few days.—I am, my dear Father, your affectionate Son-in-law,　　　　JAMES HOWE."

The above is so intimately connected with the important event shortly to follow that it is quoted almost entire. Mr. and Mrs. Howe did return to Berbice, in time for him, as well as his father-in-law to do what prudently and consistently they could, in aiding the friends from England to obtain interviews with whom they desired to communicate. In May, 1837, the

"Court of Policy being about to make a law that no one should speak in the chapels but an ordained minister, which would have excluded the catechists, as well as such visitors and ministers from the Society of Friends as Messrs. Scoble and Sturge, &c., from speaking ; Mr. Wray and the missionaries agreed that an appeal should be made against it, and to do this, Mr. Wray and Mr. Howe went as a deputation to Demerara." *

Thence, it is thought, they brought the seeds of the disease which soon was to close the earthly career of both ; of him, the father-in-law, whose course, at longest, could not be far from the finish ; and of him, the son-in-law, who was but little more than well launched on a course which already promised to be that of one of the most devoted and intelligent missionaries, in one of the best West Indian spheres that then existed.

But we must leave her who in one short week lost Father and Husband, who was herself present amid all the sad scenes of sickness, nursing, death, and lamentation, to give the details. Mrs. Tuckett had been staying with her mother in town. She writes :—

"They returned home 1st June, I think.† It was on a Wednesday. It was service evening ; my father preached as usual ; Mr. Howe and myself engaged in preparation for return-

<hr>

* Mrs. Tuckett's First Letter.
† It would be 31st May.

ing to 'Hanover' with our two children" (a bright boy, John Wray Howe, born about April, 1835 ; and baby girl, Rebecca Ashford Howe, three months old) " next morning.

"At family worship that evening (I remember it distinctly), I handed the Bible to father. 'Give it to your husband, my love,' he said, and, across the table to James, 'Will you conduct worship, my son?' After singing a hymn (our usual custom, for mother had a sweet voice), my husband opened the Bible and read the 37th Psalm, my father remarking 'How appropriate!' Mr. Howe concluded with prayer. We said 'good night' to each other, and that was the last time we met as an unbroken household.

"In the night my husband was seized with a fit of violent ague. I got up, wrapped him in blankets, and sat by him the rest of the night. I should say I had called mother, and she gave him the usual dose of calomel. Early in the morning the Doctor was sent for, but the fever increased. The day before my father returned from Demerara, the Governor had called. He wished to see him, and he asked mother to request him to call as soon as he returned home. In consequence of this, father walked to Government House on Thursday afternoon. On his return he seemed so exhausted that mother requested Dr. Hollingworth, who was just leaving Mr. Howe's room, to see him. The Doctor said he had been doing too much, and must have rest and go to bed at once ; which he was glad to do. Medicine was sent, but it was the beginning of the end ; fever came on and he became very ill. Mr. Howe also grew worse ; no remedy would break the fever.

"On Sunday both pulpits were vacant. The people came from 'Blairmont' and other estates, to see their beloved pastor ; those likewise who belonged to father's congregation flocked in, all in deep grief. Mr. Howe would see his beloved catechist, Thomas Lewis,* and one or two more. He sent to the people, by them, loving messages, and offered an earnest prayer that 'the Great Shepherd would take care of the flock.' He was calm and collected to the end, which took place on 6th June. Mother often ran down to his chamber during his illness, but she could not remain long from my father. Of all he said to her respect-

* "Toby" of former days. See Chap. ix. of this work.

ing myself and his two children, I cannot write. His end was peace. His anxiety was for the Mission. 'If it had pleased God,' he said, ' he would have liked to have been spared longer to work; but God's will be done.' And then he prayed for *him* who should take up the work he loved so well.

" During Mr. Howe's illness my father was intensely anxious. The Doctor begged mother to say as little to him of Mr. Howe's state as possible ; but to mother's surprise he said to her, ' my love, let our dear James be buried by the side of our other children, and when I am gone put me by his side ; he was a man after my own heart ; we dearly loved one another.'

" My father, just at the time my husband died, was better, that is, the fever had left him ; but it soon returned with increased violence, and delirium came on. He fancied himself in his beloved pulpit preaching, and preach he did, and prayed for God's blessing to rest on the Mission ; then, mistaking the missionaries for the gentlemen of the Anti-Slavery Association, he addressed them on the slavery question, earnestly entreating them to use all their influence to bring about complete emancipation. This state of things continued for some hours, after which he fell into a sort of stupor, and all was quiet for a time. Mother had but just left the room, when he opened his eyes, looked round at Elizabeth and myself, who stood by his side fanning him, said, ' Where is mother ?' and immediately, with a last effort, he raised himself, threw his arms round us both, and said, ' My dear children, my work is done ; I am going home.' He fell back, and before mother got into the room he was gone ; and the Mission had lost its true and faithful servant.

* " The attendance at the funeral *was very large*. At my father's request he was carried to the grave by the Negroes, and over it they sang : 'Salvation, oh the joyful sound !' A singular circumstance happened in the evening. Some, unable to attend the funeral, went then to the burial ground. To their astonishment they found a man with a lantern busily at work boring holes in the coffin with an augur. Stopped in his proceedings he turned out to be the Veterinary Surgeon, a white man, and well acquainted with my father, but an infidel and a phrenologist. Horrified by such proceedings, the people

* Third Letter.

hastened to Mrs. Wray, to inform her of the circumstance. Mother sent for the man and inquired his object. He replied that he greatly regretted it should have reached her ears, but that his intention was to have taken up the head of Mr. Wray and, after due examination, to have replaced it in its former position in the coffin. He assured her that it was from no disrespect, for he had been a great admirer of Mr. Wray; that he had long made him an object of special study; had noted his wonderful patience under insult and provocation; his great kindness to all, even his enemies; his intense hatred of oppression; but that, notwithstanding all, he always kept his feelings under strict control; in fact, that Mr. Wray was a mystery to him, he could not understand how any one could be so patient; and he had long determined, if he ever had the opportunity, to satisfy himself by a careful examination of Mr. Wray's head. He begged mother's pardon—he hoped, as he intended no disrespect, she would forgive the outrage. My mother told him, among other things, that in the study of her husband's character he had quite forgotten that Mr. Wray was a Christian, which would explain all." Mrs. Tuckett adds to this :—" My father's rule of life can be read in 2 Tim. ii. chapter, 24, 25 verses. Had he been less gentle or less patient, he could not have lived in the Colony, for hundreds looked for his halting."

" Of the grief of the people I can give you no idea. On the Sabbath after his death our house was crowded from morning to night with silent mourners. The people came and sat on the floor in the chamber where we were ; these, after a time, would give place to others, and so until evening came on. None spoke a word, for their grief was very great."

Tombs were erected over the graves of the lamented dead, each bearing a simple inscription of name, &c.* The people

* Sacred to the memory of the Revd. John Wray, the first Protestant missionary to British Guiana, and minister of Union Chapel, New Amsterdam, Berbice. He was born at South Skirlaugh, near Hull, England, December, 1779 ; and died at New Amsterdam on the 8th June, 1837.

Sacred to the memory of the Revd. James Howe, Son-in-law of the Revd. John Wray, and first pastor of the church assembling in Hanover Chapel, Berbice. He was born at Sheffield, England, 5th July, 1803 ; and died at New Amsterdam on the 6th June, 1837.

collected money also for marble memorials, to be put respectively in the two chapels where they had more statedly ministered. The Society drew up the inscriptions, and the tablets were sent out, to the disappointment at first, says Mrs. Tuckett, of the bereaved people, who had been thinking of figures or busts, and with their grievance came, as usual, to Mrs. Wray. With more reason and wisdom than appears on the surface, she told them such could not be, and read and explained Exodus xx. chapter, 4, &c. verses, to them; with which they were satisfied.

With a copy of the principal one (kindly forwarded by the Rev. L. Crookall), than which nothing can better express the character and work of the pioneer, as they have grown upon the writer during the preparation of these memoirs, he closes the present chapter :—

"Sacred to the Memory of Revd. John Wray, the first Christian missionary to British Guiana, whose unostentatious but firm and constant friendship for the afflicted and the oppressed, whose steady promotion of Education, and faithful and affectionate preaching and teaching of the Gospel of Christ, which he exemplified by a holy, active, and blameless life, during a period of thirty eventful years, secured for him the esteem and confidence of all classes of society, and the grateful love of the people of his peculiar care ; and by the Divine goodness rendered him the honoured instrument of enabling many to look from amidst the toils and sufferings of the present state, to the glories and blessedness of immortality.

"He was born at South Skirlaugh, near Hull, England, December, 1779, and died at New Amsterdam on the 8th of June, 1837.

"'The minister of Jesus Christ to the Gentiles, ministering the Gospel of God, that the offering up of the Gentiles might be acceptable, being sanctified by the Holy Ghost.'—Rom. xv. 16.

"In grateful and affectionate testimony of sincere regard for his disinterested benevolence, and veneration of his Christian character, this tablet is erected by the members of the Church and congregation assembling in this place, and by his friends in the Colony of Berbice."

CHAPTER IX.

WHAT REMAINS—CONCLUSION—CHRISTIAN MISSIONS NO FAILURE.

WHAT REMAINS.

Temporary Arrangements—Return of Mrs. Howe to "Hanover"—Thomas Lewis, Catechist—Deaths of Mr. Parish and John Wray Howe—Return of Mrs. Howe to Town: of Mrs. Wray and Family to England—Residence near Exmouth—Sufferings—Deaths of the Youngest—Removal to Truro—Death of Mrs. Wray—Marriages and Deaths—Rebecca, Sole Survivor—The Mission at Present.

The dead buried, the desolation was there, and long before tombs could be built or tablets raised, came the question immediately, in view of the great congregations and numerous schools now bereft—What was to be done until fresh aid arrived? Three missionaries were left each at a station not so far from town ; the chapel there, frequented by numbers of the well-to-do and white inhabitants as well as by hundreds of others, claimed the first thought ; and it was therefore arranged for a missionary to be in New Amsterdam each Sabbath ; Mr. Parish, the schoolmaster, doing what he could in pastoral work, and Mrs. Wray all she could in the many ways of usefulness which were so customary to her.

"It was necessary," writes Mrs. Tuckett, "though very painful, that I should return to 'Hanover' and endeavour to keep the people together, for it was quite evident the remaining missionaries could but seldom visit the station. So, with my sister Elizabeth and my two little ones, we returned to my solitary

346

home. We had for our help and comfort our catechist, Thomas Lewis, a good and faithful man, about whom I must say a word."

He was none other than Toby, mentioned in a former chapter as a Mohammedan boy taught in Africa, before his capture and sale into slavery, to read the Koran; and long years afterwards one of Mr. Wray's most diligent scholars, "greedy," as were many of his fellow-slaves, a fine intelligent people, to be taught.*

"After Mr. Howe took over Hanover, these were drafted over (from the church in town) and formed into a church by my father. Toby had always been a leader among them, teaching the ignorant, &c., with great zeal ; so, as soon as my dear husband got to know his worth, his whole soul revolted at the idea of his being a slave. But how to procure his freedom was the puzzle. At last Mr. Howe thought of a plan. Mr. Howe studied at Hackney College, and he was intimate with the Rev. Thomas Lewis of Islington (predecessor of the Rev. Dr. Allon). He would write to him and ask his church to free Toby ; and that on his freedom he should take the name of Thomas Lewis. This was generously done, and Thomas Lewis became the catechist for Hanover ; and a most efficient helper he proved to me in my desolate home.

"So time went on : the chapel continued to be well attended ; the classes were kept up ; Thomas Lewis visited among the people in the week ; Elizabeth and I kept up the large daily school which Mr. Howe had commenced ; and when any of the people could come to us of an evening, we taught them to read."

But desolations had not ceased. In town, on 2nd July, less than a month after the former losses, and within five months after his arrival, Mr. William Parish, four days ill of fever, died. A useful and zealous labourer, and most successful in the education of the young, he passed away in the faith and hope of the Gospel, leaving another widow and fatherless child, and the Mission more than ever shorn of help. And as to "Hanover," Mrs. Tuckett continues :—

* *The Evangelical Magazine*, 1836-37, contains a letter and utterances of his, and particulars of his redemption as here briefly detailed.

" But in February 1838 another severe trial was sent to me in the death of our much-loved boy, John Wray Howe. He was often attacked by fever ; and as we had no medical aid on the coast, I thought it best to send him to his grandma—the change might do him good. Thomas Lewis, of whom he was very fond, was going to town, and I gave the child in his charge. The change seemed for the better ; but soon fever came on, with convulsions, and, before I could reach town, he was gone.* I was doubly bereaved, but we found our heavenly Father faithful to His promises : 'a stronghold in the day of trouble, a refuge from the storm and tempest.' I have often thought since, we loved him too much. A very precocious child, he was quite a companion to us in our lonely home.

" I remained at Hanover until another missionary arrived, when I returned to my mother, who likewise had removed from mission house and settled in another, quite expecting to live and die in Berbice, and all of us willing to continue in the work. But it was not to be. In 1840 the aspect of affairs changed. Mother was dismayed at what she both saw and heard ; the people were discontented, and altogether things looked so black (not from persecution : that she could have borne) that she felt she could not live on and witness the disgrace of the Mission. She made up her mind to return to England with her children, and wrote to the Society for their permission. This was most kindly given, and with many tears and regrets we left the land of her adoption.

" Most kindly cared for by the Directors, after a short time we left London. Mother's near relations were all dead, her nephews and nieces scattered abroad ; she was sore at heart ; England was no longer home.

" But at " Point-in-View " near Exmouth, the Rev. Mr. Mercer lived, an old friend who had been a missionary in Trinidad, but was not allowed to continue his labours there ; had visited us in Berbice " (about 1824), " but then there was no opening, and had

---

* Buried near his father. Inscription on his tomb : " Sacred to the memory of John Wray Howe, infant son of James and Rebecca Howe, born 2nd July, 1835 ; died 16th February, 1838. ' He was the only son of his mother, and she was a widow.' ' The Lord gave and the Lord hath taken away ; blessed be the name of the Lord.' "

returned to England years ago. He wrote to mother persuading her to come to Exmouth as the most suitable climate for us poor West Indians; so to Exmouth we went, and there lived three years.

"Emily, born I think in 1824 or 1825, did not, to the best of my recollection, accompany us, or if she did, she was shortly sent back to Walthamstow to the school for Missionaries' daughters. She had been a sweet child and dearly loved by all who knew her. From her earliest infancy she had showed a decided love for good things, so that father, who was so exceedingly cautious in these matters, believed her to be a child of God from her infancy. At Walthamstow she displayed a truly Christian character. She was very useful among her companions. Mr. Freeman was highly pleased with her; she joined the church of which he was pastor, and gave great satisfaction to her kind teachers. But, alas for us! she was, after perhaps a sojourn of two years (my memory is not clear), taken ill apparently of a cold which many of the other girls had had, and recovered, and no fear was felt for her. But fatal symptoms quickly set in, and before we heard she was seriously ill, she died. Those around her were quite unprepared for such a termination, but so it was. It was a terrible blow to us. It was winter. Mother was ill of bronchitis; my sisters felt with me that we could not leave her, and as Emily was gone and we could be of no comfort to her, we did not go to the funeral. Mr. Freeman buried her in the full and certain hope of a glorious resurrection unto eternal life. We had many letters from those who knew and loved her, full of kindness and sympathy. She used to say that when she was old enough she should go out as a missionary. She loved to assist her parents, even in early infancy, in teaching the people about Jesus.

"Mother's health was very bad; she felt the cold intensely; and our cup of sorrow was not yet full. In 1843, less than a year after Emily's death, it pleased God to send me a very heavy trial in the death of my dearly loved Rebecca Ashford Howe at the age of six years. Like her young aunt she early loved good things. But it was a great sorrow, and though so many years have passed, I cannot recall it without emotion. My own health gave way, and it was considered necessary that I should have a change of scene.   Mother therefore made up her mind to leave Exmouth.

"Some friends of ours, Mr. and Mrs. Tuckett, were about leaving Exmouth for Truro, Mr. Tuckett to take charge of the Baptist church there ; and they thought Truro, being inland, would suit us better than Exmouth. So to Truro we went to see if it would. We all liked the place and dear old Mr. Moore, Independent minister, who with his family were very kind to us. Mother's health improved somewhat. She was still an invalid but always cheerful, and we had in time a good many friends. Of young people she was very fond, and they enjoyed her conversation.

"Subsequently Mrs. Tuckett, whose children had all died in infancy, was herself taken with a long illness (consumption), lasting over twelve months, of which she died. Afterwards Mr. Tuckett and I married. We have one son and two daughters.

"My dear mother, who lived to see two of my children, after a short illness (bronchitis, to which she was very subject), died on the 4th November, 1850. She could not speak much, the disease prevented it ; but she repeatedly thanked her heavenly Father for all His goodness to her and hers, and left her testimony to His faithfulness. To a friend who came to see her and who ofttimes did any business for her, when he asked her if he could do anything then or after : 'Thank you, my good friend,' she said, 'my affairs are all settled both for time and eternity. I have no wish unsatisfied. God has abundantly satisfied me ; I shall awake in His likeness.'

"Only a few months before her death Mr. Tuckett had resigned the pastorate at Truro, and we had removed to Kingsbridge, Devonshire. I was immediately sent for, and great was her delight as she clasped me and my two little ones in her arms and said : 'God has given me more than I asked ; I did not expect to see the children.' It being Saturday, my dear husband could not accompany me, and travelling then was slow work. He came on Monday, but she had fallen asleep.

" After her death my two sisters, Elizabeth and Jane, returned with us, and for some time lived with us. My eldest sister, Elizabeth, took up her abode entirely with us ; Jane went to reside with a friend, and afterwards married Mr. Goss, who soon died, leaving her a widow. She now lives at Exeter, very near us, on a small annuity. Elizabeth, born 18th May, 1810, died just three years ago this very month (August, 1888). With many tears we laid her to rest till the morning of the resurrection, when He who said 'I will come again,' fulfils His promise and returns to raise His dead saints and change His living ones. She was a great loss to me, for we had been scarcely separated through life."

So writes this Christian lady and aged pilgrim, herself born in October, 1811, when that devoted mother was left all alone in a strange and unfriendly land ; the father having suddenly voyaged to England, as we have seen, to save the infant Mission ; and now, sister Jane (Mrs. Goss) having died at the close of 1890, she remains sole survivor of her family ; an instance truly, as were her late surviving sisters, of the way in which some are brought through the diseases and deaths of a most trying clime, not to speak of other dangers on land and sea ; and as truly a monument of the blessing bestowed in response to the prayers and faithful efforts of pious parents, though surrounded so utterly by what was shameful and cruel and wicked, to train their children in the way they should go.

To have thus trained, &c., such a family, would be to have lived for great blessing to the world. But the fruit of the pioneer's life and work extends, of course, far beyond any domestic circle, as it does any results apparent in his own day, or confined more immediately to his own Mission. Known only to One who knows all, are the many tokens on earth and in heaven of that work pursued in such faith and patience by him who was the forerunner.

Many worthy men have followed in his train. Larger and handsomer structures have succeeded the chapels built in his time ; that at New Amsterdam, capable of accommodating well on to 2000 persons ; where also, amid memorials of others who have followed and fallen in the work, is placed the marble tablet commemorating his worth.

Natives, for the most part, have now taken charge elsewhere. Schools and colleges, in large measure, exist; places of worship of different denominations are found throughout the Colony.* Numbers of these receive State-aid, according to a system established about 1824 by the slavery power, with a view to keep out missionaries; and they only await the cessation of subsidies from the Colony-chest to become, as in the case of Jamaica and elsewhere, more flourishing than heretofore; perhaps, too, more charitable. For even yet ecclesiastical bigotry and the remaining prejudices of fashion and of faction would ignore the missionary work of the past. But chapels and schools, and ministers and mission-grounds, and many a mound-marked grave of husband or wife or child who has fallen, tell of those that went forth when no other human eye was there so to pity, or human arm stretched forth there so to save. And these witnesses cannot be ignored.

Some of the many things else which the pioneer had his share, perhaps no small share, in bringing about, will be found intimated or more plainly implied in the short series of Contrasts which will both serve to illustrate the changes that have taken place, and, with brief remarks, will form our

CONCLUSION.

*Quotation from Motley—Painful Details: Need of Narration—*THEN *AND* NOW: *Contrasts as to :—*(1) *Humanity;* (2) *" The Missionary Smith " ;* (3) *Military Force ;* (4) *Education ;* (5) *Public Worship;* (6) *Circulation of Scriptures ;* (7) *Commercial Affairs and Social Life.*

Christian Missions no Failure—Pioneers thereof not to be forgotten.

" ARE these things related merely to excite superfluous horror? Are the sufferings of these obscure Christians beneath the dignity of history? Is it not better to deal with murder and oppression in the abstract, without entering into trivial details? The answer is, that these things ARE the history of the Netherlands at this epoch; that

* See Appendix B.

these hideous details furnish the causes of that immense movement, out of which a great republic was born and an ancient tyranny destroyed. It was exactly because the movement was a popular and a religious movement that it will always retain its place among the most important events of history. Dignified documents, state papers, solemn treaties, are often of no more value than the lamb-skin on which they are engrossed. Ten thousand nameless victims, in the cause of civil and religious freedom, may build up great states and alter the aspect of whole continents.

"The nobles, no doubt, were conspicuous, and it is well for the cause of the right that, as in the early hours of English liberty, the crown and mitre were opposed by the baron's sword and shield. Nevertheless they were directed and controlled, under Providence, by humbler, but more powerful agencies than their own.

"Nor is it, perhaps, better to rely upon abstract phraseology to produce a necessary impression. Upon some minds, declamation concerning liberty of conscience and religious tyranny makes but a vague impression, while an effect may be produced upon them, for example, by a dry, concrete, cynical entry in an account book." — Motley's "Rise of the Dutch Republic," chap. 3.

Dealing with some of the records of such a life has been far from a pleasant task. Necessarily referring as they do to evils, to sin and ignorance, to oppression and cruelty so extreme ; the question of saying anything, and if something, then how much or how little, has often loomed and gloomed. But, without some detail, how could the pioneer's life and work be at all understood ? Is it right or well to ignore, to be oblivious or ignorant of the past ? Scripture and experience do not favour such neglect. Besides, the pain can be as nothing to his and theirs who had to live for years among the shocking circumstances ; or even theirs, the toiling anti-slavery statesmen and friends who, when preparing evidence, had to wade through masses of paper filled with details so revolting, as once, at an important crisis, sent their leader, Mr. Buxton, a man of the strongest, but sickened at heart and spent with toil, into such condition of apoplexy and apparent death, as, for more than three days, to be watched by affectionate wife and anxious friends, before a sign of returning consciousness appeared.* It was, nevertheless, with some sense of sympathy found, that the writer recently perused the words by a distinguished author of a distinguished book, cited at the head of this *Conclusion;* and it is in the spirit of such words that, in the first contrast between THEN and Now, he goes on to record what will convey some idea of the sights and sounds which, without seeking, might encounter a missionary in those days and in that region of which we have been treating. They are a few particulars from the private diary of John Smith, Wray's worthy and virtually martyred successor at Le Resouvenir, and are part of a selection by Mr. Wallbridge, who had Smith's diary before him as he wrote. Not the worst things of West Indian slavery, such as we could quote from other pages in our possession, they are occurrences *on the spot*, and will suffice. Le Resouvenir, as an estate, it should be remarked, had passed into other hands than those of its original proprietor, Mr. Post; other estates are also referred to.

I.—HUMANITY.

"*Sunday, 4th May*, 1817.—Mr. B. called to-day, he complains much of the hardness of his situation. He says the master is very severe, and that they work from five in the morning until seven or eight at night. He says he has seen the master, and manager likewise, order the negroes to have fifty or one hundred lashes without any apparent provocation. When either is in a bad humour he will vent his spite on the negroes."

"*Wednesday, 3rd September.*—Saw some negroes working in irons, and one whose skin was entirely cut off his back with the whip. O slavery! thou offspring of the devil, when wilt thou cease to exist? Never, I think, was my sense of vision more disgusted with the degradation of the human species, or my feelings more keenly touched."

"*Monday, 10th August*, 1818.--Hark! I pause in the midst of

* "Life of Buxton," Chapter xi.

this (making note of a tremendous thunderstorm which had occurred in the night) to count the lashes on the naked slave. This is the first thing on Monday morning. When the flogging was over, Mrs. S., who was in the adjoining room, called out to me, 'Did you count those lashes?' 'Yes.' 'How many did you reckon?' I said, 141. I then asked her if she had counted them. She said, 'Yes, I counted 140.'"

"*28th January*, 1819. — Was informed that the Governor (Murray) had expressed himself much displeased at my informing the Directors of the Missionary Society that the planters made their slaves work on the Sunday last year. If I were not in a West Indian Colony I should be surprised to hear such vile and false accusations as are alleged against the missionaries."

"*Monday, 29th November.*—Went to the back of the plantation to see the negroes who have the small-pox. They are in a most wretched hovel. I am not surprised at one woman having a locked jaw. I wonder they are not all dead. I could not get into the place. The entrance is not larger than the door of a dog-kennel, not room inside for them to stand up, and scarcely room for them to sit up. No light but what comes in at the hole left for a door, and the rain dropping upon them from the roof, and nothing but a litter of leaves for them to lie upon. I never saw dogs put into a worse place. Add to all this that the doctor has not been to see them at all ; this the manager told me, and the negroes say the same."

"*Tuesday, 1st May*, 1821.—The flogging of the negroes so much annoys and affects me that I can think of little else." (An entry preceded and followed by particular instances.)

"*24th July, Saturday.*—The negroes are worked so hard that they have no time to come to me for instruction, and for me to go to them is impossible." "Besides the smallness of the congregation, which is very discouraging" (he is referring to weekday evenings), "we are much annoyed, during the evening services, by the noise of the cattle-mill grinding the coffee, and often by the flogging of the negroes, the cracking of the whip, and the cries of the people ; and, in addition to this, the noise of the crapeaus, the frogs, and the clouds of flying beetles driving against one's face, and getting down one's neck and bosom, besides the host of mosquitoes, render evening services at this season extremely irksome. I scarcely know what I preach for, or what I pray about."

Amid more or less of such circumstances must John Wray have toiled, as did his successor, before August, 1823, when, as a climax, came the shameful events, the diabolical cruelties and slaughter, so thoroughly exposed and powerfully denounced by Lord Brougham, in his famous speech during the Commons' debate, June, 1824, on the Trial, &c., of the Rev. John Smith, as quoted in our 5th chapter.

With all which, contrast the following from the *Demerara Chronicle*, of Saturday, 6th August, 1887, reported of the Colony and of the same East Coast :—

"On Monday, 1st August, the anniversary of Emancipation in the West Indies, the old slaves resident on the East Coast were regaled with dinners in honour of the Queen's Jubilee, at plantations Bel Air, Nonpareil, and Hope. Such entertainment was suggested as a fitting way for the old folk to celebrate the Jubilee by, we believe, Mr. Daly, Inspector of Villages ; and Mr. Quintin Hogg, ever ready to further a philanthropic movement, promised to provide the funds, and warmly seconded the proposal, which was as heartily carried into effect by the managers of the three estates. To prevent as few as possible from being absent, arrangements were made for taking the old slaves to and from the different places of rendezvous, and the Coast was divided into three districts, of which the above-mentioned plantations were the centres. At Bel Aïr there were 99 emancipated slaves present ; 127 slaves sat at the Nonpareil banquet, and 13, unable to attend, had their dinners conveyed to them by friends."

Similarly at plantation Hope, and, to sum up in a word, clergymen took the chairs; ministers and gentlemen, the speaking; ladies presided at the tables; choirs led the singing; entertainments of music and magic lantern followed all; and an address to the Queen, drawn up and read by Mr. Hogg, was voted with acclamations, and signed by a number of the guests, who were equally hearty in thanks to their generous entertainers.

A difference truly! and in how many circumstances! "Tell it not in Gath," however, for not the least difference is in the amount of reference to Missions, presented by the respective extracts from Diary and Chronicle. Judging by the report of the newspaper, Missions were unnamed at the celebration. There was no allusion to them. Not a thought went back to the men, not a word was spoken of those, to whom, under God, so much of change for the better was inaugurated and was due. Yet, on that very Coast, in that very neighbourhood, it was that John Smith toiled and fell; that, long before then, Hilbertus H. Post had sought the good of all, and John Wray had begun his work as " Pioneer Missionary."

II.—"THE MISSIONARY SMITH."

Our second contrast refers chiefly to the same coast and neighbourhood, and to the same John Smith. It might be titled, "The Tables Turned"; and consists of several items, penned years ago by the present writer, on the fly-leaf of his copy of "The Demerara Martyr," a volume given him when in Demerara, 1861, by the esteemed author, the Rev. E. A. Wallbridge.

"It is worthy of remark :—

(*a*) That this volume was penned in the house in which a bitter opponent of Mr. Smith wrote against both him and the Missionary system.

(*b*) That though no monument was allowed over Mr. Smith's grave, nor even a mark to distinguish it, a large chapel, and also schools (in the city of Georgetown), have long borne his name.

(*c*) That the chapel in which Mr. Smith ministered, and which was taken from the missionaries, was, after a lapse of years, restored ; was afterwards removed and re-erected on land given by the brutal captor of Mr. Smith.

(*d*) That Missionaries, whom it was determined to expel the country, became, after a time, greatly increased in number ; many of their stations are now (1877) supplied with native pastors, and are self-sustaining.

(*e*) That the land in which no slave was to be taught reading, has now schools and colleges sufficient and adapted to all classes.

(*f*) That a near relative of the Rev. W. S. Austin, the Chaplain who befriended Mr. Smith and had, in consequence, to leave the Colony, is now, and has long been, a chief dignitary of the Episcopal Church there.

(*g*) That Mr. Arrindell, the legal adviser of Mr. Smith, and who, as a result, for a while lost nearly all his practice, died in the year 1863, Chief-Justice of British Guiana."

"How hath the oppressor ceased."—Isa. xiv. chapter, 4 verse. ·

"He hath scattered the proud in the imagination of their hearts," and "exalted them of low degree."—Luke i. chapter, 31, 32 verses.

We cannot add that the sentence against "the Missionary Smith," still standing in the national records, has been reversed, as long since ought to have been the case ; but we may say that for many years now, and universally perhaps, he has been deemed innocent of the charges brought against him, if ever his alleged guilt were, by any one, really and intelligently believed.

III.—MILITARY FORCE.

Our next Contrast refers to the amount of Military Force employed for the peace, &c., of the Colony, and will be given, with slight verbal alteration, in the words themselves of the Rev. John Foreman, as printed in his "Echoes from Slave-Time."

"At the time of the Queen's Jubilee, I heard some jocular remarks made concerning 'the Queen's troops,' no less than two dozen soldiers, who formed the Guard of Honour on that occasion. They were laughed at as 'our brave defenders.' It is, however, a proof of the security of life and property which now exists, in striking contrast with the insecurity which was felt in slave-time. Never, I suppose, in the English history of this Colony, had we so small a number of 'regular soldiers' in it. Our armed police will be pointed to, and rightly so, as a very important organization for the maintenance of order. But it should not be overlooked that a large majority of the rank and file of our armed police force are the descendants of the slaves of a by-gone time; or that, in the 'good old days,' besides the regular forces, there was the Militia, which did not then exist in British Guiana on paper only, as it does in 1888. There were, however, in slave-time, European troops stationed, not only in Georgetown and at Mahaica, but in New Amsterdam; Fort Wellington, too, West Coast Berbice, was occupied by soldiers. When I first knew Fort Wellington, since at various times altered, it consisted of a centre building and two wings. The centre had been the officers' quarters, the two wings were used as barracks for the rank and file.

"When the Rev. John Smith was arrested in 1823, a troop of cavalry and a company of infantry were employed in this service; now, in the Jubilee year of Freedom, less than two dozen soldiers are deemed sufficient for the needs of the Colony."

IV.—EDUCATION.

A fourth Contrast will be found in the matter of primary or elementary Education. What the first efforts at teaching to read cost the Pioneer, and the Governor's threat to John Smith of instant banishment, should his Excellency hear of his teaching a slave to read, our readers will have learnt. But for further vivid illustrations, we adduce two or three facts for which we are again indebted to the Rev. John Foreman and his "Echoes from Slave-Time."

"The only school on the estates of those days was one known as the 'picaniny' or children's gang. These little ones were turned out early in the morning, in a state of nudity, to do any kind of work that such labourers could perform. Their driver was generally an old female slave, who was armed with a tamarind whip with twisted ends, which she used on their backs to make them work faster. Or she would order one of them to be seized by the others, thrown face downwards on the ground, and whilst held by them in that position, she administered 'chastisement' to the offender. I believe in work, and in children being taught to work, not, however, by such means as the above; but what

I want to point out is that there was no teaching slaves' children to read in those days. Schools for children (estates') began to exist during the 'Apprenticeship' times, 1834-38.

"When residing on the West Coast of Berbice, and talking to some of the old people about their having been taught to read in slave-time, they shook their heads, and one of them said :—'You should see so-and-so's back.' I asked, 'Why?' 'Because,' was the answer, 'he would slip off Hope and Experiment at night, and come here and get a lesson from the teacher, and so when they caught him, they flogged him, and then put him in the stocks.'

"On this West Coast of Demerara, I was greatly amused some years ago, at hearing one who had been a slave describe the difficulties he and others had in concealing a First Book, published by the Sunday School Union, containing the Alphabet, &c. Their clothing was of the scantiest — too scanty to hide even so small a book. Hence it was hidden sometimes in a bundle of grass ; at others, in a piece of bamboo, or in a hollow branch of a tree. One moonlight night he was telling the others the names of the letters of the Alphabet, when an overseer suddenly appeared and caught them in the act. Next day the whole company was taken to the manager's house and flogged, the reader getting a double portion, being flogged the first and again the last of the batch. This man occasionally got a pass to go and hear the Missionary. He endeavoured to carry away as much as he could of what he heard, and then to tell it, as opportunity offered, to his fellow-slaves. This came to the manager's knowledge, and calling the man, he said to him : 'William, how much does the Missionary pay you for teaching the people?' The reply was, 'Nothing, Sir.' 'And how much does Mr.—— (the attorney of the estate) pay you?' Again the reply was, 'Nothing, Sir.' 'Then,' said the manager, 'I 'll pay you ;' 'and after having me flogged,' said William to me, 'he made me for a week dance an hour a day on the treadwheel.' A kind of dance that few dancers would admire.

"When Mr. Hermanus Post began at Le Resouvenir to teach some of his house-slaves to read, he was called an incendiary, a firebrand, a revolutionist, and other hard names.

"A strange contrast this," adds Mr. Foreman, to what took

place seventy years afterwards in 1887, for then, there was paid out of the taxation of the Colony, "grants to primary schools, about £23,840, and for Inspectors and District Officers, &c., about £2660 ; altogether the sum of £26,500."*

There are, besides, schools and colleges for secondary or higher education ; and, of course, on Sabbath days, Sunday schools for all classes.†

V.—PUBLIC WORSHIP.

A fifth contrast will be found in the lonely position of Mr. Wray and the first missionaries, as ministers of religion, with their difficulties in obtaining meeting-places of any kind, illustrated by the present memoirs ; as compared with the list of ministers, places of worship, &c., copied from the British Guiana Directory for 1891, and, with other statistics, forming Appendix B to this work.

VI.—CIRCULATION OF THE SCRIPTURES.

The Bible Society and its efforts afford material for our next contrast. Both Mr. Wray, as we have seen, and his successor on Le Resouvenir, Mr. Smith, began to receive consignments of Bibles and Testaments, of various sizes and languages, which were sold at prices accordingly ; part of the price, in cases of necessity, being remitted, and in other cases the books being given as presents. In harmony with one great aim of the Bible Society, the prices ruled low, much lower at that time than the prices of Scriptures sold at the stores, when obtainable there ; which was not always, sometimes not readily, the case.

But let us enter the Court-house, Georgetown. It is 17th October, 1823, the fifth day of the trial, by Court Martial,

---

* For long, the day schools at the missionary stations took the lead both in efficiency and numbers ; declining "Grants-in-aid," until the religious difficulty was more equitably settled than at first.

† See Appendix B.

under an order of Governor Murray (an illegal tribunal, however), of John Smith on the charge of inciting to insurrection.
The prisoner is there—a weakened, sick, and soon-to-be-
dying man ; worn with years of toil, spent in a trying clime,
for the good, temporal and eternal, of men, chiefly the down-
trodden and oppressed ; now also suffering from prolonged
imprisonment and anxiety ; from the unmerited opprobrium,
generally, of those in power, in the planting and slave-
owning interest ; and after one of the most serious and tragic
occurrences in the Colony—and the witness under examination is one of his deacons, named Bristol.

"Prosecutor asks—'Did you see any members of the church pay
for psalm books, Bibles, and catechisms?'

(Here the prisoner put in the following objection)—I am
not tried for obtaining money under fraudulent pretences, and
therefore object to the question as being wholly irrelevant.

COURT ADVISED.

The Court conceive the objection quite inadmissible.*

"Answer—'I have seen the members of the church pay for
Psalm books, catechism books, Bibles and other books.'

"'Does the prisoner always sell and never give his Bibles to the
people?' 'A few are given as presents.'

"Seventh Day.—Same witness under cross-examination by the
prisoner. 'How much have you seen paid for each and every
one of the sort of books sold by Mr. Smith?' (Witness details
hymn books, Bibles, Testaments, spelling books, catechisms, sold
at different prices, told in Dutch money, according to kind, &c.)

"'Did the prisoner sell the same sized Bibles to all persons, at
the same price?' 'No, there were smaller Bibles at f.12 : sometimes, if you come to buy a Bible for f.14·10, and be short
5 stivers or f.1, he would pass over that, and let you have it without the 5 stivers or the guilder.'

* The sentences braced were not in the imperfect copy of the trial
furnished officially by the authorities to the Home Government and
laid before Parliament, but in the more complete copy received by the
Missionary Directors and published by them.

"'How large were the Bibles that were sold at 12 guilders?' 'About the size of the (royal octavo) book produced.'"

It can hardly now be credited that such a Court, specially constituted and professedly for such a purpose, could be spending its time over such and similar details. But the object was, as other evidence was so scant, to lay hold of anything that seemed likely to cast a slur upon the maligned missionary, seemingly with a design to show that he took advantage of the people and tried to make some gain out of them. Hence the scraping together of such matters, so rightly objected to by the prisoner as irrelevant. But he has nothing to fear on the point. Relegating to a note a little of what the witness Bristol, twenty-one years afterwards had to say about the scene,* we here adduce what the prisoner, "the missionary Smith," said upon the subject in his defence of himself, made on the fourteenth day of the trial, 1st November, 1823. Saying generally at the outset, "the manner in which I have pursued the object of my mission deserves some notice. Having learned what kind of services had been performed by Mr. Wray, my predecessor, I endeavoured to adopt and follow his plan," then going through particulars he comes to—

"Fourthly, my selling books to the negroes has been spoken of with disapprobation; the books were Bibles, Testaments, hymn

---

* "In the month of October, 1848, Bristol called on me (Rev. W. G. Barrett) at my request. . . . He is an intelligent and well spoken old man. The substance of his statement to me is this:—'When we went into the Court we were daunted; there were so many people there, and the gentlemen kept making signs and threatening the witnesses. The white people in the Court were so anxious to catch everything against Mr. Smith that they wrote down more than the witnesses said.' . . . 'On my conscience, I do not believe that Mr. Smith had anything to do with the rebellion. The white people hated him because he taught the negroes to read; we never saw a minister take such pains with the people as Mr. Smith; the people loved him, but the managers did all they could to annoy him.' This is the unterrified testimony of Bristol."—"Demerara Martyr," pp. 110, 111.

books, spelling books, and catechisms. The Bibles and Testaments were from the Bible Society; they were sent with invoices of cost and charges, allowing me, however, a discretionary power in the disposal of them. When it appeared to me that the applicants could afford to pay the full value of the book, I charged a guilder for a shilling in the invoice, which, with the charges and the difference in exchange, was about their value. When the applicants could not afford to pay the full price, they had the book for what they could afford, frequently for half-price. Testaments I sometimes gave away; but for the Bibles something, I believe, was always paid. No one, to my recollection, ever said he could not afford to pay either the whole or part of the price; though I frequently asked them when they applied. The other books I was obliged to pay for before they came from England; of course I could not afford to give those away, and charged for them at the same rate, a guilder for a shilling.

"Of catechisms, I have given away at least 1000. Had I sold a thousand Bibles, and each of them at double the price I did sell them at, yet, I would ask, What would that have to do with the the charge (against him)? The negroes *purchased* them voluntarily, and had I forced them to purchase, and discontent had arisen therefrom, surely the consequences of that discontent would have fallen upon myself and not upon their masters.

"In selling the Bibles, I have done no more than follow the instructions of the Bible Society, and the practice of many clergymen of the Church of England—one of whom feared not to sell Bibles in this Colony."

The whole is a sad and shameful spectacle, only relieved here and there by such things as the sterling common sense and Christian straightforwardness of the prisoner. But now let us turn to a more grateful scene in that same city, in the new City Hall, but in 1889, as briefly conveyed in the Bible Society's *Monthly Reporter* for November of that year.

"The Demerara *Daily Chronicle* of 10th July gives a full account of an immense and enthusiastic meeting of the British Guiana Auxiliary Bible Society, held in the new and handsome Town Hall, in Georgetown, on 9th July.

"The Town Hall was opened on 1st July; and the Lieutenant-

Governor, Sir Charles Bruce, K.C.M.G., who presided at the meeting, expressed his pleasure that the first public meeting held in the building was on behalf of a Society which everywhere aims at elevating and uniting those of every race. It was computed that nearly 1000 people were present in the hall, and that something like double that number had been excluded from the inadequacy of the building to hold any more. The Chairman thought it was the largest meeting he had ever presided over in the Colonies, and that in the matter of order it could not be surpassed."

VII.—Commercial Affairs and Social Life.

Our final contrast will be found in commercial affairs and social life. It must be but a glance. Slavery and godlessness are no friends to the spread of improvements, of healthy commerce, or of geniality and respect between class and class.

Accustomed then to treat men as mere machines, save the stimulus they could feel from the whip, and sharing in a mother country's protective duties, great was the outcry of impending ruin as about universally to fall when that mother country emancipated the slaves, and when, later still, under a more enlightened policy, it removed protective duties. True, twenty millions sterling were paid to the slave-owners, and, protective duties removed, other advantages had been bestowed. But the thoughts and ways and habits of the old system were not put off in a day. Absenteeism with its evils, peculation by numerous underlings, and gross abuse of the poor slaves left in their power, were not to be readily surrendered. Yet, how could abiding prosperity be expected otherwise? Selfish pleasure - seeking, profound ignorance, bestial indulgence, utter irreligiousness, and blasphemous profanity, do not contain the promise of steady, upright, considerate, thoughtful men of business and members of the community. A people are neither established nor exalted by unrighteousness.

But in response to the complaints of West Indians, the Home Government stood firm. The lessons to live and labour and exist as a community, and carry on affairs like other lands where civil freedom and absence of monopoly are in the ascendant, had to be learnt; and the writer of this has some recollection how that, therefore, Lord John Russell, as he then was, or some other member of Government, in response to complaints from the Sugar interest, pointed out how little progress—*e.g.*, in improving machinery—the planters had made. That would be years ago, in the "forties," probably about 1847.

Meanwhile, old things have been passing away, doubtless with much moaning and groaning in the process, not as once and on every hand, of slaves under the cruel lash or other torture of driver, overseer, or manager, at times of all three together; but of men and communities once petted and privileged, learning to stand upright, and to approve the things that are more excellent and honourable and humane and right and equal. Much remains to be done, but what helps are at hand, already there, or with promise of forthcoming; pile-driver, steam-navvy, or some modifications thereof, for digging the drains or fortifying the dams; land-culture delivered from the degrading associations of slavery; allotments multiplied with the growth of population; not to speak of the means of education and religion, &c., already and long enjoyed.

The following extracts, however, from the pen of the Lieutenant-Governor, Sir Charles Bruce, whose speech has just been quoted, but still more recently published in an article by him in the *English Illustrated Magazine* for February, 1891, tell the advance that has been made in commercial, &c., particulars, and seem pregnant with promise of much more.

"In the year 1827, the Colony exported 70,000 hogsheads of sugar, nearly 16,000 bales of cotton, and over 8,000,000 lbs. of coffee. In 1887, the export of sugar amounted to nearly 150,000 hogsheads, but cotton and coffee have for nearly fifty years ceased to be of appreciable account as exports. In addition to sugar, rum, and molasses, the Colony now exports timber, shingles, balatta, and gold. With these sources of wealth, the future of British Guiana is intimately concerned ; but sugar has been admittedly the main stay of the present fortunes of the Colony. The success of the sugar industry has been due to a combination of fortunate circumstances, and while recognizing the influence of late causes to which allusion will be made, we can hardly over-estimate the credit due to our Dutch predecessors for the scientific and technical skill with which they designed and carried out the original settlement of the country."

" If British Guiana has escaped the very serious consequences which have followed the depression of the sugar industry in the West Indian Islands, this result must be credited to the courage and energy with which the proprietors of estates have met difficulties which, for a time, made success seem impossible. The burden of the initial cost of the introduction of labour called for a large investment of capital at a time when the very existence of cane-sugar industry was in danger. The enormous increase of the beet sugar crop steadily lowered prices, and it was only the most intelligent efforts in the direction of economy, and the introduction of improved methods, that enabled the planters to maintain the position of Demerara in the front rank of enterprise and excellence. But the introduction of improved methods involves a large outlay in the erection of new machinery, and the enterprise of experiments often costly and not always immediately successful. Fortunately, the principal plantations of British Guiana were in the hands of wealthy proprietors, whose independent resources carried them in safety through the ungenial season of adversity which for a time imperilled their fortunes, and threatened the abandonment of a large area of the Colony. Among those to whom the Colony is chiefly indebted for enterprise and liberality in the introduction of improved methods, a prominent place will be universally conceded to Mr. Quintin Hogg, who has spared neither money nor his own intelligent energy, in introducing and perfecting the new process by which sugar is extracted from the cane by diffusion.

"The recent discovery that the sugar cane produces fertile seeds, seems to open to the industry a future of boundless horizon, and the planters of British Guiana may be confidently expected to turn to profitable account the experiments now being carried on, to ascertain the conditions most favourable for the production of improved species of cane from seed."

As to race, &c., differences, Sir Charles writes :—

"The people of Georgetown, in familiar parlance, are spoken of as whites, blacks, coloured, Portuguese, and coolies. The residents of British Guiana in using these terms do not associate with any of them an inherent idea of superiority or inferiority. The African descendants of pure blood are called 'blacks,' those of mixed origin are spoken of as 'coloured.' It may occasion some surprise, but I make the statement with all confidence, that in British Guiana, as in the other British Colonies with which I am acquainted, the merits of persons are judged with little or no prejudice on account of colour. The proprietors of estates in the selection of persons to fill positions of trust and confidence, consider the qualifications likely to ensure a successful outturn. Merchants are guided by similar considerations." "In the management of estates and in the business of commerce, the African descendant is coming steadily to the front. And the same is true of his position in the learned professions and in public affairs. No Mayor of Georgetown has been more popular or more respected in public and private life than a coloured mayor whose recent death was regretted throughout the Colony. He was, by profession, a solicitor, and as a confidential friend and adviser there was certainly no one whose services were in such universal request. As a general rule, in the intercourse of 'whites' and 'blacks' of equal advantages of education and position in British Guiana, there is no sense of superiority or inferiority on account of colour either on the one side or on the other."

Christian Missions, a failure ! Offspring of ignorance and selfishness surely, is the saying. Assuming that the land on which we tread and older times are out of count, the assertion remains as base-born. Eldest of them barely a century's age, what have modern Missions not accomplished? What suspicion and exclusiveness, what bigotry and meanness at home have they lived down! What neglect and mistakes and disputes in management have they suffered! What desolation by disease and death, what unworthiness of some agents and occasionally sad lapses into gross iniquity of others have they survived! What obstacles of greed and tyranny, monopoly and strangeness, barbarity and cannibalism have they overcome! What persecutions have they and their converts endured; cruel mockery and imprisonment and death in the West Indies, in Burmah, Madagascar, Central Africa; not to speak of the loss of caste and banishment from home which Christian baptism in India generally means! But where is the Atlantic and Pacific slave-trade now? Where slavery itself, in the West Indies, the two Americas, in South Africa, and the Mauritius? Where now are the isles undiscovered of the South Seas, or those on which our mariners dare not land? Where are the cannibals of Owhyhee and Feejee, of New Zealand and, in part, of New Guinea? Where is the India forbidden to missionaries by an East India Company, or a China and Japan forbidden to foreigners altogether? Where now that blank space in the map of Africa, gazed upon with curious wonder in our younger days, as it had been by others long ages before, and continued to be until less than a generation ago? ALL GONE. Not gone, indeed, all and simply through the work of modern Missions; but how large a share in the change they can rightly claim! In how many cases, have their agents been the pioneers! And what an immensity does even their share imply of languages mastered, of books and schools, of lawful trade and commerce, of the ways and works of true civilization; yea, moreover, of heathen idols utterly abolished; of Scriptures spread, of meetings multiplied for the worship of the living God; of the knowledge of a Father reconciled, of an incarnate, sinless, crucified, risen, ascended Son and Saviour, of a regenerating, sanctifying Spirit; of souls renewed and sins forgiven; of men and women once far off, walking with God, or, rescued from depths unspeakable of suffering and degradation, sitting at Jesus' feet clothed and in their right mind! And all advancing quietly, it may be, but surely.

A failure, of course they are, when many fall in the field, bitterly lamented! But then others step forward, and, sooner or later, fill the gaps. A failure, of course, just as Christianity is a failure!—that is, just as bread is a failure in sustaining life when not forthcoming, or when made to conceal and convey the deadly poison, or when its loaf is flung as a missile of offence and hurt: just as water fails to quench the thirst when it is allowed to ripple on untouched, or, falling drop by drop, is turned into torture, most exquisite, of the Romish Inquisition.

But if Christianity means the living Christ, and if the words which He speaks are "spirit and life," receiving which, "a man hungers not nor thirsts again," but "has in him a well of water springing up unto everlasting life;" then, preaching Christ and conveying His words to the perishing, missions are no failure any more than the Gospel ceases to be "the power of God unto salvation to every one that believeth." What has thus renewed many an individual soul, is able so to bless and is so blessing many another. What has thus restored and purified many a single life, can be and does become the salt of a community. In many a case, despite the crowd of wicked and worthless fellow-countrymen, who for purposes of trade or pleasure, of exaction or vice, have followed him, have been there and stood by his side to counteract his efforts, has the missionary lived to see such fruit of his labours.

But of those in the past, *distinguished forerunners* in the work, though he was not called to the business of translation, or invention, or exploration, which some had to undertake; yet in trophies of Divine truth and grace among the lowliest of men as well as among those of higher rank; the result, under God, of toil pursued with such prayer, and faith, and patience (to say nothing of the multitude of other benefits that came of his exertions), none perhaps had a greater share than he, the papers of whose earthly record are before us. Out of the long night of travail and gloom, the light of his morning had begun to rise before he passed away; and he was recognized as "a repairer of the breach, a restorer of paths to dwell in." Among the elder of his compeers, however, and lacking the publication of his promised volume, he has more than they come to be forgotten.

Why should any of these noble leaders in missionary enterprise, which the century has seen, be forgotten; their memoirs, chief and foremost men though they were, afforded no prominence now, but put aside as a tale that is told? Is the need of them and of their example, their experience and the rest, all of the past?

Remembered or forgotten, however, at last "they that be wise (the teachers) shall shine as the brightness of the firmament, and they that turn many to righteousness, as the stars for ever and ever." And when in that day, with beams of the brightest and steadiest these shall appear; not the least lustrous among them, we are persuaded, will be seen the Pioneer of Christian Missions in British Guiana—JOHN WRAY.

APPENDIX A.

JOHN WRAY'S DRAUGHT OF PREFACE TO HIS PROJECTED
HISTORY OF THE MISSION.

THE following work has been compiled at the request of some
highly respected friends in England, and encouraged by an
affectionate resolution of the Directors of the London Missionary
Society, who conceived a history of the Mission to this Colony is
very desirable. The individual who has drawn it up has been
connected with that great Society for upwards of thirty years,
twenty-eight of which have been spent in British Guiana ; and
though called to pass through various trials during that long
period, he has never repented of the choice he made. He did not
indeed expect to be spared so many years, and from his delicate
state of health when he left his native land, his friends hardly
supposed that he would reach the place of his destination. He
has, however, been spared to the present period, and has
enjoyed a very large share of health during his long abode in this
Colony. He makes no pretensions to authorship, having always
been actively engaged in promoting the great object of his
Mission ; for the truth of which he believes he can confidently
appeal to the inhabitants among whom he has lived, in instructing the ignorant, in visiting the sick, and in preaching the Gospel
of Jesus Christ ; and he feels thankful to God for the measure of
success which, by Divine assistance, has attended his labours and
the labours of others who have been united with him in the same
work, especially his late beloved friend the Rev. John Davies.
And though he has met with great opposition, he rejoices that
the following work will show that from the commencement of the

Mission many respectable planters, and merchants, and governors, greatly to their honour, have rendered the most important services to the Mission, and have liberally supported it by their subscriptions.

Though the author makes no pretensions to literature, yet he possesses one qualification, of having heard with his own ears and seen with his own eyes most of the facts he relates. It has been his practice to keep a journal of the principal transactions which have transpired during his residence in the Colonies, and generally to note down any interesting facts which have been related to him by some of the oldest planters and others respecting the early history of the Colonies. He has also preserved many documents, letters, and papers, which have greatly assisted him in compiling the work, and has also been accustomed to make extracts from the various works he has read on West Indian subjects, and he has thought it his duty to read every book on the West Indies within his reach, and to make himself as fully acquainted with West Indian controversies as he possibly could. For the first three Chapters, containing the early Statistics of the Settlement of the Colonies, he must depend on the testimony of others, and has diligently examined all the books he could obtain, as well as seeking information from all classes with whom he has conversed who were able to give it. In an early period of his residence he had an opportunity of frequently conversing with Mr. Post and others, respecting the Settlement of the Colonies. He also possesses a number of the late Mr. Post's Letters, from which he has made large Extracts, which he believes will afford great satisfaction to all the friends of Missions. The first three Chapters have also been submitted to A. Van Ryck de Groot, Esq., late acting-Sheriff of Berbice, who has spent a long life in public offices in the Colonies, especially in Essequibo when it was a distinct Government, and whose knowledge of that part of the Colony, as well as of the Indians, is very extensive. He has kindly promised several facts and reviewed the whole. After all the care that has been taken, doubtless many errors will appear of which the Writer is unconscious, and as he disclaims every pretension, except a simple narrative of facts, he shall be very happy to be corrected by any in the spirit of candour. He has avoided as much as possible giving offence to any, even to those who have opposed him the most ; yet he has felt it his duty, particularly when connected with the late Crown Estates, to relate facts which have given him much pain, but which relation was necessary to entitle him to the character of an impartial historian, as well as to vindicate his own conduct. He, however, is conscious that nothing has been over-coloured. On the other hand, he has always felt great pleasure in recording those acts of humanity and hospitality he has witnessed. The Work being published in the form of a Journal generally, will perhaps contain many repetitions, which could hardly be avoided ; but yet this seemed to be the most interesting, and perhaps the only form in which it could be presented to the public.

BERBICE, 18*th January*, 1836.

APPENDIX B.

Demerara, Essequibo, and Berbice, when united under one Governor, March, 1831, contained a population of 98,000—viz., 3529 Whites ; 7521 Free, Coloured, and Black ; 86,950 slaves.

According to the Census of 1881, they contained a population of 252,186. Of these, 149,639 were born in British Guiana—of whom 7656 were Aborigines, Indians "wandering in the almost limitless forests" ; 14,768 were born of immigrants from India, 841 of those from China, and 5047 of those from Madeira.

Of those *not born* in the Colony, 65,161 were from India ; 4393, from China ; 6879, Madeira and the Azores ; 18,318, the West India Islands ; 1617, Europe ; 205, North America ; 5077, Africa ; and 897 from other places.

Education is chiefly denominational. During 1889, Government grants were made to 163 Schools, and amounted to about £23,500. In Georgetown are 23 Schools, and New Amsterdam, 7. In the country, Demerara has 63 ; Essequibo, 29 ; Berbice, 35 ; besides several schools in Essequibo and Berbice among the Aboriginal Indians.

Ordained Clergy and Ministers are about 92 ; in addition to whom are a number of lay-assistants—such as preachers, catechists, missionaries.

The original Mission Churches formed by John Wray and others, in connection with the London Missionary Society, are most, or all of them, Congregational Churches, and form the Congregational Union of British Guiana. The Union includes about 42 Chapels large and small, and 15 ordained Ministers. They have steadfastly declined State-aid.

The following also are voluntary Churches :—

Presbyterians,	.	.	1 Chapel, 1 Minister.
Baptists,	.	.	2 Chapels, 1 Minister.
Moravians,	.	.	2 Chapels, 1 Minister.

The following numbers, if not quite correct, are closely approximate :—

Church of England, 13 Parishes, 62 Places of Worship, 30 Ministers.

Annual Grant from Colony chest about £9600, in addition to pensions, and £2000 paid to the Bishop by the Imperial Government.

Church of Scotland, 10 Parishes, 20 Places, 11 Ministers.

Annual Grant, about £2700, in addition to pensions.

Roman Catholic Church, 16 Places, 15 Ministers.

Annual Grant, about £2300.

Wesleyan Methodist Church, 5 Circuits, 10 Ministers.

Annual Grant, about £1340.

Evangelical Lutheran Church, 1 Chapel, 1 Minister.

Note.—State Grants to Religion ceased in Jamaica about 1870. Ten years afterwards, in a Paper by Sir Anthony Musgrave, K.C.M.G., Governor of Jamaica, and read before the Royal Colonial Institute, he says, "The manner in which the people support their religious institutions, deserves note and praise."